She wanted more than just empty memories!

Melanie drifted out onto the lawn of the colonial mansion, her eyes sweeping past the elegantly manicured grounds to the exotic landscape beyond.

Darkness was falling softly over the lonely African bushveld. The rising moon bathed the land in unearthly light. All seemed enfolded in peace, and inevitably, Melanie's thoughts turned toward Luke.

She owed so much to him. Luke had changed her; he had made her life worth living again. Now she only wanted to stay with Luke, to find a place in his future. Perhaps it wasn't an impossible dream!

Smiling softly, Melanie turned back toward the house....

D0869749

Where the South Wind Blows

by

ANNE HAMPSON

Harlequin Books

TORONTO • LONDON • NEW YORK • AMSTERDAM
SYDNEY • HAMBURG • PARIS

Original hardcover edition published in 1975
by Mills & Boon Limited

ISBN 0-373-02272-7

Harlequin edition published July 1979

Printed in U.S.A.

CHAPTER ONE

To HAVE BEEN JILTED once was humiliating enough, but to have it happen a second time was sufficient to make even a girl like Melanie become embittered. She stared with disbelieving eyes at Robin, her lovely features drawn with pain.

"It isn't true," she whispered. "You don't mean it, do you?"

The young man shifted from one foot to the other, a deep frown on his face.

"It's just one of those things, Melanie. Far better that it's happened now than when we were married."

She swallowed, but the lump in her throat remained. Why make any effort at all to speak? She had been through all this before—and after that experience she had vowed never to let a man hurt her again. Yet here she was, four years later, experiencing the same pain in her heart, the same sense of loss and failure, the same sense of humiliation.

And the girl who had taken Robin from her was none other than the one who had taken Giles—her own sister.

"I must go." She looked at him just once before, turning on her heel, she left the hotel lounge in which she and Robin had so often met.

She went down to the powder room, intent on applying a little color to her cheeks, but on searching in her handbag found that she had left her blusher at home. She took out a comb and drew it lightly through her honey blond hair, making a cold and calculated assessment of her looks as she did so. High cheekbones and a clear pale skin, a wide and generous mouth, eyes that matched the cornflower blue of her suit. She was passable, she told herself, but Romaine was beautiful—Romaine who from her early teens had been able to take her choice of the boys at the grammar school that she and Melanie attended.

With a deep sigh Melanie put away the comb and, closing her handbag, went up into the foyer of the hotel. The bus stopped just along the road and she was lucky enough to arrive at the stop just in time to catch the one going to Warford. Why Warford? Her aunt lived there—Aunt Cissy who would comfort her....

"Darling!" Aunt Cissy threw her arms around Melanie even before she had stepped into the hall. "My love—but how wonderful to see you! Bless you, child, for remembering to come and see an old woman like me. Now that gadabout sister of yours hasn't been to see me since the day of her birthday—no, I tell a lie; she came on Christmas Eve and brought me a tablet of soap someone had given her at the office—for a Christmas present, of course. It stank! I shredded it up and used it in the washing machine. She got nothing in return, so I don't expect she'll come this Christmas Eve. What am I rambling on about? Come in, love, and tell me all your news. How is that charming fiancé of yours? You haven't much longer to wait for the great day, have you? About six weeks, isn't it?"

By this time Melanie had managed to get into the living room, and she turned to her aunt as the old lady followed closely behind.

"It's all finished, auntie...." And although she had meant to hold on to her control Melanie found herself weeping on Aunt Cissy's shoulder.

"My love! Oh, my dear, dear love—not again!"

"Robin's fallen in love with Romaine."

"Not again!" repeated her aunt and then, hastily, "What I mean is—Romaine hasn't stolen your fiancé a second time?"

"It's true, auntie." Melanie took the handkerchief offered and dried her eyes. "I've just been with Robin and he told me that he and Romaine are getting married as soon as Romaine's divorce goes through."

"The bitch!" declared Aunt Cissy, her pale gray eyes blazing. "Oh, but I wish she were here at this moment! I'd slap her face, believe me!"

"I'll get over it, auntie." The handkerchief changed hands again and Melanie sat down on the shabby couch under the window. "But I'll tell you this: no man—I repeat, *no man* will ever have the chance of doing this to me again!"

"I can't say that I blame you for feeling bitter, dear, but on the other hand I can't imagine you remaining single all your life. It's no fun, pet, and so once you get over this you must begin looking around again."

"Never!"

"I wonder," mused her aunt, bypassing this vehement exclamation, "how Giles is feeling now? I'll wager he regrets throwing you over for a girl who was going to want a divorce so soon."

"I hope he's suffering!"

"Darling, this is not you at all," protested her aunt, looking into her tear-stained face. "Giles was such a nice boy."

So was Robin, according to her aunt.

"You like all men," returned Melanie, but her aunt instantly denied this.

"There's one or two I don't like at all," she said forcibly, "and one of those as I've said is that arrogant nephew of my cousin's—you know, Luke Shadwell, who grows trees or cereals or something in South Africa?''

"I've never met him, you know that. Has he ever been to England?"

"A couple of times, when you were too small to notice. He was a youngster then, working for his father. Then the old man popped off and Luke was suddenly rich—farming in a big way, so Gertrude tells me.''

"Aunt Gertie's coming home, you were saying the last time I was here?"

"Yes. You'll like my cousin, Melanie. However, enough of that for the present. Let's have a cup of tea, shall we?''

"Thank you, auntie. That'll be nice.'' Melanie rose at once to follow the old lady into the kitchen. "Aunt Gertie lived with Luke and his father, didn't she?'' Melanie was talking in order to forget her pain, talking about people whom she had never met but had heard about from time to time when she had visited Aunt Cissy, her mother's sister, who was the eldest of a family of nine. But they were a scattered family, most of them having settled abroad, and Aunt Cissy was the only one of her mother's family with whom Melanie had ever been close. A widow, she was a very sprightly seventy-year-old and, in her own words, "game for anything.''

"That's right. Biscuits, love?'' And when Melanie shook her head, "Don't let this darned business send you off your food, sweetie. Have a biscuit, just to please me.''

"All right, I will.'' Melanie was putting crockery and spoons on the tray, while her aunt was making the tea. "Why is Aunt Gertie coming home?''

"Can't stand the place anymore—that's what she says, but I'm of the mind that she's had enough of that nephew of hers. Darned autocrat, he is! Thinks he's the only man in Africa who knows about growing citrus fruits!''

"Citrus fruits?" frowned Melanie, preparing to take the tray into the living room. "I thought you said he grew cereals?"

"And trees."

"I imagined the trees were for timber!"

"He grows anything, but he does have a lot of citrus groves."

"How long has he owned the farm?"

"How long since his father died? About six or seven years...." The old lady frowned in thought, the teapot lid poised above the pot itself. "Luke was twenty-four and Gertrude mentioned in one of her letters recently that he'd just had his thirty-first birthday, so he's been in charge for seven years—yes, that'll be about right!"

The lid was placed on the pot and Aunt Cissy followed her niece into the other room. "Now isn't this cozy...? Oh, my love, I do keep on forgetting your sorrow. Try to forget the wretched boy—he can't be worth having anyway!" Melanie looked away and began pouring the tea. "As for that madam of a sister of yours—well, all I can say is that the way she's going on she'll have had at least a dozen husbands by the time she's my age! How old is she now?"

"Twenty-six."

"Ah, yes, two years older than you. I tend to forget her age because I never buy her a present on her birthday. I don't know what your mother would say to her daughter's wicked ways."

"Nor father," sighed Melanie, wishing she had parents to whom she could pour out her unhappiness. To live with someone would help, too, but Melanie lived alone in a small apartment that she had furnished with some of the things she had bought when engaged to Giles. She liked old furniture and had acquired several small pieces that she treasured despite the memories they evoked sometimes when she had sat on her own in the evenings—this before Robin had come into her life and managed to make her forget her vow never to allow herself to be hurt again. Well, this definitely was the last time!

"Come again, dear," urged her aunt when at last Melanie was leaving. "It's a pity you can't live here, but you'd be too far away from your work."

"Yes, I'm afraid so. Goodbye, auntie. Take care of yourself."

"I make sure about that, my love! As a matter of fact, I'm thinking of going on a cruise."

"You are? But when?"

"Don't know, but I want to do some more traveling before I get old. I'd have gone to see Gertrude if she hadn't been coming home; I did send her a hint in one of my letters recently, but she didn't answer. I suppose it's that fellow, Luke. He'd not want her to have a visitor; it would upset his bachelor existence, I expect."

"But he's used to having a woman in the house."

"One woman, yes, but from little bits I've pieced together he wouldn't want two."

"Would you like to go to Africa, Aunt Cissy?"

"I've always wanted to go to Africa, my dear."

"Well then, why not ask outright if you can have a holiday with Aunt Gertie, before she comes back—in fact, you could come back together. I'm sure Luke Shadwell won't mind too much."

"No?" The pale eyes rolled skeptically. "You don't know him! He's a real menace, from what I can gather from Gertrude's letters." A deep sigh and then, "No, I'd better book the cruise; it would be safer."

"I'll come over on Sunday, if you want me to?"

"If I want you to! Dear child, you must come on the weekends now that you're not going over to Robin's place. By the way, what are you going to do with all that stuff you've been collecting for your bottom drawer? You want to sell it, child, and take a darn good holiday!"

"I'm in no mood for holidays," was Melanie's forlorn reply. "But I shall certainly think about selling all that stuff I've been buying over the past six months."

IT SO HAPPENED that the following morning, when she was having her cup of coffee in the staff room, Melanie heard someone say: "Jean's getting married in three months. Poor girl, she's having a dreadful time trying to buy things for the home; everything's so expensive these days. I do pity the young ones who have to start from scratch."

Jean worked for the manager and at lunchtime Melanie sought her out, with the result that Jean and her fiancé came over that very evening and took everything that Melanie had to sell—lovely stainless steel cutlery, a dinner and tea service, cut glass dishes and beautiful table linen. There were sheets and other bedding, kitchen utensils, and, still in store but paid for, a stove and a washing machine. All these items had been bought by Melanie, while Robin had in store a bedroom suite and all the furniture for the sitting room and dining room.

"Is there anything else?" Jean asked eagerly as her fiancé just as eagerly loaded up the car. "I mean—have you any furniture for sale?"

"No, but my ex-fiancé might have," replied Melanie in a fit of pique. "I'll write down his address for you."

And so it was that on the following Sunday Melanie

was able to tell her aunt that she had sold practically everything that she had had in her bottom drawer.

"Good for you! There's nothing like making the break clean! And now I have some news for *you*! I think I shall be going to Africa after all."

"You will?" Melanie was not at all interested; her mind was on Robin and the happy times he and she had had each weekend. Mrs. Lowry, his mother, always invited her and she would arrive on the Friday evening and leave after tea on Sunday, Robin bringing her home in his car. Saturday was usually a shopping day, with Robin as eager as she to look around for nice things to buy for their home. Sometimes his mother would come with them and always she would buy some pretty ornament or small kitchen utensil and make them a present of it. In the evening Melanie and Robin would go to the local dance, and on Sunday they would do some gardening in the morning and take a walk in the afternoon. There was nothing exciting in all this, but Melanie was satisfied. Robin was not overromantic, but once again Melanie was satisfied. Companionship was important and both she and Robin were good conversationalists.

"Yes, dear, I think I'm to realize my ambition after all!" Clearly Aunt Cissy was excited, and feeling rather guilty at her lack of interest, Melanie determinedly put all thoughts of Robin from her and listened with more attention to what her aunt had to say. "You see, Gertrude had apparently missed my little hint that I was telling you about, but when she read the letter over again she felt rather guilty about the omission in her answering letter and so she mentioned this to her nephew. And what do you think?"

"He said it would be all right if you went over for a holiday."

"Right first time! Well now, seeing that it appears to

be all right with him I shall go off in the morning and book my seat on the airplane.'' The pale eyes shone and the rather prim little mouth was pursed in a smile. ''What a fortunate woman I am! I only wish I had the money to take you along....''

Aunt Cissy allowed her voice to come slowly to a stop. She looked sharply at her niece. ''You've sold your bottom drawer. Then why not come with me?''

Melanie stared.

''I can't do that, auntie. What about my job?''

''We'll only be away for about a month—''

''I can't take a month off—and in any case, if I know you, auntie, you'll stay on if you find you're liking it. Remember when you went to Canada to stay with dad's sister?''

''Oh, that? It was different. Luke won't want to harbor me for more than a month at the most. Come on, Melanie, the change'll do you the world of good!''

''No.'' Melanie shook her head, but her voice was far less firm than before. ''It's quite impossible. A month? No boss would grant that.''

''Jobs are ten a penny anyway, so what will it matter if he gives you the sack?'' Aunt Cissy looked hard at her. ''Didn't you say the other week that this new boss of yours was rather horrid to you all?''

''I did, yes, but....'' By now Melanie was weakening rapidly, for the picture of a month's holiday was attractive in that it would surely help her to forget this terrible ache in her heart. Life was a drag, and there was ever before her the picture of Robin and Romaine going around together; there were the murmurs of sympathy or, worse still, the compassionate or pitying glances of her friends. ''I'll think about it, auntie,'' she found herself saying, ''Yes, I really will.''

"Then think quickly, dear, because I'm off to book my ticket tomorrow, just as I said."

"I can't make up my mind as quickly as all that. I must find out how I'm to go on at work first."

Her boss definitely turned down the idea of Melanie's having a month's leave, but after some considerable thought she decided to hand in her notice. She had arranged to telephone her aunt and this she did, in her lunch hour.

"He's accepted, but I must work for a fortnight,' she told her aunt, who could be heard to sigh impatiently.

"All right," came the voice at last. "I'll postpone it. But you're sure you can be away by a week next Saturday?"

"Yes, definitely."

"Very well, then, I'll book the tickets and you can settle up with me later." A pause and then, after having mentioned the price of the return tickets, "You have sufficient money? If not, I can perhaps manage to let you have a little—"

"I have plenty, thank you, Aunt Cissy. I've not only got the money for the bottom drawer, but also my savings."

"So you have! Well, believe me, it'll be money well spent, for you'll probably not have an opportunity like this again. Gertrude is returning with us, by the way."

HAVING ARRIVED at the airport in South Africa at seven in the morning, they still had a nine-hour journey by train before transferring to the car that was to meet them.

"It's Gertrude!" cried Aunt Cissy excitedly, waving an enormous handbag in the air. "And who's that with her? I do believe it's Luke—yes, by Jove, it is!" Melanie stared as the tall lithe figure of Luke Shadwell came leisurely toward them. In a flash she had taken in the bronzed face, lean and long; the dark brown hair waving at the front and sprinkled with a lighter color at the temples—the result of the sun, she surmised. The square and massive shoulders, the arrogant set of the head upon them, the swing of an arm while the other hand was in his pocket—all of this she absorbed. But when he came closer she examined the eyes, unable to determine their color, for one moment she thought they were brown, the next yellow. Eventually she decided that they were a tawny brown. His mouth, firm but faintly sensuous, was set, unsmiling.

Melanie transferred her gaze to the aunt she had never met. She saw a chubby-faced woman with bright shining cheeks, a faintly hairy chin and thick bushy eyebrows. Her hair was white and thin, her eyes a sort of dull blue. She looked jolly and Melanie liked her on sight.

"We're not really aunt and niece," she was saying to Luke as the introductions were being made, "but no matter. Luke, meet my new niece, Melanie Burbank."

A brown hand was extended and a dark head was inclined slightly. The tawny eyes were mocking, surely? Melanie tilted her chin and decided she disliked the man intensely. Wincing as her hand was taken, she flashed him a glance; the lean unsmiling countenance had arrogance written all over it.

"Shall we be moving?" he said when it seemed that the two cousins were intending to stay there chatting for the entire evening.

"But of course," from Aunt Gertie, pushing an arm through that of Aunt Cissy. "Oh, my, but it's so nice to see you—and you, of course, my dear," she said over her shoulder to Melanie. "I've heard such a lot about you from Cis. I know all about your recent disappointment and I do commiserate with you!"

Melanie, aware of the man's eyes upon her, looked away to where the crowd jostled to board the train. The platform was open to the sky; palms waved in the breeze, while underneath them flowers bloomed in gay profusion. The small, neat town of Rayneburg was well known for its attractive railway station. There were also good shops and a bank. A library, well stocked and run by an English couple, stood proudly on a small rise almost in the center of the town square; the Jasmine Club occupied another rise just to the east of the square. Here, Aunt Cissy had told Melanie, were held dances and parties—so Gertrude had informed her.

"Can we sit together in the back?" inquired Aunt Cissy of Luke. "We've such a lot to talk about...."

"Most certainly."

And so Melanie found herself reluctantly taking her place beside the driver who, without so much as a glance in her direction, let in the clutch and the car slid almost noiselessly from the earthy parking space on which it had been standing.

They had fourteen miles to go and the road was covered with a light brown dust, which formed clouds behind the car as it sped along. Melanie already felt uncomfortable, for she considered the welcome sadly lacking—on Luke Shadwell's part, that was. His aunt's character was very different and Melanie wondered how she had managed to get along with Luke for so long. Melanie had gathered that she was a sort of house-keeper, yet not treated as a servant in any way what-soever; in fact, she seemed to be quite happy, and Melanie was puzzled as to the reason that she was leav-ing. It certainly did not appear to be for the reason put forth by Aunt Cissy—that she had had enough of the arrogant Luke Shadwell.

Dusk was falling and suddenly the shapes of some distant kopjes looked weird and ominous in the mysterious gloom that precedes the onset of night. They were passing through a region of bush veld where the colours reminded Melanie of submarine shades—blue greens glowing, and various shades of indigo. The veld seemed limitless, filled with primitive mystery, a realm that called, yet terrified. She knew a sense of loneliness even while she was with these other people; felt the pressure of a great solitude descending from the void that hovered all around.

From the back of the car chatter persisted and yet Melanie was deaf to it, her whole being affected by the peace of this strange land to which she had come... with the idea of forgetting, if only for a time, the heartache and humiliation she had so recently suffered. At the very thought of the male sex she turned her head, seeing Luke Shadwell in profile. Cold the lines and chiseled by a classical tool; the head was held rigid, the hands resting lightly on the steering wheel. Too self-assured by far, she decided. Here was another who would beckon and entice—and then toss aside. Or perhaps he was too self-reliant, too caught up with the more prosaic things of life, and had no time for the vagaries of emotional ties. Cold....

She herself would be cold from now on, insensitive to the attractions of men like Giles and Robin'... and Luke Shadwell. Yes, he had attractions; this she could not deny. But not the particular kind that would ever touch her. Other women must have fallen victim to his handsome face and noble bearing; others must have found a challenge in his austerity, and made attempts to break it down. Was he immune, she wondered. Or did he make full use of what prodigal nature had so abundantly portioned out to him?

That he must inevitably become aware of her fixed attention did not dawn on her until he had actually turned his head. She then moved hers, lowering it and concentrating on a pretty bracelet she wore, a birthday gift from her aunt a month or so ago.

"You're very quiet, Miss Burbank." The low-toned voice held an offhand quality that—for no reason that she could explain—piqued her, and she frowned.

"I like being quiet." She had checked the curtness that threatened to creep into her voice, remembering just in time that she was to be his guest.

"Refreshing—for a woman," he returned sardonically. "They more often like to make themselves heard."

Was he alluding to the chatter coming from the back of the car? Melanie was glad that neither woman had heard what he said.

"You sound as if you haven't a very high opinion of women, Mr. Shadwell." She felt that, could she see his eyes, a gleam of humor would be revealed.

"They're useful, in their place. The trouble is, they do not always know their place."

Her eyes glinted; she would very much have liked to let him know *her* opinion of *men*. The idea of spending a month in his home was far from attractive and she began to wonder just what their relationship would be by the time she was ready to leave. She rather thought that both he and she would breathe a great sigh of relief when that day arrived.

Darkness was falling softly over the bush veld and with the diminishing twilight rose the moon; shapes and textures changed, like a landscape receding into a mist. The moon, incomplete like a disk that had been bitten into, shed a dim light on the distant mountains and on the forest of trees below them. Then suddenly scudding clouds obscured the light and the mountains were embraced in the gentle cloak of darkness. All seemed wrapped in a sort of primordial peace, and despite her hurts and bitter memories Melanie found herself entering into a state of quiet repose, which was still enveloping her when Luke Shadwell's house was eventually reached.

Lights flared from several windows and it was not difficult to pick out the patrician lines of a colonial mansion, nor to visualize the exotic surroundings in which it was set. Figures moved past the windows, figures that, surmised Melanie, were Luke's servants.

She was right; Elizabeth, a plump and smiling black woman, was told to show her to her bedroom, which was at the end of the house, with its view to the west. She would see the sunset from her window, she mused, looking around her as Elizabeth put down her suitcases and began to unpack them without even asking her permission. Melanie shrugged and concluded that this sort of thing must be usual when guests arrived. There was a bathroom off the bedroom and she entered it, its elegance startling her, for she had not expected anything quite so beautiful. The suite was in a color between mushroom and peach, the carpet and walls in off-white. Gold-plated taps and shower attachments, a stool and matching linen basket completed the picture, and Melanie had to admit that, if this had been planned by Luke, then she had to give him credit for having excellent taste.

When Elizabeth had left the bedroom Melanie, having already taken a shower, put on a crisp cotton dress—one of the many she had collected for the honeymoon that had been planned—and a pair of white leather sandals. Her hair shone after the brushing she gave it, and because she envisaged a remark from her aunt if she looked pale, she applied the blusher to her cheeks and a little color to her lips.

Not beautiful like Romaine...but passable, she decided, not by any means for the first time. Romaine... and Robin. In spite of her determination to put them out of her mind, she found that the tears were close—too close, and she blinked rapidly in order to prevent them from falling onto her cheeks. But her heart was torn, and going over to the window again, she stared out, only vaguely aware of the bulky baobab trees that formed grotesque shapes in the mothy darkness of the garden.

She was totally possessed by misery; it formed a suffocating lump in her throat, and the pain was almost physical as she swallowed over and over again in an effort to dislodge it. Romaine and Robin.... Even now, it did not seem credible that her sister had managed a second time to steal her fiancé. Her thoughts flew to Giles, and to the scene when he had confessed that it was Romaine whom he really loved and, therefore, would Melanie be a sport and release him without any fuss? Melanie did just that, but it had taken her a long, long time to get over it, especially as she continually had to endure seeing him and her sister together. She had not attended the wedding; she was not having people casting her commiserating glances in between the admiring ones they gave to Romaine, who had looked both beautiful and regal in her flowing white wedding gown. And now the divorce was going through....

A gong sounding from somewhere in the house brought her back to her surroundings, and stepping back, she drew the curtains together and with a last glance in the mirror left the room and went downstairs to the hall. Luke Shadwell was standing there, very smart and handsome in a loose-fitting tropical suit of fine beige linen. She saw something she had not noticed before—the cleft chin and the crinkly fan lines at the side of his eyes, caused, she surmised, by his narrowing his eyes against the glaring sun. He seemed to have been waiting for her, she realized, and offered an apology for being late.

"You're not late," he told her courteously. "We're just going in to dinner."

"Aunt Cissy—is she down?"

"Both aunts are down—and still chattering about old times." He was moving away and she followed. The dining room, elegant and lit by candles, was smaller than she would have imagined it and she realized that it had been planned for intimacy of atmosphere rather than for the accommodation of large numbers of people. Here again she had secretly to admit to his good taste, for everything was delightfully blended—the damask walls and the thick pile rugs on the polished block floor, the Edwardian-type dining chairs and table, the matching sideboard on which were silver dishes and spare cutlery.

"Where have they got to?" Luke glanced toward the open window, a slight frown on his face. "Sit down, Miss Burbank; I'll have Disraeli go and look for them. They went off into the garden a few minutes ago."

"Disraeli?" echoed Melanie, staring, and for the first time she saw the hint of a smile curve the sensuous mouth.

"One of the houseboys," he elucidated. "The blacks give their children the most famous of names. Another of my men—one whose work is solely outside—is called Gladstone."

She still stared, but this time she was noting the color of his eyes again, deciding that it could change with his mood. Just now they were definitely brown, light brown, and expressionless.

A few minutes later, the "two aunts," as Luke appeared to have named them, appeared from the stoop and without apologizing sat down at the glittering dinner table.

"Oh, but we've had such a natter!" exclaimed Aunt Cissy. "How glad I am I came! Melanie dear, you don't look too happy. What is it? Come, dear, you must enjoy yourself, mustn't she, Luke?"

"I sincerely hope that she will enjoy her stay," he replied with cool courtesy. "I like to think that all my guests leave with only pleasant memories of their visit."

How formal! Did the man never unbend? Melanie watched him from her place opposite; he was stiff and cold and unemotional, she had already decided. And yet there was that mouth—it seemed to brand him as a man who, put in the right atmosphere, could be as ardent as the rest.

"Your thoughts, Miss Burbank," came his quiet voice across the table, "are plainly most absorbing." Half statement, half question; she strongly suspected that his words had been spoken merely for politeness, for the two aunts were so deep in conversation that it was impossible for Melanie to interrupt. That she had no desire for speech was of course not known to Luke, and so it was understandable that he should be a trifle concerned that she was having to sit quietly and listen without joining in.

"They were rather absorbing," she returned, and did wonder what his reaction would have been had she revealed those thoughts to him. Instead she changed the subject and, assuming an interest that she was far from feeling, she asked about his work.

"I grow timber and other products, but mainly I'm interested in citrus fruits."

"Oranges and lemons." She looked at him. "I was on holiday in Cyprus once and saw lovely orange groves near Famagusta. They were a very attractive sight."

"Ripening citrus fruits are indeed a most attractive sight," he agreed, and then added, "I also grow *naartjes*, which are tangerines." His eyes wandered, first to his own aunt and then to hers.

His lips pursed and she said without thinking:

"I don't suppose you're too happy at having three women in your house?"

His straight dark brows lifted a fraction.

"Now, how am I to answer that, Miss Burbank?"

Melanie felt the color rising in her cheeks."The question wasn't very tactful, I'm afraid."

"Most untactful," he retorted, unsparing of her feelings.

"Aunt Cissy was not too sure about your wanting to have us," she said frankly. "She gave me the impression that you didn't care for your bachelor existence to be disturbed."

Luke's firm mouth twitched.

"Aunt Gertrude obviously gave her a picture of a staid, middle-aged bachelor, fixed in his ways, resentful of any deflection from routine or interference with his peculiar little eccentricities." He paused, looking at her with a sort of quizzical interrogation. "Might I venture to ask if the picture fits?"

Melanie looked at him with an expression of censure.

"What are you expecting me to say to that, Mr. Shadwell?" she could not help saying, and to her surprise he laughed.

"Your counteraction's approved," he said, watching as she toyed with the crisp bread roll on her plate. "So we're both intending to respect our roles of guest and host? Politeness shall prevail, whatever lies beneath in the way of our private opinions of each other?"

Melanie's back stiffened and her chin lifted.

"That," she told him shortly, "is far from tactful!"

The tawny eyes widened, subjecting her to an intense and arrogant stare. However, whatever he had intended to say was not to be voiced because at that moment Aunt Cissy, having caught the rather angry exclamation of her niece, turned her head and said:

"What are you two doing—having a quarrel already?"

"Quarrel?" repeated Melanie. "No, of course not."

"You were raising your voice, dear, and I just wondered," said Aunt Cissy apologetically.

"Poor Melanie is perhaps suffering from 'mandislike,'" suggested Aunt Gertie, "and who can blame her? Luke," she continued in her rather forceful voice, ignoring Melanie's discomfiture, "you must make allowances for the child."

His eyes flickered with interest as they moved from Melanie's flushed countenance to the rosy glowing face of his aunt.

"Must I? Now why is that?"

"I—it doesn't matter—I mean, it can be of no particular interest to Mr. Shadwell," put in Melanie, her color mantle deepening now, but with anger.

"Mr. Shadwell? Good gracious, child, he's Luke! You're cousins!"

"Several times removed," supplemented Aunt Cissy, "but cousins for all that."

"I asked why I should be expected to make allowances for Melanie." He saw the start given when he mentioned her name, but ignoring Melanie altogether, he gave his whole attention to his aunt. "Is there something I ought to know?"

"Well, yes, I believe there is, just so that you will be kind and understanding to the child—"

"Aunt Gertie, *please*! Mr. Shadwell doesn't want to know—"

"Oh, but you're mistaken," came the cool, determined interruption. "I most certainly do want to know."

Melanie looked daggers at him, her mouth tight. But there was nothing she could do, as his aunt was already giving him the sad story related to her by Aunt Cissy both in her letters and, Melanie suspected, again by word of mouth soon after the two had met. Come to think of it, there *had* been a short interlude of whispering in the back of the car as they were all being driven from the station to Luke's home.

"And so you see, Luke, you must try to make the child forget, since after all, that's the reason for her coming here."

"I see...." His eyes rested on Melanie's face, which was now resuming its pallor as the color faded from her cheeks. "*Two* disappointments in love. How very extraordinary," he added thoughtfully as his flickering glance took in the clear-cut contours of her face, the large, widely spaced blue eyes, the high wide forehead, creased a little now as if betraying pain. "Yes...most extraordinary." He frowned, and then added, in a casual tone now, as if he were shrugging the matter off as of no real importance, "Oh, well, it might well be third time lucky."

"*Third* time!" Melanie threw him a deprecating glance and added vehemently, "I'm not such a fool as to run my head into a noose *ever again*!"

CHAPTER TWO

THE NIGHT WAS moonless, but stars glistened from a deep purple sky; the lonely bush veld was silent, enfolded in peace with only the chirping of cicadas to give evidence of life out there in the beautiful grounds of the house.

Melanie stood on the rear stoop, her mind back-switching to that first evening, just a week ago, when she had been so embarrassed by the story that Aunt Gertie had told to Luke. He had been different since then, adopting toward her a sort of condescending kindness and sympathy that aroused in her nothing more than a burning resentment. She had no need of his sympathy; she had no wish for his kindness. Her experiences had been humiliating enough without this added feeling of debasement that his conduct was causing her. If only she had thought to make known her desire to her aunt— but it was a debatable point whether or not she in turn would have persuaded her cousin to keep silent. Aunt Cissy certainly would have acknowledged Melanie's wish, but Melanie suspected that, charming as she was, Aunt Gertie had a liking for the dramatic, whether it be related to circumstances or merely gossip.

She turned suddenly, her spine tingling; she knew that step and wished she had gone straight to her room instead of coming out here for a breath of fresh air, and for a break from the incessant chatter of the two aunts.

"Hello, there. All alone in the dark? Why don't you

switch on the light?'' Luke reached above his head and the lamplight flared on the stoop. ''Mind if I join you? Your aunt and mine haven't stopped talking for a week. It gets a little wearing, as I suppose you, too, have noticed.'' Cool and casual tones, yet distinctly edged with that inflection of sympathy.

She froze, but managed to answer in a calm and even voice, ''Of course, Mr.—''

''Can't we have Luke for a change?'' he cut in with some asperity. ''The aunts think you're crazy!''

''Very well,'' she conceded, ''I'll try.''

''Don't strain yourself,'' he responded with swift sarcasm. ''Addressing me as Mr. Shadwell won't help in your defenses, you know.'' He came and stood beside her; Melanie wanted to move away, but for the sake of manners she resignedly stayed where she was. He seemed too tall altogether, when he came as close as this, and she disliked intensely the hint of shaving lotion or some such that reminded her of heather moorlands and mossy mountain streams. Yes, she *hated* it! Or did she...?

''My defenses?'' she repeated as the meaning of his words drifted slowly into her consciousness. ''What do you imply by that?''

''You're so transparent,'' he answered, hitching up a trouser leg and resting his foot on the lower rail of the stoop. ''Your fear's so great that you're all tight and hard inside.''

''Fear?'' she echoed with a frown. ''Fear of what?''

''Don't put on that air of perplexity,'' he almost snapped. ''You can't deceive me so easily. You know darned well what I mean.'' She had the grace to blush, and his smile was one of satisfaction as he noticed this heightened color. ''You seem to regard all men as potential breakers of hearts.''

"Nonsense!" she contradicted, "I do not! In any case, what men have I met, other than you?"

"You were at the club in Rayneburg twice during this past week," he reminded her. "I watched you with young Van de Westeyn; he wanted to be friendly, but you treated him as though he had the plague. And then there was young Groenewald. He was genuinely trying to make you welcome, and what did you do?"

"I c-can't remember."

"Liar!"

"Well. . .surely I can please myself! I've no wish to dance or even to talk to them!"

"Then why go?"

"Because you said you didn't want me to be left here—it wasn't right that you, as my host, should take the aunts and not me."

He gave a small intake of breath, denoting his impatience with her.

"You're the strangest woman I've ever come across," he told her. "Are you intending to be like this all your life?"

"I am," she answered briefly and very forcibly.

"Why," he suggested with a satirical smile, "don't you consider taking the veil?"

Melanie colored.

"Such sarcasm is in very bad taste," she said. "You seem to have forgotten what you said about each of us respecting the other."

"Guest and host—yes, I'm glad you reminded me. All the same, we haven't been exactly polite at times, have we? You are, of course, to blame for the most part. You're so touchy, so liable to shrink and then to expand—"

"Must you talk in riddles?"

"You flare up for nothing," he told her, bypassing

the interruption. "But first you curl up inside yourself, trying to find protection, rather like the little creatures that encyst."

"Thanks!"

"Don't mention it."

Melanie said, a curious light in her eye, "I don't understand you at all."

The tawny eyes portrayed amusement. "Do you want to?" he asked, and she gave an impatient shrug of her shoulders. Civility was so very difficult to summon on occasions like this.

"Not particularly," was her blunt reply. "Nevertheless, it might be more comfortable for both of us if we kept to the prosaic, and the uncomplicated."

"Prosaic? Just the sort of word I'd expect you to use."

"You wouldn't expect me to use the word romantic, would you?"

"Never—at least, not in this mood you're in at present. Tell me, how long did it take you to get over the first break?"

"Giles?" The word came out unbidden and Luke's eyes flickered with interest. "Three and a half years—about."

"Dear me! What fragile hearts women do have. Did yours really take over three years to mend?"

The color in her cheeks deepened. "I'd rather not talk about it." She stared up at him in wordless misery for a long moment before adding, "It isn't easy to talk about it at any time, but now...."

She paused and Luke prompted quietly, "But now—what?"

She shook her head and frowned. "It's harder still to talk to someone who can't even begin to understand."

"What makes you so sure that I won't understand?"

he asked, and she thought she detected an edge of irrita-
tion to his voice.

"You're—" She stopped, biting back the words that
rose to her lips.

To her amazement he finished for her: "Hard and
unfeeling, insensible to the troubles of others." Crisp
the tone and short.

Melanie nodded despite his glinting expression.
"That's right. I would also have added the word *emotionless*."

A silence ensued, a strange uneasy silence as far as
Melanie was concerned. She was experiencing something that savored of a warning, vague, indefinable—
yet troublesome. It was as if Luke were smoldering
beneath this cool and placid exterior.

"Emotionless, eh?" And now the voice, though still
quiet, contained a strange vibrancy that caused a tingle
to run the total length of Melanie's spine. "That, my
dear Melanie, is a very dangerous thing to say to a man
who has any self-respect at all."

"Oh. . . is it? Why?" This was spoken slowly, for she
was attempting to analyze his words. "I—"

"Yes, it is. Because, you see, he will in all probability
have the urge to disprove your statement." She stepped
back swiftly as the warning took shape in the form of a
flash of perception, but she could not escape the hand
that shot out and jerked her in no gentle fashion until
she found herself hard up against his sinewed body. Her
face was brought up with even less gentleness as, catching her hair, he pulled it back, and the little cry of pain
she uttered was stifled as his hard, demanding mouth
came down on hers. She struggled wildly but in vain,
twisting this way and that, determined to break free.
But his hold was like a hawser, his mouth sensuous, his
body deliberately pressed close to hers. Released at last,

Melanie leaned back against the rail of the stoop, fighting for breath, her eyes flashing fire. In Luke's eyes was a sort of amused triumph; he was still close but not touching her.

"You utter cad!" she cried, tears of mortification streaming down her face. "How dare you, a stranger, act like that!"

"Stranger?" he asked with a lift of his brows. "I was under the impression that we are cousins—er—several times removed, as your aunt remarked."

"I hate you! I only wish I could leave your house at once!"

"Too late, my dear, far too late. We'll talk about it in the morning—if you're still of the same mind, that is." His mocking eyes looked her over before settling on her tear-stained face. "You might on reflection decide you liked my kisses, and wish to stay—"

"You self-conceited, pompous overbearing creature! It's no wonder you're a bachelor—for I'm sure no woman in her right mind would even give you a second glance!" She spoke wildly, saying anything that entered her mind regardless of whether or not it made sense. For all she desired was to lash out at him with her tongue, to let him hear things about himself that would ring in his ears for a very long time to come. Her mouth was bruised, her bones aching. Her hatred for him and his sex consumed her and she went on, finding adjectives that, had they all applied, would have surely branded him as the son of Satan himself. "I shall tell my aunt about this!" she blazed at last. "And she will in turn tell it to your aunt!"

"I don't think you will, my dear—"

"And don't you call me your 'dear'!"

"My, but what a temper you have! Be careful, cousin of mine, for I might just turn you upside down, throw you across my knee and give you the beating of your life.'' As he spoke he was breaking off a branch from the bougainvillea vine that wound luxuriously around a white stone pillar supporting the stoop. With deliberate flicks of his fingers he was stripping the branch of its flowers and leaves while Melanie watched, fascinated, unable to escape because he was standing in front of her, and she knew, somehow, that if she ventured to move he would prevent her from doing so.

"You. . . you w-wouldn't dare,'' she stammered when at last, the branch fully stripped, he held it out for her to see.

"Dare what?'' he inquried challengingly. "Dare what, my dear?''

She blinked, not at all sure if he was teasing her or determinedly serious.

"You wouldn't dare to. . . to t-touch me. . . .'' Her voice trailed away and she paled as she noted his slanting glance.

"You do ask for it, don't you? Are you daring me, Melanie?'' he added in an almost gentle tone. "Well, are you?''

She swallowed and shook her head.

"N-no,'' she stammered meekly.

"Sensible girl.'' The stick was tossed away, right over her head. "Incidentally, I wouldn't have used the stick— my hand would have been more than adequate.'' Again the glint in those tawny eyes. He took a step toward her, but she made no attempt to step back this time. Her hand was taken again and she made no protest when he bent his head and kissed her quivering lips. "Why so docile?'' he wanted to know, but answered before she had time to do so, "You're learning, little one—learning that what I want I shall have, even if I take it by force. Much more comfortable, wasn't it, to abandon the struggle?''

She flashed him a glance of hatred.

"I shall leave here first thing in the morning, whether my aunt agrees to come with me or not!"

BUT OF COURSE she did not leave, did not even think of leaving. She had—apart from that mortifying incident—been enjoying the holiday, inasmuch as she could enjoy it with her mind so often going back to Robin and his treatment of her. The country drew her and she had walked a great deal since coming here. The silence and the peace were especially attractive and she was not in the least troubled by the fact that she was more or less on her own, the two aunts having become such bosom friends that they were always together. Sometimes Aunt Cissy would suggest that Melanie come into town with them when they went shopping, but invariably she refused, preferring to wander along the dry stream bed and find flowers she had never known before, or sit quietly and watch the brightly plumaged birds flitting around among the gum or cypress trees, their lovely wings flashing in the sunshine. Luke, aware that she could ride, had told her she could have Sanaan, a gentle mare that he kept specially for any lady guest who might desire to take a canter along the dusty road that flanked the river bed.

"I'd like to take advantage of your offer if I may," she told him stiffly three days after the incident on the stoop. "Will one of the men saddle her for me?"

Luke had come from the fields where he had been with the men pruning the lemon trees.

"I'll get her ready for you," he offered, his eyes faintly mocking as they looked into hers. "Coming round—at last?"

Melanie counted ten before she spoke.

"You couldn't expect me to forget *that* in a hurry, could you?"

"Shouldn't bear malice." he returned carelessly. "Come on, then, and we'll see to Sanaan."

He saddled the mare for her and then gave her a hand up, even though she did not require his aid. "Where are you going?" he asked.

"Just along the road and back."

He hesitated.

"If you wait a minute I'll come with you."

"It's not necessary for me to be on a leading rein," was her sarcastic rejoinder. "I wouldn't like to keep you from your work."

His eyes glinted dangerously.

"You're forgetting that pact we made—about respect and all that."

"I'm sorry. I do keep forgetting that I'm a guest in your house and therefore I must treat you with some semblance of respect."

"Some semblance?" he echoed. "If it's such a strain, then don't bother. It lets me out, so we'll cut even."

She bit her lip.

"I'm sorry," she said again and, flicking the reins, cantered away, leaving him standing there staring after her, a deep frown on his face.

She galloped along the river bed, under the shade of the gums and, later, the willows. Reaching a pool that had not dried up, she reined in and dismounted.

Sanaan was tethered to a tree close to a lush patch of grass, which she instantly began to crop. Melanie, in slacks and a white short-sleeved shirt, sat on a boulder and gazed into the pool. She could see life, but it wasn't in the form of fish. However, she found interest in the way the little wriggly creatures got around so swiftly in the water. Black butterflies flitted around among the crimson flowers and birds came close to her feet in their search for insects. A deep hush blanketed the landscape—like the silence of eternity, she thought, and realized that dusk was very close. She rose and rode on instead of turning back; she wanted to find the swallow hole down which the river plunged.

She had been riding for no more than ten minutes when she heard the cadenza of a waterfall, breaking in on the vast silence. And there it was, dramatic, awe-inspiring, as the water, coming from a higher level, plunging over a hard bank of rocks, cascaded down and disappeared into the swallow hole, leaving the rest of the bed dry, downstream from the swallow hole. Melanie stood in the gathering shadows watching the last rays of the dying sun as they painted the mountains with rose and gold and palest yellow. Tall palm trees swayed, their dark fronds, speckled with crimson stolen from the sun, silhouetted against the darkening sky. The veld became insignificant as the shadows deepened, colors changing from the green of tropical grasslands to drab fawns and browns and a dull sort of emerald. Over the vast landscape night was falling and stars were already peeping through the purple velvet sky.

Turning, Melanie began to gallop back, but she suddenly knew fear as, with the moon obscured by cloud, the world around her was growing darker and darker with every moment that passed. Sanaan stumbled and whinnied and almost stopped; Melanie coaxed her on, but it was clear that the mare did not like the darkness—not when she was in territory that was unfamiliar to her.

How stupid, Melanie chided herself. She was unable to see at all now and she felt sure that the path had run out. Or, more correctly, she had lost it, taking a fork instead of keeping to the main route. She reined in and slid down from the horse's back, patting her reassuringly and murmuring to her in soft and gentle tones. The mare nuzzled against her shoulder and whinnied again.

Moving cautiously, but still holding on to the reins, Melanie thought she had found the path and, remounting, she cantered along, sure that she had the right path now. But time went on and no sign of lights appeared to tell her that she was nearing the house. Fear caught her and she stopped again, all sorts of visions running through her mind, visions of wild animals and snakes, of natives on the prowl. Her heart naturally began to beat overrate and her nerves played her up repeatedly; she saw many strange shapes, which afterward she was fairly sure did not exist at all.

What time was it? She had no idea, but felt sure that it must be almost dinner time and there would be near panic when the two aunts were informed that she was missing.

She was just about to remount when she heard a call and, too unutterably relieved to speak, heard it again and again before she was able to make her voice loud enough to be heard. The voice came nearer and nearer until at last she was able to recognize it as that of Luke. How mad he would be! But she was not concerned with his reaction to her foolishness in not returning in time; she was far too relieved at the idea of his finding her at all, for she had in her wild imaginings found herself spending the night out here in the wilderness of the primitive bush veld.

"What the hell—" Luke spoke savagely as he came up to her, a powerful flashlight in his hand. It shone directly into her face, and instinctively she put up a hand to shield her eyes. "Are you quite out of your mind? What in the name of Hades made you stay out here all this time? And why didn't you keep to the path, as you told me you were doing?"

"I somehow lost it," began Melanie. "I'm terribly sorry—"

"Sorry! Do you realize that you've got your aunt and mine worried sick?" In his fury he lifted a hand and she stepped to one side, half expecting a slap on the arm. "Come on, give me the reins, and you get up on her back!"

"But—"

"Up, I said, and no arguments!"

She obeyed at once and nothing more was said between them until they arrived on the homestead, where every light had been turned on. The two aunts and four servants were there, on the wide white steps, and there were cries of relief from Aunt Cissy, which were echoed by her cousin in an even louder voice.

"My love! Oh, but we thought you were never coming back!"

"I wondered if we'd ever see you again!"

"You found her, boss. I knew you would."

"Miss, I'm glad to see you back." It was Elizabeth, and she came forward to smile at Melanie.

What a fuss! Melanie had never felt so guilty in her life. She could see her watch now and was horrified to discover that it was almost nine o'clock.

"Is Luke putting Sanaan away?" asked Aunt Cissy. "Oh, but he was worried. What happened, child? Did you miss your way?"

Melanie nodded, unsure of whether she was glad or not to have the opportunity of getting in a word of her own.

"I feel so guilty and foolish. I hadn't meant to stay out until dark, but it came down so suddenly."

"You know by now that it comes down suddenly," snapped the voice from behind her, and she turned to look up into the angry face of Luke. How forbidding he appeared! His face was tight, his jawline taut, his eyes glinting with anger. Regardless of her aunt's presence he set into Melanie, and before she quite knew it she was in tears.

"Luke," intervened Aunt Gertie severely, "that's enough. Melanie's gone through enough out there on her own, without your laying into her like this. She's exhausted and I expect she was very frightened, so leave her alone. Go upstairs, dear, and freshen up. We haven't had dinner yet—"

"You haven't?" she interrupted without thinking.

"Naturally we haven't!" snapped Luke wrathfully. "You've had everyone running around looking for you! Dare to do anything like that again and you'll answer to me! All right," he added with increasing anger, "you can dry those eyes! Tears have no effect on me whatsoever, not in these sort of circumstances. Upstairs— and don't keep us waiting long!"

"Luke," protested Aunt Cissy, "do have a little pity for the child. Melanie, dear—"

"Yes, auntie," she returned wearily, "I'm going to tidy up. I'll be down in less than ten minutes."

Dinner was a quiet meal, with even the aunts being rather subdued by the frowning countenance of the master of the house.

And when it was over Melanie went straight to bed, weary and unhappy and blaming Robin for it all. She could not sleep and after trying for over an hour, she got up, slipped into a negligee and stepped out onto the veranda that ran outside her window. How cool the night, and how silent. Twinkling lights in the very far distance signified the existence of a native village and across the lonely bush veld there drifted the weird and primitive notes of a native drumbeat. It fell, muffled, on the sweet-scented night air, mingling with the unmusical whirring of the cicadas in the tall cedars at the far end of the garden.

A sound altogether different caught Melanie's ear and as it drew nearer she realized it was a vehicle of some kind. Then light flared and a ranch wagon crunched to a halt in the floodlit driveway close to the front of the house. Two young people got out, a man and a woman. Melanie heard them being introduced to her aunt as Jancis and Edward Beaufort, brother and sister. The girl was dressed in slacks and a dark shirt, her brother in slacks and a sweater. Luke appeared; there was some chatter and laughter, with the voices of the two aunts rising now and then above the others. Then they were all on the stoop, sitting with drinks and enjoying a chat in the cool of the late evening. Melanie heard her name mentioned by Aunt Gertie, who said that she had been lost and so had gone early to bed.

"Oh, how dreadful!" It was the girl who spoke and she sounded genuinely upset. "It must have been terrifying for her. I hope, Luke, that you didn't scold her."

"What makes you think I'd do a thing like that?" he asked, and Melanie gave a little gasp at the bland way in which this was said.

"I know you, Luke—your infernal temper, that is. Did you scold your cousin?"

"Dreadfully, dear Jancis. That's why the child's gone to bed. She couldn't stand his scowling countenance any longer."

Voices now were lowered a little and Melanie lost most of the conversation. But just as she was going in again she heard Edward say:

"We hear you're going back to England, Mrs. Noden. Is that right?"

"Yes, Edward. I'm getting on a bit and I feel I should be retiring. It's not that I work hard here at all, but I do do a little for Luke. If I go he can then get someone else."

"You've done more than a bit," contradicted Luke.

"You did everything for father before he died and I'm exceedingly grateful to you. Also, you know how I feel about your leaving; you can retire here, for Elizabeth and the houseboys can do all that's necessary."

"It's kind of you, dear Luke, but I do want to be with my people—and live in my own country for a while."

"It's understandable," put in Jancis. "If you've lived here all your life as we have—and Luke, of course—you don't want to live anywhere else. The heat and drought and the loneliness don't affect you at all, simply because you're used to it."

"Well, I'm used to it by now, but all the same, I want to go home."

"She's coming back with my niece and me," Melanie heard her aunt say.

"When will that be?"

"In about a fortnight's time, or just over."

"So soon? But you've only just come. A month isn't anywhere near long enough! Why don't you stay for Christmas—it's only three months away."

"Well...*I* could, but my niece might not wish to. However, it would be nice to have Christmas in the height of summer. I'll put it to her in the morning."

Melanie turned into her room, her eyes glinting and her mouth tight. Her aunt could stay if she wished, but she herself had no desire to spend another two months under the roof of the vile-tempered, overbearing Luke Shadwell.

CHAPTER THREE

SHE WAS UP as the dawn broke, having slept badly, her uncontrolled thoughts flitting all the while between Luke Shadwell and Robin. She squirmed at the memory of Luke's ruthless scolding; she shrank from the memory of the scene in which Robin had, without any prior warning hint, told her that he had fallen in love with her sister. Life seemed to hold nothing for her at all and she wondered if she would ever have an anchor, and what form it was likely to take. True, she could make her home with her aunt, but that could not be for always.

After taking a bath and getting into slacks and a shirt, she went down into the garden. It had rained violently during the night and now the earth smelled fresh, and the dust had been laid. The air was heady and cool, for the sun was still very low, having come over the horizon in a glorious blaze of fiery crimson that flared in a great arc across the brittle sky. Melanie strolled through the lovely grounds, glancing back now and then to appreciate the homestead from different angles: white Dutch-gabled, it was indeed a stately home with its impressive pillars and wide shining steps, its portico and elegant balustrade and lofty stoops. Ancient, magnificent trees surrounded the grounds, which themselves were a paradise of subtropical trees and shrubs.

She loitered by a bed of canna lilies and was just bending to touch one when she realized she was no longer alone. She stiffened and turned. Luke was there, the picture of health and vitality, his bronzed face turned toward the sunrise, his eyes narrowed against its fiery glare. He was in shorts and a dazzling white shirt, and one hand was tucked casually into his belt.

Her color rose, which was natural, since leaping out from her subconscious was the incident of last evening.

"You're up early," was his casual comment as he examined her face in a critical way.

"I woke very early, and this seemed an excellent opportunity for a contemplation of nature...." She trailed off, surprised that he should be showing amusement. He was, though, for his mouth was twitching and his eyes glimmering slightly.

"Prettily put," he remarked. "I could add to it if you wished."

"I don't understand...?"

"Melanie," he said, trading his humor for impatience with the rapid change of mood that only a man of his personality could effect, "what makes you assume that obtuseness, which is so profitless simply because it doesn't deceive me in the least?"

"All right, I do understand, then," she almost snapped. She was angry at having her solitude broken into, especially by Luke, who was the last person she would wish to spend her time with. "And what would you add, might I ask?"

"I would add more in the way of atmosphere. You came out in order to appreciate the bountiful gifts that nature can provide; you wanted to watch the sunrise alone, to smell the delightful scents or flowers drenched in rain, to wander in the fullness or the peace around you, to drink in the exotic beauty of the scenery—"

"You should be a poet," she broke in sarcastically.

"I hadn't finished," he said shortly, with another

critical examination of her face. "There's nothing poetical in what I have to add." He paused, offering her time to comment, but she gave a small and impatient shake of her head. Why didn't he go, seeing that he was fully aware of her desire to be alone? "You wanted to do all those things, and yet you intended wallowing in your misery, half of your mind given over—willingly— to the misfortunes you've suffered." Again he paused and now his eyes were hard and censorious. "Do you believe you're the only one who's suffered?"

"No, of course not! But to be... be jilted twice! What about my pride?" Anger surging even higher, she glared up at him, her small fists clenched at her sides. "You talk as if I'm making a martyr of myself! But then you have no understanding, no heart!"

"I wouldn't agree, Melanie." And suddenly his tone was gentle, and although she had in her anger turned from him she knew instinctively that his eyes had soft- ened, too. "But I would admit to a measure of impa- tience. You came here to help in the forgetting, didn't you?"

"It was mainly that, yes."

"But you have no intention of forgetting. On the con- trary, you allow your mind to dwell on what has hap- pened to you. Correct me if I'm wrong." And because she still avoided his eyes, he took her by the shoulders and turned her around to face him. Her head was bowed; he tilted it up and instinctively she caught at his hand, which was under her chin. She let go as if it were hot, realizing what she had done. Her color fluctuated delicately and she saw his gaze assume a most odd expression. Her eyes were clouded with pain and her lovely mouth moved spasmodically. "I tried to be kind," he was saying after a long moment of profound silence, "not only because Aunt Gertrude asked me to, but because I wanted to. But you refused to respond—''

"Because I don't want your pity!" she flashed, stepping back so that some little distance was put between them. "I don't want anyone's pity. Would you, in similar circumstances?"

Without hesitation he shook his head, but immediately went on to say that he had always assumed that women were different from men in that respect.

"I assumed that, being the gentler, more emotional sex, they instinctively wished for sympathy when troubles beset them. I suppose," he added reflectively rubbing his chin, "that it's all part of the male instinct to protect."

Melanie stared then, her eyes wide and disbelieving. Here was a different slant altogether on his character! Never would she have given him credit for traits such as he was revealing in this conversation. His expression, too, was faintly troubled; and the softness that she knew would be in his eyes was most certainly there as, looking down at her, they seemed to smile even though they were grave, as well.

Her own voice softer now, having lost all trace of anger, she was moved to say, "I'm sorry, Luke. I didn't understand. . . ."

"But you do now?"

She nodded. "I think so."

"And you admit that I was right when I said you're dwelling on your misfortunes?"

Again she nodded, moistening her lips.

"I suppose you're right," she answered, but grudgingly for all that. And she did decide to add, "I can't just put it from me like turning off a tap. I was in love with Robin."

"But he wasn't for you, Melanie," he pointed out. "Had you and he been meant for one another, then nothing short of death itself would have separated you.''

Again the seriousness of his words and the manner of their delivery surprised her. The cold, hard logic of them did not; it was exactly what she would have expected of him.

''Nevertheless,'' she returned obstinately, ''I can't just accept this and, all in a moment, forget that I ever cared for Robin.''

Luke said quietly, ''Would you have him back, were he to come to you at this very moment?''

She gave a start, blinking her lashes as she endeavored to provide a truthful answer to this.

''I don't know—''

''Oh, yes you do! You would *not* have him back.''

''But if he explained that he'd made a mistake...?''

''For you, Melanie, there is a standard set in your mind. This fellow Robin falls short—excessively short—of your high standards. Forget him; he was never worth a thought of yours.''

Melanie said nothing, but she reflected on what he had been saying. She knew that she ought not to take Robin back, should he come to her, but she was not sure whether she would be able to build up a sufficiently effective defense against his persuasive powers, for these had always been strong, as was proved by the way he had led her from the path she had chosen after her first disappointment in love—when she had lost Giles to her sister.

''I think I'll carry on with my little stroll,'' she said quiveringly at last. ''Talking about Robin doesn't do me any good at all.''

''On the contrary, I believe this talk has done a great deal of good. Do you mind if I stroll along with you?'' he added after a pause. Melanie had taken a few steps already, but she stopped, staring with a sudden frown at the lovely canna lilies in the border beside her. Behind them a scarlet hibiscus shone in the early crimson light and a small protective hedge of oleanders sent forth their sweet elusive perfume onto the fresh morning air. She wanted to be alone! It was an urgent desire coming from the heart.

And yet, for some incomprehensible reason, she found herself saying:

"No, of course I don't mind."

"Good." He was all brisk all at once. "I wanted to talk to you about a problem that's come up." He fell into step, adjusting his speed to hers. "I've a very good friend who has recently lost his wife. He has a little girl of six and a half who happens to be fond of me—for some quite inexplicable reason," he added with a sort of grim humor. And then he paused and Melanie glanced sideways at him, wondering where all this was leading.

"He—Kevin—has to go to England in about a fortnight's time to see to all the legal aspects of a big transfer of land and other assets into the hands of his brother, whose trustee he has been since the boy was small. This brother is now twenty, at which age he comes into a huge fortune, left by an aunt. The aunt also left a fortune to Kevin, who was old enough at the time of her death both to come into his own inheritance and to be trusted to look after that of his young brother."

Again Luke paused and Melanie waited, bewildered by these confidences and now certain that they were leading up to something of importance—importance to her personally. "Kevin has excellent servants, but he can't leave Deborah with them—it wouldn't be fair in any case. He can't take her with him because his whole time will be taken up with this business he has to do. So," added

Luke slowly, "he has asked me to have her, believing that Aunt Gertrude would be here. Well, as you know, she's returning with your aunt in two weeks' time, so there won't be any women here, either. I practically gave him my promise when he asked me a few weeks ago and I don't feel like going back on it. Melanie, would you care to stay and care for Deborah?"

She looked up swiftly, shaking her head.

"No, I couldn't. You see, I have my apartment...."

"Your aunt said that you had to give up your job in order to come here."

"That's right; there are no problems about a job, but my apartment. It's coming winter in England and there's no heat on. Everything will get damp." She frowned in thought. "This little girl—as she's obviously been used to having only her father—and the native servants, of course—her position wouldn't be any different here, would it?"

"Her mother's been dead only just over six weeks, and in consequence her father's given her the whole of his time. I would not be able to do this, since I have my work to do. I did in fact sound out Aunt Gertrude and she was not at all taken with the idea or having a child on her hands for two whole months—"

"Two months? That's a long time for her father to be away."

"There's a vast amount of work to be done, apparently, for this aunt left over a million pounds to this young nephew. Yes, Kevin will be away for about a couple of months, if not a little longer."

Melanie stopped by a high trellis on which was draped a lovely bougainvillea vine, its lilac flowers making a magnificent display against a background of cypress trees. She said thoughtfully, "Aunt Cissy might like to stay—"

"She would like to stay; she told me last evening after my visitors had gone—I had a couple of young friends of mine drop in after you had gone to bed," he explained, and Melanie nodded before admitting that she not only knew this but had been on the veranda when they were all talking. "You probably heard her saying it, then?"

"Yes, but I decided there and then that no matter what Aunt Cissy decided I was going home at the end of a month."

His lips twitched.

"I can't say that I blame you, Melanie. I had no right to lay into you like that, especially before the aunts. I apologize, but must add that if you do anything like that again I'm quite likely to be even more angry than I was last evening."

Not a very gracious way to apologize, she thought, but made an apology of her own for all that. "I ought to have considered the inconvenience to others," she owned guiltily. "There won't be another time, Luke."

"Good girl!" He flicked a hand, asking if she wished to carry on walking. "We've no need to confine ourselves to the garden," he added. "We can go beyond; it's still too early for breakfast."

"Very well, we'll walk a little farther."

Once through the gates they were on a stony ocher-colored lane just wide enough for a car or ranch wagon. It ran through Luke's lands, and as mixed farming prevailed in this particular region, there stretched away—on both sides of the lane—the emerald green mealie fields, tall healthy plants with their slender leaves rustling in the breeze. Away to the west were great expanses of citrus trees and in the opposite direction lay the vast region that was given over to forestry. Melanie could understand why Luke was unable to give Deborah the attention that she obviously needed at this sad time in her young life. He talked now, and she learned that although her aunt had expressed a desire to remain long enough to see a South African Christmas, Aunt Gertie desired nothing more than to be in England for that festivity. And so it had already been decided that the original arrangements still stood.

"So you see," continued Luke, with a certain degree of persuasion but with no sign of anything that could even remotely be described as begging, 'I'm enlisting your aid. I did mention to your aunt, after mine had gone to bed, that I was intending to put this proposition to you. She was of the opinion that it would do you good to stay."

"In order to forget," Melanie commented with bitterness as once again the face of Robin came into her mental vision.

"Deborah needs someone, Melanie." Gentle the tone, but not persuasive this time. He was making a statement that she could muse over or ignore, whichever she chose.

She slanted him a glance and he turned his head, the tawny eyes examining, as they so often were. She knew she was pale, that in the harsh morning light the dark rings beneath her eyes would not be exactly enhancing to a face that was in her opinion only "passable." What she did not know was that her sadness had about it a sort of appeal, that the distress portrayed by the quivering of her lips lent a certain beauty to them to which Luke was no means blind.

"The apartment," began Melanie. "I don't want to leave it all that time."

"I see," he said crisply with a sort of grim resignation. "Forget it, Melanie—forget I ever asked you to stay."

THAT EVENING there was a dance at the Jasmine Club, and although Aunt Cissy maintained she was far too old to dance, she nevertheless wanted to go. Obligingly Luke offered to take her and Aunt Gertrude. Melanie refused, saying she preferred to stay in and read.

"But, dearest," protested her aunt, "you'll be lonely all by yourself."

"I don't want to dance," she returned in firm implacable tones.

Luke, turning from his contemplation of two children who had come from the native hut where they lived and were in the field with their father, said coldly: "Melanie must do as she pleases. She's my guest and as such her wishes must be observed by everyone."

Aunt Cissy looked askance at her, her lips forming a big surprised "ooh" while her cousin, more familiar with her nephew's moods, observed rather dryly: "You two've been at it again, eh? I asked you to be kind to the child."

The child.... Melanie drew in her breath. In normal circumstances she might not have minded this expression, but of late she had begun to resent it, and at this moment she was actually riled by it. However, she let it pass naturally, and she also let pass Luke's remarks. But on finding herself alone that evening, she began to wonder if she really wanted it that way. It was so quiet, for the houseboys had long since gone off to the hut they occupied among the little cluster of native huts a quarter of a mile or so along the lane. Elizabeth was in, though, for she was a widow and had a bedroom in the house.

Melanie picked up her book and tried not to allow her nerves to trouble her. She had turned several pages when it dawned on her that she had not taken in one word of the text. She laid it aside and leaned back in the big armchair, wondering what Elizabeth was doing there at the far end of the rambling old house. The curtains were closed, but suddenly she wanted them open, so that she could see outside.

Apart from the flickering lights from the native village there was nothing to see—except for the stars, and the indistinct outlines of trees and kopjes and the grotesque shape of the distant massif. Cicadas trilled into the cool night air, but except for this the silence was intense. Never had she experienced such total isolation, such frightening aloneness as she was feeling now. Her heart began to thump and it took all her restraint to stand still and not to turn and run to find Elizabeth.

Impatiently she closed the curtains, feeling sheepish at her fear, but try as she would she could not settle down, and at last she decided that there was nothing wrong in going along to find Elizabeth. Alternatively she could ring the bell and ask for a drink of tea or something, but she just had to move, so she went along the corridor to the kitchen. It was in total darkness, and in a sort of frenzy she snapped on the light.

"Elizabeth," she called, going toward the door of the room occupied by the woman. "Elizabeth—you're not asleep, are you?' Her voice sounded cracked and hoarse even to her own ears and she made a tremendous effort to steady her nerves. "Elizabeth!" Still no answer and her heart seemed to be rising, slowly but relentlessly, into her throat. "Elizabeth...." Melanie turned the handle and pushed the door inward, feeling with trembling fingers for the light switch. There—she had found it!

The room was empty and in a flash Melanie recalled Luke's passing remark that the woman was keeping company with a man from the village. But she had gone out without permission, of that Melanie was convinced, for Luke would never leave his guest alone in the house.

Back in the large well-lighted sitting room she felt a bit better, but not for long; the idea of being so far from people she knew and so near the native village terrified her, even though Luke had told her that the natives were to be trusted. Supposing one or other of them should decide to come prowling around, believing the boss had taken all his guests into Rayneburg and that the house was empty. This and other unlikely thoughts flitting through her mind, Melanie was soon in that state where she was ready to imagine anything. She listened until the ringing silence of the bush veld out there brought an ache to her ears. She moved around the room, glancing at the clock. It would be at least another three hours before the others would be back. Three hours....

She flung aside the curtains again, and then, driven by some force she could not control, she opened the window and stepped out onto the flower-strewn stoop. Light flared from the room behind, flooding the space in front of the house. Melanie stood very still, staring out into the awesome blackness, trying to pick out shapes again. Yes, there they were; once her eyes had become accustomed to the darkness she could discern them. The grove of eucalyptus trees, too, to the left of her and fringing the eastern side of the garden. Luke had told her that these immigrants from Australia were to be found in many parts of South Africa now, and on the veld these flowering gums were certainly a familiar feature of the landscape.

Suddenly she froze, the hairs on her arms and at the back of her neck standing straight up. Her heart shot right into her throat again and her legs went like jelly. No, she told herself, it was not a low insidious growl that she had heard. But there it was again—much closer and not a growl at all, but the bloodcurdling echo of a jackal's mournful cry. Swallowing in an endeavour to dislodge the blockage in her throat, Melanie stepped back into the room and closed the window. But as she made to draw the curtains she saw the two flaring headlights of a car and seconds later the long sleek vehicle ground to a standstill close to the front door.

"Luke!" she cried and, without any warning at all, sank gently to the floor as blackness swept away all conscious thought from her mind.

She was lying on the couch when she came round; the light was dimmed, only one standard lamp being left on, and that had had a cloth of some kind flung over it.

"Wh-what happened?" she asked weakly, but even before he had time to say anything she had added, shuddering as she did so, "I was terrified, Luke. I was quite alone...."

"I know,'" he returned grimly. "I completely forgot that Thursday's Elizabeth's night off. That's why I'm here; I remembered while I was at the club." He had a glass in his hand which, presumably, he had had ready beforehand. "Drink this and talk afterward." Gently he eased her up on the cushions.

"You came away—because you remembered?" She stared into his eyes and decided that they weren't tawny at all, but a soft and warm shade of brown. "That was kind of you—very kind."

"Drink your brandy," he ordered roughly. "It wasn't kind at all. You know full well that you resent kindness. I returned because it was my duty to do so. Drink it, I say!"

"If it's brandy it'll make me sick—"

"At once!" he cut in, but she shook her head.

"I'm all right now, Luke," she assured him, and held out the glass for him to take from her.

His eyes glinting and, she decided, not of a warm

brown color after all, he told her in no uncertain terms
that if she did not drink the brandy right away he would
pour it down her throat. He looked as if he would, too,
and so she obeyed, shuddering and pulling a face and
saying that it burned her mouth and throat.

"And now," he said when she had drained the glass,
"you can tell me what it was that caused you to faint?"

"You."

"Me?"

"I was terrified, and when I saw your car I was so
relieved that I . . . I—well, I just lost consciousness."

He shook his head as if this made no sense to him at
all.

"What were you afraid of—apart from being alone in
the house, that was?"

"All sorts of things. . . ." She stopped, ashamed of
her fears and in consequence loath to talk about them.
But she might have known that Luke would force it all
from her by the simple expedient of prompting her each
time she made a break in her story.

"So you tied yourself up into tight little knots of fear
for no reason at all?"

"I feel so very foolish about it all—now that you're
here." This last phrase was spoken without thought,
and he smiled a grim smile and said:

"So for once you're glad to see me, eh?"

Melanie looked at him, her mind not totally clear yet.
She thought he was far too big and overpowering,
standing there, looking down into her pallid face,
examining her as if he desired to know exactly what was
going on in her mind.

"I was never more glad to see anyone in my life," came
her honest reply at length. And then, more in order to
stall any sarcastic comment that might be forthcoming as
a result of her words, she asked him to sit down.

"Sit down?" He looked puzzled. "Why?"

"I don't like you standing...." Her voice trailed away and she put a hand to her head. "I think I'm going to pass out again," she said, but Luke had hold of her, his hands beneath her armpits.

"No, you're not! Just hold on—tell yourself that you're not going to faint." Commanding was his tone, imperative the manner in which he held her. Within seconds she was managing to produce a wan little smile.

"I'm fine now. Thank you very much, Luke." She felt at peace, so safe and comfortable here on the couch with Luke's strong arm around her. "I'm so sorry to be such a nuisance."

"You're sure you're feeling better?" he wanted to know, ignoring her last remark. "If you are I'll go along to the kitchen and get you something to eat. You had scarcely anything at dinner time."

She blinked at him. "How do you know?"

"I'm not blind," was the caustic rejoinder. And then, "Oh, yes, I was aware, also, that you pretended to eat, but what you took on your fork wouldn't have satisfied a child."

"I wasn't hungry," she owned, amazed that he should have been so interested as to watch what she was eating. "But I am a little hungry now."

"Good. Would you like some coffee with your sandwiches?"

She smiled at him as he straightened up, acutely conscious of the fact that his arm had been removed from her back.

"Yes, please," she said. "A milky one, if you don't mind?"

"Not at all; a milky one it shall be."

On his return with the tray Melanie inquired about the aunts.

"I'm going back for them," he told her. "It wasn't fair to expect them to come home at this hour. They're having the time of their lives."

"They are?" Melanie had picked up a sandwich, but it was now poised half way to her mouth. "But Aunt Cissy said she wasn't going to dance."

"She was certainly dancing when I came away," he said with some amusement. "She and Aunt Gertrude have found themselves two nice elderly English gentlemen who are on holiday here—at least," he amended, "they're touring in a Land Rover and decided to stop overnight in Rayneburg, so they naturally attended the dance." He paused, taking possession of a chair close to the couch, and he watched her for a moment as she bit into the sandwich. "You know, Melanie, if you weren't so stupid you'd have been with us, and you wouldn't have had the scare, either."

"I know." She fell silent, wondering whether he was considering her a nuisance. "I'm sorry, Luke, that you had to come home."

He said slowly, "And I'm glad that I did. I'm glad, too, that you didn't add that I had no need to have come."

"No, I wouldn't dream of saying that, because it wouldn't be true. I've already admitted that I was relieved to see your car out there."

"Why were you at the window anyway?"

"I kept wanting to know what was going on outside."

"Nothing goes on outside—unless we have a marauding tiger, and then we all go out to get him."

"A tiger?" Once again her sandwich was poised as she stared at him with wide, frightened eyes. "I didn't think you had tigers in Africa?"

"We call leopards tigers," he explained. "Sometimes

we have one around, but as I've said, we all go out—
with guns, of course—to catch him.''

"Is he dangerous?"

"He comes after the sheep and, unlike a lion who kills
only when he's hungry and intends to eat his kill, the
leopard will kill for the sheer joy of it, as will your
English fox. I lost no less than sixteen sheep one night.
We got the leopard, but not until a week later when he
came along to try his luck again.''

Melanie took her coffee from the tray and began to
drink it, her mind confused by this change in her own
attitude towards Luke. She tried at first to explain it by
the simple truth that she had been so glad to see him that
gratitude was now her dominant emotion. But, strangely, it was more than gratitude that affected her at this
time. She was in a mood of pleasant acceptance of his
presence; she *liked* being here, on the couch, with Luke
not very far away.

"I expect I'm not yet myself," she murmured, quite
unaware that she had spoken her thoughts aloud—
unaware, that was, until she heard him say:

"You still feel groggy? Would you like to lie down for
half an hour or so before we go out?"

"We?"

"I'm not leaving you alone a second time," he told
her grimly. "When I remembered that it was Elizabeth's
night off and I decided to come back at once, it was my
intention to go along to the native village and bring
Elizabeth back before I left for Rayneburg to pick the
aunts up, but now that I've seen how you are I have no .
intention of leaving you.''

"I'll be all right if Elizabeth's here," she assured
him. "Yes, if you'll go along and fetch her...." She
came to a slow but definite stop on seeing his expres-

sion. "All right," she said, "I'll come to Rayneburg with you."

He glanced at his watch.

"Do you want a rest first?"

Melanie shook her head. The sandwiches and coffee had done wonders for her, she told him.

"And the fresh air will do the rest," was his answer as, rising, he took up the tray and disappeared through the door. On his return Melanie was standing up.

"I'm fine," she asserted, a little surprised that she wasn't weak in the legs. She looked up at him, her eyes soft and limpid and faintly pleading. "Don't tell the aunts that I fainted, will you?"

He shook his head.

"Not if you don't want me to," he promised.

"Thanks a lot." He was ready to go, but she hesitated. "And thank you for...for...everything," she murmured, and Luke, although exhibiting some measure of perplexity at this rather cryptic sentence, asked no question at all but merely took her arm and, reaching the car, helped her in and tucked a rug around her legs and feet.

"Comfy?" he inquired as he slid into the driver's seat.

"Beautifully comfy," was her swift and frank reply.

What she didn't mention was that, for the first time in weeks, she no longer felt the leaden weight of dejection dragging at her senses.

CHAPTER FOUR

IT WAS FOUR DAYS later that Kevin dropped by with his young daughter. Melanie was in the garden, spread out on the finely cut lawn sunning herself, and she looked up on hearing the car. The aunts were having an afternoon nap, and as Luke was out somewhere among the citrus trees Melanie naturally got up, grabbing the beach robe that lay on the grass beside her and donning it over her rather scanty sunsuit.

"Hello." Kevin spoke before she had time to do so. "You're Melanie, Luke's cousin. He told me about you; you're here with your aunt."

"Yes, that's right. We're here on a month's holiday." She flung out a hand in a little helpless gesture. "I don't quite know where Luke is. Was he expecting you?"

"No, I was going into Rayneburg and decided to make a detour and drop in on him."

"Can I offer you anything, er, a drink?"

"I'll be glad of one," he answered, and then, looking down at the pretty fair-haired child at his side, "'Say hello to Melanie. This is my daughter, Deborah."

"Hello, Deborah." Melanie smiled and took the small hand that was extended to her.

"I want to see Uncle Luke." The child glanced all around; it was plain that she felt shy with Melanie. "Where is he?"

"I'll get Elizabeth to bring your drink onto the stoop," offered Melanie. "And then I'll send Gladstone to see if he can find Luke." Gladstone, she had noticed, was in the kitchen garden, pulling up weeds that had sprung up after the rain.

"Thank you, Melanie." Kevin, a man of about thirty-eight years of age, was of average height and weight. He had a look of sadness on his tanned face and his gray eyes were shadowed. Deborah, too, seemed sad and thoughtful; she held tightly to her father's hand as they walked over to the stoop.

"Would you like coffee, or something stronger? If so, perhaps you'd help yourself, as I'm not sure where everything is. And Elizabeth is not allowed to touch the intoxicants."

"Coffee will be fine. And for Deborah a glass of lemonade, if you have it."

"I'll tell Elizabeth."

"Is Uncle Luke coming?" she heard the child ask as she went from the stoop into the house to ring the bell. "I want to talk to him, daddy."

"So you shall, darling. Melanie will find him for you."

On her return Melanie was able to inform Kevin that Gladstone knew exactly where to find his employer and so Luke should be appearing within the next ten minutes or so.

Meanwhile Melanie sat with the visitors and tried to chat with the child. After a short while she did manage to make some headway and after that it was quite easy.

"I'm going to stay with Uncle Luke while my daddy's away in England," she told Melanie.

But her father interrupted to say: "We're not quite sure, pet. If Uncle Luke's too busy, then he can't have you...." He tailed off and a small sigh escaped him. His eyes were troubled and thoughtful; he moistened his lips once or twice as if he were under the effect of some nervous complaint.

"Can I come with you, then?" Deborah was asking. "I'd like to go to England and see my other uncle."

Melanie looked at her as she picked up the glass and took a drink of the lemonade. The pale gold hair was long but tied back with a blue ribbon; the eyes were a deep blue, large and widely spaced. A little retroussé nose and a pointed chin, a clear pale skin—altogether a very attractive child, was Melanie's assessment.

"Ah, here's Luke now!" Kevin announced, and Deborah clapped her hands together as she turned her head to see him cantering along the driveway, at the end of which Kevin's car was parked. A few seconds later Deborah was being swung high into the air, and watching Luke, Melanie felt a strange, restless sensation that she failed utterly to comprehend.

"And how's my best girl?" demanded Luke as he held her above his head. "Been good for your daddy?"

"I'm always good," she laughed. "Aren't I, daddy?"

What a change in the child, thought Melanie as the laughter of both Deborah and her captor rang out. She was certainly very fond of Luke, and very much at home with him. At length he put her back on her feet.

"I see that you've been looked after," remarked Luke approvingly as he noticed the empty coffee cup and glass. "Melanie's been doing the honors. Thank you." he added, glancing at her. She flushed a little and lowered her long lashes.

"I'm glad you could be found," she murmured, rising to go. "I myself had no idea where you were, but Gladstone knew."

Luke merely nodded his head; he was interested in what she was wearing, and she instinctively hitched the front of her beach robe together. The shaft of a smile touched his lips and her color fluctuated.

"Are you going?" he asked when she began to move. "There's no need for you to do so."

"I want to get dressed," was her reply, and Luke shrugged his shoulders.

But then he said, "What do you think of our little Deborah?"

"She's—charming."

Kevin interposed, "Don't flatter her, Melanie; she delights in it."

"Melanie's nice," interrupted Deborah. "I like her very much."

"Thank you, Deborah," returned Melanie with a swift spontaneous smile. "Shall I come back when I'm dressed?"

"Yes, please, and we can go and look at the flowers."

"Very well, I'll not be long." Conscious of Luke's eyes on her, she seemed compelled to glance his way. She could not help but note the question in his eyes and she turned away quickly, fearing she might weaken and consent to remain and take care of the child.

She was almost dressed when there was a quiet knock on her door.

"Come in," she called, expecting to see Elizabeth, or perhaps her aunt. It was Luke, and she glanced down with some dismay at the dainty underslip she wore. "Oh. . .!"

"Put something on," he said without so much as an apology for the intrusion. "Here—" Having picked up the beach robe he tossed it unceremoniously at her. "I want to talk to you."

"If it's about Deborah—" she began.

He interrupted her, "You know very well it is. Melanie, I'm asking you once again—will you stay for a couple of months and look after her? No, don't interrupt yet," he almost snapped as she raised a protesting hand to stop him. "I've had a word with your aunt and she's willing to go along once a week and see to your apartment—to put some heat on for an hour or two and make sure everything's all right."

He stopped then and waited, his austere features set and yet faintly drawn with anxiety. "Apart from anything else," he continued when she did not speak, "you'll be doing something fine, something noble. That child needs a woman, Melanie, and it so happens that fate has willed it that you happen to be here at this particular time." Again he waited. "Well?" he said impatiently when a few silent moments had passed.

She had put on the robe, but she still felt inadequately dressed. However, he had other things on his mind then the female figure and she felt her blush fade as she and he stood staring at one another.

"I really don't want to stay—"

"You're refusing?" His eyes rakcd her and there was a bite to his voice.

She felt an onrush of guilt and was angry because of it. "Although I'm sorry for both Deborah and her father, I don't see that their misfortune's my affair."

"I see!" His face became an unpleasant mask. "That is your final word?"

"Luke, I do wish you'd try to understand—"

"Was that your final word?" he interrupted impatiently.

"You're making me feel dreadfully guilty," she complained. "After all, it's only chance that I'm here at all."

His eyes flickered over her contemptuously.

"You have an opportunity of doing something good and fine, as I've said, and yet you turn it down, for no reason at all that I can see."

Melanie bit her lip till it hurt. It was a most strange thing, but while one half of her was more than willing to do as he asked simply because she was so sorry for those two out there, the other half of her was sending out warning lights, telling her to beware, instilling in her an acute sense of danger.

"I don't know what to do," she quavered. "My conscience tells me that I should stay, but—"

"In that case, stay," he broke in firmly. "Because if you don't, then that conscience is going to trouble you for a very long time to come!"

IT WAS THE MIDDLE of November and Melanie and Deborah were sitting under a mango tree, Deborah with her chin in her hands and Melanie leaning against the trunk of the tree, reading to her. Earlier they had been into Rayneburg—Melanie driving the ranch wagon with which she was now familiar—where they had bought, among other things, several glossy children's books and also some paints with which to color some of the pictures that had been left specially for this purpose. There had been heavy rain recently and the tributary of the Limpopo River was now a pretty stream with shining water dancing over the boulders and thick vegetation growing along its banks. The swallow hole farther upstream could no longer take the volume and so the surplus water was allowed to flow on, rushing down a steep gradient before reaching the area that ran through Luke's rich and fertile farmlands.

"I wish we could go into town again," Deborah said when at last the story of the "White Princess" was finished. "I want to see if there's a letter from my daddy."

"We asked this morning," Melanie reminded her. "I doubt very much if there'll be one today now. We'll go again tomorrow, I promise."

But when they got back to the homestead and Luke heard of the child's desire go into town again, he himself offered to drive in.

"We'll all go," he decided, "in the car."

"I like going in the ranch wagon, Uncle Luke, with Melanie driving."

"You're going in the car, with me driving."

"Oh, all right. But can I sit in the front with you both?"

"Of course; you're only a little one." But as he said this his eyes traveled to Melanie and she flushed as he slid them over her slender, graceful figure. "Yes, just a little one."

What was happening to her that she could be happy like this, she was asking herself as she sat in the front of the car, with Deborah between her and Luke. Robin seemed totally unimportant; in fact, his face was becoming vague and she had to work hard when on occasions she wished to see a clear picture before her. It must be the job she was doing, she told herself, the worthwhile job of caring for a motherless child while her father was away. On his return, he had told Luke, he intended employing a nanny for the child, and he added that while he was in England he would probably advertise for someone.

"The mail has come, after all." Luke had gone into the office and he emerged holding several envelopes, one of which he handed to Deborah and one to Melanie.

"It'll be from Aunt Cissy," she said, her eyes lighting up. But their light faded instantly as she saw the handwriting.

"Something wrong?" Luke asked, forgetting about his own mail for the moment.

She nodded, her throat having gone dry so that speech was delayed.

"It's from my sister," she told him.

"*The* sister?"

"I've only one. Romaine, who took Robin from me."

"And Giles," murmured Luke, and automatically she nodded her head. She did not want to read the letter and wished she could destroy it. Yet it must contain something of vital importance, simply because it would never otherwise have been sent, not with things being as they were between the sisters. There had been the initial rift, which was bad enough, but this latest act of Romaine's had, as far as Melanie was concerned, meant a complete break; she wanted nothing more to do with her sister. "Come on into the café and you can read it. Deborah, leave yours a moment and we'll find a comfortable place to sit."

This was done in no time at all, and while Deborah sat quietly in a corner reading the long letter her father had sent, Melanie was reading hers.

"They've split up," she said at last, and Luke jerked his head, again forgetting his own mail.

"Robin and Romaine?"

She nodded, wondering if she were as pale as she felt.

"Romaine's written to say it was all a mistake and that she's sorry. Robin wants me back."

"So...." The sensuous mouth hardened, the jaw went taut. "And you—what do you think about the idea of picking up a whole lot of broken pieces and trying to put them together again?" The sarcasm in his voice could not possibly escape her, but strangely it did not annoy her in any way at all.

"I can't come to a decision until I've thought about it."

His eyes glinted, hard as agate. "You're willing to think about it?"

Melanie shook her head impatiently. "I'm confused, Luke. Please don't ask me any more questions about it."

"As you wish," he agreed, but his voice had an edge of steel—cold steel.

"I'd like a lemonade, please." Deborah's voice, speaking to the waitress standing by their table, cut into the uneasy atmosphere that had arisen between Luke and Melanie, and Melanie gave a sigh of relief.

"What will you have?" Luke asked her coldly.

"Just a cup of coffee, please." Why was she now so dejected after having been happy just a short while ago? She would still have been happy had not this letter arrived.... And so the thing to do was ignore it—toss it away and pretend it had never arrived. She did just this, a wastepaper basket being conveniently placed by a potted conifer at the side of the table. "Well," she said with satisfaction, "that's that!"

Luke glanced up from the letter he was reading.

"You've made your decision—so quickly?"

She nodded and smiled, little realizing how different she appeared from what he had seen in her face a few minutes ago.

"Yes, I have."

"And you look as if you've shed a ten-ton load."

"That's exactly how I feel!" Her lovely mouth curved and then her smile had spread to laughter. "I'm free of him," she said. "Oh, but you have no idea what that letter has done to me!"

"If it's freed you, Melanie, then that's good news. I shall take you to the club tonight, just to celebrate that freedom."

Her eyes lit up. "That's nice of you, Luke."

"Just a cousinly gesture," was the strangely caustic rejoinder.

"Thank you." Her voice had lost a little of its verve, because of his tone and his expression and because he had instantly dropped his eyes to his letter again.

"WHAT SHALL I WEAR?" she was asking herself later when, having bathed Deborah and put her snugly into bed, she had read to her for a while before putting out the light in the dainty little bedroom that the child occupied. "I think my plain black velvet skirt and my white lace blouse."

Luke'e eyes flickered over her as she came down to the hall where he was waiting for her, looking far too attractive in casual slacks and a white safari jacket. His thick hair was brushed back, but even as she looked an unruly lock came forward. Carelessly he flicked a finger under it, but he had no sooner put it back than it had fallen again.

"You look wonderful," he told her, and yet somehow she thought she detected a hint of mockery in the compliment. Unfathomable man, who could change moods so swiftly. He baffled her in his manner toward her—though still that of the host in his concern for her comfort, it was also one of faint familiarity, a familiarity that she shied from, remembering the incident of the kiss, which occurred very early in their acquaintanceship. He had obviously enjoyed it and he could one day decide he would like a repetition—and this she meant to avoid. There would be no affairs for her, however superficial and fleeting. She was finished with men forever; the realm of love and romance and marriage was not for her, simply because she had no intention of embarking on the journey that would take her there.

"Thank you, Luke," she said, forcing a smile. "I'm sorry to have kept you waiting."

"It's of no matter. I expect Deborah took a great deal of your time?"

"She likes me to read to her for a while, and I couldn't disappoint her just because we were going out."

"I've given Elizabeth instructions to listen for her; she'll not wander off or anything like that."

The car was standing at the front door and within half an hour of getting into it they were at the club, having driven along a road where one or two stately white bungalows had recently been built, and farther along, some palm-shaded huts where native Africans lived. The night was cool but not cold, with a new moon hanging in the great purple vault of the star-spangled sky. As they got out of the car a wispy cloud spun a veil right overhead and the stars behind it took on the appearance of a handful of pearls.

"What a glorious evening!" someone was remarking as others, too, got out of a car. Someone else spoke and there was a general air of jollity as laughter rang out from the babble of voices, both male and female.

Luke helped her from the car and closed the door.

"A drink first?" he asked as he guided her into the lounge. Several people hailed him and nodded to Melanie, whom they knew because she had been to the club with Luke and the two aunts several times since that night of terror when she had vowed never to be left alone again.

"Heard from Kevin?" asked a bronzed South African fruit grower, Jan Woebecker.

"Yes, and so has Deborah."

"Sad business. Will he get a nurse for the child?"

"He has that idea in mind. Melanie, what would you like?"

She told him and they took their drinks over to a

table, which at first they had to themselves, but within a few minutes they had been joined by Edward and Jancis, whom Melanie had met previously at a club dance.

"How nice to see you!" exclaimed Jancis. "Can we sit here?"

"Please do." Luke had risen and was now asking what they were drinking. While he was away Edward became caught up with one of his friends and Melanie found herself alone with Jancis.

"How's Deborah?" asked Jancis conversationally. 'I expect she's missing her daddy."

"Definitely; she asks about him every day. But she's not unhappy, which is a blessing."

"You're very modest, Melanie. We all know how much you're doing for the child." Melanie merely colored and Jancis went on to explain, "Luke's told us all about it. He thinks you're doing a wonderful job." The girl looked oddly at her and then, "How do you find him—Luke, I mean?"

Melanie looked at her with a puzzled expression. "I don't understand...?"

"He's so impenetrable, with his armor of arrogance and air of superiority. Oh, I know he's your cousin, but you must be regarding him in the light of a *man* for all that."

Melanie laughed and said, "He is a man, so how else would I regard him?"

"You know what I mean. If I were living in the same house as him I'd either break him or be broken myself. I have tried from time to time, but—" helplessly Jancis spread her hands "—I've never made any headway, so I've come to the conclusion that only rare and porcelainlike beauty can melt him."

"What makes you say a thing like that?" Melanie's thoughts flew to Romaine—whose beauty had been described as "porcelainlike" by a well-known portrait painter in England.

"Well, because he did once fall for a girl like that."

"He did?" Melanie wondered why she was so interested in Luke's past love affair.

"Yes. She came from Scotland, I think, to spend a winter here with some relatives who have now left these parts. She and Luke were seen together all the time and it was fully expected that he would marry her, but something happened and the next thing we knew was that she had gone home, and she never came back."

"When was this?"

"About three or four years ago. I must admit that I was glad it fell through because I then felt I had a chance again—I'd been doing a bit of chasing before this rare beauty appeared—but he wouldn't fall. He reverted right back to the unreachable god who sits high on his pedestal and won't even bend to let you touch him."

"So he's been in love...."

"Unbelievable as it seems, yes, he has!"

Luke came back and the four of them chatted casually. Then Melanie found herself in Luke's arms, following him as if they'd danced together all their lives. He seemed happy, content; she knew she was happy, and at peace with the whole world.

They danced together for most of the time and then, just before the end, Luke said they would go outside to take a breath of fresh air before the last dance, which was a waltz.

"What a lovely evening I've had!" she told him enthusiastically. "I can't think how I've recovered so quickly, not when it took me three years—and more—over Giles." So easily she could talk about those two who had let her down!

"But you didn't have any help the first time."

"That's true. Coming here has certainly been good for me."

"And now you're almost ready for that third time I mentioned."

She stiffened and the blood within her seemed to freeze.

"I most certainly am not! I meant what I said about never letting a man hurt me again. What kind of a fool do you take me for?" She had stopped under a high palm tree, and Luke was beside her, tall and austere as he looked down and saw her face in the dim light that had escaped from an uncurtained window of the club.

"My mistake," he said crisply. "Bad joke, wasn't it?"

"Exceedingly bad."

A silence fell, uncomfortable and long. Melanie knew a sense of loss; she knew anger, too—anger against Luke for saying something that had spoiled the pleasure she was experiencing. The night was no longer magic— even the sky was losing its starry splendor as soaring domes of cumulonimbus clouds gathered with ominous intent.

"It's going to rain," she mentioned, quite unnecessarily but for something to say. Luke continued to walk on, his eyes staring at nothing in particular. "I think we ought to go back."

"If that's what you want." And without more ado he swung around and began to retrace his steps, striding out so swiftly this time that she had to skip to keep pace with him.

They reentered the club and danced the last waltz. Melanie spoke to him several times but received monosyllables in reply, and she eventually abandoned the attempt to recreate the happy atmosphere that had prevailed before they had gone outside for that stroll.

"Thank you for taking me," she said when they had arrived back at the homestead.

His gaze was stony as he replied, "Think nothing of it. I hope you enjoyed it."

"Of course." She knew she was not convincing. "It was a most pleasant change."

His mouth curved in a sort of mocking half sneer. "You're remembering to be polite all at once."

Melanie said bluntly, "You spoiled it by mentioning my readiness for another gamble with love."

"Gamble?" His stony gaze was riveted upon her. "Is that how you regard it?"

"It's most certainly a gamble," she asserted, "and one at which I could never be the winner."

Impatience was written all over his face.

"Isn't that an assumption that is rather absurd?"

It was Melanie's turn to exhibit impatience.

"It might appear absurd to you, but to me it's logical that I should have come to the conclusion that I'm unlucky in love."

He said nothing for a moment and she dwelt for a space on what Jancis had told her about Luke's own love affair. Perhaps he was thinking about it at this present time, since his expression was so grim.

"You're a strange girl," was all he said. He and she were in the sitting room and the curtains were wide apart; a flash of lightning warned of the storm that was to come. "You've allowed yourself to become so embittered by these two experiences that you can't even see straight."

She looked up at him. What exactly did he mean by that?

"I admit I'm embittered—and so would you be," she added indignantly as he lifted his brows on hearing her first words. "What makes it all worse is that in both cases it was my own sister who caused the break."

"Your sister...." He appeared to be diverted by this. "What is she like?" he asked, at the same time looking intently at her, examining every feature of her face— the high cheekbones, the flawless skin, the lovely blue eyes, limpid in the shaded light coming from the solitary wall light on the opposite side of the room.

"Very beautiful." She paused a moment before deciding to add, "Hers is a beauty usually described as a rare, porcelainlike beauty. A portrait painter once described her in that way."

His eyes flickered and she wondered if her words had recreated the memory of another girl with that particular kind of beauty. This time his face showed no sign of the grimness that had possessed it a few moments ago, but his expression could certainly be described as reflective.

"You do know," he said at last, "that you yourself possess a rare kind of beauty?"

She started, and then colored daintily. His expression changed rapidly and what she saw there brought an even deeper flush to her cheeks.

"I'm...passable," she managed to say, and at the rather scolding lift of his eyebrow she added, "That's how I always describe myself."

"Ah—how *you* describe yourself. But then, Melanie, you are not in a position to judge."

"Are you trying to flatter me, Luke?"

"I'm stating a fact."

She shook her head to throw off that statement. "I'm not what anyone would describe as beautiful."

"You have no faith in my assessment, then?" The eyes were brown now, and narrowed.

"That's a difficult question, Luke. If I say no then

you'll accuse me of impoliteness; if I say yes then surely I'm immodest?''

He laughed unexpectedly.

"You're an obstinate child, Melanie, and I do think the day will come when I shall carry out my threat."

"Threat?" she blinked. "What threat?"

"To beat you, for I'm certain it's the only way to deal with a girl like you."

Her cheeks, already fused with color, became hotter than ever.

"You wouldn't dare to touch me!"

"That's too confident a statement by far, let me warn you. If you continue to crouch inside your little walled-in fortress, then I shall set about blowing it up...." He paused to wag a long brown finger at her. "And in the process, my little one, you're going to get hurt! And I'm not so sure that I oughtn't to begin right now!"

Although her nerves instantly sprang to the alert, Melanie had no time to benefit from the warning as, with as little heed for gentleness as on that previous occasion, he had jerked her to him and, taking her chin in a ruthless grip, he pressed his lips to hers. As before, she began to struggle, but Luke was even more forceful now than he was then and her action seemed to infuriate him. "You'll get hurt, I'm warning you!" he said between his teeth before his cruel mouth crushed hers again. "And I'm also warning you that you'll reciprocate!" he told her as at length he held her from him.

Melanie was fighting for breath, but his eyes remained hard; she put a soothing finger to her lips but the action only served to bring a smile of mocking triumph to his mouth. Her slender body quivered in his arms, but his reaction was merely to tighten his hold unmercifully. Thoroughly shaken, Melanie thought for a second of Robin, who, not being romantic, had kissed her without passion or desire. This man's kisses possessed both. . . and in no mean quantities, either!

She said quietly when at length he decided to release her, "I shall never reciprocate; and in fact, I can't see why you should want me to. If it's an affair you want, you should find someone with more to offer than I." She turned from him and moved away toward the door. "I can't leave Deborah now," she said, and her voice trembled as the tears trickled down onto her cheeks. "But I might as well tell you that, had I known what I know now, I would never have consented to stay in the first place."

Coldly he looked at her, and she did wonder how he could be so heartless.

"I'd kissed you before then," was his stiffly spoken reminder.

"I didn't expect there'd be a repetition."

"No?" He seemed to give a small sigh, but she could not be sure of this. "Then you're even more stupid than I thought you were."

She frowned. There was some subtle implication in this, she knew, but being so shaken by the scene just enacted, and so utterly tired and dejected, she merely bade him a curt good night and left the room.

CHAPTER FIVE

WHETHER OR NOT Luke had been worrying about the possibility of her going back on her word about not leaving Deborah, Melanie did not know, but just before lunchtime the following day he approached her as she was in the garden, with Deborah at her side, picking some French beans. They were for the evening meal, and as it was a pleasant task Melanie often went out and gathered the vegetables that Gladstone grew with such care and pride.

"I'd like to speak to you," he said, glancing at the child. "Deborah, run along inside to Elizabeth."

"Now, Uncle Luke?"

"Yes, now."

Without another word Deborah went, and Melanie, straightening up at last, nervously smoothed her dress— just for something to do. Her face was flushed by the memory of last night; her eyes were just a little too bright.

"I want to say that I'm sorry," was the surprising manner in which he began. "It was inexcusable of me to treat you like that. I ask your pardon."

She looked up into his austere countenance, wondering just what the apology had cost him. A great deal, she suspected, and swiftly on this came the probable reason for the apology.

"I wouldn't have left," she said in a low and husky tone. "So you needn't have worried."

He seemed to swallow hard before saying, "Am I forgiven, Melanie?"

"Of course."

"You were so happy at the dance, and then I spoiled it." He was not in any way humble, yet undoubtedly he was in a softer mood than usual. And now she grasped it all! He was being kind again—after having forgotten his aunt's request for him to make life easy for her. She supposed that on both those occasions when he had treated her so abominably he had been in the kind of mood where he wanted to do a little petting; and she, Melanie, had just happened to be there—on hand, as it were.

"Are you going into Rayneburg at all today?" she asked, anxious to change the subject. "Deborah wants to buy some wool. She's suddenly decided to knit you a scarf."

"Me?" He shook his head. "I don't want a scarf."

"Oh, yes, you do. Deborah's knitting you one, so of course you want it."

"Of course," he agreed, and then, "I wasn't going into town, but I can do. Are you coming, as well?"

"Not if you're going. I'd have gone had you been too busy."

"What are you going to do, then?"

"Wash my hair for a start."

"So my taking Deborah off your hands will give you a little time to yourself?" He frowned and added, "I should have thought of this before—"

"It doesn't matter. I manage to get through all my own little jobs without much trouble. Besides, it won't be for much longer now."

Silence—strange and uncomfortable. Melanie looked up to see the most odd expression on Luke's face. And for one unaccountable moment she had the most convincing notion that he did not want her to leave—not ever. . . .

"What time do you want me to take her?" he asked brusquely. "I can't go immediately after lunch, but I shall be free from about two-thirty on."

"That'll be fine. Any time that suits you."

Lunch was a far more pleasant meal than breakfast had been, as then Melanie and Luke weren't on speaking terms and it was Deborah's voice that was heard throughout the meal. But now Luke and Melanie chatted—just as if nothing untoward had happened so very recently, she thought. They were on the stoop at the back of the house; it was cool and the fresh breeze blew along its length. The lunch was a typical South African one of fresh grapefruit followed by pumpkin soup. Cape snook was the fish course and then lamb cutlets, sweet potatoes and fried eggplant rings—these with a green salad, which was followed by corn on the cob flavored with butter and salt and pepper. Luscious papaw was the dessert being served with lemon juice and sugar.

"Ooh, that was good!" exclaimed Deborah, patting her stomach. "I think I'll go out and play now." She glanced at Luke. "Please may I leave the table?" she asked primly as she noted his expression. He nodded his head.

"You may. Be ready to go out when Melanie calls you."

"Yes, I won't go far."

Off she went, singing to herself, and when she was out of earshot Luke said seriously, "Thank you, Melanie, for staying."

She was unable to answer, yet she could not have said why. Her throat felt blocked; her thoughts flitted around and she saw herself getting ready to leave, saw

Luke taking her to the railway station, saying goodbye.... She was on the plane, flying away...never
to return. She frowned at these thoughts and endeavored to distract her mind by an interested contemplation
of the garden with its glorious riot of color—cannas,
bougainvilleas, English roses, hibiscus blossoms and
the fiery red gold of the flowers of the flamboyant
tree. The sun was high and as its rays filtered through
the waving palm fronds undulating patterns of light and
shade streaked across the velvet lawn. The melodious
sound of the houseboy singing mingled with the whirring of cicadas and the breeze as it drifted between
the leaves of the vine that shaded the stoop. Over the
veld, heat shimmered, and the mountains burned in the
sun.

Melanie, suddenly acutely conscious of a strange and
baffling emotion rising uncontrollably within her,
became staggered by the knowledge that she had no
urgent desire to leave here, after all. It was so beautiful
a land despite its many disadvantages. But she liked the
isolation, the warmth of the sun on her body, the balmy
evenings and flaring sky at dawn. She was happy living
in such a luxurious house, happy when in the garden, or
walking beside the riverbed. Happy....

"What are you thinking, Melanie?" Luke was sitting
back in his chair, one leg bent and resting on the knee of
the other. His hand gripped his ankle tightly and she
noticed the veins standing out between knuckles and
wrist. "You look so very serious."

She hesitated, unwilling to confess the truth. But after
a moment she shrugged and said frankly, "I was thinking how happy I am here."

His eyes widened.

"But only an hour or two ago you implied that you
were impatient to leave?"

"Yes, and I suppose I am...and yet..."

"You've changed your mind?" he asked curiously.

"Not exactly. In any case, I couldn't stay indefinitely. But I am growing to love this place."

"The house, you mean?"

"That, as well."

"As well as what?"

"The countryside. And I love the sun, and even the rain." She looked at him in some bewilderment. "I suppose a country like this, with its mystery and magic and exotic flowers and trees, gets hold of you and you know that when you leave there'll be a wrench, just as if you're pulling up roots that have grown despite your initial conviction that nothing of this nature could possibly happen." She had no idea why she spoke like this; it was too intimate by far. Her intention must always be to hold on to her reserve where Luke was concerned—although she felt sure he would never again give her reason to fear his attentions.

"So you've already sent down roots?"

She moistened her lips, reluctant to be drawn deeper into this subject.

"I supoose I must have done," she admitted at last.

"I wonder why?"

"I can't explain, even to myself." She stirred uneasily on her chair. "It isn't an easy thing to explain, Luke. All I know is that I shall remember this all my life."

His eyes were inscrutable, yet she had the impression that beneath the cool unruffled exterior there burned a strong emotion.

"Something is disturbing you," he stated, but she shook her head immediately.

"Nothing is disturbing me," she returned. To her relief the conversation ended there because Deborah, tired of what she had been doing, came on to the stoop to say, "Melanie, please come and play with me until Uncle Luke's ready to take me shopping."

THE NEXT FORTNIGHT passed uneventfully in one way, but in another it was memorable. For during that time a sincere friendship had grown between Melanie and Luke. They would walk together of an evening when Deborah was in bed; they danced at the club; attended parties given by the neighbors; gave a small dinner party themselves, with Melanie helping "just as if she were the lady of the house" Luke had said, but teasingly. For Melanie there were moments of great pleasure...and there were moments when there would creep over her an indefinable longing...and a desire. She was proud to be with Luke when they visited or went to the club; she was content to be with him on those evenings when they sat on the stoop in the cool of the summer evening—for the South African summer was well under way now— talking quietly, just the two of them. Luke asked about her life—her childhood and later. She found herself keeping nothing back.

For his part Luke also confided, but he was never quite without reserve and it was as if he were guarded in his every word, his every act. Sometimes—especially when she mentioned her intention of never taking any more chances with men—he would adopt a satirical or mocking mood; sometimes his mood would be a teasing one; but on occasions it would be almost tender. And it was at these times that Melanie would know a recurrence of that yearning, that strange desire that defied interpretation. Confused, she would lie awake at night and make a concentrated effort to reason out the cause of her troublesome emotions. And, just as she was giving up, there would invariably come to her those scenes when Luke had forced his kisses upon her. She would feel them again, but they were never quite so rough, nor were his arms quite so hurtful, as they had been at the time.

It was in early December that the letter arrived, the letter that not only threw her into confusion but that also seemed to tell her that the pleasant days she had known were definitely at an end.

"What on earth's wrong?" demanded Luke rather anxiously as he noted her sudden pallor and the way the letter fluttered in her hands. "Bad news...from your aunt?"

She shook her head, dazedly staring up at him.

"Romaine's coming here—and Robin."

A frown that was almost a scowl appeared on his brow.

"Whatever for?"

"I can't think what they hope to gain," she faltered. "But Romaine says that, as she's the cause of the break, and that as Robin wants me back, it's her duty to do something about putting things right between Robin and me, so she's taking her holiday now, and so is Robin."

Luke's eyes narrowed.

"They want to come here—to stay in this house?"

"Romaine hasn't said so. I expect they'll stay in Rayneburg."

"This sudden decision results from your ignoring the previous plea," he said almost to himself. "Perhaps it would have been better if you'd replied to this Robin's letter, telling him once and for all that you're finished."

"It's too late now," she told him. "They're arriving on Monday—"

"Next Monday?" he cut in. "No, it can't be!"

"The day after tomorrow," she said, glancing again at the date that Romaine had given. "There isn't time to stop them, is there?"

"Not now." He held out a hand. "May I look at the letter?"

"Of course." It changed hands and for a space there was silence in the room. Melanie brooded; she was thinking of Romaine's perfidy, and of the attitude of indifference that her sister had adopted on that first occasion when she had told Melanie that she and Giles were in love.

"We couldn't help it," Romaine had told Melanie with a careless shrug of her beautiful shoulders. "We both tried to fight it, but really it was silly of us, because we knew all the time that we were meant for each other."

The divorce, wondered Melanie—was it still going through, or had Romaine decided that it was Giles she wanted after all?

"You're right about the date of their arrival," said Luke as he handed back the letter. "I thought you must surely have made a mistake."

"I don't want them to come." Melanie looked at him with eyes shadowed by distress. "Romaine and I mean nothing to each other anymore."

"And Robin?" he inquired brusquely, his keen scrutiny watching for any signs of a change of expression.

"He means nothing to me anymore...." She stopped, aware suddenly of a sensation of insecurity and doubt, and she knew that during the past two weeks she had been growing so close to Luke that she had come—almost unconsciously—to rely upon him, to feel sure that if anything went wrong he would be there to put it right. He had become a prop, but now he seemed a world apart, and all because Robin had been mentioned. Why should Luke erect a barrier? Or was it she herself who was erecting a barrier? "I don't want them to come," she cried with urgency in her voice. "Why should I have to be troubled by them?"

"You've no need to be troubled by them," was Luke's quiet, unhurried comment. "When they arrive, you can state firmly that there's no room here for them and send them off to Rayneburg—"

"But they'll want to talk! That's the whole purpose of this visit."

"True, that's their purpose, but it need not affect you."

"I shall have to see them, Luke," she murmured in despair, and all at once his arm was around her shoulders.

"No such thing, Melanie," he said gently. "If it isn't your wish to see them, then all you have to do is give me the authority to send them away."

She looked gratefully at him.

"Will you do that for me, Luke?"

"I shall be delighted to send them away," was his grim rejoinder. "They're not welcome, and therefore we shall let them see this."

Melanie turned toward him, her face lifted as she gazed into his eyes—eyes that were definitely of a soft brown color at this moment. Her heart seemed to contract and a smile quivered on her lips. She felt safe again, secure because of his arm around her and the look in his eyes, and because there was about him something that stamped him as a protector.

"I'm most grateful to you," she murmured. "I feel as if a load has been taken off my shoulders."

His smile was spontaneous; she had never seen him smile quite like this before.

"Dear Melanie, if I can take a load off your shoulders, at any time at all, then I shall be very happy to do so."

Dear Melanie.... Her heart contracted again; she knew a sort of exquisite pain...and again that indefinable longing. What was it, she was asking when, quite without warning, she felt Luke's arm tighten around her and, quite without warning, he bent his head and kissed her gently on the lips.

"Oh...I...." Confused, she twisted from his side, the color fluctuating in her cheeks. Luke's eyes were almost tender as they settled on her face.

"Yes?" he prompted in some amusement on noticing her loss of poise.

"You...you shouldn't h-have kissed me like that."

"No?" he challenged with a lift of his brows. "You prefer my former technique?"

"No...." She lifted a hand to her cheek as the color rose even higher. "No, certainly not!"

He laughed and flicked her hair carelessly with his hand. She noticed the attractive crinkly lines at the corners of his eyes.

"Little one," he said softly, "you're quite enchanting."

What she would have said to this she did not know, for at that moment Deborah appeared on the scene and the intimate situation was brought to an abrupt end.

"WHAT TIME will they be here?" Melanie was asking at eight o'clock on the Monday morning. "I'm all on edge, Luke." They were having breakfast together, Deborah having had a late night on the Sunday and in consequence being still asleep. "You did tell me, but I've forgotten."

"The plane was due to arrive at eleven o'clock last night, and I calculated that they would be another eleven hours getting here, so we should expect them around lunchtime or even a little before."

"They might have stayed the night somewhere."

"I rather think that they'd sleep on the train. As I

told you, I called and was told that there was a train that they could catch almost immediately after landing. It seems feasible that this is what they would do, having themselves worked out all these times beforehand. Your sister was sure of arriving here sometime today."

Melanie nodded, glancing at the clock.

"I wish I could add a few hours onto the time, for then it would be all over—the ordeal, I mean."

"There isn't going to be any ordeal, Melanie. I shall see that you're spared any upset at all."

Her eyes smiled at him across the table. She was so content to have him take the burden; and what was more, it seemed the natural thing for him to do!

It was in fact almost three o'clock when the car turned into the driveway and slid to a halt at the imposing front of the homestead. Melanie was at a window of one of the bedrooms, her heart racing with almost sickening speed. She saw the driver get out, his intention being to inquire as to whether or not this was the right house, but Luke was there at once and within seconds Robin was out of the car and introducing himself to Luke. All he received as he held out a hand was a casual nod, the hand being totally ignored. Melanie could imagine him going red, and his temper rising. Where was Romaine, she wondered, puzzlement taking possession of her as Robin and Luke began talking to one another. And then Melanie saw that Romaine was actually in the car, but lying back against the cushions. Luke's glance into the car was followed by a spread of his hands, and the next moment she heard him in the house. He called her name and she emerged from the room.

"Your sister's been taken ill in the hired car," he informed her. "She'll have to be brought in and a doctor sent for." His tone was grim and so was his expression.

Nevertheless, he was resigned to having Romaine and Robin in his house. "There's nothing else for it, Melanie," he said, "for after all, she is your sister."

She nodded her head. "Under these circumstances there isn't anything else we can do, as you say. She isn't very ill, is she?"

"I can't say. She's just lying there and Robin says she's been complaining of stomach pains."

"I see." Melanie found that she was being torn between acute dislike of the idea of having Romaine here and deep anxiety as to the cause of the pains.

She followed Luke, her heart still racing. She dreaded the meeting with Robin and anger rose within her at his action in coming here, intruding into her life just at a time when all was running smoothly, when she was finding contentment and pleasure in the relationship that had grown between Luke and herself.

"Melanie!" Robin came forward, hands outstretched, his whole attention with his former fiancée. "My dear Melanie, forgive me—"

"Hadn't you better attend to this young woman?" broke in Luke curtly. "If you and the driver will bring her inside, I'll go and instruct my servant to prepare a bed."

"What's wrong with her?" Melanie asked, thankful for Luke's interruption but at the same time aware that she herself was fast regaining her composure as far as her attitude toward Robin was concerned. She spoke to him now, going on to ask how long Romaine had been feeling unwell.

"This came on about an hour before we left the train," he replied impatiently, his eyes still on Melanie's face. "I suppose we ought to have done something about it then, but I was anxious to arrive here before dark."

Melanie looked contemptuously at him, then went to the car. Romaine smiled weakly at her as she moved on the seat toward the door that Melanie had opened for her.

"Didn't you care about Romaine, and the fact that she was in pain?" asked Melanie of Robin.

He shrugged, but before he had time to answer her Luke spoke again and the next moment had left Robin and the driver to see to Romaine.

Two or three minutes later Romaine was sitting on the couch in the living room, looking all around her with appreciative eyes before, finally, she looked up into the handsome face of Luke Shadwell. And here her gaze remained fixed, and the beautiful lips curved in a smile as enchanting as ever. Robin was outside, paying the driver, and Melanie watched her sister intently as she made a play with those enormous eyes of hers. Luke's face was impassive, yet Melanie could not for the life of her imagine his being immune to such incredible beauty as that possessed by Romaine. And quite without warning her heart sank right into her feet. Romaine here... Romaine, whose particular type of beauty was that most admired by Luke....

Where had she been drifting, Melanie was asking herself much later as she sat in the bath, perfumed soapsuds floating on the water all around her. She and Luke had come far in the past couple of weeks, and although it was not possible to measure the depth of their friendship, she now knew that this friendship was carrying her, by the most gentle and pleasant means, on to a far different relationship with the man who was, in effect, her employer.

And now Romaine was here.

Little beads of perspiration stood out on Melanie's forehead and she wiped them away with the sponge.

They came again and she told herself that the water was too warm. But no, it was not that at all. Useless to deny that a great fear had entered her, a fear of what Romaine could do to her, even yet again.

She must be kept warm and quiet, the doctor had said after giving Romaine an examination. It was nothing more serious than a touch of food poisoning that was already clearing up. Nevertheless, Romaine must not be moved for at least three or four days, the doctor had advised, and although Luke was angry about this he agreed to allow her to stay. But Robin he would not tolerate and without so much as an apology sent him off to find accommodation in Rayneburg. Robin had tried to insist on speaking to Melanie in private, but Luke had refused absolutely to listen, and the result was that Robin, after deciding that a show of temper would get him nowhere with a man like Luke, had gone away. But Melanie knew that he would endeavor to contact her in some way, perhaps tomorrow, by which time he would have hired a car that he himself could drive, rather than hiring a car with a driver as he had done when coming to the homestead in the first place.

Romaine stayed in bed for dinner that evening, but by lunchtime the following day she was up, and although her face was pale she appeared to be in reasonably good health. She ate a little food, watched by Luke who, Melanie noticed—or believed she noticed—was fascinated by Romaine's beauty. He certainly seemed unable to bring his attention from her, and Melanie, left to her own reflections, wondered just how long it would be before Luke found himself falling victim to her sister's undeniable charms.

This time, thought Melanie, there would at least be no humiliation, since she was, after all, only an employee of Luke's, the girl who had acceded to his request that she should extend her original stay in order to take care of Deborah. Yes, if Romaine *should* ensnare Luke, there would be no humiliation such as had occurred twice in the past.

CHAPTER SIX

So DETERMINED was Melanie to be on the defensive that she never stopped to calculate the effect this changed manner of hers would have on Luke. All she did know was that the rather wonderful interlude was at an end, that a glance in the mirror told her that the sparkle in her eyes had died, leaving them dull and lifeless. Romaine's, on the other hand, were more attractive and expressive than ever as she made a play with them at every opportunity when she was in Luke's company. Watching him and Romaine together, Melanie began to convince herself that Romaine must captivate him—that she intended to do so. In consequence Melanie herself withdrew, enclosing herself within a protective armor of coolness and indifference.

Robin arrived just before dinner, having had difficulty in hiring a car in Rayneburg. The maid let him in and came to Melanie to inform her that he was waiting in the sitting room. Luke was out and Romaine languidly resting against the cushions in the big chair that had been put on the stoop for her.

"Melanie...." His voice seemed to break after the one word was spoken, but he came toward her with outstretched hands.

"It isn't any use, Robin," she returned without any thought of sparing him. "I don't want anything more to do with you."

He stared, his eyes as dull as hers.

"What have I done?" he cried, putting his hands to his face in a gesture of despair. "That damned sister of yours caused it all! I can't think now how I came to be infatuated with her. I should have known better, after what happened with Giles—"

"Shall we not go into this?" she interrupted in calm and quiet tones. "Whatever the cause of the break, it can't make any difference to the way I feel at the present time. I don't love you, Robin...." She stopped and looked directly into his face, waiting for him to complete the action of lowering his hands. They came to rest on his neck, and he stood there, a figure of dejection and despair. "I mean that—I don't love you. So you see, there isn't anything for us to discuss, is there?"

He swallowed hard and allowed his hands to drop to his sides.

"I can't believe that a love like yours has died," he said hoarsely. "No, I can't believe it, no matter what you say."

That he was deeply penitent was plain, and that he was suffering was equally plain, but Melanie felt no pity in her heart for him. But neither did she experience any resentment. She was thinking of Luke, and the way her life had changed since the friendship had developed between them. Yes, life had become worth living all at once.... But now she was right back to where she was a few weeks ago, shielding herself from hurt, determinedly forcing herself to keep her thoughts from drifting along the pleasant lines whereby they would give her a picture of a future with Luke. Yes, she had known for a few days now that she could have forgotten the pain of the past unfortunate experiences and become all in all to Luke. And he was also coming to care.... But Romaine was here! Into her mind this stark fact was thrust and she actually felt a physical indrawing of herself—like a creature that encysts, Luke had said when describing her attitude, and this was how she felt at this moment. She wanted nothing so much as a shell around her, a shell that nothing could penetrate.

"I can't think why you decided to come all this way." Melanie spoke at last and Robin looked at her. "It was a waste of time and money."

"I believed I could win you back."

"With Romaine's assistance." Melanie's voice was bitter.

"It was her idea, in fact. She had been to see your aunt, who told her about your staying here to look after a child. I don't think it was your aunt's idea for us to come—"

"I'm quite sure it wasn't. Did my aunt happen to mention that I was working for a particularly attractive and handsome man? A wealthy man?"

"That's not like you, Melanie," he protested. "Are you suggesting that Romaine came here with the idea of stealing yet another man from you?"

"I would be a hypocrite if I denied that the idea has come to me. On the other hand, she couldn't steal Luke from me simply because he and I are nothing more than employer and employee." She wondered if she had gone pale; she felt as if the color was fast leaving her face.

"Romaine's intention was solely to try to bring us together again. Much as I dislike her now, I have to give her credit for genuinely regretting what she did to you."

Melanie was shaking her head from side to side. "I don't really believe this. I'd rather believe that Romaine wanted to have a holiday at someone else's expense. I expect you paid for this trip?" she added, looking questioningly at him.

He nodded. "Of course I did. It would have been worth every penny had you come back to me." He took a step toward her and extended his hands again. "You can't have stopped loving me," he asserted with a sudden frown. "It was so strong and beautiful—"

"Strong?" she echoed, lifting her brows. "Had it been strong I couldn't be standing here telling you that I no longer want anything to do with you."

Robin bit his lip and turned from her to stare out over the lovely garden. Melanie followed the direction of his gaze, marveling at her own detachment. In fact, she felt detached from everyone in the house except Deborah; she felt she would not care if she were to find herself quite alone with the child. Robin sighed a deep and prolonged sigh, but still she remained unaffected. The color in the garden was of far more interest to her than the man standing there, his face drawn and his hands clenched at his sides. The sun was dropping swiftly behind the mountains and a spectral flare of crimson was already searing across the African sky. Closer to, beyond the blossom-festooned stoop and the low grenadilla hedge, the borders were bright with flowers— cannas and Watsonias, roses and allamandas—while towering above them the palms swayed gently against the sky, and now and then an elusive bird cry would create a mental picture of gay-plumaged wings being caught by the orange glow of sunset.

"I still think we could come together," Robin was saying quietly. "We should try, you know, Melanie, because you and I once had something very precious."

She did not answer at once, for she was still gripped by the beauty before her. The day was going down in a crescendo of glory and the spectacle was too good to miss. The nearby trees were fading rapidly from view, as were the foothills of the mountains, and the veld flowed out in a seemingly endless vista, wrapped in that elusive violet that was all a part of the theatrical splendor of twilight. In the garden itself dappled shades gave the impression of approaching magic and mystery.

"I have no inclination to try," she told Robin at last. "My decision is made and nothing can alter it now."

He looked at her, noting the pallor and the faded expression in her eyes.

"You were so happy once," he said regretfully. "I've made you sad like this."

"I'm not sad," she was quick to deny. "I've got over it and at this moment I feel nothing but indifference. It seems that we never loved at all."

It was true, and yet she felt she ought by right to have experienced some sort of regret, however slight. For she did care deeply at one time and the future had held no fears for her happiness as Robin's wife.

"I've realized too late just how deeply I love you, Melanie."

"You thought you loved Romaine," she could not help reminding him. "What happened that you and she came to discover that you weren't in love after all?"

"I don't know...." He shook his head. "I really don't know, Melanie. It came all at once; we both felt it together and decided to talk about it. I knew then that it was you I loved, that it was always you." He glanced pleadingly at her, but noting her expression he looked away quickly, his shoulders sagging. "It really is the end, isn't it?" he said, and Melanie nodded her head without hesitation.

"It is, Robin." And now she was able to inject a note of gentleness into her voice. "You shouldn't have come." A small pause and then, "What will you do while waiting for Romaine? You could take a tour for a couple of days or so. They run them from Rayneburg."

"Do you think I'm interested in things like that?" he returned bitterly. "No, I expect I shall sit in my hotel room and spend my time reflecting on what might have been had not that sister of yours decided to flaunt her charms in front of me! I expect she's busily engaged in the same damned tactics with your handsome employer." It was a statement, and one that occupied Melanie's mind long after he had gone. And when Luke came in and smiled at her Melanie failed to respond, resolving not to allow herself to be affected in any way by his attractiveness or his approach.

He frowned and said, "What's wrong, Melanie? You seem out of sorts, somehow." He had come to her just as she was about to go to her room to bathe and change. How good-looking he was! And his eyes were soft and searching, concern in their depths. She remembered her first impression of him, admitting to the noble lines and impressive bearing, but branding him cold, austere, unfeeling.

"Robin's been here—"

"Robin? I wanted to be in when he arrived! When he didn't appear earlier I concluded that he wouldn't appear at all today. What had he to say?" The voice was harsh, the eyes like steel. Melanie looked up at him and knew a hurt inside at this change in him, even though the change was caused by Robin and was not the result of any displeasure that she herself might have incurred.

"He wanted me back."

"Wanted?"

"I told him it was finished."

"Good girl. I must admit that I wondered how his pleading would affect you."

She managed a weak smile and said, "You didn't imagine I'd take him back, surely?"

He paused a moment, his face wearing a preoccupied look.

"Women are such funny creatures," he asserted at length. "They appear to know, deep inside, that things will go wrong, yet they will make the attempt to put the clock back. I find this most frustrating, since it's something a mere male can't combat.''

His face was still preoccupied and for some moments she studied his expression. Then she said, quite out of the blue and without knowing by what force she was impelled, ''Have you ever been in love, Luke?''

At this he came from his reverie and looked at her, his eyes faintly smiling.

''Tell me,'' he said, ''what do you think?''

She colored delicately and replied, ''It was an impertinent question, wasn't it?''

''Not in the least; it shows you're interested. Yes, as a matter of fact I was in love once. Does that surprise you?'' he added with a touch of amusement that sent her heart out of control, for he was so profoundly attractive when in this faintly humorous mood.

''I'm not surprised,'' was all she said in answer to his question, and of course he then wanted to know what had prompted her own question in the first place. ''I just wondered,'' she said, hoping he would not, with his keen perception, suddenly guess that she had gained some information from Jancis.

''You're most restrained, aren't you, Melanie?'' Luke was still smiling with his eyes and she glanced away.

''I don't know what you mean. . . .''

''Aren't you curious to know what she was like?''

''The girl whom you loved?''

''That's right.''

''What was she like?'' Melanie then asked obligingly, waiting to hear that the girl was similar in appearance to Romaine.

But all he said was, ''She had a beauty that was, for me, at that time, quite irresistible.''

"What happened?" Melanie supposed that she should tactfully have relinquished the discussion before this question was voiced, but she was indeed curious to learn more about Luke's love affair. "I mean, why did you part?"

"She, like you, was passing through the stage of recuperation after a broken engagement. She and I found much to attract one another and as far as I was concerned our future together was settled, although at this time I hadn't proposed. She was not ready, in my opinion," he added, and still again he was smiling with those tawny eyes of his. "However, she received a letter from her former fiancé, who vowed he had always loved her and that his jilting her was a mistake. She went back to him as fast as the plane would take her," he ended, and now his mouth was curved with humor.

"He blamed her for everything, I expect?"

"He did." Melanie wondered what Luke would say were she to repeat what Robin had said about Romaine's trying out her charms on Luke.

"I'm very glad that you sent him off," was all Luke said before, swinging the door inwards, he passed through it, closing it quietly behind him.

ALL THROUGH DINNER Romaine displayed her charms, and Luke was undoubtedly interested in the way she talked and smiled. Melanie knew once more that sinking feeling in the pit of her stomach and the dejection of spirit. Luke spoke to her several times, but she answered in monosyllables until in the end he confined his conversation to Romaine. This was formal, it was true, but gradually Romaine managed to dispel the coolness and even gained so much ground that she made Luke laugh on one or two occasions. His keen eyes seemed to examine intently every line and contour of Romaine's face;

he looked at her eyes and her mouth and her lovely hair,
all in a way that convinced Melanie that—inwardly at
least—he was filled with admiration for her beautiful sister. As for Melanie's attitude toward her, it was aloof but
not hostile, cold but not icily so. She had been genuinely
worried at first as to the reason for the pains suffered by
Romaine and she was still faintly anxious, having noticed
her once or twice putting a soothing hand to her stomach.

However, Romaine's adroitness with the male sex had
remained unimpaired and when dinner was over and
they all retired to the stoop Melanie was not long in saying her good nights and going to her bedroom. Once
there she burst into tears, and for a full minute wept as
if her heart would break. No use pretending that she did
not know the cause of her tears. She was in love with
Luke. . . and she was about to see him fall madly in love
with her sister. This she knew without one atom of
doubt, she told herself. They were together now, in the
romantic setting of flower-strewn veranda and luxuriant
moonlight and stars, which were an implacable part of
the magic of Africa.

Why couldn't Robin have accepted the inevitable without coming out here with Romaine, intent on bringing
about a reconciliation? And Romaine. . . ? Knowing her
so well, Melanie could not give her credit for even the
slightest measure of repentance or the desire to make
amends by coming over to assist Robin in his efforts. No,
it would be more logical to assume that it was Luke who
had unwittingly drawn Romaine to Africa. Melanie dried
her eyes at last and after bathing her face and hands got
into bed. She would read, and forget all about those two
down there, for after all there was really nothing she
could do to prevent Luke from falling in love with Romaine. Twice before Romaine had without effort taken
the man Melanie wanted, and she would do so again.

THE FOLLOWING MORNING Melanie went riding with
Deborah, and having wandered farther afield than usual
they came upon a little pool around which bloomed a
veritable botanical garden. The walls on three sides of
the pool were covered with lichens and mosses and
dainty cushions of flowers formed in patterns that set
off the color contrasts to the most impressive advantage. Deborah was delighted, and after they had dismounted and tethered their horses they sat down on a
rock and listened to the melodious sound of running
water as it cascaded down one of the mossy walls and
splashed into the pool.

"Isn't it beautiful?" exclaimed Deborah when the
sunlight, escaping through the waving heads of the gum
trees, sent ripples of silver over the surface of the pool.
"I must tell my daddy about this when I write to him
tonight!"

"Tonight?" Melanie looked around and added, "I
thought you wrote to your daddy yesterday afternoon?"

"I did, but I lost the letter, so I'm going to write
another after I'm in bed."

"Uncle Luke thinks you go to sleep after I've put out
the light." Melanie was smiling; she knew full well that
Deborah often became active after she, Melanie, had
said good night and snapped off the light. "If he happens to notice that you've put on the light again, he's
likely to be cross with you."

"I know, but you won't tell him, will you?"

"Of course not. What else are you going to tell your
daddy?"

"About Auntie Romaine—"

"Auntie Romaine? Who told you to call her that?"

"She did; she said she's going to stay with Uncle Luke
for a long time, so I might as well call her Auntie Ro-

maine. Isn't it a beautiful name? I wish I was called that, and I wish I was beautiful like her. Hasn't she got pretty hair?''

"Very pretty." Melanie spoke briefly, her mind on what the child had said. "I don't think she is staying with Uncle Luke for a long time. She's leaving just as soon as she feels better." Romaine was feeling better already, completely better, but as the doctor said she must not be moved for three or four days she would of course be staying, but only for that time.... Only for that time—if Luke decided she must go. But Melanie was so sure that he would ask her to stay on for awhile longer. What would be the eventual outcome? Would the relationship reach the stage where Luke would ask Romaine to marry him? Melanie felt the tears prickling the backs of her eyes and resolutely shut out any picture of a marriage between Luke and her sister. Romaine had mentioned the divorce to Melanie, quite blatantly admitting that she had made a big mistake in marrying Giles in the first place.

"It'll be through in a couple of months," she had said carelessly. "We've arranged one of these 'do-it-yourself' divorces and it takes only a few months."

"You've been separated for two years, then?" This Melanie had not known, so little interest had she had in her sister's activities.

"Of course. I told Aunt Cissy, but she obviously hasn't passed on the information to you."

"She wouldn't—not under the circumstances."

"You're still mad at me for pinching your fiancé? All's fair in love and war, you know."

This conversation had taken place just after breakfast that morning, when Luke had left the homestead and Romaine was preparing to settle down on the stoop, where she would be waited on with drinks and other refreshments by Elizabeth. Melanie thought about it now as she watched Deborah chasing a butterfly. It was almost within her grasp when it escaped by fluttering away over the pool, and Deborah gave a little cry of disappointment.

"But if you had been able to catch it what would you have done with it?" Melanie asked, and Deborah said she would let it go again.

"I wouldn't like to keep it in a cage, or anything like that," she added, her eyes wandering to where the bright little creature made dancing shadows along the edge of the pool.

"If you were to touch it, even, you would injure it, Deborah," returned Melanie seriously. "The wings of moths and butterflies are very fragile indeed."

"Oh.... Then I won't try to catch any more, because I would cry if I hurt one."

Melanie smiled, aware of a longing within her and an errant thought that brought back Giles and the idea that, had she and he married, then it was most likely that she would by now have had a child of her own. Well, that was a dream she once had cherished, a dream that had died on the day that Robin had told her that their engagement was at an end. And yet.... Yes, there had been Luke, and a sweet elusive notion that with time he and she might get together. Nothing concrete, no word from him that might have given her a clue to his intentions, but somehow that lovely friendship had come to mean much more than it appeared on the surface and in fact Melanie had begun to admit that neither Giles nor Robin had ever affected her in the way Luke was doing. The pleasure of his presence; the quiet walks under the velvet sky when Luke would stop now and then to point out the various stars to her; the odd daytime stroll when, after a recent shower, the fields and pastures were brightened and the grass lush and green. So many memories in so short a time—and not one moment of dissension, no evidence of Luke's manner of cold austerity.

"I think," she said to Deborah at last, "we ought to be getting back." Rising as she spoke, Melanie untethered the horses and began to stroke Sanaan's neck while waiting for Deborah to join her.

"When my daddy comes home can I still come sometimes and stay with Uncle Luke?" The child spoke as they moved away from the pool. "I want to come to this lovely pond lots more times."

"I expect you can stay with Uncle Luke, but of course I won't be here to bring you along to the pool."

"You won't be here?" Deborah's wide forehead creased in a frown. "I want you to live with Uncle Luke always."

"That isn't possible, Deborah. I stayed only so that I could look after you while your father was away. As soon as he returns I shall be leaving."

"Will you ever come back?"

"No, I don't think so."

Deborah's frown deepened.

"I'll tell Uncle Luke I want you to stay," she decided, her firm little chin tilting up. "He loves me and so he'll let you stay forever!"

Forever.... Yes, she could spend the rest of her life here, in this beautiful country with its sun and warmth and mountains and forests. The homestead was like a dream house with a fairy-tale setting. And then there was Luke....

She made no answer to what Deborah had said and for the next twenty minutes or so neither spoke very much at all. Only on their arrival back did Deborah begin to chatter—this to Luke, who was standing on the stoop talking to Romaine. Dazzlingly beautiful and immaculately dressed, Romaine made Melanie feel like a tramp, and she became acutely—even painfully—conscious of her dusty slacks and sweat-stained shirt. Her hair, too, was far from tidy, and when she saw Luke's eyes move from Romaine's lovely face and figure to her own, she blushed hotly and, turning away, excused herself and left the two adults and Deborah on the stoop.

But in her room she heard Deborah's voice clearly, as the child spoke first to Luke and later to Romaine.

Deborah was saying that she wanted Melanie to stay for always, and that Uncle Luke must make her. Luke said something to this, but his voice was so low that Melanie missed the words completely. But she heard drifts of what Romaine was saying and she gathered that her sister was making it very clear to Luke that it was impossible for Melanie to remain in Africa. There was Aunt Cissy, who depended on her, and in any case Melanie would never be happy and settled in any country other than her own.

Listening, Melanie felt only bitterness at these untruths—or perhaps she ought to be more generous and term them "assumptions." Romaine had no idea whether or not Melanie could be happy and settled in any country other than her own. Also, Aunt Cissy had never depended on anyone; she liked to see Melanie, but she had never once intimated that she *needed* her. However, it did not matter what Romaine said, for Melanie had no intention of trying to prolong her stay in Luke's house.

After washing and changing she would very much have liked to escape somewhere on her own, but as Deborah had finished chattering she was told to go to Melanie and be bathed and made to look pretty.

"And then we'll go off to Rayneburg," added Luke with a glance at Melanie. "I've a little shopping to do."

"Oh, dear," sighed Romaine, leaning back and crossing her shapely legs one over the other. "Am I to be left all on my own?"

"Perhaps," suggested Luke, "you'd like to go to your room and lie down?" He sounded anxious, to Melanie's ears. It never occurred to her that he might be carelessly indifferent as to how Romaine should spend her time.

"Yes, I might do that," Romaine answered languidly, her lovely eyes resting on Luke's face. "Then I shall feel brighter when your friends come this evening for a sundowner."

"Friends—?" Melanie glanced at Luke. "You have friends coming in this evening?" She felt hurt that he had not mentioned this to her but yet had done so to Romaine. "Who are they?"

"Charles and Jancis, and one or two others. You've met them all at the club." He was subjecting her to a searching scrutiny and she did wonder if he noticed the dark rings under her eyes, which a few minutes previously she had endeavoured to camouflage by the application of a little face powder. Her eyes, she knew, still wore that dull expression and altogether she felt glaringly inferior to her beautiful sister. That Luke must be aware of this played so deeply on her mind that she retreated into a sort of defensive silence, which she maintained throughout the drive into Rayneburg.

When the car was parked Luke turned to her and said, his eyes narrowed and faintly cold, "What's wrong with you, Melanie? Why the protective armor again? I believed I'd broken through it, but now you're right back to where you were at the beginning."

"I'm all right." Unconsciously she injected a note of

agression into her voice. "I don't know why you should trouble yourself about me and my...my moods."

"Moods is certainly right." He looked away for a second to where Deborah was standing, staring at a dog that was sitting in the back of one of the parked cars. "Snap out of it," he said, and this was almost an order, spoken with an authoritative inflection in his voice. "Romaine won't be here much longer, if that is what's upsetting you."

"She won't?"

"No, she won't." Frowning at her, Luke added, "Why do you ask that?"

"Deborah seemed to think that she was staying for some time."

His eyes opened wide.

"It's the first I've heard of it. As far as I'm concerned she leaves immediately the doctor declares her fit to be moved."

"You don't believe she's fit to be moved now?"

"I do, but I can't very well order her out, can I?" He sounded impatient and his mouth had hardened. Undoubtedly he was not feeling in the best of moods himself. "The doctor will come by tomorrow and—I hope—will say that Romaine can leave for the hotel in Rayneburg."

Melanie said nothing; she was mentally listless, so convinced that Romaine had already progressed more than halfway toward her object of drawing Luke's interest to herself. Luke sighed impatiently at her silence and, calling Deborah to him, took her hand and began to stride away toward the street in which the shops and the bank were situated.

"Shall I take Deborah?" asked Melanie as they came from the parking lot into the tree-lined road. "You'll be better able to do your shopping then."

"Have you anything to buy?"

"One or two items, yes."

"Very well." He arranged to meet them at the hotel, where, he said, they would have afternoon tea. His tones were curt, his whole manner aloof. Melanie told herself that he had not adopted such an attitude with her sister. No, with Romaine he would be all softness and concern, just as he was when asking if she would like to rest in her room during the afternoon.

"Can we go to the toy shop?" Deborah wanted to know when Luke had left them. "I want to buy some chairs for my dolls' house."

This was a pleasurable task and Melanie entered into it with enthusiasm. There were several types of chairs from which to choose and both she and Deborah took some time to make up their minds. In the end both agreed that the upholstered ones were the best, but when it came to paying Melanie found to her discomfort that she had not enough money; she had left her purse at home and all she had with her was a small sum that had been dropped into the center pocket of her handbag.

"We'll come back," she was saying when she became aware of Robin standing at the end of the counter, his face turned toward her, his ears alert. "The little girl's uncle will pay—"

"Allow me to pay!" Robin took a few steps to reduce the distance between them. "I have a note here. Is it sufficient?"

Melanie was shaking her head, but the assistant had already taken the note.

"I prefer to wait," she snapped. "Luke will pay."

"Melanie, please let me pay. It's for the child, not for you."

She turned from him and said, "I want nothing to do with you, Robin. I shall be obliged if you'd go away."

He remained at her side.

"I love you," he said simply, and there was no mistaking the catch in his voice. "For God's sake, give me another chance! I've been through purgatory these past couple of days."

She turned then, and flooding over her was the memory of the happy days they had spent together. She recalled those weekends when she had become so welcome a guest at his parents' home. Having no home or parents of her own, she had been ever grateful for the security that those weekends had provided. She had had an anchor at that time; now she had nothing and she floundered, lonely and dejected. Robin seemed suddenly to be a straw to which she could cling—a straw that could perhaps lead her to the anchor for which she craved.

"It could never be quite the same," she murmured, not meaning him to hear this uttering of her thoughts. "One can never completely mend a break such as that—"

"I love you," he repeated, and although this time there was a distinct note of eagerness and hope in his words, he was careful to hold back any trace of confidence that might otherwise have crept into his voice. "That, surely, is the important thing."

She looked into his eyes and said with a deep and trembling sigh, "I don't love you, Robin—not anymore."

He swallowed hard.

"You did once and you can again," he stated. "I'd take the chance on it, Melanie."

"I can never love you—not now." Her thoughts flew to Luke and she knew that he and he only could have won her heart completely.

"The lady's giving you your change." Deborah, tug-ging at his trouser leg, brought Robin's attention from Melanie and he held out his hand for the money the assistant was offering him. He thanked her, speaking well above the whisper he had been using when speaking to Melanie. "Shall we go now?" asked Deborah, her small parcel clutched in her hand. "I'm ready for my tea."

"It's too early yet." Melanie smiled down at her and took hold of her hand. "We'll go and do my shopping and then it might be time to meet Uncle Luke."

"May I come along with you?" Robin's voice pleaded, and unable to refuse him, Melanie said yes, he could come along with them.

"This evening," he was saying about an hour later when, the shopping finished, they were on their way to the hotel, "will you let me take you to the club? There's a dance on, and you do remember how we used to enjoy dancing together." He stopped rather abruptly as he noticed the sudden stiffening of Melanie's features. "That wasn't tactful, was it? I'm sorry, dear, if I brought back memories that hurt."

That, she thought, was even less tactful, but she made allowances for his present emotional condition. He was unsure as to whether or not she would in the end be persuaded to take him back, to promise that she would try to recapture the happiness that had been theirs before Romaine had decided that she wanted Robin, as she had previously wanted Giles.

"I don't think I want to go to the dance this evening," she said after a long moment of indecision. "I feel I ought not to make any arrangements without consulting Luke."

"Luke? But surely he doesn't control your evenings—your leisure time?"

"No, of course not...." She trailed off, reflecting

that of late the evenings had been spent with Luke, pleasant hours of quiet companionship that had on one or two occasions lasted into the morning hours. It had been as if neither she nor Luke had wanted to bring the pleasure to an end by saying good night. "But we've never really fixed my hours, or my time off."

"I don't see any difficulty. When Deborah's in bed there isn't anything to keep you, is there?"

She shook her head, but thought of leaving Romaine alone with Luke. Not that it would be the first time the two had been alone together. But Melanie was remembering that all unconsciously she had left Giles alone with Romaine.... However, if Luke was to fall victim to her sister's charms, there was nothing Melanie could do to prevent it. It was as though, where Romaine entered into it, Melanie must admit defeat at the outset. She was no match for Romaine simply because she lacked the essential weapon, which was beauty. True, Luke had said she possessed a certain beauty, but Melanie suspected that he was just being kind because she herself had declared that she was merely passable.

"I suppose I could come out with you...." She had uttered the words before asking herself from where they were coming. She had no real desire to go dancing with Robin; on the contrary, she would prefer to retire to her room and be alone. But for some reason she could not understand words came to her lips unbidden and she found herself uttering them.

"You'll come?" Eager now, Robin risked touching her hand. "Dear Melanie, I'm so much happier than I was an hour or so ago. Shall I call for you about seven?"

"That's far too early. Deborah doesn't go to bed until that time. I usually read to her for about half an hour, and then I shall have to get ready—"

"Eight o'clock, then?"

"Yes, eight or just after."

Deborah was running on ahead, but now she turned and ran back.

"I'm very hungry! Please let's get there quickly!"

"We're still a little early," Melanie told her, glancing at her watch. "Uncle Luke said four o'clock and it's still only a quarter to."

"Well, we can wait for him. Besides, he might be there early and he won't like waiting for us."

"Very well." Melanie turned to Robin. "Goodbye. I'll see you later."

"Fine." He paused and then questioned anxiously, "You'll not change your mind?"

Melanie shook her head. "No," she answered firmly, "I'll not change my mind."

CHAPTER SEVEN

LUKE WAS ALREADY in the hotel lounge when they entered. Deborah immediately informed him of all that had happened.

"And then the gentleman went off on his own, but he was nice to pay for my chairs, wasn't he?"

"Very nice." Curt the words and cold the glance he sent in Melanie's direction. "I would have paid, you knew that."

"I told Robin you would pay, but he insisted. The woman behind the counter took the money from him so there was little I could do."

"Nonsense! You should have refused to take the money!"

"I didn't take it," she protested, loath to say anything that would lead to a deterioration of the position between them.

"You allowed him to pay!" He seemed disproportionately angry about Robin's payment of the money and Melanie once again endeavored to smooth the matter over.

"I couldn't cause a scene in the shop, could I?"

"Don't you like that gentleman to pay for my chairs?" interrupted Deborah. "You see, Uncle Luke, Melanie had left her purse at home, so she hadn't enough money, and it was lucky that her friend came along because he had plenty of money."

"You said you weren't having anything more to do

with the man," snapped Luke, ignoring what Deborah
had said. "There should have been no difficulty about
your refusing to allow him to pay."

Melanie fell silent, wondering how she was to inform
Luke that she had consented to go to the club with
Robin that evening.

"Shall we go in to tea?" she asked, going on to say
that Deborah was hungry.

"They'll bring it to us in here." Luke beckoned and a
waitress appeared. "We'd like afternoon tea brought to
us here," he said. The girl produced a notebook and
took the order. When she had gone Melanie sat back in
her chair and watched as Deborah took out the chairs
from the parcel she had already opened.

"Do you like them?" she asked, lifting her small face
to his. "Melanie helped me to choose them. There were
a lot more, but we liked these best."

Luke took one of the chairs and appeared to be examining it as to the quality of workmanship, but Melanie
sensed his lack of interest aware that his mind was on
Robin and his intrusion into her life again after she had
said, quite firmly and finally, that she wanted nothing
more to do with him. She decided to tell him that she
was going out that evening, but it took several attempts
before the words could be forced out. And when at last
they were, they contained an element of defiance and
challenge, since it had nothing to do with Luke anyway,
and so he had no right either to approve or disapprove
of her decision.

"You've accepted an invitation to go out with him!"
Luke stared unbelievingly at her across the table. "I
don't think I've heard aright?"

She colored, angry with him, but even more angry
with herself for allowing him to affect her like this. He
might almost be in a position of total authority over her,
she thought.

"It'll be a change," she muttered defensively.

"From what?" His narrowed gaze held hers and she knew full well what he meant.

"Romaine's here," she began.

He interrupted her. "Answer my question!"

"Uncle Luke," protested Deborah, her eyes suddenly filling up, "I don't like you being angry with Melanie and shouting at her like that. She hasn't done anything wrong—have you, Melanie?"

"Deborah, be quiet. Your tea will be here in a few moments; I want you to eat it without talking, understand?"

Deborah pouted, but the stern inflection in Luke's voice was noted and the child's voice was meek when she spoke.

"All right, Uncle Luke. I won't talk while I'm eating."

Luke returned his attention to Melanie. His eyes were narrowed, his mouth tight.

"Perhaps," he said stiffly, "you'll now tell me what you meant about its being a change?"

"I didn't mean it would be a change from . . . from those evenings that . . . that you and I spent together—"

"You're not being at all clear," he cut in coldly. "It seems to me that you prefer this fellow's company to mine?"

"That's not true," she denied indignantly. "But Romaine is here, and therefore you are occupied with her."

"I . . . ?" Luke's eyes opened very wide indeed. Melanie saw the astounded expression in them. "Why the devil should you infer a thing like that?"

Melanie shrugged her shoulders in what was meant to be a careless gesture. "I expect you and she have a lot in common."

"Indeed?" His eyes were now notably alert, and his

head moved almost imperceptibly as if he were mentally reaching a conclusion. "Perhaps you will explain just what your sister and I could possibly have in common."

Melanie swallowed, her color deepening under Luke's interrogating stare.

"She's very beautiful. Men can't resist her." This was not the right thing to say, but Melanie saw no reason to withhold from him what he already knew. "I expect you enjoy her company," she ended, and once again his head moved slightly.

"I think I understand." Curt the tones, but his eyes had lost some of their hardness. "Melanie, if I don't end by beating you it will be a miracle—" He stopped abruptly as Deborah, glancing up swiftly on hearing this, opened her mouth to utter a big "Oooh" of astonishment and censure. "Here's your tea," he told the child. "Start on the sandwiches, not the cakes!"

Deborah blinked at him, her eyes filling up again. Melanie looked angrily at him and fully expected that he would say something soothing to the child. But he was staring at a spot behind her, and when automatically she turned her head she saw Robin sitting at a table in the corner, a good distance from the table that they themselves were occupying.

"Robin is staying here," she began, but Luke instantly interrupted to say that he was well aware of that fact.

"Seeing that I sent him here I ought to know!" he added scathingly. "What would you like me to do now—invite him over so that we can make a nice friendly party for tea?"

"There's no need for sarcasm, Luke."

"Are you really intending to go out with him this evening?"

"Of course, I promised."

"Then there's nothing more for me to say!" Picking

up a sandwich, he began to eat it, but the very idea of food sickened Melanie and all she had was a cup of tea. This scene had hurt unbearably and she did wonder in her confused mind just why she had agreed to go out with Robin when she had no real desire to do so. She expected it was a sort of defensive tactic instigated by her conviction that Romaine must inevitably captivate Luke. Yes, that was it! She wanted more than anything to conceal from both Luke and Romaine that she had any feeling for him at all. In this way she would be saved embarrassment, and Romaine would never know that, for the third time, she had been able to come right in and, without the least effort, rob her sister, leaving her with nothing but emptiness and humiliation.

No word was spoken between Melanie and Luke on the journey home, and when at last they arrived at the house Melanie took Deborah off to the room that Luke had set aside as a playroom. There she and Deborah sorted out the furniture in the dolls' house and added the new chairs. Despite her dejection Melanie could not help but find pleasure in this task, and later, when she was ready to go out, she was quite surprised to find, on glancing in the mirror, that the dark shadows were no longer to be seen and that her eyes were a little brighter than they had been of late.

ROMAINE WAS IN the sitting room and she glanced up as her sister entered. Melanie was wearing a long dress of dark blue brushed nylon with a high waist and frilled bodice trimmed lavishly with white lace. The neck was high, the sleeves full at the top but tight-fitting from just above the elbow down to the wrist.

"Going out?" queried Romaine. "You never mentioned it at dinner."

"I'm going to the club." Moving into the middle of

the room, Melanie stood there looking down at her sister, reclining there on the couch like a beautiful model of perfection, right from the crown of her golden head to her shapely ankles and tiny feet.

"The club." Romaine frowned slightly. "I must go there at the first opportunity."

"You'll be returning to England once you're fully recovered, surely?"

"Not on your life!" Romaine gave a spurt of laughter before adding, "I want to taste the sort of existence one has in this part of the world. Luke's my ideal man and I want to know what sort of social life I shall have if I decide to marry him."

"If *you* decide?" Although Melanie's voice was calm and steady, her nerves were rioting and her heartbeats were far from normal. Romaine married to Luke.... "Aren't you taking a lot for granted? You've known him less than three days."

"What has time to do with it? I have Luke in the palm of my hand already, so I'm not contemplating any difficulty in bringing him to the point of a marriage proposal." Again the laugh; it grated on Melanie's senses and she glanced through the window into the darkness, wishing she could see the lights of Robin's car appearing along the tree-lined driveway. "I never have difficulty with any man, do I?"

Melanie looked at her with contempt.

"It would be to your credit if you looked around for your own man instead of indulging in the hobby of stealing mine."

"So you've fallen in love with Luke?"

"Certainly not!"

"But you've just admitted it, my dear sister," purred Romaine. "However, it's of no matter since you can't have him now that I'm here. No, don't interrupt,

Melanie! I *know* that you've fallen for him simply because no woman could possibly live in the same house as Luke and remain immune to his devastating charm. Why, all the women in the district must have had a go at winning him, for he's certainly a prize and no mistake!''

"How crude you are!''

"And how slow *you* are! If I'd been with Luke for only half the time you've been with him I'd have been married to him by now.''

Melanie sent another glance toward the window. What had happened to Robin? He was already five minutes late.

"You take a lot for granted, Romaine. Luke isn't like the others, you'll find.''

That the wish was father to the thought Melanie would not have denied, and she was not surprised when Romaine said, "You're hoping that I'll fail? No chance, Melanie. I can have any man I want—*any man*!'' There was no comment from Melanie and she went on to say that already Luke was profoundly interested in her as a woman. "He's falling fast,'' continued Romaine with a sort of exultant confidence. "I can guarantee to be able to twist him right around my finger within a week.''

Melanie said, her face white as the trimming on her dress, "You're not expected to be here for a week.''

"I shall make sure that I'm here for much longer than that.'' A small pause and then, "My, but how pale you are! Foolish girl, to fall in love so often! Especially when you know very well that I can take your man every time. Believe me, Luke is mine already, so you might as well forget all about him. I was interested when Aunt Cissy told me about this wealthy South African farmer with whom you were staying. I didn't at all like the idea that you might marry wealth when I myself have not managed to do so yet. Aunt Cissy could have bitten out her tongue—I saw that at once—but the damage was done. Did you know that she was half hoping that you and Luke would get together?''

Melanie turned away, her whole mind and body affected by her sister's heartlessness and total disregard for her discomfiture and distress.

"I think I'll wait on the stoop for Robin—"

"Robin? You're going out with Robin, after saying you didn't intend taking him back?"

"I still don't intend taking him back."

"He'll be hoping—if you start going out with him again."

"It's only for tonight." Melanie made a move toward the French window. "He's only staying around because he thinks you'll be returning to England with him."

"Then he's in for a disappointment. You might tell him, if you don't mind, that I'm not intending to return for some considerable time, so he can go just whenever it suits him to do so." Casual the tone; it seemed impossible that Romaine had been so attracted to Robin that she could have taken him from her own sister.

"I still believe you're taking too much for granted. Luke hasn't asked you to stay, has he?"

Romaine laughed and sat back even more comfortably against the cushions. There was no doubt, thought Melanie, that she made a most alluring picture, and it would not be in the least surprising if, as Romaine had said, Luke was already falling in love with her. In fact, it would be surprising if he had not been falling in love with her.

"You're trying to convince yourself that he isn't interested, aren't you?' sneered Romaine. "Yet deep down inside you you know very well that I'm well on the way to success. Silly child! Aren't you sorry that you allowed yourself to fall for him?"

"I didn't fall for him!" flared Melanie, quite unable to endure any more of this kind of talk. "He isn't my type at all!"

"No?" Romaine's voice changed with startling speed. "Luke isn't your type, Melanie?" The voice was now soft and attractively husky. "But how strange. Who, then, is your type? Robin, with whom you're going out this evening?"

Melanie scarcely knew what she was saying as she replied, a tremor of passion in her voice, "Yes, of course Robin's my type! It should be obvious that he is!"

"And not Luke?"

"I've already said so! Luke's the last man I'd be likely to fall for!" That should sound convincing, decided Melanie, congratulating herself. And she turned then, intending to make her exist through the window—but she almost collided with Luke. He had been standing there for the past few seconds; she was never so sure of anything in her life.

And Romaine had known he was there.

"Your boyfriend's waiting," was his icy comment as his hard eyes ran over her figure. "He came around the wrong way and he's at the back. I've told him to come around to the front." And with that he strode past Melanie and went through the room into some other part of the house.

"You're very clever, Romaine, I'll grant you that," said Melanie bitterly. "How could you be so vile as to make me say things I didn't mean?"

"So you do love him? Oh, well, he wouldn't have looked at you anyway, and most certainly not now, when he can have me."

"One day," predicted Melanie, looking straight at her, "you'll be sorry for what you've done to me."

Romaine merely grinned and said carelessly, "I doubt it. I'm not the sort to have qualms of conscience; it's far too uncomfortable. Life is for living, Melanie," she added, her eyes glinting with a sort of defiance that Melanie had never seen before. "I intend to live, and to enjoy every single moment of my life." She glanced at the closed door and for a second or two she seemed to become thoughtful. "Luke will be exciting, and I don't believe I shall ever tire of him. If I do, his money will compensate and I shall have a good time on that...." She stopped, for Melanie had turned away and was leaving the room by the French window.

"Ah, there you are!" Robin's eager voice jarred on Melanie's nerves and she would have done anything to be able to make some excuse and send him away. But she could not, since he would be utterly hurt and miserable. So she went to the club, and danced and smiled, and when the evening came to an end she knew that Robin was more than a little optimistic about a reconciliation.

On the way back to Luke's home she mentioned this, and Robin admitted that he hoped for total forgiveness on her part.

"Oh, I can forgive you," she readily answered, "but I can never care as I cared before."

"If you take this attitude you won't," was his rather gentle rejoinder. He was cautiously handling the car as he drove it along a road where tall palm trees swayed in the night breeze and where here and there lights could be seen twinkling from the windows of the smart bungalows that were built on the low rises and in the valley.

"I don't think I ever cared as strongly as I should have done, Robin," she told him seriously, and he turned swiftly, a frown on his forehead.

"What exactly do you mean by that?" he wanted to know.

"I've got over it so quickly."

"More quickly than you got over Giles." A statement, and it brought to mind Luke's comment that, in the case of Giles, she had had no help.

"I've had things to take my mind off it this time."

"Such as?" A faint trace of stiffness had crept into his tone.

"I came here, for one thing. It was all new and interesting."

"And there was Luke Shadwell."

She swallowed and remained silent for a space.

"Yes," she agreed at length, "there was Luke Shadwell."

"I see...." The stiffness remained in his voice, but now it was accompanied by a hint of despair. "You're in love with him?"

"No—oh, no! Of course not!"

"But you've just admitted it—almost."

She supposed that this was true, but she now wished only to refute the idea she had given him.

"I meant that he offered me employment, looking after Deborah."

"Your aunt told this to Romaine. But that's not the whole situation, is it? You've come to care for Luke?"

"Luke isn't interested in me," she told him quietly.

But with a quick perception for which she would not have given him credit he said, "Not since Romaine came here, eh?"

She supposed she was going pale, as she usually did when her nerves were being tested like this.

"Shall we change the subject?" she asked. "I have no wish to discuss either Luke or Romaine."

He was silent for a space and then said, almost harshly, "She'll set out to get him, that's for sure! And when that woman spreads her tentacles there's no escape. I know, and so does Giles! He, poor devil, has to make a new future for himself, having lost four years of his life—no, *wasted* four years! I suppose, considering this, I myself should be thanking my stars that she threw me over before a marriage could take place!" He was bitter and furiously angry, but he certainly was not experiencing any real hurt because of what Romaine had done to him. "She'll go on and on ruining men's lives! A woman like that ought to be put away!"

"She'll settle down eventually, I expect."

"Never! If she manages to get Luke Shadwell it'll be his money that'll keep her with him—I'd wager my last penny on that!"

He drove with rather less care and on taking a bend the car skidded.

"Be careful," she warned, "these roads are treacherous in the dark."

He steadied the car, but his temper was such that it was some time before he began to drive with any real care.

"So my cause is definitely lost," he said at last. "You could never forget Luke, not after once having cared for him."

She said nothing, hoping he would allow the subject to drop, but her hope was in vain.

"Robin," she pleaded after he had been muttering about his lost chances for a while, "please forget the whole thing. I don't wish to talk about it—I've already told you this."

"Has any man been a greater fool than I?" he said, ignoring her plea. "How could I have come to lose a girl like you?"

Melanie decided that silence on her part was the only effective way in which she could put a stop to Robin's comments, so she sat back and, folding her hands in her

lap, tried to relax, to steal a little of the peace that surrounded her in the darkness that enveloped the veld.

And Robin, too, fell silent, speaking only when they
pulled up before the front door of the homestead.
Lights were on and through the window Melanie could
see Luke and Romaine sitting there, each with a glass in
hand. So the guests had already left.

"There she is," was Robin's angry and disgusted
comment. "Playing her usual game—the game she must
inevitably win! Why are men such damned idiots!" He
snapped off the headlights and turned to Melanie. "So
this is goodbye—really goodbye?"

Suddenly she was filled with pity for him; it overrode
all other considerations and emotions. His dejected
voice smote her, his very manner, with shoulders sagging and mouth drooping, went straight to her compassionate heart. She had no other desire at this moment
than to comfort him and impulsively she said, "While
you're here, Robin, I'm quite willing to go out with
you—if you want me to, that is?"

"If I want you to! Melanie, you're an angel! Yes,
dear, we'll go out together while I'm here."

"Do you know just how long you're staying?"

"I haven't made up my mind. It hasn't anything to do
with that bitch of a sister of yours; she can make her
own way back—if she's intending going back, that is! I
was staying only in the hope that you would come to
me, that we could get together again."

"I thought you were waiting for Romaine."

"Perhaps I was at first, but now that I see she's trying
out her tactics on your handsome Luke Shadwell I'm
not interested in seeing her safely home."

"You should never have come, Robin," she said
gravely. "It must have cost you a lot of money...?"

"What does money matter? It would have been worth

a thousand times more had I been successful in my mission.''

That, she supposed, was gratifying, yet it made no impression on her. She was immune to the fact of his loving her—immune, that was, as regards any reciprocation on her part.

"I'll say good night." Melanie managed a weak smile as she turned her head toward him. "Thank you for taking me."

"Can I see you tomorrow evening?"

"Yes, I suppose so."

"Same time?"

She nodded her head. "Where shall we go?"

"I'll take you out to dinner."

"Then I'll put on a long dress."

He smiled at her in the dimness of the car.

"You always look so lovely in an evening dress, Melanie."

"Passable," she said briefly, her eyes wandering to the window and to the beautiful girl sitting there opposite to Luke, with the light just in the correct place to enhance the clear unblemished skin of her face.

Romaine had once said to Melanie, "You're trouble is that you haven't either technique or finesse in your dealings with men. Whatever the occasion you should position yourself so that every advantage is derived from the light and shade of the room, or other place in which you find yourself. Quite often you look positively plain, and all because you haven't taken the trouble to ensure that you're positioned correctly in relation to the light."

"Not passable," declared Robin with a hint of anger. "You always used to say that."

She shrugged and, opening the door, slid from the car.

"Good night, Robin," she said, and scarcely waited for his answer as she moved away from the car.

It turned and disappeared along the driveway. Melanie went up the steps of the stoop and stood by the rail, staring out over the gardens to the veld beyond. The loneliness was intense, breathless; the shapes of the kopjes and baobab trees became mysterious in the implacable moonlight. A few pinpoints of silver filtered through the moving foliage of palm and bamboo—lights from the native huts that lay beyond Luke's one cropped area of alfalfa and soya beans.

She turned, nerves tingling, to find Luke standing in the frame of the open window. Even in shadow his face showed up harshly and his mouth was tight, matching the taut line of that strong, inflexible jaw.

"I hope you enjoyed your evening." He spoke with icy politeness and she remembered with poignant regret that he had heard from her lips words that had not been true—words spoken in self-defense, and put into her mouth by her sister who knew that Luke was close enough to overhear.

"Yes, it was most enjoyable, thank you, Luke." She looked at him, desperately wanting to undo the damage that had been done earlier—damage to his pride, mainly, for it could not have been pleasant for him to hear that he was not the type that appealed to her.

"I'm delighted that you're so happy." Sarcasm, surely, since she was certain that she was looking far from happy. Luke's eyes flickered over her and she felt stripped. In consequence color flooded her cheeks and all she desired was to escape. But this was not possible, with Luke standing in the window like that. She realized suddenly that she was in the full glow of the light from the room behind; it was not a position in which Romaine would have found herself—no, not in a harsh light such as this.

Instinctively Melanie would have turned from him, but he was speaking again and she was forced to look into his face. "Have you made another date with him?"

She nodded, but then kept her head averted. "Yes, as a matter of fact, I have."

It seemed an eternity before he spoke.

"I conclude that you've decided to take him back?" Strange the inflection in his tone; it mingled with the harsh undertone and she wished she could have grasped its meaning.

"No, not at all," she replied softly, her eyes straying once more to the girl in the room behind. Romaine was becoming restless; it was clear that she was feeling herself neglected, and she would be hating it. "I promised to go out with him while he's here," added Melanie, and heard an exclamation escape him. As before, she wished she could be given some insight into what went on in his mind.

"And how long is he staying here?"

"I don't know."

"Until you're in a position to go back with him," rejoined Luke in harsh and frigid accents. "I hope you'll honor your promise to stay until Deborah's father returns?"

"Certainly I shall! And as for returning with Robin, I've no intention of—"

"Of picking up the threads?" he cut in almost savagely. "But he's your type—I overheard you say so to your sister." He waited, and she saw a nerve move in the side of his neck. "Well, have you nothing to say to this?"

Automatically she shook her head, asking herself just what she could say. Luke had heard and that was that. A denial would be useless under these circumstances.

Luke would not believe her and he could not be blamed for any skepticism he might display.

"No, Luke, I've nothing to say."

He raked her face contemptuously.

"You'll go back to him," he asserted harshly. "Before you know where you are you'll be wearing his ring again!"

She said, scarcely knowing why, "I suppose it would provide me with an anchor."

"Undoubtedly! And as that appears to be all you require from marriage, then it should, after all, work out very well."

"Security's important." Again she knew not why she spoke like this. She supposed that it was because she was indifferent to the conversation, desiring only to bring it to an end.

"All-important, obviously. Well, Melanie, I wish you luck!"

So sharp and angry was his tone that she thought he would have turned from her and reentered the room where Romaine was waiting for him. But he stood motionless, staring past her at the scene on which she herself had been looking a short while previously. Clouds shifting across the moon created patterns on the ground and on the low hills, so that they became covered with a patchwork quilt of contrasting light and shade. Along the dry stream bed palms and bamboos moved gently, blanking out the lights from the huts now and then. The silence was profound, unearthly.

"I think I'll turn in—it's getting late." Melanie was all awkwardness, just as she had been in the very beginning.

"You're right, it is late." Still he did not move; he seemed wholly unaware of the girl sitting in the room, but he also seemed unaware of Melanie herself as he said, so softly that she had to strain hard to catch the words, ". . . willing to accept second best . . . simply for security."

"What do you mean by that?" she wanted to know and as he jerked visibly, she knew he had in fact been murmuring his thoughts aloud.

"By second best?" He gave a shrug and said without much interest, "Second best's sufficient for your present needs, so you'll marry Robbin—who after all is your particular type," he added, and she did wonder if she detected a hint of bitterness in his voice. Something about him made her think of his own unproductive love affair. He had got over it without too much trouble, she decided; but then men seldom experienced strong emotional feelings—they very soon allowed other things to become superimposed on any hurts they might happen to sustain. How easy it was for them! Melanie almost wished she herself were a man.

"I'm going in," she said again, and this time Luke moved to one side, making room for her to pass him. "Good night, Luke." A moth flew close to her before settling on a small branch of the bougainvillea vine curling its way around one of the tough wooden pillars of the stoop. The little creature's eyes burned like rubies and they seemed to be looking right at her. Automatically she moved a finger close to the bough and the moth flew off again. Luke watched intently, but Melanie never glanced at him again as she went past him and into the room. She heard his good night, glanced at the petulant face of her sister, then passed through the room to the corridor outside.

CHAPTER EIGHT

ROMAINE HAD SOMEHOW managed to convince the doctor that she was still unfit to be moved. To Melanie the whole situation was ridiculous simply because it was plain to her that her sister was totally recovered, and had been so after the first couple of days. But she groaned when the doctor touched her stomach, and shuddered as he drew away. His brow was furrowed and it did seem that he would advise hospital treatment.

Watching Romaine intently, Melanie saw that she had grasped the doctor's anxiety; and in order to forestall any suggestion that she should go to the hospital, Romaine said silkily, fluttering her beautiful lashes so that the poor man was brought instantly under her spell, "I've had this before, doctor, and it does last for a week or ten days, usually. It'll go, believe me. There's no need for any real anxiety. It's just that I always have to rest—but not in bed, of course," she was quick to add.

Melanie could not help but allow her lips to curve in a gesture of contempt. Romaine had no intention of staying in bed, not while she could spend her time more profitably in ensnaring Luke.

"Very well," said the doctor at last. "I'll come in again in a couple of days and I hope by then that you're feeling much better." He turned to Melanie, a frown on his brow. "If the pain recurs you must get in touch with me at once."

"I'm quite sure it won't recur," she could not help saying. "My sister will be quite well by the time you call again."

His frown deepened. He said censoriously, "You don't appear to be sufficiently concerned about your sister, if you don't mind my saying so, young lady!"

Melanie colored a little while Romaine, reclining against the silken cushions on the settee, grinned behind the doctor's back.

"Take no notice of Melanie," she purred as the doctor turned toward her. "She's never really understood me, and in addition she's rather hard—no compassion, doctor."

Melanie gasped and stared at her. Romaine seemed to be having the greatest difficulty in suppressing laughter. And when the doctor had gone she did in fact burst out laughing, and continued to laugh for as long as Melanie's indignation remained visible in her expression.

"You have no sense of humor at all," she gasped. "Oh, Melanie, what you do miss in life! It can be fun, you idiot, so why don't you break out of that web of misery that surrounds you and look for a little enjoyment?"

"Do you really consider it funny to say things like that about me?"

"I consider it funny that the silly old fool believed me! You know, Melanie, all men are fools—utter fools! You can do exactly what you like with them!"

"If it so happens that you have the necessary beauty to reduce them to slaves," was Melanie's contemptuous rejoinder. "It's always been easy for you, but as I said, the day will come when you'll be sorry for all this."

"Rubbish! Ah, here's Luke. My, but what a handsome man he is! I know I've said this before, but every time I see him striding along like this, dressed in tight slacks and an open-necked shirt, I feel I could fall madly in love with him. He's the typical outdoor man, tall and brown and strong! And where did he get those looks? I daresay he had French and Flemish ancestors—many of these Afrikaners have. Do you think he'll be glad that I have to stay on for a while?"

"I've no idea what his reaction will be. You implied that he was falling in love with you, so in that case he's bound to be glad." Of course, he himself could have invited Romaine to stay, and he probably would have done so, decided Melanie, convinced as she had been, right from the start, that Luke was bound to fall in love with her sister.

"The doctor's been, I see." He looked questioningly at Romaine, his eyes fixed on her lovely face. Melanie, clad in jeans and short-sleeved blouse, felt a wave of inferiority sweep over her when presently Luke transferred his gaze from the seductive vision of Romaine to Melanie herself. That he was comparing, she had no doubts at all. She knew he found her drab, uninteresting, plain, whereas he found Romaine alluringly beautiful in her tasteful, well-cared-for clothes. He found her intelligent, attractive...desirable. It had been so with Giles, and then with Robin—so it *must* be the same with Luke.

"I've to stay for another few days." Romaine told him, in her best musical tones. "I'm dreadfully sorry, Luke, but I'm sure you won't really mind my being here."

"Not at all. If you're not fit to be moved then of course you must stay."

"Melanie doesn't like the idea—"

"I didn't say so!" cut in Melanie with a flash of indignation. "It has nothing to do with me, in any case."

"No, it hasn't, has it? Luke's the one who's being inconvenienced." Romaine looked covertly at him from under her thick dark lashes. "I feel so well, and that's the annoying part of it all." A small pause and then, "Do you think I could go to the club?"

"Club?" he frowned, while Melanie, dwelling on what Romaine had just said about feeling well, wondered what the doctor would have to say were he to hear his patient talk in this vein. "If you're unwell then obviously you can't go out."

"The doctor hinted that I could."

"The—" Melanie pulled herself up short, but she could not disguise her expression.

Looking from one sister to the other, Luke said softly, "*Did* the doctor hint that you could go out?"

"I've just said so." Blatantly Romaine came out with the repetition of the lie she had already told. She looked straight into her sister's eyes, challengingly. "He suggested that it would do me good."

Luke's eyes narrowed. "And yet he says that you can't be moved from here?"

"I think he's anxious that I won't be cared for properly if I go to a hotel." Romained produced a devastatingly attractive smile, and watching Luke closely, Melanie noted the admiration that entered his eyes. She moistened her lips, for her mouth felt parched. And she turned away and left them together.

Deborah came to her shortly afterward, a writing pad in her hand.

"I can't spell Romaine," she said. "I can't spell all the other words, but I do want to spell Romaine right. It's such a beautiful name, isn't it?"

"Yes, Deborah, it is." Melanie spelled it for her and watched as the childish letters took shape. "Is there anything else you would like me to spell for you?"

"Some words, yes. But it doesn't matter if they're not all right. Daddy says he doesn't mind so long as I write to him."

"You write very often indeed. You like writing, don't you?"

"Yes, but I like drawing best. I wish my daddy was back home, because I haven't seen him for a long, long time." The child's lovely big eyes were shadowed and Melanie caught her close, with a protective arm around her shoulders.

"Daddy will be with you very soon now, darling. And then you'll be going back to your own home."

"Will you come to see me? I'll make you a pie, because mommy showed me how to bake—with flour that makes pastry."

"I'll be going back to my own home, Deborah, so I'm afraid I shan't be able to visit you.' '

"I don't like you going away." Deborah sucked the end of her pencil and frowned. "It's a very long way, you said."

"A very long way. I have to go on an airplane."

"Like daddy?"

"Yes, that's right." Melanie looked down; Deborah was still close, clinging with one hand to her skirt while holding both pad and pencil in the other. And it was like this that Romaine found them as she came from the sitting room into a small cozy room that Melanie and Deborah used quite frequently.

"What a charmingly domesticated scene!" she exclaimed. "What's wrong with the child?"

"Nothing," answered Melanie abruptly. "Did you want something, Romaine?"

"I want to speak to you in private."

"You can talk before Deborah; there can't be anything important that you wish to say to me."

"You're the most unfriendly sister imaginable. Your trouble, Melanie, is that you're totally unrealistic. Why on earth you should continue to have a grudge against me I don't know! If it's Giles, then all I can say is that you didn't miss much! He's enough to drive any woman to distraction with his erudite notions that he's forever pushing at you. I'm all for an intelligent conversation, as you know, but Giles was more than even I could stand!"

Melanie said nothing and her sister added, "As for Robin—well, he's yours if you want him—" Romaine broke off and spread her hands in a gesture of asperity. "There's been no real harm done if you look at the situation with an enlightened attitude. Your engagement was broken, it's true, but you've said yourself that he's still your type. So it seems logical to me—and sensible— that you and he get together again." Still Melanie said nothing, and Romaine ended by stating that to take Robin back was the best thing Melanie could do because time was going on and if she was not careful she would end up on the shelf.

"That won't trouble me," was Melanie's immediate retort. "In fact, that's where I intend to end up."

Romaine shrugged and said again that she wanted to speak to Melanie alone. "Would you like to run away and do your writing somewhere else?" She gave Deborah a dazzling smile to which the child responded at once.

"Yes, of course," Deborah answered obligingly. "Shall I come back in a few minutes?"

"Yes—but not too soon."

Melanie watched Deborah leave and close the door behind her. Then she looked at Romaine and said, "What is it that's so important?" Romaine looked at her through narrowed eyes.

"Have you told Luke everything?" she asked, and the tone of her voice was neither pleasant nor smooth.

"What do you mean by everything? He's aware that you stole Robin—"

"You know what I mean! Have you told him about Giles as well as Robin?"

"He knows about Giles, too."

"You rotten little telltale sneak! Did you have to open up and let him have the whole story?"

"What is this all about?" demanded Melanie, her anger rising.

"I dislike intensely this atmosphere that Luke creates. I'm not used to being an object of suspicion and contempt!"

Melanie's eyes widened.

"So things are not going quite as smoothly as you would have me believe? You've hinted that he's falling in love with you, but it looks rather as if that's not quite true, I'm thinking."

"I haven't said that things aren't going smoothly," denied Romaine, and it was easy to see that she was furious with herself for the way she had handled the matter. "Luke can't help but fall in love with me, simply because he's no different from the rest. However, I sensed from the first this thread of censure and faint contempt in his manner and it suddenly dawned on me just now, when I was asking if I could go to the club, that he knew far more about me than I wanted him to. For if he didn't, he wouldn't be so difficult to manage."

"What you're trying to say, Romaine, is that you've discovered all at once that here's a man who can see through you." Melanie realized that her heart was beating too quickly, and all because she was beginning to have doubts as to whether Luke was falling in love with Romaine. "Luke's no fool, and he most likely suspected that you were telling a lie when you said that the doctor had given you permission to go to the club."

Romained colored with temper.

"You certainly put suspicion into his head with your unguarded exclamation." She drew closer and her face almost touched that of her sister. "I'd have killed you if you hadn't pulled yourself up before you'd given me away!"

Melanie stepped back, shaken by this vicious mood of Romaine's. "Don't be melodramatic," she said, then added, "I did pull myself up, so why this unnecessary show of temper?"

"I'm not satisfied with the situation as it is! Luke's filled with pity for you and he's blaming me for your two broken engagements!"

Melanie could see the whole picture clearly. Romaine was trying out all her wiles on Luke, but he was not falling as quickly as either Giles or Robin—or any of the numerous other men who at various times had fallen beneath the onslaught of her charms. This kind of situation would not suit Romaine at all. However, the chief thing that occupied Melanie's mind was the mention of pity. Luke was filled with pity for her.... She had said from the first that she did not require his pity, and she would tell him so again—and without much delay!

"If there's nothing more you have to say, Romaine," said Melanie at length, "then I'll go to Deborah."

"I have just one thing to say! It's time you began thinking of going home!"

Swift anger brought the color to Melanie's cheeks.

"I shall go when I'm ready—and not before!"

"I can look after Deborah." Romaine's own anger faded and she spoke in quieter, less hostile tones. "Be a sport, Melanie, and tell Luke you want to go home with

Robin. I'll let him know that I don't mind seeing to Deborah until her father returns.'' She looked almost pleadingly at her sister. "You can't gain a thing by staying. And in any case I'm sure you're anxious to get back to England. Go with Robin and make a fresh start. You were happy with him once and you can be happy again.''

Contemptuously Melanie's gaze swept her figure.

"You want the way clear—that's it, isn't it?''

"I'd certainly like to have Luke all to myself. Melanie, please do as I ask. Luke's the only man for me, and while you're here, reminding him that you were treated badly by me, I shan't be able to make much progress.''

"So you admit you treated me badly? That's the first time you've had the decency to own to it.''

"I suppose I was rotten. But this time I'm not doing you any harm. Oh, I know you've fallen for him, but as he hasn't fallen for you, your case is hopeless, isn't it? And anyway, Robin's the one for you; recent events have proved it. Sorry I won't be at your wedding, but—'' She stopped and turned her head. "Oh, hello, Luke. Melanie and I are just exchanging confidences.''

"So I gathered,'' he replied with an icy inflection. "I heard something about a wedding?'' His eyes, glinting like points of frost, settled on Melanie's hot face. She was acutely conscious of his coldness, but what mainly occupied her mind was Romaine's assertion that he pitied her. "Whose wedding?''

"Melanie's, of course,'' came the answer purringly from Romaine. "She and Robin have made up.''

Silence followed. Melanie decided without hesitation to refrain from any denial of what her sister had said. In this way she would be proving to Luke that she was not in need of his pity.

"Is this true?" he asked at last, and his tones were ones of quiet unruffled hauteur.

"Yes, er, yes, it is true."

"Congratulations," he said, and left the room.

"Are you going home?" Romaine wanted to know, and Melanie nodded her head.

"It'll be for the best." She looked at her sister, but for the first time Romaine could not meet her gaze. "I hope I never cross your path again," Melanie announced, and with this she also left the room.

LUKE CAME TO HER in the garden the following afternoon. She glanced up to note with some surprise that there was a strange hint of grayness about his face that she had never seen before.

"I'd like to know when you're thinking of leaving," he said frigidly. "Your sister has offered to stay on and look after Deborah." He was frowning and Melanie believed she now knew the reason for the gray tinge to his face. He was worried about Deborah.

"If Romaine's willing to stay on then I'm free to leave just whenever I wish?" She heard the calmness in her own voice and marveled at it. But she realized that her mind was lazy, unwilling to exert itself in any way at all. She was in the depths of an apathy from which she had no especial desire to emerge, since this was a more comfortable state than full consciousness and the acutely painful knowledge that Luke and she were now irrevocably separated.

"Of course," he returned briefly, his eyes hard and cold as they looked down into hers. "I expect you're eager to get back and get the wedding plans moving. Will you be married before Christmas?"

"No, certainly not before Christmas." And not ever, she thought, but did not speak this aloud. "When is

Deborah's father expected to be back? It can't be long now, surely?''

"He wrote to say there's been some delay. He's not expecting to be back until the week before Christmas."

Although it seemed to Melanie that there was now nothing more to be said, Luke remained at her side, much to her surprise. She felt awkward, yet recalled the lovely evenings she and he had known, intimately friendly evenings when awkwardness on her part was nonexistent. They were strangers at this moment—strangers who were separated by the wide gulf of her own defensive attitude and Luke's unfriendliness. But what did it matter? She would soon be gone from here and she and he would never meet again.

Gone.... She would miss this beautiful country with its special form of tranquility and peace. She looked out now, over the wide veld, and the deep solitude seemed to take her protectively to itself. It spread like a veil that takes over when the gentle state of slumber prevails. She glanced up to where a trail of shifting clouds portended rain—much-needed rain that would leave the earth and its fruits smelling fresh and clean. She thought of what might have been had not Romaine appeared, to cause this rift between Luke and herself.

"What are you thinking, Melanie?" Luke's voice was almost gentle now, surprising her into a swift glance of perplexity. Why the sudden change from the frigid and almost hostile tones he had used a few moments ago?

"I was thinking of this place," she replied with honesty. "'I've grown to like it very much."

He looked oddly at her.

"You've no need to leave it," he reminded her, still in the same quiet unhurried tones. "It's your own choice entirely."

She nodded, but it was an automatic gesture.

"It's for the best, Luke," she said, her eyes pensively resting on the bright-plumaged bird that had flown across the sunlit garden to settle on the mimosa bush close to where she and Luke were standing.

"Would you care to explain why it's for the best?"

She could only shrug her shoulders, for she could scarcely tell him what was in her mind; tell him that she was leaving because she had an idea that he and Romaine would get together and that she, Melanie, had no desire to stay and watch this happening.

He spoke again, saying that she must tell him quite definitely if she was leaving, so that he could give Romaine her answer.

"I'm definitely leaving," she told him after the merest hesitation.

"Very well." The tone was cold again and Melanie turned away, unable to bear the icy expression that she knew she would see on his face.

Romaine appeared a moment or two after he had gone, triumph on her face.

"So you've told Luke you're leaving. Sensible girl! You should get in touch with Robin at once; there's sure to be a train leaving Rayneburg before the weekend."

That she was being pushed away was more than clear to Melanie, but she was indifferent to this fact.

"I'm seeing him this evening; that will be soon enough."

"But if you went to Rayneburg now you might be able to save some time."

Melanie looked straight at her. "You're in a great hurry to get rid of me, aren't you?"

"I certainly shall feel more comfortable when you've gone," was the frank and brutal admission from Romaine. And then she added, a curious expression on her face, "Are you really intending to marry Robin?"

"No, Romaine, I am not intending to marry him!"

"How sad...how very sad. I almost wish I hadn't broken it all up. However, I wouldn't then have met Luke, would I, because you'd never have come over here." Melanie said nothing and Romaine added callously, "I have a lot to thank you for, Melanie, since but for you I wouldn't now be in the happy position of being the prospective bride of a wealthy and handsome man like Luke Shadwell."

"Does it ever occur to you, Romaine, that you yourself might one day have competition?"

Her sister's eyes opened very wide. It was clear even before she spoke that such an eventuality had never for one moment occurred to her.

"Me—have competition? It's the most unlikely thing in the world. When men fall for me they don't get up in a hurry."

"Giles tired of you," Melanie could not help saying, simply because she had had far more than she could take and because she did in fact feel—for the first time in her life—that she wanted to inflict a real hurt on someone.

"He did not! *I* tired of *him* and you know it! How dare you suggest that he was the one who decided to end our marriage!"

"Oh, well, it isn't of any importance now. But what about Robin? That break, I believe, was mutual?"

"Partly," was the grudging admission.

"So he did tire of you—"

"No!"

"It might interest you to know," went on Melanie, still in the mood to hurt, "that Robin now dislikes you intensely."

Her sister's face turned crimson.

"You and he have been talking about me?"

"Naturally—under the circumstances. Robin's in a regretful mood and now admits that what he felt for you was nothing compared with what he felt for me." She noted the fury in Romaine's eyes and was glad she had been able to affect her in this way. It was high time that she knew what humiliation felt like.

However, whatever Romaine would have answered to this was never uttered, for at that moment Deborah came racing from the direction of the house, a letter fluttering in her hand. She had been to town with Jancis, who, having dropped in on a casual visit on her way into Rayneburg, had offered to take Deborah with her as the child wanted to see if there was a reply yet to the letter she had written to her father.

"What do you think!" she exclaimed, waving the letter in the air, and in reality offering it to Melanie. "I asked daddy if you could stay forever and look after me, and guess what he said?"

Melanie's nerves tingled, for there was only one answer—judging by Deborah's animated expression and the way she danced excitedly around from one small foot to the other.

"He agreed that I should stay and look after you."

"Yes, that's right!" Deborah pressed the letter into Melanie's hand. "Read it! I'm so happy now! Are you happy, Melanie?" No anxiety as to whether or not Melanie would accept; it was taken for granted by the child that, her father having said yes, there would be no difficulty from Melanie. "Read it quick!"

Taking the letter, Melanie began to read, aware of her sister's interest—angry interest.

The wording was tactful, Kevin merely saying that, if Melanie would agree, then he would be delighted to have her stay to look after Deborah. But she might not want to stay, he had gone on to point out, ending by promising to write to Melanie and see what she thought about the idea. It was a simply written letter, naturally, but the warning was there, the warning that Deborah must not assume that Melanie would stay; she must wait and see how Melanie felt about the proposition. But Deborah in her excitement had missed the warning, which was understandable, thought Melanie as she handed back the letter.

"Are you happy?" the child repeated, her piquant little face all aglow with expectancy. "You see, I'm writing to daddy now and I want to tell him that you're as happy as I am!" Still no response from Melanie, who was trying to picture what her life would be like working as nanny to Kevin's young daughter. It would be a full-time job, although there would be a few hours off during the day when in a few month's time Deborah went to the small school in Rayneburg. Yes, it might be a pleasant position... if it weren't for the misery of constantly seeing Romaine and Luke together. And later, if they did get married.... No, decided Melanie, she could not accept this position. And yet, as she stared down into that happy little face, she had not the heart to see that happiness wiped away and that shadowed expression reappear in Deborah's lovely eyes—that expression that both she and her father had worn on that first occasion of Melanie's meeting with them. "Please say you're happy," Deborah was saying in a beseeching tone. "You will stay, won't you?" she added anxiously, as a sudden doubt entered her mind at last. "I want you to stay with me—always."

And after only the merest hesitation Melanie took the child's hand in hers and said with a smile, "But of course I shall stay, Deborah, but I won't promise for how long. However, I shall stay until your daddy makes some suitable arrangements for you." To her relief, that satisfied the child, who in an affectionate gesture brought Melanie's hand up to her cheek.

Romaine, who up till now had merely been the scowling onlooker, angrily reminded Melanie that she herself was now employed by Luke to look after Deborah.

"You've sacked yourself," she snapped. "In any case, I thought you were most eager to get back to England?"

"I'm no longer eager," returned Melanie, and marveled at the way she now felt. It was as if a load had been lifted from her mind and body; she no longer dreaded seeing Romaine and Luke together. On Kevin's return she would be living in his house and she need never set foot in Luke's home ever again. "No, I'm no longer eager to leave, Romaine. I've grown to love this country and the opportunity of this position is one I don't intend to let slip by."

"But what about me? I'm supposed to be looking after the child." She was crimson with fury, a circumstance that left her sister strangely cold and indifferent. "If you think Luke will allow you to change your mind about leaving then you're mistaken—he won't! Besides, he believes you're marrying Robin!"

"What's the matter, Melanie?" cried Deborah, obviously frightened by Romaine's temper. "I don't want her to look after me."

"I'm looking after you, darling, so stop worrying." With a gentle hand Melanie brought Deborah to her. "We'll be staying with Uncle Luke until your daddy comes home, and after that we'll all be living in your house."

"I shall see Luke about this," flashed Romaine. "He's offered me the position and I intend to keep it!"

Melanie looked disgustedly at her. "See Luke," she said coldly. "I'm quite sure that in any case of choice between you and me he'll do the obvious thing and ask Deborah which one of us she wants.''

"He'll do nothing of the kind. He'll *tell* Deborah whom she shall have, and it'll be me—just you wait and see!''

"I have no option but to wait and see," rejoined Melanie unconcernedly, and then, to Deborah, "Jancis has gone, I suppose?''

"No—oh, dear, she asked me to say she wants to speak to you importantly. She's on the back stoop.''

"She has something important to say to me?''

"Yes, and she says she's dying for a cup of coffee, as well!''

CHAPTER NINE

WHEN MELANIE MENTIONED to her sister that she might one day have competition it never for one moment occurred to her that this would ever happen, either now or at any other time. But the first thing Jancis said when Melanie ran up the steps to the stoop was, "What do you think! Fay Champion's back in Rayneburg! Fay's Luke's old flame—I told you about her, if you remember? She arrived this morning, having traveled throughout the night on the train. I saw her when Deborah and I were in town this afternoon and we had a chat."

Melanie's mind computed swiftly and she was soon recalling Luke's admission that the girl possessed a kind of beauty that he had been unable to resist. He admitted that he had been in love with her and had intended asking her to marry him. However, he had also said that when she recently suggested coming out to see him, he had informed her that he was no longer interested. He seemed pleased that she had accepted this and not wasted time in coming over. But, it would appear, the girl had changed her mind.

"Her relatives no longer live here, you said?"

"That's right. However, she made several friends while she was here and she's staying with the Marshalls—you've met them at the club, I expect?"

Melanie nodded her head. "You've had a chat with her, you said?"

"Just a couple of hours ago." It was clear that Jancis

was faintly amused by what was happening. "She's as beautiful as ever, and I'm pretty certain that she's here after Luke."

Melanie glanced curiously at her. "You don't seem too troubled about it?"

Jancis laughed.

"She can't hurt me this time; I've got over whatever it was that I felt for Luke." She glanced up to see Romaine approaching, her book in her hand. The sun had tanned her arms and legs beautifully, and she made a most charming picture of feminine allure—charming enough for a glossy magazine, mused Melanie, wondering just how she was going to take this latest piece of news. And what of Luke? What would be his reaction? Melanie felt that the whole situation would have been extremely amusing had she herself been totally aloof from it, unaffected by the charms of Luke Shadwell. "My case was hopeless," Jancis was saying, her eyes still on the approaching figure of Romaine, "so there was nothing to be gained by harboring optimism, was there?"

"No, there wasn't." Melanie frowned at the thought that Romaine might decide to join her and Jancis on the stoop. However, the girl merely lifted a hand to Jancis and went into the house.

"Isn't Romaine joining us?" Jancis asked the question a few moments later, after Melanie had requested Elizabeth to bring coffee and cakes out to the stoop. "She'll not have gone into the house because of me, surely?"

"You mean that she would consider she was intruding?" Shaking her head before Jancis could answer, Melanie went on to add that Romaine probably wished to wash and dress now that she had finished her sunbathing.

But within about ten minutes or so Romaine did come out, much to Melanie's surprise.

"Do you want some coffee?" Melanie, desirous of keeping from Jancis the strain existing between Romaine and herself, forced a smile to her lips.

"Please." Romaine sat down opposite to Jancis, her eyes almost insolently examining her from head to foot. "And a sandwich," she added as Melanie rose to go inside to seek out the servant. "Ham if you have it."

When Melanie came out again Jancis and Romaine were talking, although one glance at Jancis's face was sufficient to tell Melanie that she was not enjoying Romaine's company.

"Elizabeth will be out directly with your coffee and sandwich." Melanie's voice was stiff now; she was angry that Romaine should have intruded when she knew full well that she would not be welcome.

"I'd better be going," said Jancis eventually, glancing at her watch. "Shall I see you at the dance on Saturday evening?"

"I expect so." Luke would have been taking her, mused Melanie, had not Romaine appeared and upset everything. As it was, Robin would be her escort.

"I expect Fay will be there—but meanwhile, you can expect her to be calling on her old flame!" Jancis gave a laugh, but all Melanie's attention was with Romaine, who on hearing Jancis's words had jerked upright in her chair, her eyes wide and puzzled. "I wonder whether they'll really get together this time? Everyone in Rayneburg will be agog at the reappearance of Fay! They'll guess she's after Luke."

"Fay...who?" The two words came from stiffened lips. In fact, Romaine's whole body seemed to have become taut and the color was fast leaving her cheeks.

Jancis looked at her as she rose to her feet. Romaine

was still sitting upright and she lifted her face as Jancis spoke.

"Fay Champion. She was once practically engaged to Luke. . . ." Jancis's voice retreated slowly as the truth began to spread through her mind. "Are you all right?" she asked, and it was easy to see that the question was put merely in order to give her time to recover from the embarrassing position in which she found herself. Her glance went swiftly to Melanie, whose face was impassive.

"This Fay," said Romaine, ignoring the question. "She was practically engaged to Luke, you said? When was this?"

"Oh, some time ago," replied Jancis, endeavoring to assume a casual manner. "I expect it's all over, really—"

"You remarked that she's after Luke," came Romaine's almost harsh reminder. "Where does she come from? England?"

"Scotland." Jancis moved uneasily and once again her glance shot toward Melanie.

The plea was so obvious that without hesitation Melanie rose and said, "I'll come to the car with you, Jancis. Excuse us, Romaine; Jancis has to go. She's in a hurry."

"But—"

"Sorry!" It was a curtly spoken word and without any further interruption from her sister Melanie led the way down the steps and then walked beside Jancis to the station wagon that was parked at the front of the house.

"Lord, what a fool I am! I had no idea your sister had fallen for him."

Melanie turned to her and said, "It was so obvious, then?"

"But of course it was! I'm terribly sorry, Melanie, for my lack of tact—"

"Don't worry about it," interrupted Melanie. And she decided to add, "Romaine and I don't get along all that well, so you haven't upset me in any way."

"I didn't think you got on too well." Jancis stood by the door of the vehicle and looked searchingly into Melanie's face. "You're not alike in any way at all—if you don't mind my saying so."

"She's very lovely," murmured Melanie. "That's the chief difference between us."

She noticed Jancis's brows being raised and was not altogether surprised when the other girl said, "It's a matter of opinion, Melanie. However, I won't embarrass you by going into that part of it. What I will say is that in many other ways you and she are vastly different." A small pause and then, "You know, it could be quite hilarious—two bitches fighting one another! It's usually one bitch to one heroine. Still, Fay's so nice that I suppose you could put her in the heroine's place...." She stopped and then said, "I've been most untactful again, haven't I? Obviously you wouldn't class your sister as the bitch."

Faintly Melanie smiled. "I haven't thought much about it," she lied, automatically pulling open the door as Jancis made ready to get into her vehicle.

"There's Gladstone," remarked Jancis with a laugh. "What a card he looks in that hat!"

Following the direction of her gaze, Melanie saw Gladstone in the shrubbery. He was wearing the brightly colored straw hat that had belonged to one of Luke's visitors—female visitors. It shaded his head and eyes from the sun, but it also gave him a comical appearance that afforded him as much amusement as it afforded those who saw him wearing it. Deborah was with him,

Melanie noticed as the child emerged from behind a bush. She was holding a doll, but she was intently watching all that Gladstone was doing. She would be coming with her letter, thought Melanie, and turned to say goodbye to Jancis.

"Deborah'll be going to school soon, won't she?" Jancis asked, and Melanie nodded her head.

"After Christmas—I think it's about the eighth of January that the school starts." A small pause and then, "I'm staying on to become a sort of nanny to her. Her father wants me to."

"Really? But how splended! I'm glad you're not leaving us, Melanie." Jancis was in the driver's seat and just about to start the engine when Luke appeared from over a rise. He was on a horse, cantering leisurely along the edge of the field of alfalfa.

"I expect Deborah's delighted that you're staying on." Jancis took her hand from the starter and Melanie realized that she was intending to await Luke's arrival so that she could impart her news.

"She is," said Melanie, then added, "it was dreadfully sad about her mother. How old was she?"

"About twenty-six or seven. Tumor on the brain; it was all over and done with in a matter of hours. She went into a coma and never regained consciousness. It was a terrible shock to everyone, because she was a girl who was always full of life. Kevin won't get over it for a very long time to come."

"No, I shouldn't think he would. Deborah's different—children are, of course. She talks about her mother at times, naturally, but her eyes don't fill up as often as they did."

"Thanks to you, Melanie." Jancis was watching as Deborah, having seen Luke, raced away toward him. On reaching her he dismounted and Melanie could

imagine her telling him about the letter she had received.
Luke glanced over to where the two girls were standing,
Jancis having got out of the station wagon. He waved a
hand, then walked the horse, Deborah riding on its
back.

"I've told Uncle Luke!" she exclaimed when presently she and Luke had reached them. "He says he's very
glad, and I'm glad, too!" She was lifted down, but
Luke's eyes were fixed on Melanie, the most odd expression in their depths.

"I thought you had altogether different plans," was
his comment after he had sent a smile in Jancis's direction.

"Well, er. . . ." Melanie had no answer; she had been
thinking about it for the past few minutes, wondering
what she was going to say to Luke when, having learned
of her change of plan, he asked about Robin. "I felt I
must stay," she murmured lamely, wishing that Jancis
were not here.

"I see," he said abruptly with the sort of inflection
that clearly stated that he did not see at all.

Jancis spoke at last, watching in some amusement as,
after imparting her news to Luke, she saw the increduli-
ty appear in his eyes.

"Fay—here!" he repeated. "You've seen her, you
say?"

"Today." Jancis couldn't resist adding mischievously, "There's only one reason why she should be here,
Luke: she still loves you!"

Luke's eyes narrowed as he said, "Don't be facetious,
Jancis! Fay's here to see old friends—and I don't happen to be one of them!"

With a shrug of her shoulders Jancis said carelessly,
"We shall see, Luke. And now I really must be off! See
you on Saturday, Melanie. So long for now!"

"Goodbye." Melanie waved as the vehicle turned out of the driveway into the road beyond.

Luke spoke then, his voice abrupt and puzzled.

"You've definitely decided to stay here to look after Deborah permanently?"

"I don't know about permanently. For one thing, Deborah's father hasn't yet written to me to ask me to stay."

Luke's eyes flickered angrily.

"You're evading the issue," he told her sharply. "Are you or are you not going to marry Robin?"

The question she had of course expected; it was bound to come, as a natural consequence of her change of plan regarding Deborah.

"I d-don't know," she stammered. "Deborah needs me." She ended on a lame note and heard the indrawn breath that was a sign of Luke's exasperation.

"Am I to take it," he snapped, "that Deborah is more important to you than Robin?"

"That's not a fair question—"

"Answer it—before I do you some damage!"

She stared, her nerves alert, her eyes wide with astonishment at this loss of control. For assuredly he was in a temper. She saw that his eyes were tawny—burning too, like smoldering ashes suddenly fanned to life. She prudently decided to be honest with him.

"I'm not going to marry Robin," she said quietly, and before she could even take a guess at his intention she found her shoulders seized and she was shaken so violently that the tears sprang to her eyes and within seconds had flooded onto her cheeks.

"Uncle Luke!" cried Deborah, starting to cry. "Stop hurting Melanie! She's crying—look! I don't like you anymore because you're cruel!" And she turned and raced toward the house as fast as her legs would carry her. Vaguely Melanie was struck by the fact that the child meant to bring some help.

"Look what you've done now!" he thundered and gave Melanie another shake.

"I?" she gasped, sweeping away the tears with the back of her hand. "You're the one who's to blame—entirely!"

"What did you mean by telling me that damned lie about marrying Robin?" His face was taut and grim, his whole attitude menacing as he stood over her, too tall by far, too overpowering and aggressive.

"I don't understand you at all," she began, but got no further because Romaine came from the house, walking swiftly toward them, Deborah by her side trotting to keep up with her.

"What's happening?" Romaine took in the scene— Luke furiously angry and Melanie still weeping. "Deborah tells me that you've shaken Melanie?" Romaine's eyes glittered as they moved from her sister to Luke. "Is this true?"

Luke turned to her, slowly.

"Quite true," was his brief and curt reply.

"Well," began Romaine hesitantly, "that's not very nice."

"Please go away," snapped Melanie. "This isn't your affair!"

A shrug from Romaine and then, "If that's how you feel I will go away!"

"And you can go, too," Luke told Deborah, but the child looked up at him, reluctant to leave.

"You won't hurt Melanie again?" she asked.

"No, I'll not hurt her again."

"All right then, I'll go!"

When they were alone Luke said softly, staring down into Melanie's moist, unhappy eyes, "I hope, Melanie, that the shaking will be a lesson to you not to tell me lies."

She averted her head, avoiding that stern and accusing stare. But she was puzzled in the extreme, since it could not matter to Luke whether or not she was intending to marry Robin...unless.... She glanced up then and caught her breath. Thoughts rioted and she was recalling the fact that all was not going smoothly with Romaine in her attempts to bring Luke worshipping at her feet. Melanie had experienced a slight doubt about the likelihood of his falling for her sister, but later she had once more become resigned, remembering, as she so often did, how easily Romaine had succeeded with Giles and Robin. Why should Luke be any different, Melanie had asked herself.

Luke was speaking, reminding her, in the same quiet accents, that she had not responded to what he had just said.

"I didn't think it mattered—about Robin," she murmured defensively.

"Why did you tell me that lie?"

"Because I didn't want your pity—"

"My pity?" he broke in, surprised. "When have I offered you pity?"

"At first you did, and then—"

"True, at first I did. But this is not 'at first,' is it?"

"Romaine said—" She broke off, this time of her own accord, but Luke was not allowing her to hold back what she had intended to say.

"Romaine said what?"

For a long moment Melanie remained stubbornly mute, pretending that she was interested in the little green lizard that was darting around on the dusty path. Its tongue flicked out with the customary speed of creatures of its kind and Melanie knew that each time this happened it was more than likely that a tiny insect was taken into the lizard's mouth.

"Romaine gave me to understand that you were feeling sorry for me," she offered when at length it seemed that she would be forced to answer his question.

"I've never told Romaine that I'm sorry for you," he returned crisply. "She's obviously misled you."

"Perhaps." Melanie frowned a little. "Does it matter?"

"You obviously considered it did, seeing that you went to the trouble of lying in order to prove to me that you didn't need my pity." He paused a moment, watching her changing expression. "Yes, Melanie, I can see through you. But I wish I could see more!" he added unexpectedly, and without affording her the opportunity of responding to this he took up the horse's rein and strode away toward the paddock, where two other horses were cropping grass.

It was early evening when Romaine sought out Melanie in her bedroom, merely tapping on the door panel before entering. Brush in hand, Melanie turned in some surprise, angry spots of color fusing her cheeks when she saw who it was who had entered without so much as a request.

"What do you want, Romaine?" she demanded. "I'm busy!"

"I'd like to know what was going on between you and Luke! But that's only one thing I've come about!" Romaine's face, red with anger, appeared far from beautiful, especially as her mouth was twisted and her eyes smoldered viciously. "Why should he be shaking you, that's what I want to know!"

"Then ask him." Turning again, Melanie began

vigorously to brush her hair, her anger revealed in every single stroke.

"So you won't tell me?"

"Romaine," said Melanie without turning around, "will you please leave this room!"

Romaine's reaction to this was to take a few steps that brought her closer to Melanie.

"The other thing I've come about is the nasty way you have of twisting things around to suit your own purpose!"

"Just what are you insinuating? Come to the point quickly before I order you out!"

"You got in the first word with Luke!"

"About what?" Melanie could see her now, through the mirror.

"Deborah!"

"Oh, that? Yes, he knows I'm taking up the position of nanny to her."

"And staying here in the meantime! The position was mine and I told him so!"

"You did?" Melanie now swiveled around on the stool. She was extremely interested in how Luke had taken this. "And what did he say?"

Seething as she was, Romaine had difficulty with her speech.

"That you must stay. I've lost the job."

"You never really had it, did you?" No answer from Romaine and Melanie added, "One can't lose a position that one has never occupied." Melanie was musing once again on the difficulty that Romaine appeared to be having with Luke. With any other man she would have achieved her object long before now. Melanie had said that Luke was not quite like the rest; she had not believed this at the time, but she did believe it now.

"I shall find some way of remaining here," flashed Romaine after a long silence. "If I'd taken that position it would have given me time—" She stopped, coloring vividly as she realized what she was saying.

"You've never before needed time," Melanie could not help pointing out. "Either you're slipping or Luke is tougher than you bargained for."

Romaine stared, since this was the first time Melanie had ever spoken in this particular way.

"You've changed," she said, and there was a pettish note to her voice. To Melanie she had never appeared so hateful as now, and all Melanie desired was to escape, to retreat to some safe place where she would never set eyes on her sister again—never as long as she lived. Yet, conversely, regret hovered in her heart and mind as she thought of what might have been had she and Romaine been comrades and friends, sharing experiences and confidences. But for as far back as Melanie could remember they had lived their lives apart, and the climax of this disunity had occurred when, for the second time, Romaine had ruthlessly set out to take Melanie's fiancé from her. And even now she was determined to have Luke, despite the fact that she had guessed that Melanie was by no means indifferent to him.

"If there's nothing else you want to say to me," said Melanie, beginning to brush her hair again, "then please go—" She broke off as a reverberating noise outside brought a jerk of warning to her brain. "What on earth was that?" The shuddering trees were the answer. A storm was brewing, a terrifying African subtropical storm. Luke had mentioned them to her, but assured her that they did not occur often. "It will batter everything down!" almost wailed Melanie, thinking of the lovely flowers in the garden.

Romaine shivered as something crashed outside.

"That sounds like a tree falling on the roof of the garage," she said and, turning, hastily left the room. Melanie followed more slowly, going to the sitting room where she found Luke with Deborah on his knee.

"I'm frightened of the wind!" Deborah put both hands over her ears, and leaned against Luke's chest. Melanie stood by the door staring at them, and something turned in her heart as her eyes met those of Luke. His were soft, tender; she knew instinctively that he would make a patient, loving father if ever he had children of his own.

"Are you afraid, Melanie?" he asked, and his voice was gentler than she had ever heard it. "Storms like these are rather frightening, I admit, but we have nothing to fear—not inside the house. Damage will be done to some of the buildings, I expect, but there's nothing we can do until the storm abates."

"Will it last long?" she asked, coming into the room and taking possession of a chair.

"It's hard to tell, but while it does it'll be severe." He paused a moment before repeating his question, "Are you afraid?"

"Not really. I'm concerned about the flowers and bushes in the garden. And what about the native huts?" she asked as the thought came to her. "Will they withstand this wind?"

"Yes, they're safe enough." He touched Deborah's head gently with his fingers. "There's nothing to fear," he told her in soothing tones.

"Can I stay up until the wind dies down?"

"Of course you can—" Luke stopped abruptly, cocking an ear. "Is that a car?" He frowned.

Melanie nodded and, rising, went over to the window. "It's a young lady," she said, staring at the lovely creature who had stepped from the car. Fay Champion....

Luke was on his feet, having put Deborah on the couch. And a moment later the silvery voice was heard, complaining of the wind; it had literally rocked the car, Fay was telling Luke.

"I thought I'd never make it! Oh, but I'm glad to see you again, Luke!"

"You shouldn't have come...." His voice went quiet and Melanie heard no more until the pair entered the sitting room from the hall. "Fay, meet Melanie; she's looking after Deborah there." He gestured toward the couch. Fay was looking Melanie over in the most critical way, but presently she was saying hello to the child.

"Hello," responded Deborah. "Did the wind frighten you?"

"Indeed it did." The girl smiled at the child, then looked up at Luke. "I arrived in Rayneburg early this morning," she informed him.

"So I heard." He was looking intently at her, but Melanie could read nothing in his expression. Her attention returning to Fay, Melanie saw the resemblance of beauty—the clear, almost translucent skin, the fragile quality that she surmised would arouse the protective instinct in any male who might be interested in the girl. Yes, she had an especial kind of beauty...as had Romaine. Melanie turned her head as her sister entered; the next few minutes ought to be amusing, but Melanie, the plain Jane between two inordinately lovely women, felt as if she wanted nothing more than to leave the room.

"Romaine, meet a friend of mine, Fay Champion." Cool, impassive tones, but Luke's eyes flickered with interest from his old love to the girl who was staring almost disbelievingly at her. "Romaine and Melanie are sisters."

"How do you do," said Romaine in acid tones. "Are you staying here, or in Rayneburg?" Her manner suggested an awkwardness that Melanie had never before encountered in her sister. It seemed as though Romaine—probably for the first time in her life—was lost for words.

"At the hotel in Rayneburg, but I'm hoping my good friend Luke will invite me to stay here." The look Fay gave to Romain was clearly a challenge. "I used to be a regular visitor here, you see, so I grew to love it."

Luke said quietly, "We'll talk about it later, Fay, when we're alone. Meanwhile, you must stay tonight, because it's impossible for you to drive back to Rayneburg in this storm."

Enchantingly Fay smiled up at him, her enormous eyes expressing pleasure and a pretty, silent "thank you."

"You haven't changed a bit! Oh, but it's good to be back in Africa!"

Luke left the room for a few minutes and the three girls were left alone, with Deborah lying back on the couch, her hands pressed to her ears. Outside the wind raged, tearing at the roofs of the buildings and ripping branches off the trees, branches that now and then smacked against the window, then fell onto the stoop.

"Have you been here long?" inquired Fay, settling down into the luxurious cushions of an armchair as if she had lived here all her life. "You're looking after Deborah, Luke said, but where are her parents? I remember them well—Deb was only small—"

"Her mother died," cut in Melanie almost in a whisper so that the child did not hear. "And her father's in England on business. I've been here a couple of months or so. I came for a visit, but stayed on at Luke's request."

"At Luke's request," murmured Fay, her eyes once more examining Melanie's face. "Luke was having Deb, then?"

"Yes, her father asked him to have her, and that was why he asked me to stay. He thought at first that his aunt would be here—"

"His Aunt Gertrude? Yes, I remember her—happy little person, she was. Has she left him?" asked Fay in some surprise. "She was with his father for years and years."

"She wanted to go back to England. She's my aunt as well as Luke's, although several times removed," added Melanie with a swift smile of amusement.

"So you and Luke are cousins?" Fay spoke reflectively, her eyes straying to Romaine and flickering strangely. Romaine's face was set and stiff, her mouth tight. She met Fay's gaze and there was open hostility in her eyes. Fay seemed to shrug inwardly before transferring her attention once more to Melanie. "How do you like living here?"

"Very much. It's a beautiful country."

"It is indeed. I wish I'd never left it."

"Will you be staying long?" inquired Romaine from the depths of her chair.

"That remains to be seen. It's up to Luke."

There was an uncomfortable silence after this and Melanie at length took Deborah off to the cozy sitting room, where they sat together listening to the howl of the wind outside and the creaking of the trees as they were tossed this way and that. The ripping off of branches made a shuddering noise, and the smaller twigs still scraped against the window before ending up on the stoop where, suspected Melanie, there would be a pileup before the squall eventually died away.

"Why doesn't it stop?" complained Deborah, moving closer to Melanie. "Will you stay with me until it does?"

"Of course," returned Melanie soothingly. "In fact, I'm going to ask Uncle Luke if you and I can have our meal in here—together, seeing that you're staying up until the storm abates."

When this was put to Luke, he frowned at first, but then agreed.

"However," he said grimly, "I'm not particularly looking forward to dining with those two." His eyes were faintly amused; Melanie wondered if he knew that Romaine was equally attracted to him as Fay.

After a pause she could not resist saying, "How strange; I thought you would enjoy the company of two such beautiful girls."

All she received in response to this was a glowering look before, after stooping to kiss Deborah, he went from the room.

CHAPTER TEN

By nine o'clock the wind had died down. Deborah, dozing on the couch, was put to bed without her bath and by half-past nine Melanie was back in the small sitting room, preferring to spend the rest of the evening alone. However, it was not to be, for less than half an hour later Luke entered to inform her in frigid tones that Robin was here.

"He came in this weather?" she frowned, vexed at being taken from her book.

"It doesn't take long to get from Rayneburg. The storm's been over for almost an hour and a half." His glance was cold, his mouth compressed. Melanie apologized for Robin's presence in his house. This seemed to infuriate Luke because his tawny eyes blazed, but he said nothing and she suspected he was considering it would be more prudent to maintain a silence or otherwise he would say something he'd later regret.

"Do you mind if I see him in here?" she asked, and Luke flicked an impatient hand.

"Do just as you please. He's waiting in the hall at present."

Melanie went out to him, and invited him into the sitting room.

"Why did you come?" she asked with a hint of anger. "We weren't to meet until tomorrow evening."

"I know, but I just had to see you, if only for an hour." His face was drawn and haggard; he looked as if he hadn't slept for a week. "I can't go on like this, Melanie. I'm staying on here only in the hope that you'll change your mind and take me back. I love you," he added simply and, she knew, sincerely. How sad it all was—how sad that Romaine could break lives in the way she had done. There was Giles, thrown into the inconvenience of divorce, having wasted several years of his life, and now Robin, who without doubt would be a considerable time getting over his love for Melanie.

"I don't know what to say, Robin." Distress edged her voice and her lovely eyes held a depth of pity as they looked into his. "It's all so tragic."

He came toward her, his hands outstretched.

"There isn't any hope at all for me?"

"I've already told you this," she replied in gentle tones. "Dear Robin, I'm sorry for you, but there's no way in which I can even begin to put things right between us."

He swallowed hard.

"We were so close once," he murmured, but now she knew that he was reminiscing and that his words had no deeper meaning—no quality of hope in them. "There's nothing for me but to leave, and this I shall do as quickly as possible." His hands were still outstretched and on impulse Melanie put hers into them. She was drawn close and she offered no resistance, even though she was well aware that he intended to kiss her. It was a goodbye kiss and she would not deny it to him. His lips were gentle, but quivering, too. Melanie took her hands from his and put them around him, a comforting gesture, and he responded.

And at that very moment Luke tapped lightly on the door and opened it at once. The two drew apart, Melanie's face coloring vividly. She soon averted her head, for Luke's expression was excruciatingly painful to her—the contempt, the anger, the condemnation.

"Excuse the interruption," he said harshly, "but Deborah's awake and asking for you."

"I'll go to her." Melanie's head was still lowered. "You've been to her?"

"She called out, so I went to her, yes." And without another word he was gone.

Robin said in a slow and odd sort of tone, "Is that the way he normally speaks to you?"

She shook her head as she moved toward the door. "No, of course not. I'll be with you again as soon as I can."

It was ten minutes later that she rejoined him.

"Deborah's restless," she said. "The storm upset her and I don't think she's quite got over it yet. However, she's so sleepy that she'll go off again at once." She looked at him from where she stood by the door. "Will you have a drink before you go?" she asked, acutely conscious of the pity within her but even more aware of the desolation caused by Luke's entrance into the room at that particular moment. The fact that he despised her so much was so hurtful that she could scarcely bear it.

"No, dear, I'll be off at once." He was resigned but unhappy, so unhappy that his eyes were deeply shadowed and the sides of his mouth gray and drooping. "Goodbye, my dearest Melanie. I hope that, one day, you'll find the happiness you deserve."

Her smile was bitter.

"Robin," she said gently, "I dare not try again."

"Because of your sister, I suppose?" He, too, was showing bitterness.

"Because of Romaine, yes. She could—and would—take even a husband from me."

Robin gave a deep sigh and nodded his head.

"It's a strange thing, but once I really got to know her I saw nothing attractive in her at all, *nothing*!"

"By then it was too late."

"What a soul-destroying expression—too late."

She saw the bitterness in his eyes, heard it in his voice. She wished she could change within herself and discover that she cared. But this was impossible, and she gently bade him goodbye.

"Will you be going before the weekend?" she asked as he turned to go.

"If there's a train out of Rayneburg, but I have an idea that my particular train doesn't leave until the early hours of Sunday morning."

THIS PROVED TO BE correct. In consequence, Robin got in touch with Melanie and the result was that she agreed to let him take her to the dance at the Jasmine Club on the Saturday evening. Robin came with the hired car, which would later be picked up at the railway station by the garage proprietor who had lent it to him. Luke's car was in front of the homestead, ready and waiting to take Fay and Romaine and himself to the dance. He had not asked Melanie if she wanted to go, but when she had said she would like to go with Robin he immediately made this easy for her by ensuring that Elizabeth would not be going out.

At the club all eyes were on Fay, who entered with Luke, Romaine having gone to the powder room to see to her hair and to apply something to her face. Smiles abounded and it was quite plain that Fay's presence was causing quite a stir.

"Isn't she beautiful!" exclaimed Jancis, having come up to Melanie while Robin was away getting drinks.

"She'll get him and no mistake!" She turned swiftly on hearing a quick intake of breath. "Oh, hello, Romaine. I didn't expect to see you here—"

"And why not?" Romaine challenged insolently with eyes narrowed to mere slits. Melanie guessed that her sister had overheard what Jancis had just said.

"Well. . . ." Jancis was put out and Melanie frowned in anger that she should be made uncomfortable like this. "You were supposed to be unwell—"

"Supposed to be? I *was* unwell. The doctor was attending me! However, I'm quite all right now." Romaine's eyes had traveled to Fay who, ravishing in gold lace and with some rather exquisite jewelry around her neck and wrists, was laughing up at Luke in the most coquettish manner—a manner to which he was obviously feeling more than a little responsive. For his normally hard features were relaxed in an indulgent smile, and one arm was slid around Fay's slender waist.

"I'm glad to hear it." Having recovered, Jancis spoke in acid tones. "You'll soon be leaving us, then?"

Romaine's face was turning pale as she continued to watch the flirting activities of Fay Champion.

"That remains to be seen. Excuse me, please." And she drifted away, leaving behind an exotic whiff of perfume.

"I'm sorry," began Jancis. "I wasn't very polite, I'm afraid."

She looked genuinely distressed, and in order to put her at her ease Melanie said kindly, "Think no more about it, Jancis. As I said before, my sister and I are not in the least close. She and I have never agreed about anything and I'm very sure that we never shall in the future."

Jancis said nothing, but her eyes wandered to where Luke stood, chatting to Fay and to several others who had joined them. Romaine was standing there, on the outside of the circle, trying to edge her way in so that she would find a position close to Luke. Melanie became fascinated by this performance; never before had Romaine exhibited such lack of self-assurance, never had she been the one outside trying to get in. What was she feeling like? Undoubtedly her fury would be rising, but in all probability she would be able to control it and turn on the charm as soon as the opportunity arose.

And this she did. Having gained the position she wanted, Romaine shone up at Luke and her voice could, be heard as she asked him to get her a drink. He obliged, although Melanie had the surprising impression that it was not done willingly, but rather for the sake of appearance, since he was unable to refuse without causing some astonishment among his friends standing by.

Robin came with two glasses, saw Jancis and said, "Can I get you something?"

She smiled and told him what she wanted. She had seen him in Rayneburg, with Melanie, and when he had gone she said curiously, "He came with your sister, didn't he?"

"That's right."

"But you and he. . .?" She allowed her voice to fade and gave a deprecating shrug of her shoulders. "I'm a real nosy parker," she laughed. "I suppose we haven't much in the way of news here in this out-of-the-way place, so we all tend to want to know everyone else's business, especially the business of newcomers."

"It's understandable," returned Melanie in quiet, gracious tones. "And there is a story, Jancis, but as the telling of it would cause me a great deal of embarrassment I hope you'll forgive me if I don't relate it?"

"But of course! You make me feel awful!"

"You needn't feel awful. I will say this much: Robin came here for a special purpose, and as this hasn't materialized he's leaving in a few hours from now."

"He's in love with you, that's for sure," declared Jancis. "Oh, well, that's life! How very easy it all would be if love affairs went right!"

Melanie looked hard at her and said hesitantly, "You, Jancis...isn't there someone?"

"There was, as you know...." Her eyes wandered to the tall aristocratic figure of Luke as he walked toward Romaine, the drink in his hand. "But not now."

"This isn't the place to meet people, is it?"

"We don't get many strangers coming, if that's what you mean. I sometimes think I shall go away—to a town—and get a job in an office or something like that."

"You'd hate it!"

"True, I would." Jancis stopped as Robin appeared. He smiled rather wanly at her as he put down the glass on the table in front of her. Melanie made a formal introduction and the three chatted until the orchestra struck up, when Robin asked Melanie to dance. As Edward appeared at this moment Jancis also got up. Later, Edward invited Melanie to dance and Robin and Jancis paired up.

It was much later that Luke came to Melanie for a dance. She felt overwhelmed by shyness, tongue-tied and gauche.

"What's wrong?" he inquired, looking down at the top of her head.

"Nothing at all."

"How's the romance progressing? It's all on again, of course?"

She merely shrugged her shoulders, too dispirited to inform him that Robin would be leaving Africa in a few hours' time. He would learn soon enough. But as she watched his expression she was puzzled, for he seemed suspicious, as if, quite suddenly, he doubted that the romance was on again, as he had put it. She asked him if

he had heard from Kevin and he scowled at this unexpected change of subject.

"I've been expecting a letter from him asking me to
accept the position of nanny to Deborah," she added,
and saw the frown of puzzlement that settled on Luke's
lean and handsome face.

"I haven't heard from him lately." Luke spoke curtly
and she suspected that her refusal to answer his question
had been taken as a snub. "I imagined you'd changed
your mind again . . . ?" He was clearly perplexed that she
had not done so, and once again she felt that he was
having doubts about her and Robin having come together again.

"I shall stay for as long as Kevin wants me to." Her
own voice was curt and tight; she had no patience with
his suspicions, or his curiosity. She cared not whether
he had suddenly reached the conclusion that she and
Robin had parted irrevocably. Luke saw the indifference in her eyes and no more was said between them
until the music stopped.

Then, "Thanks," he snapped, and walked away
toward the bar. Romaine joined him and he and she
chatted and laughed for a few minutes before being
joined by Fay.

"You know," whispered Jancis in Melanie's ear,
"there'll be a scrap between those two before very
long." She was laughing with her eyes and looking
most attractive in this humorous mood. Robin joined
them and a flash of appreciation entered his glance as
he looked at the girl with whom he had had three
dances already, these when Melanie had been claimed
first by Edward, then by Van de Westeyn, and finally by
Luke. "It really is amusing, the way they glare at one
another. But you must have noticed; everyone else
has."

"No," said Melanie, shaking her head, "I haven't noticed."

"Have you noticed, Robin?" Jancis gestured with her hand. He looked across at the three standing at the bar.

"Noticed what?" he asked.

"The way Romaine and Fay are with one another."

"Oh, I see now whom you were talking about when you mentioned the word *glaring*. If you ask me, that's a mild description of the kind of looks they give to one another."

"I wonder what Luke is thinking?" mused Jancis. "He'll not be pleased, that's for sure!"

"Not be pleased?" echoed Robin in surprise. "On the contrary, I would imagine he's wallowing in the adulation of two such beautiful females." The sneer in his tone escaped Jancis, but it was vibrantly accepted by Melanie's ear. She glanced at him, saw the bitterness in his eyes, heard him say, for her benefit only, "For the first time in her life Romaine has competition. I'll wager she's reaching boiling point inside."

Despite the fact that he had spoken almost into Melanie's ear, Jancis heard him and she twisted her head sharply, an odd expression on her face.

"You know Romaine very well, don't you, Robin?"

There was silence as his eyes met those of Melanie.

"Do you mind if I tell Jancis?" was his astonishing request. And without knowing it Melanie was shaking her head. This he took as an assent, and before Melanie had time to say anything he had told Jancis that he and Romaine had until recently intended to marry.

"You were engaged—and then broke it off?" Her swift glance passed from him to Melanie and then to Romaine. "Yet you came here together?" She just could not contain her curiosity and she made no apology for it. "Aren't you upset about the break?"

His lips curved in a sneer.

"I'm not upset about the break with Romaine; it's—"

"Please, Robin," interrupted Melanie, "you've said enough."

"I'm sorry, dear." The look he gave her, contrite, regretful and pleading for indulgence—it was seen by Jancis, naturally, and her puzzlement increased.

"A mystery," she murmured, and then, "Sorry. I'm far too meddlesome; I told you this earlier, Melanie."

"You must be very puzzled," sighed Melanie, "but—" She stopped to stare at Fay and Romaine who, on their own now, were quite plainly arguing with one another. Fay was cool and arrogant; Romaine on the other hand was definitely heated, her face flushed and her eyes flashing.

"So Luke left them to it," commented Jancis softly. "And no wonder! He must be painfully aware of everyone's amusement!"

Melanie frowned as she dwelt on this; she was recalling her earlier impression that Luke was not overenthusiastic about going to the dance. The impression was born from something Romaine had said, but at the time Melanie had not taken much notice. However, she was now wondering if Luke had brought the two women merely for the sake of politeness.

"He'd no need to come," Robin was saying, his voice breaking into her thoughts. "But he did, and he brought those two, so it's his own lookout if he's embarrassed."

Jancis frowned slightly.

"Luke has always put his guests before anything he himself might want. Both Fay and Romaine are his guests, and therefore his first consideration would be for them. If they wanted to come here tonight he would feel obliged to bring them whether he himself wanted to come or not."

Robin was not interested; he was brooding inwardly and it showed in his expression. Melanie felt suddenly that the very air around her was oppressive and with a quick word of excuse she left Jancis and Robin together and went outside into the clear, serenely beautiful night. Here, away from the lights and chatter, she would find solace...peace. And so she wandered farther into the darkness of the gardens where the luxuriant vegetation blanketed the strains of the orchestra, which had struck up again after the short intermission. Robin would be all right with Jancis, decided Melanie, refusing to harbor a sense of guilt at leaving him like this. He and she would dance together and Melanie would not be missed.

Where was Luke, she wondered. She had taken a good look around the room, but there was no sign of him anywhere. Perhaps he had gone to the bar, or he might be on the verandah at the other side of the building, taking a breath of fresh air.

Finding a low rocky wall, she sat down, potently aware of the solitude that surrounded her. Close to lay the gardens and beyond them the silent bush veld, dark, mysterious, intimate. The breeze was warm and sweetly scented; it caressed her face and shoulders and tousled her long shining hair. Peace enveloped her and she knew a strange, unexpected lift of spirit. Thoughts flitted around: one second she was deciding that she must soon be writing to Aunt Cissy, asking her to send on clothes and other necessities that she would find in the apartment, and the next second she was thinking of Luke and confusedly wondering whether or not he really was attracted to one or other of the beautiful girls he had brought to the dance this evening. Two of them....

Suddenly Melanie stiffened, jerking herself upright on the wall, her ears alert. The glow of a cigarette pierced the voliage of a nearby bush and almost at once a slender figure appeared. Moonlight revealed the taut face of her sister who, arrested by the dark shadow rising above the wall, called out sharply:

"Who's there?"

"It's only me." Melanie's voice was low and slightly tinged with annoyance. Romaine's company was the last she would have desired.

"Oh—can I sit down?"

"Of course. You sound angry."

"That dreadful girl—Fay Champion! How dare she adopt so possessive a manner with Luke? Just because she knew him years ago! Did you know she left him to go back to an old flame of hers?"

"Someone told you?"

"I overheard a conversation being carried on by some of the local people." Romaine took another draw at her cigarette before tossing it to the ground and heeling it into the dust. "I can't imagine Luke taking her back after all this time." There was an unfamiliar break in Romaine's voice and it struck Melanie that she really was suffering. But whether it was pain that she suffered or the humiliation of defeat it was difficult to tell. "Have you seen Luke?" asked Romaine pettishly. "He disappeared a while ago and I haven't seen him since. I want to be taken home!"

"I have no idea where he is," answered Melanie quietly, aware that she did not like at all the idea of Romaine's use of the word *home*. This, plus the manner in which she spoke of Luke, seemed to give evidence of the fact that she already considered Luke in a sort of possessive light. It was as if she was thoroughly determined that he should be hers. What Melanie did not know was that Romaine, for the first time in her flirtatious career, was suffering the indignity of her beauty being challenged, and in addition she had just taken a defeat in her skirmish with Luke's old flame. Both these circumstances had undermined her confidence and she found herself in a position she was loathe to accept. She had to take it out on someone and her sister just happened to be at hand.

Yet she scarcely knew what she was saying as, her temper enveloping her like a net from which there was no escape, she made the wild and totally illogical statement, "This is all your fault, for changing your mind about leaving!"

"My fault?" Melanie blinked at her, as well she might. "What is my fault, might I ask?" Her very calmness riled Romaine.

"You're so cool, and arrogant! You didn't used to be like this. You were reduced to tears when I took Giles from you, and the same when Robin and I fell in love. You hadn't the courage to put up even the semblance of a fight! I hate you, Melanie! I hate you for this way in which you treat me!"

Pale, but still composed in spite of this violent show of temper and malice, Melanie returned quietly, "You're not yourself, Romaine. What's happened I do not know—although I can take a guess. But you're talking wildly, and in a way that by the morning, you'll regret. You see—" Melanie got no further; her words having added fuel to the fire of her sister's wrath, she felt herself reeling over the wall as Romaine, striking out viciously, sent her sprawling backward, her arms and legs flying. Automatically flinging one hand toward the ground on realizing that inevitably she must hit it, Melanie cried out as, the wrist bone cracking, the pain shot excruciatingly right up her arm to the shoulder. "Oh, what have you done to me?" She was gasping with pain, expecting Romaine, overcome by contrition and anxiety, to come over the wall and help her up. But there was not even a sound to reach her ears, much less any practical help as, one arm hanging helplessly at her side, Melanie managed to get to her feet.

Romaine had gone!

Thoroughly shaken by the fall, and suffering from shock, Melanie sat down again. But the pain was too much to bear, and in addition the bone was displaced and a swelling beginning to rise all around it. She rose unsteadily to her feet, and it was just at that moment that another figure appeared, a tall lithe figure that she knew so well.

"Melanie...what are you doing out here all on your own?"

"I...I came for a stroll...." Tears were streaming down her face and she turned from him, ashamed of the little access of self-pity that was affecting her. "I wanted to be quiet for a few minutes."

To her surprise Luke laughed—a harsh laugh, yet edged with amusement for all that.

"Funny thing, so did I—" He broke off as, a stab of pain shooting along her arm, Melanie uttered a little sobbing moan. "What's wrong?" His eyes scanned her face as she turned. "Are you ill...?" He saw, then, the arm that she had now brought up and was holding against her chest, the other hand beneath the wrist, supporting it. "What have you done?" He stepped closer, his tone changing, his attitude one of deep concern. She lifted her eyes in the moonlight and he saw the tears glistening on her lashes.

"I fell off the wall and I think I've broken my wrist." Her voice faltered and another little moan escaped her. "It's dreadfully painful, Luke. It needs some sort of treatment, I think."

He had hold of the wrist and his strong fingers probed, causing her to flinch.

"Hospital treatment," he decided. "Come. I'll take you in the car."

Once she was seated in the car Luke wanted to know how she had managed to fall off the wall. He was driving quickly out of the club grounds and his eyes were staring straight ahead.

"I just fell," she replied. "You know how these things happen."

"No," he said, "I don't."

A trifle put out by this brusque remark, she found herself at a loss for words. And after a moment or two Luke repeated his question.

"I toppled backwards" she explained. "And naturally put out a hand to save myself."

"I see." He sounded as if he did not see at all, but no more was said and within a few minutes the hospital was reached and Luke slid the car to a standstill under a brilliantly lighted canopy extending over the front entrance of the building.

An hour later they both emerged, Melanie's arm encased in plaster up to the elbow

"Six weeks!" she exclaimed, not for the first time. "It'll seem an eternity."

"I'm sure it will," he agreed readily. "However, it could have been a lot worse; you could have fallen on your head."

She nodded and said yes, she had already thought of that.

"At least with this there'll not be any aftereffects," she added.

"For which we must be grateful."

We.... And there was in his voice something that set her nerves tingling and her senses alert.

On arriving back at the club he stopped the car under a clump of trees but made no attempt to get out.

"I don't expect you want to go back in there?" he said.

"No—but Robin will be wondering what's happened to me, so I shall have to go back in."

"Shall I speak to Robin for you?"

"If you don't mind."

He left the car and Melanie sat back, relieved that the doctor had given her something for the pain. Vaguely she wondered what was Luke's intention, but her mind felt too drugged to deal with such a question. However, on his return he stated firmly that he was taking her home.

"But what about Romaine and Fay?" she asked.

"Robin will bring them home when the dance finishes."

Melanie said without thinking, "Romaine wants to come home now."

Luke had already started the car and he continued to nose it from under the trees.

"She does? How do you know that?" Cool tones, but edged with curiosity.

"She told me earlier on that she wanted to be taken home."

"Earlier? Then why didn't she mention this to me?"

"You weren't around."

"So she told you after I had left the hall?" The car was almost at the high gate and even as he spoke Luke was turning it into the road. The lights were being left behind and after the town was skirted nothing but the dark veld lay around them, with drifting glimpses of native huts or trees or kopjes appearing, highlighted by the moon's silver rays as they pierced the thin cloud layer.

It was some time before he received an answer to his question since it was now occurring to Melanie that she was near the point where she might have to give away the fact that the accident had been caused by her sister.

"Yes, it was after you had left the hall."

"How long after?" Luke was acting rather strangely, she thought, since it would appear that he was probing far too deeply into the matter.

"I didn't take much notice of the time."

For a while there was silence between them, with Luke sitting in the most casual pose, hands lightly resting on the steering wheel, eyes ahead. The light of the headlights threw into relief the bright white bungalows that were now appearing, scattered prettily on the hillside or along the roadside. Bushes and small copses came and went, living for a bright illuminated moment before melting back into the slumbering darkness of the landscape. Moths by the hundred fluttered before the headlight glare, like snowflakes wrapped in fine gold leaf. And in the vast dark vault of the sky a myriad stars twinkled, clear and blue as the purest diamonds.

Having reached a particularly lonely place in the road Luke turned off. The car rocked drunkenly on a rutted and stony track and even as Melanie opened her mouth to ask what this was all about the car dragged to a stop and the brakes were applied.

"Don't speak," was his first command as, reaching up, he snapped on the interior light. '*I'm* doing the talking, and as I'm in no mood for subtleties I'll come straight to the point—or perhaps I should say, points, since there are several that I shall bring up. First, I want to know exactly what happened when you fell off that wall?"

"Is it important, Luke?" This stopping of the car puzzled her, as did Luke's manner, for although it was calm, unruffled, she had the strange impression that there was an unfamiliar tenseness within him. She also had the impression that it would not take very much provocation to make him lose his temper.

In fact, her question brought an impatient intake of his breath, and his voice was sharp and short as he replied, "I wouldn't otherwise have asked it, since I'm not in any mood to waste words!"

"Do you mind telling me what this is all about?"

He turned in his seat and looked narrowly at her.

Emotions stirred and she lowered her lashes, automatically fingering the hard white ridge of plaster that covered her wrist and reached right down to the knucklebones.

"A few moments before I came upon you out there in the club gardens Romaine ran past me; so great was her hurry that she didn't see me, and she was muttering to herself something that sounded like 'It serves her right.' She came from the direction of the wall."

A pause ensued as he gave Melanie the opportunity of commenting, but a silence pervaded the car as she sought vainly for words that would shield her sister. "I suggest that it was then that she told you she wanted to go home?" Again no sound from Melanie and he continued, "She had something to do with the fall." It was a statement, but Melanie automatically shook her head and said she would rather not talk about it, whereupon he nodded perceptively and told her that her reticence was adequately revealing.

"You and she had quarreled, that was obvious from her mutterings. It was also obvious that she was in a temper and I strongly suspect that Romaine in a temper would stop at nothing. And although you won't speak, I know that in some way she was responsible for your fall—I knew it almost at once, but naturally I was far more concerned with the matter of getting you to hospital than in wasting precious time analyzing the situation." He looked sideways at her, noting her pallor, and a frown crossed his face. "Either she hit out at you deliberately, or she gave you a push that caused you to lose your balance. Are you going to tell me what the quarrel was about?"

"It was more an argument than a quarrel," she said, and he uttered an exasperated sigh.

"Very well! Point two," he said abruptly, his swift change of subject giving her a jolt, "might cause you a little embarrassment. But should it also cause you to shrink away and tuck yourself into that armored shell that you manage always to keep handy, then despite the fact that you've broken your wrist I shall give you something that'll make you tingle for a week—and sitting down more than a little difficult!'' Impatience mingled with the hint of anger in his voice, but amusement was also there—and the note that warned her he was quite ready to carry out his threat. ''Point two, Melanie is: what were you doing allowing Robin to make love to you like that?''

Just as he expected she blushed hotly, but she was prudent enough not to ''shrink away... into that armored shell....''

''He wasn't making love to me—I mean,'' she amended on noting the swift and skeptical raising of his eyebrows, ''it wasn't what it appeared to be.''

''Really?'' he challenged with a further lift of his brows. ''It looked perfectly plain to me.''

''I don't understand what this is all about!'' she said impatiently. ''I'm very tired, Luke, and would like to go to bed.''

''Avoiding the issue again! Melanie, don't, I beg of you, goad me any more! You know darned well what this is all about! Would I bring you here, and sit and talk like this, if there weren't something important afoot? Open your eyes, girl, and see what you ought to have seen long ago—before that sister of yours came poking into our affairs, convincing you that she could take me from you!'' He was in a temper now, but Melanie, having fully absorbed what he had been saying, knew no fear of that temper; on the contrary, the very fact of its existence brought an onrush of pleasurable sensations such as she had known prior to the appearance on the scene of Romaine, when, her friendship with Luke being strengthened every day, Melanie allowed into her consciousness glimpses of a happy future with him here in this beautiful country.

"Luke," she faltered at last, hearing his angry intake of breath as his patience began to run out, "are you t-telling me that we—you and I—can...." She got no further because of the tightness in her throat and the fact that no words of affection, even, had ever left his lips.

"Yes," he snapped, "that's exactly what I am telling you!"

"Oh...."

"And perhaps you'll now tell me why you were allowing Robin to make love to you!"

"He wasn't, Luke. We were saying goodbye."

"You—" He stared at her. "What, then, were you doing with him this evening?"

"His train doesn't leave Rayneburg until early tomorrow morning, so he asked if he could take me to the dance." She paused, searching his face for some sign of softness, but all she saw was a tight, unreadable mask and she added hurriedly, "It was all over before he arrived in Rayneburg, Luke. I knew I could never take him back."

"Because...?"

She hesitated, but only for a moment.

"Because I'd begun to care for you," she answered simply, and the next second she was in his arms and his mouth had found her tender, quivering lips. The kiss was long and gentle, and when at length he drew away his arms remained around her.

"I was so sure, before those two arrived. But then you encased yourself almost immediately and I began to wonder if you were despising yourself—for the discovery that you still wanted Robin."

"There were so many misunderstandings," she whispered, turning her face to his, inviting a kiss. He took her lips again, but this time there was less gentleness in the pressure of his mouth on hers. Ardency and desire were no longer held back. "You see, how was I to know that you loved me?" Although it suddenly struck her that he had not as yet mentioned love, she knew there was no need for words.

"There were numerous signs that had you not been so obsessed by the conviction that Romaine held some sort of magic power over men, would have flashed out at you like a beacon on a headland. What about when I gave you that shaking?"

She blushed and said, "What about it?"

"Wasn't that proof enough that I cared? It happened as a result of your telling me that you weren't marrying Robin after all. You remember?"

Remember.... She was not likely to forget that shaking in a hurry!

"Well," she returned plaintively, "one would scarcely take such treatment as a demonstration of love!"

He laughed heartily and said, "I don't expect it seemed to be one at the time, but had you thought to ask yourself why I should have acted so, you'd have come up with the one and only answer: I was so relieved by your statement that you weren't intending to marry Robin that I just had to punish you for my previous sufferings—"

"Sufferings!"

"It might interest you to know, my girl, that I was almost out of my mind, believing that you'd marry him, accepting second best!"

"I must admit," mused Melanie after recollection had come rushing in, "that I recall being somewhat puzzled by your anger, and I recall, also, that I related it to the fault of Romaine's not being totally successful regarding her plans for you and her—" She stopped, but it was too late. Luke was nodding and his eyes had taken on that tawny hue.

"She tried, didn't she? I've never been so bored in the whole of my life. I had to tolerate her in my home, firstly because the doctor said she must not be moved, and then, later, because she was your sister. I just hoped that she would take one or more of the numerous hints I gave her and leave. She became a nuisance to me and that's why I invited Fay to stay with me." He paused, and he and Melanie just sat quietly in the car, potently aware of each other's nearness, and of the peace and silence of the bush around them. Shrubs and trees formed dark silhouettes against the purple sky; in the distance the vague outline of the mountains reared up to merge with the cloud cover above them. The silence seemed to widen before being broken as Luke murmured reflectively, "So Romaine actually admitted that things were not going her way?"

"Yes, and that's why she was so anxious for me to leave." Once again she realized she had said too much. Luke's eyes glinted, but he refrained from comment, reverting to what he himself had said.

"If she admitted that things weren't going her way, then why did you keep up that defensive attitude?"

"Because I believed she would get what she wanted in the end—"

"Stupid child! My little one, you'll be lucky if you escape my wrath!" But in contrast to his forceful threat his arms were gentle as he drew her to his breast, taking infinite care not to touch her injured hand. "What am I to do with you?" he asked with tender emotion. "For the moment, I can think only of this...." His lips, strong and cool and masterfully possessive, claimed hers and held them captive for a long, long moment. "Dearest Melanie, I love you...."

Another silence, and so Melanie never voiced what she had intended voicing—that she naturally felt convinced of Romanie's success with Luke simply because she had been so successful with both Giles and Robin.

Anyway, what did all this matter—this unhappiness of the past? It had been a prelude to this magic realm of true love and friendship in which she now found herself.

"Little one," he murmured close to her cheek, "there are several minor questions that need clearing up between us, but you're tired and need to be put to bed—"

"Put!" she ejaculated, drawing away from him like a frightened child. "Not *put*, dear Luke!"

"Put," he said inexorably, gently tapping the plaster. "You're minus a right hand, my love."

"Yes, but—"

"No buts! Obedience, little one! This is one of the first things my wife must learn!"

"I'm not your wife—"

"You will be within a week— No, my love, no arguments. I know what you're going to say: you can't get married with your arm in plaster. Well, we shall see!"

Melanie had to laugh, a happy, carefree laugh that seemed to fascinate him.

"How I've wanted to hear you laugh like that," he said, "My dearest sweetheart, I hope I shall always make you happy."

"There's no doubt about that," was her fervent rejoinder as she lifted her hand to touch his lean brown cheek. "Have I said I love you?" she asked with shy hesitancy.

"No dear, you haven't," he grinned, and she gave another laugh.

"Then I'll say it now. I love you, dear, dear Luke."

He kissed her then, and caressed her face and her neck, and lifted her hand to his lips in a gesture that savored of homage.

"What about Deborah?" Melanie was saying as they continued their journey home a few minutes later.

"Kevin will have to make other arrangements—just

as he would have done had you not appeared on the scene. There's no immediate problem, as she can remain with us until Kevin returns, which will be before Christmas so it won't be long now.''

"He'll be able to get a nanny for her?''

"Probably. However, she's used to being with her daddy—there's been only the two of them since her mother died. And in any case, she'll be going to school very soon after Christmas.'' He paused and then said, "Fay and Romaine will be told to leave immediately, though I rather think they won't need any telling when we inform them, at breakfast tomorrow morning, that you and I are engaged to be married.''

"Married...'' Melanie repeated slowly. "I can't believe it!'' The lights of the homestead suddenly appeared through the trees, twinkling and moving with the stirring of the foliage. "We're home,'' breathed Melanie, and Luke turned then and smiled tenderly at her. But he said nothing until the car had crunched to a halt and he had switched off the headlights.

"Yes, home, Melanie. We're home...together.''

Complete and mail this coupon today!

Bill

"Take a deep breath, relax and say something else."

Before Tracy could shrug him off, he added, "Pause after the first word."

"I can't." How she hated to admit she had a weakness.

He massaged her shoulders, thumbs delving deep into her tense muscles. "Think Olympic athlete. Nothing comes easy to them. And yet they triumph. Take a—"

"Will...you stop with the coaching already?"

"That was awesome." Chad moved to her side, draped an arm over her shoulder and gave her an air-stealing squeeze.

She shoved his arm off. "Seriously? Now you're being nice to me?"

"Hey, I've always been nice." Chad grinned. *Grinned!*

She wanted to slug him. She wanted to shout at him. She wanted to kiss him.

Dear Reader,

Welcome to Harmony Valley!

Just a few short years ago, Harmony Valley was on the brink of extinction with only those over the age of sixty in residence. A younger generation is moving back to town, but if the only industry around—a winery—doesn't succeed, that could end.

Before a car accident, Tracy Jackson was a rising star in the advertising world. Now she's working in slow-paced Harmony Valley as a coffee barista and waiting for her chance to get her life back on track. Travel writer Chad Bostwick has got a lead on a story in Harmony Valley, only it's not going to be a kind, fluff piece. Satire is how he's built his following. Tracy's the only person in town who realizes Chad might derail revitalization efforts. She's determined to make him see that the charm in Harmony Valley is the real thing.

I hope you enjoy Chad and Tracy's journey to a happily-ever-after, as well as the other romances in the Harmony Valley series. I love to hear from readers. Check my website to learn more about upcoming books, sign up for email book announcements (and I'll send you a free sweet romantic comedy read), or chat with me on Facebook (MelindaCurtisAuthor) or Twitter (@melcurtisauthor) to hear about my latest giveaways.

Melinda Curtis

www.MelindaCurtis.com

HEARTWARMING

A Man of Influence

——

USA TODAY Bestselling Author

Melinda Curtis

Recycling programs
for this product may
not exist in your area.

ISBN-13: 978-0-373-36783-2

A Man of Influence

Copyright © 2016 by Melinda Wooten

Printed in U.S.A.

Award-winning and *USA TODAY* bestselling author **Melinda Curtis** lives in drought-stricken California with her husband, small dog and bossy cat. Her three children are all in college in another state, which means she's constantly wondering if they're eating right, studying hard and making good decisions. Despite knowing they don't eat right, they do make her proud.

Melinda enjoys putting humor into her stories, because that's how she approaches life. She writes sweet contemporary romances as Melinda Curtis (Brenda Novak says of *Season of Change*, "found a place on my keeper shelf"), and fun, steamy reads as Mel Curtis (Jayne Ann Krentz says of *Cora Rules*, "wonderfully entertaining").

Books by Melinda Curtis
Harlequin Heartwarming

Dandelion Wishes
Summer Kisses
Season of Change
A Perfect Year
Time for Love
A Memory Away

Thanks to all the readers who enjoy the Harmony Valley series. Your kind words and love of the characters make Harmony Valley a joy to write.

And thanks to my parents, who are old, quirky and stubbornly independent, traits shared by many of the older characters in the series.

PROLOGUE

"YOUR SERVICES ARE no longer required." The chairman of the board for *Bostwick Lampoon* magazine fixed Chad Healy Bostwick with the kind of stare one gives to spoiled, stinky sushi.

"You're firing me?" A week after his father died, Chad hadn't thought he could feel any emptier. He was wrong. His insides felt as hollow as a jack-o'-lantern on Halloween. He rubbed a hand over his designer tie, just to make sure no one had carved triangular features in his chest.

"We're taking the *Bostwick Lampoon* in a different direction," the chairman said, in a voice gruff with age and years of cigarette smoke and maybe—just maybe—regret over what he was doing. Barney had been a friend of Chad's father during their student days at Stanford. He'd known Chad since the day he was born. He had to realize what he was doing was wrong.

But there was the spoiled and stinky sushi stare. And him giving Chad the ax.

A quick glance around the boardroom—at

dour and pitiless faces—and Chad realized how few friends he had left at the magazine. He reached for his coffee, misjudged the movement and grappled the cardboard cup with both hands to save it from spilling.

Silence filled the room, but it couldn't fill the empty spaces inside Chad.

"This is my company." His voice felt as weak as a fighter's jab in the last few seconds of the fifteenth round. Never mind that Chad was editor-in-chief and managed the other writers. Never mind that he wrote The Happy Bachelor On the Road—a popular travel column for the magazine. He owned 49 percent of the publication his father had started over fifty years ago. "You can't take it away from me."

But since stockholders controlled 51 percent of the shares, they could fire him.

"We're honoring your father's last wishes." Barney handed Chad a sheet of paper.

"Postmortem manifesto?" Chad perused the document on *Bostwick Lampoon* letterhead, his gaze catching on a paragraph in the middle.

My son, Chad Healy Bostwick, has done a brilliant job leading the magazine. But every so often a periodical has to reinvent itself to stay relevant. Chad is not my choice for the job.

Unable to read any more, Chad crumpled the paper in his fist.

This was the thanks he got for taking care of his father during his three-year battle with cancer? This was the thanks he got for thirteen years of service? The *Bostwick Lampoon* was a send-up of the news of the day. It was supposed to be a clever vehicle to make people laugh. Chad couldn't work up so much as a chuckle.

He used to laugh. Back before he'd had to run the company. He used to smile. Back before he'd had to fire people with kids and mortgages. He used to joke. Back before his father was struck by the Big C. The *Bostwick Lampoon* didn't like what he'd become? They'd made him this way!

Doreen, his father's assistant, led Chad out. She and a security guard stood in Chad's office as he packed his personal belongings in a single box and thought about the man he used to be. They didn't care that he took the lead sheet from his team's last story meeting. They didn't seem concerned that he might try to beat them at their own game.

At the top of the list was a small town called Harmony Valley.

CHAPTER ONE

IT WAS THE "what ifs" that drove Tracy Jackson crazy.

What if she could eat as many oatmeal raisin cookies as she liked and still fit in her skinny jeans? What if she didn't have to get up every morning at 4 a.m.? What if she'd participated in that brain shock therapy after her car accident?

Yeah, no way was Tracy going to let anyone attach an electrode to her head and send a jolt of electricity through it.

Since cracking her skull against a semi-truck, she'd gone from being a motormouth to being idle in a conversation. She talked in short sentences, especially when she got flustered. She had the occasional brain fart when she couldn't remember a word. Doctors said her progress toward beating expressive aphasia was hindered by the stress Tracy put on herself.

Stress? How about high self-standards?

Before the accident, Tracy had been among the top of her class at Harmony Valley High School. She'd been a double major in college. She'd thrived on the fast-paced, competitive jungle of a large advertising agency. After the accident, she'd used her advertising connections to land a television news production job.

Okay, so maybe television wasn't the best fit for her current verbal skill set. She'd had a meltdown live when the reporter she was working with had vomited at a crime scene. Tracy'd had to take over the microphone and she'd gone as mute as a deer in the headlights. Maybe that's why her news station job had been phased out—their way of firing her without actually firing her. And maybe being canned had forced her to sit down and think about listening to what the doctors ordered so that her life wouldn't seem like a dead end at age twenty-six, so that she could take another fork in the road and work on overcoming aphasia.

Mildred Parsons rammed her walker into the counter of Martin's Bakery in Harmony Valley, bringing Tracy back to the fork she sat at in the road. "Two pumpkin spice scones and a latte." With her poofy white curls and poofy pink cheeks, Mildred looked like Mrs.

Claus. The lenses of her glasses were as thick as ice cubes, and were apparently just as hard to see through. She squinted at Tracy and handed over her wallet. "I should have a five in there. Keep the change, dear."

"Thanks." That quarter tip would really help build Tracy's retirement fund. She took the five and handed the wallet back.

Mildred bumped against the counter again as she turned. *Bang-turn. Bang-turn. Bang-turn.* A perfect 180—not—that got her out of the way of the next elderly resident.

The morning rush was in full swing.

While Tracy made Mildred's latte, she took Agnes Villanova's order—hot green tea and a vanilla scone. Accepted Agnes' exact payment. Plated the scones. Served them. Took Rose Cascia's order—chai latte with soy milk, no scone. Admired the former ballerina and Broadway chorus girl's kick-ball change. Made change. Wondered what was keeping bakery owner Jessica in the kitchen—she could use her help.

Greeted Mayor Larry in his neon green and yellow tie-dyed T-shirt—coffee, two packets of sweetener, no cream. Smiled patiently while Old Man Takata debated whether to order the bran muffin or the chocolate croissant. There was no debate. He always went with the croissant. But his indecision gave Tracy time to make another pot of coffee.

Tracy didn't need to say much as a baker's assistant. She just had to move quickly. She was the only thing moving fast in this remote corner of Sonoma County. In a town where the average age of the one-hundred-plus residents was in the seventies, most things went at walker speed. Case in point: the game of checkers being played in the corner between Felix, the retired fire chief, and Phil, the should-be-retired barber.

The town council sat at a table in the middle of the bakery. Mayor Larry espoused the merits of controlled growth, while Rose, the no-growth advocate, tried to talk over him with her high-pitched outside voice. Eunice Fletcher sat quilting in the window seat, occasionally glancing down at Jessica's baby in a small playpen. She was about due for a coffee refill.

It was just another Friday morning in Harmony Valley. Tracy felt no stress at all.

And then *he* walked in.

Morning sunlight glinted off the blond highlights in his brown hair and outlined his broad shoulders. His eyes were the dark

brown of coffee, no cream. Those eyes catalogued everything in the bakery, as if he
thought there'd be a test later.

The conversation in the room dwindled
and died. Chairs scraped. All eyes turned toward the newcomer, because Harmony Valley
wasn't a pass-through town. It was practically
the end of the road.

"Don't. Scare. Him." Dang it. Stress jabbed
repeatedly at her stilted speech button like a
child playing ding-dong ditch. Tracy swallowed her sudden discomfort and waved the
man to the counter.

"Who came in?" Mildred asked, voice
on the max volume setting. Apparently, she
hadn't put in her hearing aids this morning,
and couldn't see through her ice cube lenses.

Mr. Golden Glow chuckled as he approached
the counter. He moved out of the sunlight and
became...no more normal. Still gorgeous. He
walked as if he owned the room, exuding a
vibe Tracy had always admired—power, pres-
tige, a winner of corporate boardroom games.
Didn't matter that he wore jeans and a polo
shirt. That walk said suit and tie. His confident air said, *"I know people who can get you
a job."*

Tracy's mouth went dry, because she needed

a better job. Unfortunately, she could practically feel the full extent of her vocabulary knot at the back of her tongue, clogging her throat.

She tried to remember her latest speech therapist's advice. *Breathe. Relax. Turn your back on the person you're talking to.*

Okay, that last one was Tracy's antidote. But it worked. Not that there were many opportunities to turn her back mid-conversation or in an argument without looking like a total jerk.

And how could she forget the advice of her speech teacher in college? *Breathe. Relax. Imagine your audience is naked.*

"What's good here?" Mr. Tall, Perfect and Speech-Robbing stepped in front of her.

Tracy's gaze dropped from his steel gray polo to the counter. Oh, for the days she dared imagine the opposite sex naked. "Coffee." That was good. Normal sounding. If you didn't count the frog-like timbre of her tone. She cleared her throat. "Scones." She waved a hand over one of the pastry cases that her boss, Jessica, worked so hard to fill.

"Why do you suppose he's here?" Rose, never shy, asked the room, shuffling her feet beneath the table. That woman never sat still.

"Maybe he's lost," Eunice piped up from the window seat.

"Not lost," the stranger said cheerfully, smiling at Tracy as if they shared a private joke.

The joke was on him. This was Harmony Valley, where people had no respect for personal boundaries and could have taught the FBI a thing or two about interrogation.

"Visiting relatives?" Mildred squinted his way.

"Strike two."

Tracy had never been a believer in eyes twinkling. But there you go. His did. Despite that power-player vibe. Or maybe because of it. Her body felt a jolt of electricity, as if it ran on twinkles, not caffeine.

Old Man Takata held up a chunk of chocolate croissant. "Health inspector?"

"Thank you all for playing." The newcomer grinned, scanning the menu board above Tracy's head while the room erupted with speculative conversation.

Tracy felt the urge to apologize for her hometown homies. "We don't get many…" She searched for the word amidst the nerve-strumming intensity of his very brown eyes. "…*strangers* here."

"No worries. I'm a travel writer." His voice. So silky smooth. Like the ribbon of chocolate

Jess put on the croissants. "I'm here for the Harvest Festival."

If he thought that would bring the room back to normal, he was wrong. The bakery customers exchanged dumbfounded glances. This was what Harmony Valley had been waiting for—exposure. No one really believed it would ever come, because the town had been off the radar for a long time. More than a decade.

When Tracy was a teenager, the grain mill had exploded. To this day, Tracy couldn't think about her mother and her mother's co-workers being burned alive without a sickening churn in her stomach. Back then, Tracy had been devastated, too young to understand the ramifications beyond the heart-wrenching grief over losing Mom. Without jobs, the majority of the population had moved away. Those who'd remained were mostly retired. But now there was a new employer in town. A winery, started by Tracy's brother and his friends. People were returning. New businesses were opening. What they needed were tourists and the dollars they'd bring. What they needed was this man and his readership—whatever that might be.

"Thought I'd come up early," the travel

writer added. "Find a room, and do a story on the town and its winery."

Mildred gaped. Rose gasped. Phil covered a snort with a cough and received several dirty glances.

Tracy sighed. Yes, there was a story here. Probably too many. There just wasn't a hotel within a thirty mile radius. Rumor had it the Lambridge twins were going to open a bed and breakfast—next spring. Mr. Travel Writer wouldn't find a room this week unless he wanted to bunk with Mildred.

"A travel writer." Mayor Larry stood in all his tie-dyed dignity, tossing his gray ponytail over his shoulder and approaching the counter. "Welcome, welcome. I'm the mayor." Larry gave the town council the high sign— a repeated head tilt toward the door, as in: *emergency meeting needed to find the travel writer a place to stay.*

But Rose only had eyes for the newcomer, Mildred was legally blind and Agnes was digging in her purse.

Larry pumped the travel writer's hand as if he drew water from a well. "Why don't you sit down and let Tracy bring you some coffee and a scone?"

Tracy held her ground because Mr. Travel

Writer didn't seem like the black coffee type. If she had to guess, she'd go with a shot of espresso with a splash of half and half. Besides, the hunky travel writer hadn't accepted Mayor Larry's offer.

"The town council meeting will start in five minutes," Agnes said, proving she'd received the mayor's message after all. "Phil, you're on the agenda today."

Phil, the town barber and the Lambridge twins' grandfather, glanced up from the checkerboard. He was the one person in the room who hadn't been staring at their visitor, most likely because the guy had crisply cut hair and no need of a visit to Phil's barber chair. "But my game—"

"Can wait." Mayor Larry grabbed Phil's spindly arm and helped him up.

Agnes, Mildred and Rose mobilized. The fire-drill search for a hotel was in full swing.

"It's not even Tuesday," Phil wailed, referring to the town council's regular meeting day as he allowed Larry to lead him out the door.

And just like that, the morning rush was over.

From his playpen, Gregory gave one of his happy-to-be-alive shouts. Eunice leaned over and quacked at the baby, eliciting giggles from Jessica's son.

Chocolate croissant eaten, Old Man Takata moved into Phil's spot with a rattle of his walker.

Before Takata could settle in Phil's seat, Felix executed a three-hop move and grinned. "King me."

"Seriously?" Takata grimaced.

The bakery quieted enough that Tracy could hear the creak of the oven door as Jess worked in the kitchen. Her speech therapist would have encouraged her to start a conversation with the newcomer, who still stood across from her at the counter and who looked nothing like a travel writer, not that she'd ever met one before. But all Tracy could think about was how normal she looked at the moment and how that image would shatter if she opened her mouth, how the warmth in his eyes would turn pitying and how low her spirits would then sink.

She said nothing, but her head began to nod as if trying to fill the silence with movement.

"I swear, I showered this morning." The travel writer tugged the placate of his polo as if airing out his shirt. "I've never emptied a room before."

"It wasn't you," Tracy fibbed. Good. Very good. She could appear intelligent. If she could just get a handle on the nervous head nodding.

"That's what my last girlfriend said." He gave a self-deprecating laugh. *"It's not you. It's me."*

Was he flirting with her?

Tracy used to love to flirt. She used to be the Queen of the One-Liners, the Princess of Comebacks, the Junior Miss of Verbal Jousting. Now she was just a head-nodding simpleton. "Latte? Sssss-cone?"

His smile softened like chocolate on a warm spring day. He probably thought he was so gorgeous he made her tongue-tied.

Little did he know, Tracy's tongue was permanently in knots.

"YES TO BOTH latte and scone." Chad introduced himself and smiled at the pretty, petite blond behind the counter. He'd spent the past month relearning the feel of lips curving upward over his teeth, the deep sound of his own laughter, the subtleties of a nuanced joke.

He'd slept in, eaten junk food and driven up the western coast from California to Canada and back again with a laptop, a small suitcase and the box he'd taken with him from the office in his trunk. He'd enjoyed the culture, sophistication and women the cities of Portland and Seattle had to offer. It wasn't until he'd returned to an empty penthouse in San Francisco that he'd remembered the story lead sheet and thought about what was next for him.

The choices he faced...

He could freelance or write for someone else. He could work in editorial for another publication. Or he could start his own travel magazine—one tailored to other happy bachelors. Take his relearned smile and remembered laugh and be so successful Barney and the *Lampoon* and the father he'd buried would regret letting him go.

And didn't that bring a smile to his face?

According to his research, Harmony Valley had nearly been a ghost town until a winery begun by dot-com millionaires had breathed life into it. A winery founded by wealthy bachelors in the middle of nowhere? Now, there was a story. The "why" behind it intrigued Chad. What did this small town have which made it special to three single men? The buzz was the town may be barely breathing, but it abounded with quirky traditions it was loath to give up.

So here he was in Harmony Valley for the Harvest Festival, hoping he wasn't too late and could beat the *Lampoon* to the story. He'd landed on a new name for his column and had the Happy Bachelor Takes a Different Path website all set up with content loaded from his experiences in Portland and Seattle. All he needed to do was press publish. But first, he needed a strong lead article. Something that set this phase of his travel life apart from the previous thirteen years.

Yep, here he was in Harmony Valley, the smallest small town he'd ever seen, looking for a unique experience for bachelors. Only problem was: he didn't write about small towns. He wrote about hip and happening urban locations that hip and happening urban bachelors wanted to visit.

This was…

Shades of his elderly parents.

Harmony Valley might just as well have been a retirement community. He'd seen a few people walking around—all white-haired, wrinkled or balding. He'd driven a circuit of the downtown blocks a time or two—there were only a few each way. There were more empty buildings than businesses. And this was the only bakery.

He glanced around. Where was the local sheriff? Where were the local trades? Where were the moms coming in to get a morning dose of caffeine after dropping off their kids at school? Where were the singles setting up shop for an hour or two to get work done and perhaps meet someone?

They were all conspicuously absent.

Still, Chad soaked in the ambience that was Martin's Bakery. In a way, it had the hidden-treasure vibe his *Lampoon* readers appreciated. A window seat with a deep cushion and pillows, a collection of tables and mis-matched wooden chairs that looked as if they'd been here for a century. The yellowed photos of bakery workers hanging on the wall seemed to prove that point. Dark brown beadboard trim was capped with a chair railing on the side wall. Three bakery cases made an L shape in the space. A large chalkboard hung on the wall behind the register. The daily special: pumpkin scones. And the coffee… Chad breathed in deeply. The coffee smelled rich and fresh, as if it had just been ground for him.

So maybe the people weren't hip. Gray and white hair, walkers and canes, polyester pants and orthopedic sneakers. At least they looked healthy. And maybe they weren't happening in the where-it's-at sense. The two old men reset their checkerboard instead of an online game. But they had a certain spunk. He just wasn't sure what Harmony Valley offered made for a good first column to launch his online travel magazine.

Chad claimed a table next to the old woman quilting in the window seat. There was a crib beside her with a cooing baby. She had the air of a talker, and Chad needed details to decide if this story was worthwhile. There was still time to drive to San Francisco for the Union Street Wine Walk or Monterey for a celebrity golf event.

The old woman's hair was an unusual color, a purplish-gray more suited to the alternative scene in Soho than a remote corner of Sonoma County. She wore bright pastels—pink, yellow, lime green. The kind of colors he associated with spring. Her complexion was free of age spots and had a healthy pink glow.

She glanced at him over the edge of her black-rimmed readers, much like a chaperone making sure he behaved at a middle school dance. "We don't get too many drop-ins this far out from the highway, especially not writers."

"I'm looking for undiscovered gems." Rare, those gems. And the places that weren't jewels? The dud locations he'd written about in the past were among his most popular columns at *Bostwick Lampoon*. Currently, the town was more dud than diamond, which cheered him up.

"We've always been a gem." The old woman stared at him, as if they were playing a game of who would blink first. "The winery is changing things here."

"For the better?" A sly opening in case she didn't want Harmony Valley to change.

"Yes." She gazed down at the baby, who gripped his toes and crooned softly. "Before the winery came to town, I'd never seen a baby born. And I'd never imagined such a beautiful creature would be the result of the horrors of childbirth."

Chad opened his mouth to reply, but said nothing. Was the baby hers? She had to be staring down eighty. His parents had had Chad in their fifties—late, but not this late. The old woman should have thought this through. Parents needed to be young enough to keep up with their kids.

She didn't notice his doubt. "I mean giving birth… The pain and the bl—"

"Eunice." Tracy delivered Chad's order with a warning for his talkative neighbor. Her shoulder-length blond hair was just-out-of-bed tousled. Her bright blue eyes reflected both intelligence and vulnerability. "We agreed. Childbirth details. Are not. Bakery. Appropriate." Tracy blew out a breath and turned to Chad, avoiding eye contact by looking at his shoulder. "Anything else?"

He brushed at the cap of his sleeve and whatever it was Tracy saw there. "No, thanks." He was grateful she'd saved him from the details of childbirth no bachelor wanted to hear. "Is the baby yours?" Because despite it being medically possible for it to be Eunice's, he sincerely hoped—for the child's sake—it wasn't.

"The Poop Monster?" Hands up, Tracy backed away. "No."

"Gregory is Jessica's. She's the owner here. I'm his godmother." The pride in the old woman's voice was unmistakable. "Isn't he the most perfect baby you've ever seen?"

Chad leaned in for a closer look. Gregory paused in playing with his feet to stare back. He must have decided Chad passed muster, because he gave him a drooly smile that plumped up his already chubby cheeks. As babies went, the Poop Monster was cute and practically the only town citizen not to run at the sight of him.

Gregory kicked his feet and made a sound like a small motorboat.

"He likes you." Eunice's gaze turned to Chad and speculation. "Do you like babies? Are you married?"

"Eunice!" Tracy froze mid-turn. She had tentative curves, as if she'd recently gained or lost weight and couldn't decide if she was going to gain or lose more.

"I don't mind questions." Questions led to conversation. Chad liked to get the measure of a town. But he couldn't seem to get a bead on Harmony Valley. Or Tracy.

"Good." Eunice removed her glasses and deposited them on her head, fluffing her purplish curls into place around them. "Men always ask about jobs. We women need more important information. Where are you from?"

"San Francisco." Who knew for how long. The penthouse he'd shared with his dad, once filled with hospital equipment and round-the-clock nurses, seemed more like a mausoleum than a home.

"Welcome to Harmony Valley." Eunice leaned forward, opening her eyes wide and

blinking slowly in a way that was oddly hyp-
notic. "Are you or have you ever been married?"

"No." *Wait a minute.* Chad sat back in his
chair. He was always looking for an angle
on a story, asking personal questions in a
way that didn't intimidate, not the other way
around. "How'd you do that?"

"It's my eyes." Eunice blinked them in
rapid succession. "They're violet, just like
Elizabeth Taylor's. I've been told they have
special powers."

Shades of retired superheroes. Chad almost laughed. Almost, because her stare had
worked on him.

"It's the shock." Tracy picked up a rag and
spray cleaner, along with a gray tub for dirty
dishes. "Of all that purple."

Eunice harrumphed, as if used to Tracy's
teasing, and then fluffed her hair again.
"Where is Jessica? She promised to try one of
my mother's recipes. I don't see Horseradish-
Doodles in the case." She stood, smoothing
her pink polyester pants and setting the orange and navy quilt pieces aside, and then
she marched toward the kitchen with a sly
half glance at Chad. "Watch Gregory for me,
will you?"

"Let's pray…" Tracy's back was to Chad

as she cleared a table in the corner. "That we never sell Horseradish-Doodles."

"Horseradish-Doodles." Chad had traveled all over the world. To the dirtiest dives and the most luxurious five-star establishments. He'd never heard of Horseradish-Doodles. "Is that a salty snack or a cookie?"

"Who knows?" Tracy shuddered.

Chad made a mental note to include Eunice and her Horseradish-Doodles in his piece.

In the playpen, the baby's kicks became more violent. He gave a little shout.

"Gregory wants you to pick him up." Tracy didn't turn around.

"I'm not sure that's wise." Chad didn't do babies. He'd heard there was a trick to it— picking them up, holding them, changing their diapers.

The old men playing checkers chuckled.

"Ah." Tracy turned and stared at Chad's shoulder once more. "You're one of *those* bachelors."

Intrigued as to how she'd lump him, Chad pretended ignorance by taking a sip of his latte.

"You're afraid babies are contagious." Tracy's smile. It was honest and mischievous. It hit Chad in the gut, warming him quicker than his latte.

Gregory shouted louder. Chad ignored him, trying to dissect the appeal of Tracy's smile. He liked women with sophistication and polish. Tracy didn't wear any makeup. Her black A-line apron wasn't sophisticated. She was as simple and homey as the town seemed to be.

Seemed? Nothing was as it seemed in Harmony Valley.

Someone called for Tracy in the kitchen.

"Go on. Pick him up." Tracy carried her loaded tray toward the swinging kitchen door. "He won't break."

"You're leaving him with me?" Chad could be a kidnapper or a child molester. He could grab the kid and be out the door before the checkers champs could say, *"King me."*

"Thirty seconds." Tracy disappeared through the swinging kitchen door. He couldn't be sure, but he thought she'd been grinning.

Gregory shrieked, a test run to a full-blown tantrum, for sure.

The old men chuckled some more. Feminine laughter cascaded from the kitchen. These people didn't think he could do this.

Chad could pick up the kid. He could change a diaper. He'd changed them for his father. He'd changed so many he'd vowed never to change a diaper again.

He bent over the edge of the crib, getting a more pungent whiff of the Poop Monster. "You don't want me, kid."

Gregory grinned and drooled. But when Chad didn't pick him up, he kicked out again, blinked like Eunice and then shrieked.

Chad felt as if he was being studied, tested and stalked. By a baby. Not to mention the women in the kitchen.

Gregory gave another shriek, and then his lower lip began to tremble and his eyes to water.

"Don't do that." Chad reached for the kid. "They'll think I'm torturing you."

Before his hands reached Gregory, the kitchen door swung open. A woman with an olive complexion and a thick, dark ponytail hurried toward the crib. "Eunice, Gregory isn't a meter you use to measure a man. I'm so sorry." She swept Gregory into her arms and spun him around. "Hello, baby mine."

Gregory rewarded his mother with a round of giggles that eased the tension in Chad despite the awful smell coming from the kid's pants.

Eunice returned to the window seat and tsked. "I had such high hopes for you, Chad."

CHAPTER TWO

"YOU WANT ME to ask Leona if that travel writer can spend the night with her?" In the barber shop, Phil Lambridge was beside himself with jealousy. He paced. He paused. He sounded as if he might cry. "Alone? Unchaperoned?"

Mildred clenched her remaining molars together so she wouldn't shout. Phil was a traditional man. He was still in love with his ex-wife twenty years after she'd divorced him. Mildred wanted to tell Phil to get over it and take one for the Harmony Valley team, to man up and do the right thing. But what good would it do? Phil would still be jealous and still walk on egg shells around Leona.

Rose flitted about the narrow shop. "We need a hotel room for that travel writer. Your granddaughters are going to open a bed & breakfast in Leona's house anyway come spring."

Agnes sat in one red barbershop chair,

nodding in agreement. Larry sat in the other red chair, nodding in agreement. Mildred sat on her walker just inside the front window watching Phil angst and pace. Phil was a tall, gangly man with limbs that moved with marionette uncertainty. He was just so...so... ridiculously endearing.

"You know how Leona is," Phil said. Given her vision challenges, Mildred could only see his sharp nose and chin. Both stuck out stubbornly. "Until those girls sign on the dotted line, that home is Leona's castle."

Everyone knew how Leona was. Bitter. Caustic. Penny-pinching. She gave no charity and expected none in return. But she lived in what had once been a mansion in Harmony Valley. She kept up the hundred-year-old Victorian like a showplace. It was their only chance to impress upon the travel writer that Harmony Valley was a good tourist destination.

"You ask her, Agnes." Phil was a cream puff. It was why Leona had kicked him out two decades ago. She needed a strong man to stand up to her.

Mildred didn't need a man. But she wanted one. And for some unknown reason, her heart was set on wanting Phil. For the life of her, Mildred couldn't figure it out. She'd been a race car driver back when men would do anything to keep women off the track. She'd been independent forever. Why did Phil and his gentle ways make her feel as if she was forty again?

"It's settled then. The town council will make the request." Mayor Larry could also be filed under "Non-Confrontational Man." He wouldn't risk alienating Leona, because she still voted. "Do what you have to, ladies. Phil and I will go back to the bakery and entertain our guest until you come up with a workable solution."

Phil moaned.

A few minutes later, Agnes parked her late model, faded green Buick in front of Leona's home.

Mildred got out using the door for support, waiting for Agnes to bring her walker from the trunk. "This is going to be a waste of time."

"Not necessarily," Agnes said. "It's a beautiful home and she doesn't get to show it off very often."

"It's not as pretty as mine." Rose had a much smaller painted lady, and a history of arguing with anyone who'd listen that hers was superior.

Even with her glasses, Mildred couldn't see the details on the Victorian, so she couldn't judge. In her eyes, Leona's home was a green hulk with white trim that towered over the back fence of Mildred's small Craftsman-style home. In forty years of being neighbors, she'd heard Leona's caustic laugh over that fence. She'd heard her sing off-key as she gardened. She'd also heard some searing arguments between Leona and Phil before their official break-up. She'd always be Team Phil.

"How many steps are there?" Mildred's annoyance increased. Growing old was a pain in the tuckus. Back in the day, Mildred would have skipped up the steps the same as Rose was doing now.

Of course, Rose had sundowning syndrome, which meant when she got tired, she got loopy. Mildred had all her marbles. The macular degeneration was stealing her vision and a car crash decades ago had weakened her knees. But Mildred would take her marbles any day of the week.

Agnes carried Mildred's walker up the steps in one hand, holding on to Mildred's arm with the other.

Leona opened the front door and stared them down. "Well, if it isn't the town council."

Mildred didn't need to see details to recognize Leona's salt-and-pepper hair in its usual tight beehive. She wore a blue dress—and heels, from the sound of her feet on hardwood—and probably had her mother's pearl choker around her neck. There was no way Mildred was wearing a skirt and heels just to hang around the house. Did the woman never let her hair down?

"Leona." Agnes had the unique talent of putting both sweetness and authority into her tone. "We've come to ask a favor."

"I will *not* contribute to the Harvest Festival bake sale."

It was hard to imagine soft-hearted Phil being in love with this dragon. She hadn't even invited them in. And Mildred was standing in the brisk morning air with her walker!

"That's not the favor." Agnes should have been mayor. There was both respect and determination in her words. Of course, she wasn't in love with Phil, so she probably had more patience for Leona than Mildred did. "May we come in?"

"If you must, but wipe your feet. I just did the floors."

Mildred navigated carefully over the threshold, wishing it'd been raining and she'd rolled her walker through the mud. Leona brought out the most uncharitable thoughts in Mildred. Her mother wouldn't have approved. Of course, her mother hadn't approved of Mildred racing either.

Leona's house smelled of furniture polish and disinfectant, sterile and off-putting, like the owner herself.

While Mildred sat in her walker, Rose perched on a black leather wingback chair nearby, unhappiness radiating from them both, like sulky children banished to the basement.

"There's a travel writer in town." Agnes shared the antique pink velvet loveseat across the room with Leona. What she didn't share was Leona's sour attitude. "You know how important getting the word out about Harmony Valley is." If they didn't attract young people to town, Harmony Valley would die with its aging citizens.

"It's important to some." Snooty. Leona was snooty. If they'd been in a car race together back in the day, Mildred would have given her a bump and sent her into the wall. "As soon as my granddaughters make me an acceptable formal offer and turn this into a bed & breakfast, I'm retiring to the city."

Good riddance.

"The thing is, Leona…" Once again, Agnes'

calm voice filled the room. "We need a bed &
breakfast for this man now. Today."

"Until after the Harvest Festival," Rose
clarified, sounding glum.

"You expect me to take in a strange man?"

Mildred nodded. She couldn't tell if anyone else did.

"You expect me to cook breakfast and
clean up after a man who isn't my husband?"
Leona sounded horrified.

Mildred nodded again, trying hard not to
smile. Was it wrong to hope the travel writer
was a serial killer? A grin escaped, because
she knew it was wrong and highly unlikely.
Mildred revised her hopes from serial killer
to him being someone who talked loudly all
the time on his cell phone. She hated that.

"We also expect you to charge him for his
stay," Agnes pointed out.

"Nine nights, I figure," Rose said gloomily.

It was the first time Mildred could remember Leona being speechless.

THINGS HAD SETTLED down since the baby test.

Jessica had taken Gregory into the kitchen
alcove for his mid-morning feeding. Eunice
was sewing in the window seat. The checkers match was still going on. And Chad was

busy tapping away on his phone, no longer interested in Tracy's existence.

Tracy condensed inventory in the bakery case, content with the silence and the lack of male attention. She was becoming good at being invisible.

The mayor and Phil returned.

Phil looked pale and more unsteady on his feet than usual. "You didn't wait for me, Felix?" He pulled up a chair to the checkers match.

"Checkers wait for no man," Felix said, absently brushing cat hair off his black T-shirt. He rescued cats and never showed up anywhere without a sprinkling of hair on his shirt.

Mayor Larry claimed a seat at Chad's table and introduced himself again. "Who do you write for, Chad?"

"I'm launching my own online travel magazine." There was a hard note to Chad's voice that contradicted his easy smile. "Until recently, I was editor-in-chief for a national magazine and sometimes I wrote for a couple of national papers."

Several heads swiveled in Chad's direction. If Felix's sage nodding was any indication, the mention of a couple of national newspapers had earned Chad some of the points he'd lost by not picking up Gregory.

Meanwhile, Tracy's stomach did a barrel roll. Chad was handsome. He was successful. He had a shiny red sports car parked out front. She bet he'd never been phased out of a job. She bet everything he'd ever wanted had been within his reach. She bet that's what she used to look like to the world—attractive, successful, on top of the corporate food chain. And now...

She gripped the hem of her canvas apron. She'd been back home since spring and had only made halfhearted attempts to land jobs in her field, most of which had ended with stilted telephone screening interviews and form rejection letters. Was she ready to get back out there and be rejected?

No. The bakery case glass needed cleaning.

Soon "out there" might be here in Harmony Valley, which would be fantastic for the town and her brother, Will, who'd risked a lot of money investing in the winery.

Mayor Larry straightened his tie-dyed T-shirt, nearly beside himself with the excitement of a national newspaper contributor in their midst. "Once you get settled, we'll take you on a long tour of the town and the surrounding sights, and give you some local history." He embellished the upcoming experience. There wasn't enough to see or hear about Harmony Valley for it to be a long tour. "We'll also arrange for some time at the winery and a private wine tasting."

Tracy tugged her cell phone out of her back pocket and searched for Chad Healy. Results came up right away—not as Chad Healy, but as Chad Healy Bostwick, the Happy Bachelor On the Road. He'd authored a long list of columns. He'd worked his way up the ranks at the spoof magazine his father had started to become editor-in-chief and acting CEO, parting ways after his father's death.

She skimmed some of his articles. His posts were well-crafted. Chad had a gift for a clever turn of phrase. A theme emerged. Sarcasm, satire, ridicule. Not surprising, given the title of his column and that he'd written for the *Bostwick Lampoon*. No place seemed safe from Chad's scathing commentary. Harmony Valley was a sitting duck.

Chad. Handsome, witty, nationally syndicated newspaper–worthy Chad. He hadn't come to rescue them. He could incinerate the town's revitalization efforts with a few strokes on his keyboard, ruining Will's winery in the process.

Who could she tell? Will was on his honeymoon.

"Larry?" Tracy forced a smile. "Can I talk to you?" She gestured toward the kitchen. "Alone?" *Before you invite Benedict Arnold into our midst?*

"Not now, Tracy." The mayor waved her off, and then thought better of it. "Tracy, can you call the winery and make arrangements for Chad to have a private tasting?" Mayor Larry used his politician's voice—equal parts self-importance and condescendence. "Tracy's brother owns Harmony Valley Vineyards."

"Part-owner." Along with his friends Flynn and Slade. But Tracy wasn't calling anyone until she sent out the SOS to the mayor. She tried again, adding a hand wave. "Larry…"

"I'll have another coffee, Tracy," Larry said firmly. "Bring Chad another…latte, was it?"

Chad nodded.

Tracy shouldn't care that Mayor Larry was digging a hole for himself. She shouldn't care that Chad would take whatever the innocent folk in Harmony Valley said and twist it around to make him look clever. She shouldn't care that he'd make fun of her hometown traditions, like pumpkin bowling for the harvest queen crown. They were silly traditions.

But she did care.

Harmony Valley may be off the beaten trail, old-school and homey, but it was Tracy's trail. Her old-school. Her home.

She planted her sneakers firmly behind the counter and glared at the enemy as she made his latte, because she knew Mayor Larry wouldn't listen to her. Not when convincing required quick, smoothly spoken words.

A coffee and a latte later, Agnes, Rose and Mildred entered the bakery.

"Good news." Agnes was all smiles. "We've secured our visitor a room at the Lambridge Bed & Breakfast. Welcome to Harmony Valley."

Who said Harmony Valley wasn't progressive? Just this morning there'd been no B&B in town.

Wait a minute. *Lambridge?* Tracy glanced at Phil. That meant...

Eunice's penciled-in eyebrows rose, as if she was just catching on, too. "But—"

"Leona Lambridge is the proprietor," Agnes cut Eunice off, looking as calm as if she lied through her teeth every day of the week.

Leona Lambridge was also the town kill-joy. She'd never bowled for the pumpkin queen crown. She didn't even hand out candy on Halloween!

Maybe not such a good idea to book Mr. Sarcastic there. "Hey...uh... Agnes..."

Agnes paid no heed to Tracy either. "She's expecting you," Agnes said to Chad. She proceeded to introduce Chad to everyone in the bakery.

"Are there other hotel choices in town?" That tone of voice. It said Chad was suspicious. It said he'd love for something hinkie to be going on.

Was it wrong to think Chad's intelligence was hot when he was the villain here? Probably about as wrong as Tracy thinking she might actually help save the town.

Save it? Who was she kidding? The only people the older town residents listened to were their doctors, and that was only half the time.

To her credit, Agnes' smile never wavered as she answered Chad. "At the moment, the Lambridge B&B is our only offering."

Rose was doing a slow grapevine in front of the pastry case, eyeing the scones that she'd passed on earlier. "You'll find a great many painted ladies in town, not just the Lambridge place."

Phil made a hacking noise, as if he was coughing up a hairball.

Mildred had planted her walker seat by Phil's table and seemed lost in thought as she stared at the back of Phil's head, perhaps pondering the need for a slap to dislodge that hairball of Phil's.

Rose held a pose at the end of the bakery case, an aging ballerina poised to leap in cargo pants and hiking boots. "You'll be here ten days, correct?"

Ten days? They were doomed.

The mayor jumped back in the fray. "Plenty of time to experience everything that makes Harmony Valley special."

True that. Special and weird and wonderful.

However, chances were slim the villainous Chad would recognize wonderful if it sashayed up to him and kissed his cheek.

The reputation-ruiner cast a glance Tracy's way. Could Chad tell Tracy knew who he was?

Would it matter if he did?

CHAPTER THREE

SOMETHING DIDN'T SMELL RIGHT.

And it wasn't the Poop Monster.

Everyone was suddenly too nice. Too kind. Too helpful.

Had someone researched who he was? The only one he'd seen using a cell phone was Tracy, and no one was paying attention to her. She had a tendency to talk slowly and hesitate over her words. Was that why the mayor had snubbed her? Was that why she lived in such a far-flung location?

The need to defend Tracy rose like smoke from a struggling flame. With a puff of exhaled air, he ignored it.

"Mayor Larry will drive with you to the B&B," the short, spritely old woman was saying. Her name was Aggie or Agnes or something.

"No need to trouble the mayor. Tracy can show me." Had Chad just said that? He glanced at the coffee barista. He had indeed.

Tracy sported a horrified look. She skimmed her hand over a bakery case. "I'm working."

"I'll cover for you." Eunice leapt to her feet without so much as a quiver of her purplish-gray curls.

"But…" Tracy glanced at each resident in turn.

"You forgot my lumbago, Agnes." Larry reached for his back. "It's why I walk nearly everywhere."

"Sorry, Tracy. We've got a game going on." Felix jumped a checker. "King me."

"No license," Phil grumbled. "No car. No ride for the playboy."

A chorus of *"Phils"* echoed through Martin's Bakery.

"Doctor's appointment." Mildred sighed, although how she could see the road through those thick glasses was beyond Chad.

"Driving her," Agnes/Aggie said, explaining everything.

"Riding shotgun." At least Rose had the courtesy to look apologetic as she twirled slowly in the corner.

Everyone else looked as if they were happy to shirk tour guide duty.

And inexplicably, Chad was okay with that.

He smiled at Tracy. "I did shower today *and* use deodorant. Scout's honor."

Tracy studied him as if he was an over-priced used car, one with high mileage and no warranty.

He studied her in return. That tousled hair. That determined jut of her chin. It was weird. Just looking at her made him want to smile. That was the point of his new life, wasn't it? He smiled.

"Fine," Tracy grumbled. "But I'm driving."

"What?" Chad's gaze bee-lined to his be-loved sports car.

"It's settled." Agnes/Aggie clapped her hands.

A few minutes later, he and Tracy stepped out on the brick sidewalk. Harmony Valley could have served as a backdrop for a Norman Rockwell painting. Old fashioned lamps lined Main Street. The buildings had brick fronts and canvas awnings. The wind blew brown and orange leaves down the road list-lessly, as if even the elements knew the pace here was slow. Tracy zipped up her tan jacket against the autumn chill, and then extended her palm. "The keys."

"To my car?" He glanced at his cherry red convertible and gripped the key in his hand. He'd ordered it custom from the factory. No one had driven it but him since he'd bought it. It required nimbleness to get in and out of. Neither a walker nor a wheelchair could fit in its trunk. "How about you sit in the passenger seat and I drive?"

"Nope." She made the gimme motion with her hand and spoke slowly. "I had an accident..." Each word she spoke was labored. "I was in the...*side* seat." She scowled, clearly not pleased with her word choice. "I don't know you. Or how you drive. Or if I can—"

"You can trust me." He gave her the grin he'd used to charm his mother's friends when they'd come over to play Bunko. "I'm a good driver."

"Don't. Finish. My sentences." She glowered at him. As glowers went, it was cute.

Chad's father had been the King of Glowers. Until the last six months of his life when he hadn't glowered at anyone. Dad's soul, his personality, his very being had slipped away, leaving Chad to wait until his body gave up, as well.

"Give me the keys." There was a pleading note hidden between the demanding words and the glower.

Chad stared at her, then at the gray-haired

MELINDA CURTIS 51

audience inside, and finally at his car. "It's a stick shift." A lost art form.

"Perfect." She breezed past him and slid into the tan leather driver's seat, leaving Chad no choice but to ride shotgun. She held out her hand for the key fob as soon as his butt hit the stiff leather.

He inserted the key in the ignition. "On cold mornings, she's a bit touchy going into third gear." He hoped Tracy wouldn't grind the clutch. He hoped the B&B wasn't far away. He hoped he wouldn't regret coming to Harmony Valley.

"I knew it." She patted the dashboard and grinned. "Midlife crisis."

"I'm thirty-five. Too young for a midlife crisis," Chad grumbled.

"Huh. Makes me wonder…" Tracy swallowed, her grin fading as she forced out the words. "What you'll drive…when the real crisis hits." She shoved in the clutch and started the engine with a roar. The grin came back. She backed out competently and sent the car forward without so much as a neck jerk or a grinding gear.

Chad's apprehension eased. "Why do I get the feeling no one wanted to come with me?"

"Leona is… She's… You'll see." Tracy

forced the words out like stale dough through a noodle press.

"Are there a lot of young singles in town?" The place didn't look like it had much night-life.

She laughed and came to a stop at the in-tersection of the large, deserted town square. It had a broad expanse of grass and a huge oak tree with a single, wrought-iron bench beneath it. Tracy glanced at him with those clear blue eyes that seemed to see so much. "Agnes is single. Rose is single. Mildred is single. Eunice, too." She smiled at her listing of old ladies. "Need I go on?"

"Please don't." He fought off the thought that he'd slipped back into his parents' world. No nightlife. No metropolitan eclectic en-ergy. A pace slower than frozen molasses. All these old people. They'd get sick. They'd drift mentally. They'd die. They'd leave be-hind friends and family with holes in their chests that nothing seemed to fill.

Suddenly, Chad didn't want to be here. He gripped the seatbelt strap across his chest.

Oblivious to his need to flee, Tracy turned right and continued to drive his car as if it was her own—a bit fast, banking into the turns. It was oddly relaxing—the ride, her youth, the way her hair dipped and tumbled in the breeze. His grip on the strap eased.

"Where'd you learn to drive a stick?" Few people had the skill anymore. His dad had taught him to drive a manual transmission on his 1967 Ford Mustang.

"First, a farm tractor. Then Mildred's Volkswagen Beetle." Tracy made another right and slowed down through a residential district.

Single-story ranches and Craftsman-style homes. Dirty windows and peeling paint. Empty driveways and neglected yards. Many seemed abandoned.

The neighborhood was an afterthought relative to the puzzling woman next to him. "Have you always struggled to get the words out?"

Tracy slammed on the brakes, sending the tires squealing, even though they hadn't been going faster than twenty miles an hour. She gripped the steering wheel and turned to glare at him. "I had an accident." And then she lifted her gossamer blond hair, revealing a ropey scar on her skull. "I have...expressive aphasia. I'm trying to be normal."

Chad was beginning to think Tracy wasn't normal. She was extraordinary.

An aluminum screen door screeched on

protesting hinges. An elderly woman stepped out on her front porch in a pink chenille bathrobe and white tennis shoes. Her short gray hair stuck into the air as if she'd rubbed her head against a balloon. "Everything okay, Tracy?"

"Yes, Mrs. Beam." Tracy glared at Chad, but her voice was sweet as sugar, and didn't sound forced.

"I could call the sheriff for you," the old woman said.

"We're fine, Mrs. Beam."

"Okay, dearie." Mrs. Beam went back inside. Her screen door groaned as if it belonged in a haunted house, and then banged shut.

Tracy put Chad's car in gear and continued slowly down the street.

It was time for a change of subject. "So your brother owns the winery. Do they make good wine?"

"Is your car fast?"

That was a good sign. "Do wine lovers come from miles around to taste their wine?"

"No. They only…soft launched." She turned to the left and parked in front of a forest green Victorian with white trim and an expansive lawn.

Chad was used to seeing narrow painted

ladies in San Francisco's Cow Hollow district, but this house was easily three times the width of one of those classics. "Impressive." Why hadn't the Lambridge Bed & Breakfast turned up on his internet search? It had a great location. It couldn't have been more than a ten minute walk from downtown. He hoped it was as nice inside as it was out.

Chad made to open his door.

Tracy put her hand on his arm, stopping him. Her touch was soft, personal when Chad had lived an impersonal life for years. "Don't hurt them."

"Who?"

"The people here." She gestured back the way they'd come and then she fixed him with a warning stare. "You're the Happy Bachelor. Well… Your columns aren't happy. They're… they're…*mean*." She made a frustrated noise, slapped her palms against the steering wheel as if unhappy with her words, and then added, "Malicious."

Chad fell back against the seat. The September sunlight fought its way through the brown and curling elm leaves, but didn't warm him.

She'd seen his columns. People usually responded in one of two ways to his travel reviews in the *Lampoon*—love 'em or hate 'em. Put Tracy in the hate column.

Chad's instinct was to laugh Tracy off, or to tell her to mind her own business, but something about her scar, the way she spoke and perhaps even the way she defended the elderly made him take a different approach. "I don't attack anyone personally. I write things the way I see them using the irony of truth."

"They won't understand." There was an entreaty in her voice, if not in her eyes, which still promised retribution if he hurt the people in town.

Chad didn't care if the locals understood or not. Having been raised by parents the age of his peers' grandparents, he was tired of making concessions for the elderly. This was his time. He'd live life and write columns his way and enjoy doing it. And yet, he didn't snap at Tracy. "You don't sugarcoat anything, do you?"

"I can't." She opened her door with jerky movements. "Not anymore." She popped the trunk for him, peering inside at his laptop bag, his travel bag and the box from the office, flaps folded and sealed.

Taking his suitcase and his laptop bag, Chad followed Tracy up the grand walk.

Huge trees, lush shrubbery and not a weed in sight. The windows gleamed and reflected the late morning sun.

The front door was open, but the proprietor seemed as closed off as the pilot's lounge at an airport. Salt and pepper beehive hair. A blue dress that hung awkwardly off her bony frame. And an air about her that said, *"Thou shalt not hug. Ever."*

Chad couldn't blame the others at the bakery for not wanting to come here. The place and the proprietor were intimidating. Why on earth was this woman running a bed & breakfast?

The proprietress opened the door wider to let him in. The hinges didn't creak, didn't groan, didn't even whisper. It just seemed as if they should have. "Welcome to Harmony Valley. I'm Leona Lambridge."

Queen of all she surveyed.

She surveyed Chad and, with a turn of her nose, found him wanting. "And welcome to the Lambridge Bed & Breakfast. I'll show you to your room." She held a stop-sign hand toward Tracy. "You may wait outside."

Chad wondered if Tracy's request to go easy on folks in town extended to Queen Leona.

He doubted it.

"I'll walk back." Tracy handed Chad his car keys and then shoved her hands in her tan jacket pockets and headed to the street. The town's young protector may look waifish on the outside, but Chad suspected she had a core of steel. That scar…

"Mr. Healy." A royal summons.

Chad turned, and crossed the threshold. The bed & breakfast had been decorated in period style. Antiques. Gilded mirrors. Ceiling medallions. It was spectacular. It smelled cleaner than a hospital room.

"I'm trying a new check-in procedure." For a moment, the ice queen's demeanor cracked. "I must find you tolerable and you must agree to pay me with cash or check at the end of your stay." She gave him a nightly rate he deemed acceptable.

"I've got cash."

"You'll do." Her expression turned icily regal once more. She led him to the grand staircase, her back as rigid as a British royal guard.

The floors creaked, but everything was clean. The stairs groaned, but the wood was so shiny Chad could almost see himself in the reflection. When they reached the second-floor landing, the house rattled as softly as a whisper and settled with a sigh, as if it'd been empty too long. It was the most welcome Chad had felt since arriving.

Leona made a noise that seemed disapproving and opened the first door. "This is your bathroom."

The horror. Chad had to share a bathroom with other guests. The normal traveler would view this as a mark against the place. Chad looked forward to the stories sharing a bathroom with fellow guests would bring. Of course, the stories would have been better if the bathroom wasn't first-rate. White on white, from the claw-foot tub to the pedestal sink to the penny floor tile and grout. Not a crack or a chip or a stain anywhere.

Leona walked farther down the hall, opening the second door "And this is your room."

Chad set his suitcase in the corner. He could tango in that room, even with a king-size four-poster bed and a simple cherry desk and matching chair. The southern-facing window let in generous amounts of sunlight. "This is nice."

"Nice?" Leona drew back as if she'd smelled the Poop Monster. "Two presidential candidates have slept in this room." Said with

pride and a bit of prickle, as in, *"And you, young man, are no presidential candidate."*

As hotel proprietors went, Leona was among the most unwelcome. But that didn't mean the experience of staying here wouldn't be first-rate. There was that decadent hotel in Cancun run by a guy who didn't like anyone. And that luxury hotel in the Rockies. The manager there had carried a shotgun everywhere, safety off. A little bristle in hotel staff added character. Maybe Harmony Valley was worth the trip after all.

"Do I need a password for the internet?" Assuming there was internet.

"The entire town has the interweb. No password required." Leona may have been shorter than he was, but she still managed to look down her nose at him. "I suppose you'll be wanting to post something on the Facebook."

Her comment explained why there was no website for the bed & breakfast. Chad kept his expression carefully neutral. "I suppose."

"Breakfast is between eight and eight-thirty." Leona walked toward the door, her steps as crisp and sharp as her words. "Eight and eight-thirty only."

So rigid. He'd rather eat breakfast at Martin's Bakery. "I'll need a key."

"To your room?" She paused in the open doorway, not even bothering to turn around.

"Yes. And the front door."

"No." She closed him in. Her heels echoed in the hallway.

"Not to either?" he called after her, receiving no answer. That's when he noticed there wasn't a lock on his door handle.

Chad smiled, got out his tablet and began making notes.

CHAPTER FOUR

"WHAT ARE YOU doing here, Sunshine?" Standing in the barn doorway, Tracy's dad tugged off his work gloves.

"I need to paint." Every nerve ending in Tracy's body crackled with tension. Above her, farm tools hung—shovels, hoes, scythes, pitchforks. She indulged a quick fantasy where she chased handsome, villainous Chad out of town with a pitchfork. But fantasies couldn't calm the need to do something, to change something, to make her mark.

She dug through some cans from the stack that was butted up against the wood wall, trying to decide what colors to use. Since the accident, Tracy painted when she was frustrated. She'd painted the small bedroom she'd grown up in—black walls and ceiling were a backdrop to a colorful, fanciful garden. She'd painted the outside walls of the barn—tomato red with rows of crops along the bottom. Who knew what she'd paint today. Or where.

"Everything okay?" As he came closer, the worry in her father's voice was palpable. It echoed in the large wooden barn and plucked the guilt chord inside Tracy.

She hated that she made him worry. "I need to paint." She faced her father, holding her hand out in the same way Leona had to her earlier. Her frustrations rattled unspoken words in her head—*helpless, powerless, weak*. But she didn't try to give them voice, because to try to get the words out would just make her feel more incompetent.

If only she could conquer her speech challenges, everything would be all right. The town council wouldn't dismiss her attempt at saving them. People like Chad wouldn't ask what was wrong with her. She'd have employers knocking down her door.

"What's the matter?" Ben Jackson stood as sturdy as ever in a brown corduroy jacket, dirty blue jeans and mud-caked work boots. His blond hair was thinning and faded with gray. Hurt filled his blue eyes. "Do you want to call Will or Emma?"

She shook her head. Her brother, Will, had married her best friend, Emma, last weekend. They were on a three-week honeymoon in Europe. "I. Need. To. Paint." Oh, the pain of sounding like a slow, broken record. The leaves blowing across the driveway outside moved faster than her sentences.

"Didn't that last speech therapist say you needed to use your words, not hold them in by painting?" Her father disregarded Tracy's attempt at boundary setting and drew her into his arms. He smelled of corn husks and dirt. The comforting smells of her childhood.

Tracy squeezed her eyes shut and clung to him, fighting the frustration of Leona's rejection and the nebulous threat that was Chad. She wanted to be the town motormouth. She wanted to shout streams of words with barely a breath in between.

Dad patted her back. "Let it out, Sunshine."

In her father's arms, she was safe. He was her magical rabbit's foot. The words spilled forth easier than if she stood alone. "I want to be able to argue again."

"With Will?"

"No." She rested her cheek on Dad's shoulder and stared at her great-grandfather's tractor. Life would be so much easier if she didn't want anything, if she didn't long for more. "I want to argue with everyone."

Her father chuckled. "So like your mother."

He kissed the top of her head. "Impatient. Railing at the world."

She admired so many things about her dad—his work ethic, his ability to keep Mom relevant, his refusal to hold Tracy during a phone interview she'd had last month. She'd wanted his arms around her so she could talk smoothly. He'd argued, *"They have to want you for who you are, warts and all."*

Tracy sighed. "I'd love to rail at the mayor and the town council and Leona and Chad." Why couldn't she say a sentence like that when she stood alone?

"Chad who? I don't know any Chad." Oh, how overly protective Dad got when it came to Tracy and men.

"A travel writer who came to the bakery today." She batted his shoulder playfully, willing herself to lighten up, too. "He makes fun of people for a living. No one would listen when I tried to warn them."

"A bully." Dad's tone mellowed. "You never had much patience for bullies. And if people don't listen, it's their fault." He put his hands on her shoulders and set her away from him. "You weren't meant to be a coffee barista, Tracy. You weren't meant to hold on to your dad to be able to get words out. You need to knuckle down and figure this thing out."

"Dad." Were all parents the voice of one's conscience? Tracy knew he was right. She needed to take charge of her life, but she was tired of failing, tired of the grand series of experiments to help her regain verbal normalcy. So she said sullenly, "The doctor recommended I slow down." Like it was the doctor's orders that she return to Harmony Valley and keep her mouth shut? She did a mental eye roll. It wasn't as if she'd pulled a muscle and it needed rest.

"The last doctor you saw told you to slow down and find a job you love. That was months ago." Dad checked his watch and glanced outside. The days were getting shorter and he always had a lot to do around the farm. "Don't use me as a crutch. Use that fancy phone of yours to find work that'll make you happy."

She'd be happy to land a job that didn't require a verbal interview. Was that too much to ask?

THERE WERE NO other guests at the B&B. No cars in the driveway or out back. The big house was silent. No murmur of voices. No scuffle of feet.

If Chad had been a nervous man—the kind that watched too many horror films—he'd have been…well…nervous. Nice quiet town. Welcoming residents. Prickly bed & breakfast owner. No lock on the door. It was a perfect setup for a clichéd slasher film, right down to the pretty girl leaving him at the front door.

But Chad wasn't nervous. He was driven to overcome the humiliation and betrayal of his father and the *Lampoon*'s board.

In order to launch his travel review site successfully, he needed interesting places and interesting characters. And he needed them the day after the Harvest Festival, when the advertisers he'd lined up expected his website to go live. So far, Harmony Valley had interesting characters in spades. Inspired, he went in search of his hostess, poking his head in every sterile room downstairs until he found her in the vegetable garden tucked into a corner of the back yard.

Leona wore a broad-rimmed straw hat and had changed from her dress into shapeless blue jeans and a long-sleeve blue chambray shirt. She looked healthy. She hadn't lost any of her mobility, or—it seemed—her intellect. His mother had been like this when he was in college—stubborn, independent, set in her routine.

Chad hated routine.

"You've got quite the green thumb." Chad sat on a wood bench in the shade of a towering pine tree near the back fence. The wind rustled through the needles above him. He snapped a picture of the house with his phone.

Leona didn't acknowledge him in the slightest. Hale and hearty, she dug her trowel in the rich brown soil and popped out a weed, root and all. Her garden was ripe for the harvest— red tomatoes, green bell peppers, green onions and several white gourds.

He decided to test how long and sharp her thorns were. "I hope tomorrow's breakfast includes a vegetable omelet."

"You'll get a meal between eight and eight-thirty, Mr. Healy." She was as brambly as the blackberry vine in the corner. She continued weeding.

Chad tried again. "There's no television in my room."

She dug at a clump of crab grass. "There's no television in the house."

Leona was a gift from heaven. His readers were going to love her. Already, Chad could see guys booking the Lambridge B&B

months in advance. They'd line up to spar with Leona.

"Do you need something, Mr. Healy?" Down on all fours, Leona glanced at him with a balance of cool rejection and regal regard.

That look said it all. He took a picture of her.

Leona got to her feet quicker than a fighter after an unexpected knock-down. "Did you just take my picture?"

"Yes, I—"

"Perverts and pornographers are not tolerated in this establishment." She gathered her garden tools with jerky movements. "I'll expect you off the premises immediately."

"But…I…" He wasn't sure how he'd offended her with a photo. Was Leona in the witness protection program? Did she believe pictures captured her soul? "I'm a travel writer. I include pictures of hotel clerks and bed & breakfast owners in my columns."

She waved aside his statement. "Your profession guarantees me nothing. You can't snap a picture of me bent over…" Her face reddened. "I will not have my…my…*derriere*—"

"Whoa, whoa, whoa. Slow down." He brought Leona's image to his screen and hurried to her side. "Look. I took a picture of your face." The queen from another century looking down her nose on her progressive subjects.

She scrutinized the photo and then said somewhat meekly—because she could never truly be meek. *"Oh."*

"I would never disrespect you in such a way." And then he added, hiding a grin, "Ma'am."

She sniffed. "Best you remember that or you'll find yourself out on the street."

Harmony Valley was turning out to be gold. Chad couldn't wait to uncover more gems. He left Leona and headed toward the town square to do some treasure hunting.

THERE WAS LITTLE more demoralizing than applying for a job you had little chance of getting.

Tracy had a job search app on her phone. She used it to find two new postings for advertising copywriters in Northern California. A few clicks later and her résumé was submitted.

"Two," she called to her father, who was tinkering under the hood of his old white farm truck.

He wiped oil from a wrench with a blue

cloth. "Are you happy? I won't be happy until you're happy."

"I'd rather be painting," she grumbled, heading up the drive.

Dad slammed the hood shut. "You know I love you just the way you are."

Of course he did. But lately, he was like her brother, Will—pushing, trying to set goals for Tracy, wanting her to reach higher. Her family didn't want her to settle for silence.

Truth be told, Tracy didn't either. If only getting back on track wasn't so hard.

She reached the end of the driveway and turned toward the Harmony River bridge and town, pausing to pluck a dandelion from the side of the road. She'd been making wishes on dandelions since she was a girl.

A few minutes later, Tracy leaned on the railing of the bridge and watched the water drift past. That shallow river was like her life. At an all time low and moving slow.

How was she supposed to get a job when she couldn't string a fluent sentence together out loud?

A faded green Buick pulled up next to her. Mildred rolled down the passenger window in front, her thick glasses nearly resting on her plump pink cheeks. Rose slid across the seat in back and cranked down the other window. Her snow white ballerina chignon had not one hair out of place.

"We're off to the doctor's office," Mildred announced. "Agnes wants to know if you need anything in town."

Agnes leaned over the center console and waved. "Isn't Chad wonderful?"

"And he's not wearing a ring," Rose singsonged.

They were trying to fix her up with the wolf in sheep's clothing? "Not interested. Have you read...his column?"

It was their turn to lack interest.

"A hardworking, good-looking man," Agnes said. "Who needs to read his column?"

"Don't set the bar too high," Mildred advised with a kindly squint in Tracy's direction. "We don't get many bachelors your age up here."

"Better snatch him up quickly." Rose nodded sagely. "You don't want to be an old maid."

"I'm twenty-six." Hardly over the hill. And certainly not stupid enough to fall for a man who made his living writing a bachelor column.

"We could give you dating pointers." Agnes

chuckled, perhaps realizing how ridiculous Tracy might find that statement. Perhaps not.

The three town council ladies drove away.

If Tracy controlled her aphasia, she'd clue everyone in to Chad's intentions. If Tracy controlled her aphasia, she'd get out of town. And she needed to get out of town or she'd be an old maid. So she needed to control her aphasia.

She'd been twirling the dandelion. She blew its seeds into the wind and began singing softly. And then louder, forcing the words out, which only made her stumble more.

CHAPTER FIVE

SOMEONE WAS SINGING the alphabet song. Someone who wasn't five. Someone who hesitated over the letters.

Recognizing that voice, Chad smiled, quickening his pace as he approached a curve in the road.

She's not the story.

He ignored the voice that usually guided him to the good stuff.

"Now I know my...ABCs." There was a pause and then a strangled, "Next time. Won't you. Sing with me." Tracy made a frustrated sound and shouted, *"Nuts!"*

Chad rounded the bend. Tracy was leaning over a rail on a bridge. She had her back to him and gripped the railing as if considering launching herself over it.

"Don't jump," he shouted, grinning because he didn't believe she planned to leap to her doom.

"There is no place..." she hung her head "...private in this town."

"You could try working on your speech therapy at home."

"I live above the bakery." Her cheeks bloomed with color and she shuffled her sneakered feet. She looked as if she wanted to teleport to another dimension. "The walls have ears."

The bridge was a narrow two-laner with a silver metal railing. It spanned forty feet. Both banks were thick with foliage and trees that created a shady oasis. But in the center of the bridge it was sunny and Tracy's hair was almost as yellow as the T-shirt beneath her tan jacket.

Again, he recognized this wasn't the story he needed. Again, he walked toward Tracy, stepping onto the bridge.

She eyed him expectantly, waiting for him to say something.

"You have a nice singing voice." He should have kept silent. Silence had served him well at the *Lampoon*. Silence created spaces others rushed to fill. But silence lacked the smiles and laughter and jokes he'd missed. "It's the truth." May as well fill the hole he was digging with her with something.

"Truth?" Tracy fixed him with a look that

said she recognized what he was filling that hole with. "You introduced yourself as Chad Healy. Not Chad Healy Bostwick."

"Healy is my legal name. My mom was angry with my dad the day I was born. She left his name off the birth certificate." And she'd been angry with Dad the day she'd died, furious that he'd never given up cigars and had developed cancer. After reading his father's last wishes concerning the *Lampoon*, Chad could understand how she felt.

With a wave of her hand, Tracy let the issue of his name drop. "What are you doing out here? Did Leona kick you out?" She didn't mince words, but she also didn't seem to realize her speech had smoothed since her acapella performance.

"No." He leaned on the railing next to her. "I'm searching for the angle I want to take on my story." Were there more crotchety people like Leona in town? Did it have more to offer than good coffee and reputedly good wine?

"You? Searching?" So much passion. It radiated from the disbelief in her blue eyes to her expressive hands. He never would've guessed all that emotion had been hiding behind the black bakery apron. "Your columns slant one way—one way!" She jabbed her finger at him, stopping just short of poking his shoulder. "You put people down. Is that why you were fired?"

The *F*-word hit him below the belt and shook his ego at knee level. Nowhere had it been reported he'd been let go. The terms of his leaving were part of his termination contract. Sure, some in the press had speculated he needed time to grieve. But no one had guessed the truth until Tracy. "I still own nearly half the company." He couldn't keep the anger from his voice.

His anger didn't stop her from punching back, saying baldly, "Ownership didn't stop them from firing you."

There was a truth for him. "Apparently, my dad wanted to take the *Lampoon* in a different direction. My services no longer fit what they were looking for." He hadn't said it out loud before. The words—though spoken quietly—seemed to ricochet between them like a flat rock bouncing across a smooth river.

"Ahh." Tracy glanced downstream. "You were phased out."

"I'm guessing from your tone you've experienced this."

Her sharp nod confirmed it.

"But I bet you weren't downsized by your father from the grave." If he'd known what Dad had up his hospital gown, he would've walked away six months ago when the old man had gone completely on life support.

No. The thought sickened him. That was hurt talking. Chad had loved his father.

Despite that love being wasted on a man with no heart, he wouldn't have changed anything he'd done for him in the last year. But he would've been better prepared for betrayal. "It's why I'm starting my own magazine. And Harmony Valley is the perfect launch vehicle." He hoped.

She'd retreated metaphorically when he'd told her about dear old dad phasing him out, but at the mention of the town she bounced back for another round. "Harmony Valley isn't what you write about. No nightclub. No spa. No chichi hangouts."

"So far, I love that it's different." Charm, checkers, a cast of personalities. The more he thought about it, the more he was convinced there was more than enough to work with here. He might write more than one column.

Tracy frowned at him and half glanced over her shoulder toward downtown, as if thinking about making a break for it.

He didn't want her to go. "You want to protect the town from me? Convince me it doesn't deserve a send-up."

She frowned the way she did everything else—wholeheartedly. Her shoulders rolled toward him, her hands fluttered, her eyes narrowed. He realized why he liked watching her. Every expression was a full-body experience, as if to make up for her brevity of speech.

"I'm not helping you. Ask Mayor Larry or Agnes."

He shook his head, not calling her out on what he suspected was the real reason she didn't want to convince him—she'd have to talk—because that was his ace in the hole. With her speech challenges, she'd never win a verbal argument with him. And if that line of thinking wasn't worthy of an entrepreneur trying to claw his way to the top, Chad didn't know what was. "The mayor wants to give me the dog and pony show."

"What makes you think…" Her gaze collided with his, simultaneously suspicious and self-conscious. "I won't?"

Earlier in their conversation, she'd been more focused on the battle and less on her vocabulary. Now she was very much aware of this war of words and she was back to stumbling.

"Tracy." He captured one of her hands the way his father used to capture his mother's hand when he wanted her complete attention. "You're the only one in town who read my columns. You and I are from the same generation." And he'd much rather be with her than the mayor. "We're in the same place in our lives. You know what singles want."

"We're not the same." She tugged her hand free. "You're having a midlife crisis."

"We can debate that while you give me a tour." He grinned. Sparring with Tracy and Leona made him happier than he'd been in a long time. At the *Lampoon* and at home, arguments had been more heated and with higher stakes.

Tracy wasn't giving in that easily. She put the back of her hand on her forehead. "So young. It's tragic. Early midlife crisis. It skews your perspective."

His perspective was fine. But his job would be easier with an inside track. And she was perfect. There was one angle he hadn't tried with her yet. "The more I know this place— more than a dog and pony show can tell me— the better chance I have of bringing people to visit your brother's winery. You want to protect his interests, don't you?"

Her blue eyes widened. "Dirty pool." She shook the rail, gripping it with fingers that might have wanted to grip his neck. It didn't take her long to make a decision. "Okay, I'll sell my soul to the devil and show you around. But only if I can read your column before you publish it."

He'd bet she didn't realize her speech had smoothed out again. Regardless, advanced reads weren't on the negotiating table. She was just like some of *Bostwick Lampoon*'s sponsors. At least the advertisers he'd lined up for The Happy Bachelor Takes a Different Path weren't that controlling. For the first time in over a decade, he had creative freedom. He shook his head.

"Then the deal's off." Tracy crossed her arms and settled her hip against the rail for a third round of drawing lines in the sand.

She made him smile and that wasn't inconsequential in these negotiations. He gave her a once over. Everything about her looked soft— faded blue jeans, yellow cotton T-shirt, a tan jacket with a suede collar. But she wasn't soft or pliant. She was strong and gutsy. "What are you doing working in a bakery?" She was parked in the middle of a retirement town miles from anywhere.

She bumped her hip against the rail repeatedly as if she was hitting her head against a wall. "Not many ad agencies…hire the speech impaired."

"Oh, woe is you. That's no excuse." He looked her up and down once more. "You're not disabled. It'd be unfair to pit you against someone with a *real* speech impediment."

Her arms waved about. Her feet shifted. Her mouth opened and closed and opened again, but nothing came out.

"Maybe you haven't noticed," Chad said evenly. "You've been talking to me on this bridge more fluently than I heard you speak this morning." He reached over and tapped her temple near her hidden scar. "You think too much and about the wrong things, except when you don't think and then the words tumble out."

She tried to walk past him toward downtown.

"Hold on. We're still negotiating."

She stopped.

And then he realized why. He'd caught her arm and pulled her close.

CHAD HAD INCREDIBLY expressive brown eyes.

In them, Tracy noted a surprised earnestness.

He stared at his hand on her arm as if he couldn't quite believe he'd taken hold of it.

She couldn't quite believe it either. Or the earnestness. He didn't care about Tracy or Harmony Valley. And he was wrong about her not being disabled, wrong about her speaking easier with him. She'd been struggling the entire time he stood nearby. And now they stood face-to-face, inches away from being kissably close.

Tracy licked her lips and inadvertently stared at his, over-thinking, just as he'd accused her.

Luckily, her cell phone rang and Chad released her. She drew a deep breath, filling her lungs with much needed air.

"Ms. Jackson, this is Sue Gaines from Three Filmers Productions." The woman spoke with a smoothly modulated voice Tracy envied. "You sent in an application a few weeks ago for a producer job?"

"Yes." Tracy braced herself for the worst. It was rare for her to get good news about a job application.

"Congratulations. You've made the short list of candidates we're considering for the position."

"What?" Tracy reached for the railing to steady herself. *"No."*

Chad didn't pretend to hide his curiosity. He tilted his head and contemplated her expression with all the seriousness of a doctor she'd once met at a speech research facility.

"Yes." Sue chuckled. "For this next round, we're asking all applicants to create a three minute video segment that tells us who you are. You may feature people and things that are important to you or that shaped who you are. But you must be on screen for at least two of the three minutes."

On screen? Tracy did a quick visual inventory of her body parts and surroundings, because she felt as cold as if she'd fallen in the river. This was an exercise she couldn't do. She'd have to turn them down. Responses formed in her head—so grateful, have to decline, chickening out.

Meanwhile, Sue was barreling on quite happily. "You'll present your video in two weeks to the interview panel in our offices. I'll send everything you need to know in a confirmation email. Good luck!"

"What's wrong?" Chad asked when Tracy disconnected the call. "You look like you lost everything in the stock market."

Tracy shook her head, still feeling cold. "I got a call-back interview. At a film production company."

"Don't you want the job?"

"Yes." Tracy longed for the mental challenge and sense of purpose the job offered. "But…" Be on screen? "They want me to… make a video. About what makes me…me." That was going to be one quiet film.

Chad shrugged off her fears. "Everybody makes video résumés nowadays. Besides, didn't you say you used to work at an ad agency? This should be right up your alley."

"They want mc. To be *in* the film." Tracy tiltcd her head back and stared at the sky. It was a clear bluc, happy sky. A sky that promised smooth sailing. Not trusting it, Tracy dropped her gaze to her sneakers. "Me. In the film. *Talking.*" A sensc of foreboding crept up her calves like delicate, determined spider legs, threatening her equilibrium. "I'm going to decline." As soon as Sue sent the confirmation email. Because Tracy had been unable to spit out the words on the phone.

Words spit about her head now: *Coward. Fraidy-cat. Spineless jellyfish. Loser.*

She hated those descriptors.

Chad bent his knees to peer into her eyes. "You're quitting?"

Quitter. Yep, that was appropriate, too.

Tracy clenched her fists, hating that label, as well. "At least, I'll have my dignity…if I bail on the interview. You, Chad the Blackmailer, don't…have dignity or respect. Certainly not mine." She dodged around him and his penetrating gaze, heading toward the bakery as she tossed over her shoulder, "Besides…technically, I can't quit if I'm not hired." That smoothly uttered sentence was a fluke, just like that job offer. She'd learned not to get her hopes up over flukes. There'd been the copywriting job last month the recruiter said she was perfect for. Tracy had sat across from her prospective boss unable to do more than nod her head and offer monosyllabic answers.

"And here I thought you were brave." Chad matched her escape pace perfectly, his tone just as hard on Tracy as she was on herself.

"And I thought you were honorable," Tracy flung back at him. It was easier to argue with him than to deal with the doubts churning in her stomach.

"I have a code. I'll take that over honor any day." He hurried ahead, as if he couldn't wait to get back to the town proper and find that story. "There's nothing wrong with it, but do you really want to make coffee the rest of your life?"

She didn't, of course. And that was what was killing her inside.

And then she saw what had him walking so fast. Roxie Knight had parked her old red truck on the corner. The truck bed was filled with small cages. Each one had a chicken in it.

Tracy told herself not to worry. Chickens might be trendy and Chad might be sneaky, but chickens didn't fly with the bachelor crowd.

CHAPTER SIX

AN ELDERLY WOMAN with short, wiry blue hair in stained blue coveralls and driving around with a truckload of chickens.

This would be fun.

Chad's inner voice had him veering away from Tracy and the disappointment he felt over her fear of a challenge. He didn't want to think about Tracy or why he cared what happened to her. He called out a greeting to the old woman, ignoring Tracy's parting shot of, *"Be nice!"* and introducing himself.

"I'm Roxie." The old woman adjusted the hang of her coveralls, wheezing as if she'd just run a race. "You must be that reporter people are talking about." She tightened a strap that held her cages down with hands that seemed plumper than fit her thin, petite frame.

Interest in a story was elbowed aside by the alarm flashing in his head, the one experienced during years spent raised by elderly parents. Roxie's shortness of breath. Her poor circulation. Was her skin pale because she didn't get outdoors? That was the argument his mother had made when Chad had asked her to see a doctor. Too late, it turned out.

"You don't talk much." Roxie hit him with a sideways glance. "Are you a friend of Tracy's? From one of those clinics she goes to?"

"No." Chad drew back. She thought *he* had speech difficulties? "I was distracted by all your chickens." He hoped to be distracted by whatever reason she had a truckload of fowl, distracted enough to ignore what he saw as warning signs in her health.

"I'm taking them to the farmers market. Getting dotty in my old age." She gasped for breath. "Let too many roosters in the hen house and ended up with too many chickens. Or so my daughter says. She made me promise—" *Wheeze*. "—to get rid of them all last time she visited." Panting, Roxie climbed unsteadily onto the rear bumper and untied a small cage with a small blue-gray speckled hen. "The load unbalanced when I came around the corner. I've just got one cage too many. Poor Henrietta." She slumped over the tailgate, balancing the cage on the fender.

"Whew. You'd think we were at a high elevation. I can't seem to catch my breath."

"Let me help." He placed a steadying touch at the small of her back. "Give me Henrietta." Once the hen was on the ground, Chad took Roxie's hand and helped her down.

Roxie's was cold. Her grip weak. Up close, her skin had an unhealthy tinge to it.

Mom, you don't look so well. Let's go to the doctor.

Tension pinched between his shoulder blades. "You shouldn't be doing this trip alone." Roxie shouldn't be doing it at all. She should be seeking medical attention.

It's none of your business. That's what his mother had said. *I may be slowing down, but everyone slows down at my age.*

He was looking at Roxie, but that didn't stop an image of his mother's face from coming to mind and replacing hers.

I could be wrong. I'm not a doctor.

It didn't feel wrong. And he would have appreciated anyone who could've made his mother see a doctor. Maybe then she'd still be alive. Maybe then he wouldn't be alone and empty.

"I'm glad you offered to come." Roxie smiled up at him mid-wheeze. "Won't take more than an hour. My friend Marty says he'll sell them for me, so it's just a drop-off."

"But…"

"Get a move on." Roxie pressed her keys into his hands, picked up Henrietta's cage and walked around the truck to the passenger side, huffing and puffing like a six-pack-a-day smoker.

Chad was dumbfounded. This was just like earlier when Eunice and Tracy left him—a stranger—with a baby. What was it about Harmony Valley that inspired such trust in their fellow man? Didn't they realize the world was a dangerous place?

And yet… His reporter instincts stood on end—*this is the story.* Chad stood still, rejecting the idea. He didn't write smarmy, feel-good pieces. He didn't do good deeds, like pointing out to someone they might be sick. Or driving them to the doctor. There must be someone in town who'd drive Roxie.

Although no one in the bakery had been willing to drive him a few blocks. The only volunteer driver, the petite woman—Aggie/Agnes—was probably still busy taking Mildred to her doctor's appointment.

Roxie got in with a mighty door slam and a raspy gasp.

The chickens in the back startled, clucked and stared at Chad as if to say, *"Get a move on!"*

The surreal moment continued to fuzz Chad's brain and make him slow to react.

Roxie's plump fingers flapped toward the open driver's window. "Daylight's burning."

Chad climbed in the front seat and inserted the key in the ignition. And then he hesitated, the good Samaritan debating with the good reporter on a deadline. "Before we go, I have a few questions."

"Shoot." Roxie rested her arms across Henrietta's cage and looked at him with faded gray eyes that matched her wiry gray hair and nearly matched the gray tint to her skin.

Her gray skin looked so much like his mother's the last time he'd seen her alive, Chad felt pressure in his chest, pressure that forced words out in a rush. "Do you live alone, Roxie?"

"Are you asking me for a date?" She snorted and then gasped for breath, pressing a swollen hand over her sternum.

Biting back a few curses, Chad started the engine. It gave a mighty cough that sounded like a shotgun blast, one that shot down the cold-hearted bachelor columnist who wanted to leave Roxie to her fate. "You didn't answer my question."

"I'm divorced." She frowned. "My daughter lives in Cloverdale where the farmers market is."

"Can you call her?"

Roxie's eyes narrowed and her pale lips pinched. "If you're thinking of kidnapping me." Gasp and wheeze. "You may as well take my chickens. My family has nothing of value to ransom me with."

Leave it, the reporter in him said.

He couldn't. Each belabored breath Roxie took seemed as if it would be her last. "I think you need to see a doctor. Shortness of breath, swollen extremities." He handed her his cell phone, trying to appear confident and commanding, because that was when his elderly parents had been least likely to challenge his decisions. "I'm going to take you to the emergency room. Call your daughter and have her meet us there."

Roxie gripped his phone. "Is this a joke?"

"No, ma'am." He turned the truck around, being careful of the chickens in the back. "I wish it was. You share some of the symptoms my mom had." He spared her a glance. "Before she died."

"I have indigestion, that's all." Roxie moved sausage-like fingers to cover her mouth.

She knew nothing of the warning signs of heart disease. "Maybe. The doctor will know for sure."

"Has anyone ever told you…you're the strangest man?"

"I've been called worse." Tracy came to mind—her stubborn chin and disagree-with-you gaze.

"But…I can't go to the hospital. My chickens…" And there it was. The denial of the need for a doctor. She was just like his parents. She'd probably put off seeing a doctor until her heart felt like it was stopping.

Well, he wasn't letting another person die on his watch. He'd risk being called wrong and foolish and a meddler. Worst case? He'd pay for her emergency room visit. "I'll drop off your chickens," Chad said through gritted teeth. "Call your daughter."

Surprisingly, Roxie did as instructed. And then she called Agnes to spread the word about the nice young reporter.

Chad may not like small towns much, but he knew how they worked. It wouldn't take long for this to get around.

Leona wouldn't bat an eye. Eunice would

reassess her opinion of him once more. And Tracy?

Tracy wouldn't believe it.

That was the only thing that lifted Chad's spirits through the next few hours.

TRACY SLIPPED IN the back door to the bakery's kitchen.

Maybe *slunk* was a better way to describe her entrance. That's what deadbeats did, right? They slunk around, avoided notice and didn't live up to their potential.

Tracy's potential had been totaled along with Emma's car in that accident.

She wanted the production job, but she didn't want to appear on film.

She wanted to prove to Chad she was brave, but she didn't want to appear on film.

She wanted to feel good about herself, but…shoot and darn. She wanted to veer right, up the L-shaped staircase to her mid-century modern studio apartment, which was way cooler than saying she had simple kitchen cabinetry from the 1950s, pink stucco walls and a pink toilet and tub, accented with pink subway tile. But there was Eunice and her purple curls in the alcove to her left, rocking Gregory between the crib and the shelves with baby toys, books and diaper supplies. And there was Jessica in the large kitchen with its four wall ovens, butcher block counters and a huge island in the middle. The paneling was dark, but windows above the staircase flooded the room with light, leaving Tracy no shadow to slink into.

Eunice and Jess looked at her expectantly.

Tracy paused near the stairs, feeling clammy from her confrontation with Chad and cowardice.

I'd rather be a coward than have no dignity.

Except Tracy suspected her fears made her dishonorable. And she'd never been a dishonorable deadbeat in her life.

"Hi." Tracy shrugged out of her jacket, acknowledging a quick escape was impossible. She flung the jacket over the dark wood banister.

"You look like someone lost your letter to Santa," Eunice whispered without missing a rock in her rhythm.

"Twice." Jess nodded, brushing her hand across her forehead. She went back to transferring mini chocolate Bundt cakes for El Rosal to cooling racks. The Mexican restaurant had a standard dessert order to be delivered every other day and Jess changed up what she baked each time.

The baby turned sleepy eyes Jessica's way. He was adorable, especially when he was sleeping.

Don't grow up, kid. Being an adult is more complicated than making sure you've got a clean diaper at the ready.

"I…" Tracy struggled with how much to tell them. But heck, why not give up the details and embrace her impending cold feet? "I have a job interview."

Jess set the Bundt pan aside. "I should be looking like I lost something. You're going to leave me and boy, will I be in trouble."

Stack guilt onto the demoralizing decisions weighing Tracy down. Jess needed her. "Don't worry. I'm not going anywhere." Tracy explained about the video.

"Don't back out. You'll do fine," Jess said kindly, because she could see a silver lining in the darkest of rainclouds. "It's the right job for you. I can feel it."

Tracy couldn't feel anything but failure, like a gaping chasm at her frozen feet. If she moved toward this job, she'd almost certainly go down, down, down. And splat.

"My father used to make family movies

back in the fifties." Eunice made it sound as if her father was a well-renowned director. "Would you like to see some? I bet you could learn something."

If Eunice's father had made artistic films back in the 1950s when Tracy couldn't bring herself to make a home video, she might have to give up looking for a new career permanently. Better not risk it. "Thanks, but no thanks." Tracy eyed the cooling oatmeal raisin cookies on the center island. Sugar always made her feel better, but sugar solved nothing. "I don't see the point...in me making the video. They want someone who can talk."

Eunice tsked. "You talk just fine."

"Not as much as before."

"You have no problem communicating with me or our customers." Jess wiped her hands on a white tea towel with apples embroidered on it, unaware that her words and Eunice's made Tracy feel better. "Nobody's perfect. My teeth are prone to cavities. Eunice needs reading glasses."

Eunice bristled. "I do not *need* reading glasses to read."

"Look at the time." Jess smiled mischievously at Tracy. "Can you drizzle icing on these Bundts while I make Duffy lunch? He'll be here soon." Duffy being Jessica's husband and the winery's field manager.

"I glob," Tracy warned, passing the cookies on her way to the sink.

"Squeeze slow, move fast." Jess wasn't taking no for an answer. She removed a tray of sourdough rolls from the oven and set them on the counter. The rolls were destined for Giordanos Café across the street for their lunch crowd.

"Duffy likes my peanut butter and jelly," Tracy said as she washed her hands.

"Not as much as he likes cream of broccoli soup in a bread bowl." Jess opened a plastic bag full of pumpernickel rounds. And then she stopped, fixing Tracy with a serious look. "You have to try. Promise me you'll try and make a video. Your brother showed me some of the commercials you worked on in the past. You were good, really good. You can still be good, just in a different way. It's like…me trying a new recipe."

"Like Horseradish-Doodles," Eunice whispered. "Something new, but still by you."

With her back to Eunice, Jess exchanged a private smile with Tracy. "Yes, it's just like that."

Under the influence of their positive words,

Tracy felt some of the weight fall from her shoulders. "All right, all right. I'll do it." Tracy picked up the icing bag and assumed the ready position, hand over the first mini Bundt. And then she hesitated, picturing globs instead of smooth thin lines of frosting.

"Don't over-think," Eunice said.

Easy for Eunice to say. She was better with the baby than with Bundt cakes.

Jess glanced up from carving a bowl in the pumpernickel loaf. She made a swift back and forth gesture with one hand. "Squeeze slow, move fast."

Tracy did as instructed, completing the task with a minimum of globs. "I can make the deliveries." The Bundt cakes and rolls.

"Okay." Jess gave Tracy a stare she probably thought was stern, but Jess wasn't the stern stare sort. "But then you work on your video. No excuses."

"No excuses," Tracy agreed, trying not to think about all the ways she could humiliate herself during this interview process, on screen and off.

"WHAT DO YOU think of Chad?" Agnes asked during their car ride back from Mildred's doctor appointment and a pleasant lunch in Cloverdale. "I'm impressed that he took Roxie to the hospital."

"Me, too." Mildred turned her face to catch the dappled sunlight through the passenger window. It was a little thing, but it made her feel alive to have the sun on her skin.

"Most men wouldn't have noticed Roxie was ill," Rose said from the back seat. Her hiking boots scuffed against the plastic floor mats, as if she was tap dancing while sitting, which she probably was.

"We didn't notice she was ill," Mildred pointed out, still smarting over the doctor telling her she needed to get out and walk more. *Walk more?* She was nearly blind and in a walker. For her, exercise was an accident in the making.

"We haven't seen Roxie in a week or two," Agnes allowed. "It makes me wonder who else we haven't seen recently."

Such were the concerns in a town with so many old people. But if they, the town council, didn't worry, who would?

"Frankly, I wouldn't have noticed anything." Much as it pained Mildred to admit. "I'm no good at spotting physical deterioration." Or sidewalk hazards. Darn doctor.

"I think Chad should stay." Rose's feet

kicked the back of Mildred's seat. "Maybe he and Tracy will hit it off."

"She doesn't seem to like him much." Agnes sounded distracted.

Mildred was distracted, too. By thoughts of romance and Phil. If only he wouldn't waste his time on Leona. If only she was brave enough to do something about her attraction. "What do you think of Phil?"

"I don't think of Phil at all." Rose was painfully honest, even when her friends didn't want her to be.

"In what context have you been thinking about Phil?" Agnes should have been a private investigator. She always knew just what thread to unravel.

"It was a general question." Mildred's cheeks felt hot. She shouldn't have said anything. She lifted the binoculars she kept in Agnes' car and looked at the road ahead. Mildred was so sight-challenged, she couldn't tell how far they were from home. This stretch of road looked the same for miles. Eucalyptus trees lined the two-lane highway flanked by vineyards. The asphalt hummed steadily beneath the tires. She put the binoculars down. "Where are we?"

"A mile from the turn-off into town." Rose

tapped the back of Mildred's seat. "I'm with Agnes. Why are you thinking about Phil?"

"He's a very nice man," Agnes said kindly. Agnes was no dummy. She probably knew now that Mildred had feelings for Phil.

"He's not always nice." Mildred wrapped the binocular strap around her hand. "But I think that might be because he's still broken-hearted over Leona." Which made Mildred as brokenhearted as a school girl over her first unrequited crush. What was wrong with her?

"Regardless." Rose sniffed dramatically, because she did so love to over-dramatize. "Men don't know how to meddle properly. Phil certainly doesn't."

"Are you sure you should be thinking about Phil?" Agnes asked, slowing to make the turn. "You just admitted he's still in love with Leona."

"There is that." Mildred sighed. "I probably need a change."

"I thought you already went through the change." Rose might remember every verse from *West Side Story*, but sometimes she was slow on the uptake.

"I'm done with menopause, Rose. I'm talking about being in a rut. I'm… I don't know. Bored?"

"Well, you've got no husband and you can't read a book or watch television." Rose called it like she saw it—with that painful clarity. "But you do have us."

Mildred was glad she was in the front seat and could hide her pain at being alone by looking out the window. Not that she could see much of anything.

"I can't remember the last time your daughter came to visit. And you don't even have a dog." Rose was on a roll, flattening Mildred further in her rut.

"I am forsaken," Mildred murmured. Her daughter was too busy living a full life and who was Mildred to complain about that? She'd left home at eighteen and hadn't looked back. Ever.

Agnes turned left toward Harmony Valley. As usual, she hit the pothole with the edge of her right front tire. "Let's not get maudlin."

At their ages, no one wanted to be maudlin. But at their ages, sometimes you couldn't help it.

"I was thinking I'd like to start dating." Mildred might just as well admit it.

"Don't tell me you want to date Phil?" Rose sounded horrified.

"He's a good-looking man," Mildred said

stubbornly. Or at least he had been twenty years ago when she could see him.

Agnes patted Mildred's shoulder. "But Phil's emotionally unavailable."

"Leona has the house. He has no one." Mildred squared her shoulders. These were her friends. They were supposed to accept her fragile feelings and insecurities, not bash them. "Maybe if he had someone, he'd get over Leona once and for all."

"You're breaking up the band." Rose sighed heavily. "We're a threesome."

"I just want to feel alive again." Before she fell while following the doctor's orders, broke a hip, and died. That was how Kiley Anderson kicked the bucket. Six months from fall to death. "Is that so bad?"

"No," Agnes said, slowing some more as they passed the stark white building that was Snarky Sam's.

"Well, if we're being honest here…" There was a breathy quality to Rose's voice, as if the forthcoming admission was as much a cherished secret as Mildred's fascination with Phil. "I've often wondered what it would be like to kiss Rutgar." The blond, bearded, large-as-a-mountain mountain man who lived atop Parish Hill.

"You probably couldn't find his lips beneath all that beard," Agnes pointed out.

They all laughed like the band of silly schoolgirls they'd once been.

CHAPTER SEVEN

"MR. HEALY, YOU cannot bring that chicken into my house." Queen Leona sure knew how to put on a hero's welcome.

"Leona, it's been a long day." Chad set Henrietta's cage on the porch in the fading afternoon sunlight. "Roxie gave me this hen as a thank you gift." And then he raised his voice, when he hadn't done so all day. *"For saving her life!"*

It scared him that he'd been right. Roxie needed three stents for three blocked arteries. She'd cried. Her daughter had cried. Chad had left them at the hospital to drop off her chickens. Before he'd left, Roxie had insisted he take Henrietta as a thank-you gift. And yes, her daughter had looked at him sympathetically, shaking her head as if giving him permission to refuse. But what could he do? It might be Roxie's last wish.

Leona opened her mouth to say more, but Chad cut her off.

"What I need is a warm, safe place to keep Henrietta." At least until he could figure out who to give her to or how to convince Roxie to take her back. "Maybe that shed of yours in back has room."

The bed & breakfast owner shook her head from side to side as if the swivel point was the pearl choker about her neck. "Unless you want chicken for breakfast, you'll store that thing at Roxie's."

He was tired, emotionally wrung out, and the drive-thru burger he'd eaten on the way back wasn't sitting well. It wasn't worth arguing with Leona. "Where does Roxie live?"

"Three blocks up Madison. You can't miss the house. She hung fishnets on the fence." Leona shut the door.

The wind rustled through the trees, sending leaves fluttering like golden snowflakes to the ground.

Grumbling about queens and their royal subjects, Chad picked up Henrietta's cage and returned to Roxie's truck. When he turned the key, the truck shuddered, coughed and died as surely as he'd expected Roxie to earlier. Several unproductive key turns later and Chad stood next to his little red sports car.

The one with narrow front seats and no room for a walker, a wheelchair or a chicken cage.

Henrietta strutted back and forth in her metal crate, making worried noises.

"I guess we're walking, Henrietta." Thankfully, his readers couldn't see him now.

He picked up the three by two cage and started walking. The hen nestled into the corner near his hand. Her blue-gray feathers were soft against his fingers. Henrietta had the personality of a hesitant kitten. She deserved a nice home. Chad envisioned her living in a coop on his penthouse's back patio.

What is wrong with me?

He was thinking about adopting a chicken. Where was his big city indifference? The Happy Bachelor didn't do pets. He didn't drive old ladies to the hospital. And he certainly didn't let a hotel proprietor get the best of him.

A block later, he spotted Tracy sitting on a curb, scribbling in a notebook. He didn't like to acknowledge how relieved the sight of her made him feel.

"If you're counting cars driving by," he said. "I'm betting you haven't counted one." There was no traffic in Harmony Valley.

Loyal bird that she was, Henrietta clucked as if laughing at his bad joke.

Tracy didn't chuckle. She barely looked up, perhaps hoping he'd walk on by. She wasn't getting that lucky.

"Hey, I recognize that expression of yours." He set the cage on the sidewalk and sat next to Tracy. The cement was cold, but not as cold as a hospital chair. "That's your over-thinking face." He'd never run into anyone who was as set on defeating herself before the game ever started. "What are you doing?"

"I'm scripting my video." Her chin jutted out and her eyes burned hot blue. "Isn't that what you wanted?"

He hadn't really wanted anything. She was a stranger, same as Roxie. And as soon as he left town, she'd be a memory, same as Henrietta. That didn't stop him from glancing across the street, curious as to why Tracy would choose to sit here.

And then it was his turn to chuckle. They sat across from an elementary school. "Don't tell me you're starting at the beginning of what made you who you are today? First grade teacher, perhaps?"

From the wash of color on her face, he must have been close.

"Don't be a cliché," he said. That was a fate worse than death for a writer. Most likely for videographers, too. He held out a hand for her notebook. "Let me see your other ideas." If she was like other writers he knew, she'd have a list somewhere on those pages.

She clutched the book to her chest and glowered at him.

He worked hard to keep from smiling. She'd never be good at glowering, not with those petite features and big blue eyes. "If you won't show me, cough up the next idea on your list."

"No."

Henrietta settled deeper into her corner and made soft noises like a toy train on a circular track. He hoped she was hunkering down from the increasing intensity of the wind and not laying an egg, which would only fall to the pavement.

"If I had to guess," Chad said, returning his attention to Tracy. "It'd be something by the river." There weren't many things around town that might have shaped who Tracy was.

The glower disappeared. Tracy's shoulders drooped around the notebook.

Chad sighed. "I can only hope you'll work through the predictable dreck before you film."

"Sometimes…*often*…it takes writing dreck to be inspired." The droop undercut the confidence in her words. She wasn't convincing anyone, least of all, herself. "I'm not worried about what my topic will be…so much as how I'll deliver it."

There it was. A long sentence. And if her droop was any indication, she didn't recognize it.

Tracy laid her temple on her knee, facing away from him. "I was going to do a test drive tomorrow morning at the park by the river. I'll take a break from the bakery at eight and the light will be fabulous coming off the water."

Henrietta made a derisive noise before Chad could. Tracy had no inspiration, no plan and at this rate, no chance at grabbing that brass ring.

Like me.

The burger flipped in his stomach and he shook his head, trying to shake off the doubt.

Not like me.

Chad had inspiration—Harmony Valley. A plan—a website and advertisers. And a very good chance at grabbing that brass ring.

Tracy turned back to him and said begrudgingly, "What you did for Roxie was nice."

He smiled. "I bet you hate to admit that."

That won a grin out of her. "Harmony Valley brings out the best in even the worst of people. And now you've found your story."

She didn't understand him or the Happy Bachelor at all.

Chad stood and collected Henrietta. "I haven't found my story. There's no reason why people should visit this town. In Napa, the accommodations are more luxurious, the winery choices more numerous, and the nightlife…well, it exists."

"YOU'RE A HYPOCRITE." Tracy got to her feet, stiff from having sat so long on the cold curb. "You want everyone to think you're this insensitive. Witty. Self-centered bachelor. And yet…you took an old woman—*a stranger*—to the ER." And he'd encouraged a coffee barista—in a haughty, superior way—to reach for the stars with more than a clichéd, halfhearted effort. "And then there's this chicken…" Tracy faltered. One, because she didn't know why he had a chicken. And two, because she'd spit out a really long speech, without stumbling too much over her words.

Not that Chad seemed to notice. He was walking away from her, broad shoulders tall beneath that black leather jacket. "Henrietta is a thank-you gift from Roxie. It would break my code to trash a gift." His back was rigid. His tone was frosty. But the indignation in his next words were fluid and hot. "And Leona refused to allow Henrietta on her property. What harm could a small chicken in a cage do to the B&B?"

"They can dig up a yard worse than a dog after a gopher," Tracy said, marveling at his big-city ignorance. But it was the indignation over the chicken that got to her. She wouldn't have expected the Happy Bachelor to care what happened to a stranger, much less a hen. It made her trail after him as if she was one of his flock. Besides, he was from the city and there was livestock at stake. "You don't know anything about chickens, do you?"

"They get up early and they lay eggs."

The farm girl in her rolled her eyes. "And the care and feeding…?"

Chad's steps slowed to a stop. He turned to look at her, a complete contradiction—a stylish city slicker carrying a chicken. "Roxie isn't coming home for at least two weeks. What will I…" He glanced down at the small bird, concern etching faint lines from the corners of his eyes. "I can't even keep a house-plant alive."

"I can help you get her settled. About her long-term future? Lots of people have chickens," Tracy said reassuringly, stopping a few feet from him. Her father had gotten rid of his hens when Tracy went off to college, claiming there'd been too many eggs for one man to eat. But there were others in town with coops. She'd even heard the winery had gotten some recently. "For now, she's safest at Roxie's." The sun was setting. For certain, there was still a chicken coop and some grain at Roxie's.

"Thank you," Humble Chad said.

Humble Chad. His eyes didn't twinkle and his cocky boardroom demeanor was conspicuously absent, but Tracy found this side of him just as appealing. If only he wasn't the Happy Bachelor.

An orange tabby ran across the street, darting beneath the bushes bordering an abandoned house. There were more empty houses and empty lots about than elsewhere in Harmony Valley.

Tracy glanced around. She seldom came to this part of town. And now, with grief thickening in her lungs, she remembered why. A road to the right led to what was left of the grain mill. The silo's skeleton rose like an empty castle turret above the swaying trees. A romantic image for such a horrible end.

Chad followed the direction of her gaze.

"That's where my mom was killed." A chill reached deeper into her bones than the brisk autumn wind. "They say the explosion happened so fast…" As fast as Tracy's car accident. "They couldn't have done anything." So many dead.

Chad nodded as if he understood. And then he said the nicest thing. "She'd be proud of you."

The cold, thick feeling in her lungs spread into her throat. "For some things," she choked out. Her academic achievements. Her rise in the advertising world. Perhaps not the temptation to settle nowadays. "She'd have liked you prodding me…to do my best. But not—"

"Let's just leave it at that, shall we?" He started walking.

Tracy didn't look at the mill again, but she felt her mother's presence—or rather the lack of it.

They walked in silence to Roxie's house. Henrietta was happy to be in her large coop. Tracy showed Chad where the grain bin was and told him how much food to give the hen. They latched the gate and went their separate ways. The Happy Bachelor walked off, shoulders hunched in his jacket.

Only then did Tracy remember she'd told him she was filming in the morning and begin to feel guilty.

Because she'd lied.

CHAD WAS DOWNSTAIRS in the Lambridge B&B's dining room at 8:01 on Saturday morning, feeling like a bear awakened too early from hibernation.

The formal dining room was as stuffy and stately as the rest of the house—a cherry dining set that could seat twelve, dark wainscoting, forest green striped wallpaper and a large brass chandelier. How different it might feel with other guests at the table.

He'd slept restlessly on the lumpy, squeaky mattress that probably hadn't been replaced since the last presidential candidate had come to town fifty years ago. Yeah, he'd looked it up.

And during his sleepless night, he'd read about the care and feeding of chickens, had a circular debate with Tracy—in his head—about the Happy Bachelor's code of ethics in columns, and researched ways to conquer expressive aphasia.

He'd also sat at the keyboard for hours trying to start a column on Harmony Valley. His attempts had failed. He might even say they'd failed miserably. Every time he felt he was on to something, Tracy's disapproving glower popped into his head. Not that he was panicking. It was a week until the Harvest Festival and eight days until his web page went live. But he was beginning to feel stressed.

"I like a man who's prompt." Leona wore a brown sheath dress and low black heels. Her hair was pulled back so tightly from her face, it seemed to lift the wrinkles above her brows. She retreated through a swinging door, returning almost immediately with a small white plate—almost a teacup saucer—and a mug of black coffee.

Chad stared at the one mini quiche, the one mini bran muffin and the cluster of five green grapes. "This is it?"

Leona had turned to leave him. She spun back, resting a hand on one hip. "This is a bed & breakfast, Mr. Healy, not a Las Vegas buffet."

"This won't hold me." He'd gotten up early and went for a jog. He'd fed Henrietta. He was ready for eggs and sausage, biscuits and gravy, coffee and creamer.

"I never said I'd hold you." Leona left him, unaware of the double entendre of her words.

The quiche was gone in one bite. The muffin in two. The coffee smelled bitter and the grapes were sour. This would've been a sorry state of affairs if Martin's Bakery wasn't within walking distance. Besides, he needed to find a repair shop for Roxie's truck.

But first—since he was out—he might just as well go by the park next to the river and see what Tracy was up to. He was learning his way around town. He took the alley behind Main Street to reach the park. It was empty, but Tracy had mentioned the light on the water.

Chad veered onto the path across the sparse grass, drawn to the birds singing by the river. He passed a rusty swingset, an equally rusty pushable merry-go-round, a couple wooden picnic tables carved with initials, and lots of trees—poplar, oak, eucalyptus. Finally, he reached the bluff overlooking the water and nearly fell over the edge.

Tracy wasn't there, but immediately below him, on a narrow strip of dirt beach, a naked man was doing yoga. He was old, fit and had a long gray ponytail.

"Good morning, Chad," the mayor said, as if he did naked yoga with an audience every day.

"Good morning," Chad blurted, backing away from the view. "Sorry to interrupt."

"Want to join me?" Larry called after him.

Naked yoga with another dude? "Nope." That was a definite man-code breaker. Chad's pace picked up, not because he was embarrassed— although there was that—but because he'd been set up.

By Tracy.

CHAD ENTERED MARTIN'S and drew a deep breath. Ah, coffee. The morning's lifeblood. A glance around the bakery revealed many of the patrons from the day before. The checkers match was on between Felix and Phil. Eunice sat in the window seat wearing Easter Egg colors that complimented her purple hair. Two men stood drinking coffee and talking near Eunice. The taller, more solid-looking of the pair held Gregory with the ease of parenthood.

There was a line to place an order, and Chad got in it, smiling. He'd left the *Lampoon* offices wanting to smile and laugh and joke more. With the exception of Roxie, Harmony Valley was giving him that. And now, he had to decide what kind of payback to give Tracy, the prankster.

He moved forward and the first pastry case came into unobstructed view. Forget another breakfast quiche. The pastries in the case looked decadently large. They'd hold him. He gauged the distance between he and Tracy. Her arms were slender, but they could hold him, as well.

Whoa. Where had that thought come from?

Granted, Tracy was attractive and engaging, with a good sense of humor. And granted, he enjoyed her company when they weren't arguing about him being an evil overlord. But she wasn't his type. She wasn't a polished, driven go-getter. And yet, in that instant, Chad's perspective changed. She was… datable.

When it was finally Chad's turn, guilt was written all over Tracy's face as she stared at his shoulder. "The usual? Latte and pumpkin spice scone?"

"Latte and a cinnamon roll, please." The cinnamon roll was the largest item in the bakery case and smelled heavenly when compared to the mini bran muffin. "So... I didn't see you filming yoga down by the river this morning."

She had her back to him while she steamed his milk. She spared him a glance, biting her lip. And then she smiled, not in the least apologetically. "I'm sorry?"

Chad felt that smile deep in his chest. "You're not."

Her smile widened. "I'm not." She returned her attention to his latte. "I read more of your columns." If that was her opening salvo of the day, she'd have to add context and criticism.

"My readership might be interested in a place where they can do naked yoga."

"You wouldn't." She turned. Her eyes were wider than those in the smiley face she'd made with milk on top of his wide-mug latte.

A fully dressed mayor appeared next to Chad. "I was serious about my earlier offer. Yoga is invigorating down by the river. I'd wear clothes for you, Chad."

"He doesn't make that offer...to just anyone," Tracy ribbed, not that the mayor paid her any notice.

But Chad did. Her banter, her ability to pull a prank. They combined to fill his chest with warmth.

"Let me know if you change your mind." Larry set two dollars on the counter. "Do you think your article on us will be picked up by any of those national papers?"

Stress pinched more than his shoulder blades. It wrapped around Chad and squeezed.

"I couldn't say," he wheezed, worse than Roxie had yesterday. Chad swallowed and tried again. "I need to learn about the town's character, the festival, the winery—"

"Flynn." The mayor waved over one of the men standing near Eunice, the one with reddish-brown hair and no baby in his arms. He introduced him as one of the winery owners. "He'd like a tour of the winery, Flynn. He's comfortable with Tracy if you can't spare the time."

"I'll ask Christine when he and Tracy can taste." Flynn didn't question Tracy's inclusion, despite her propping her fists on her hips and huffing at the mayor after she'd given him his coffee and sugar packets.

"Excellent." Larry pumped Flynn's hand. "Text Tracy a time to take him over."

"Before we roll out the red carpet…" Tracy held up several sheets of paper. "I printed some of Chad's columns." She offered them to the mayor and Flynn.

Chad leaned forward to murmur, "I hope you picked some that make me look good."

"You wish," she murmured back.

Whatever columns she'd chosen, whatever the mayor's reaction, it wouldn't change what Chad wrote.

"I don't need to read those, Tracy." The mayor was in pompous mode and discounted Tracy too easily. "And neither does Flynn. Chad's written for important newspapers." The mayor drew Flynn away to talk with the man holding the Poop Monster.

Tracy dropped the papers into the trash with a defeated sigh.

Chad's cell phone rang. It was one of his sponsors. A sponsor call on a weekend wasn't a good thing. "Marty, what's up?"

Marty McPhearson was the media buyer for an online travel clothing company—No Wrinkles. He'd once been a drill sergeant and his voice rasped with rough peaks and deep valleys. "My boss is giving me grief about our spend with you."

Chad gripped the counter and looked up. His gaze met that of a man in a sepia-tinted photo with his shirtsleeves rolled to his elbows and the heels of his hands deep in dough.

Chad hadn't expected the *Lampoon* to lose an advertiser without a fight. The advertising business was a personal one. Chad had a friendly business relationship with Marty. Another editor at the *Lampoon* had a friendly business relationship with Marty's boss. But he'd thought the window to backing out had closed.

"I defended my spend with you, Chad. But without subscription and readership numbers, I'm not in a good position." Marty cleared his throat, but it didn't seem to make any difference in his gruff voice. "You know I hate to ask this, but I could do with some stellar advance content to prove I'm spending the company's money wisely."

Chad opened his mouth to say no, but Marty beat him to the punch.

"Without it, I may have to back out."

Chad's grip on the counter tightened. If No Wrinkles backed out, others might, as well.

"I need your best stuff, Chad. And I need it yesterday."

Nothing he'd written in the past month was good enough. Chad had a sinking feeling his best stuff had yet to be written and it'd be written about Harmony Valley. "Tuesday," he choked out. "I can get you something by

Tuesday." He disconnected and scowled at the phone.

"Tuesday deadline?" Tracy placed an oatmeal raisin cookie on the plate next to his cinnamon roll. "I thought you worked for yourself."

"Advertising supports blogs. One of my sponsors wants a taste of my magazine before I go live."

"Did you find your story?" There was too much superiority in those blue eyes.

"Did you find what makes you...you?" he countered.

"You found your story yesterday. With Henrietta." That superiority spread to her smile. "You're just too stubborn to admit it."

"That strong backbone of yours has been strengthened by accidents. First your mother's. Then yours." It was a guess, but the words felt right. A woman as soft-looking as Tracy didn't develop a foundation of steel by facing sunshine and rainbows every day.

"You need help." Her smile hardened. "I could help you write your column."

"And I could help you write your video script."

The mayor clapped a hand on Chad's shoulder. "I'm glad you two are offering to help each other." His smile was oil-spill slick. "Tracy can show you around town, tell you about the festival and take you wine tasting. And you can help her with that interview video she's stressing about."

"How did you…" Tracy's gaze cut to the window seat. "*Eunice*."

"You may be talented," Eunice said sweetly. "But Chad's been in the paper. Popular ones."

The room erupted with agreement that boxed up his and Tracy's objections before they'd ever been spoken.

"You can start now. I'll man the counter." Eunice scurried over, immediately brightening the space with all her spring color.

Not two minutes later, Chad and Tracy stood outside the bakery zipping up their coats.

Tracy glowered at Chad. Her expression wasn't so cute anymore. Not when his breakfast and latte weren't outside with them.

She took one look at his face and rolled her eyes. "Like this was my fault, Mr. Hotshot Newspaperman."

CHAPTER EIGHT

"I DON'T NEED your help." Tracy wanted to make that perfectly clear to Chad, because annoyance was wreaking havoc with the caffeine coating her stomach.

"Likewise," he said. "It was easier not to argue."

"Agreed." Not that they were out of the meddlesome woods. Harmony Valley residents loved to butt in. But his comments inside the bakery still rankled. "I am *not* shaped. By accidents."

Chad didn't miss a beat. "And I am not writing about a chicken."

While leaves danced gracefully down the street, Jessica came out with a tray she'd loaded with Chad's order, plus an espresso and two oatmeal raisin cookies for Tracy. "I'm surprised you let them bully you into a partnership."

"I prefer to think of it as a strategic escape." Chad claimed a wrought-iron chair at one of the small sidewalk tables. "There is no partnership."

Tracy dropped into a chair across from him. The nip in the air was already creeping around her toes. "You don't understand...how things work here. These people. Can be stubborn."

"What's there to be stubborn about?" Chad asked. "It's none of their business."

"They're talking about screening Tracy's interview video for editorial purposes." Jess set their drinks in front of them. The smiley face on Chad's latte had morphed into a wobbly frown. "Saturday night after the Harvest Festival dance."

Annoyance doubled down in Tracy's stomach. Chad smirked.

Their plates came next, delivered with Jessica's remorseful smile. "And they want a reading of the article Chad writes before it's released. Eunice offered to read for you at the dance, Chad, but I bet as soon as Rose hears about it, there'll be a fight."

Chad stopped smirking. "I'm not giving them anything to read."

"They'll ask for it. Every morning." Tracy broke a cookie in half. "Plus I think...Mayor Larry heard you say...Tuesday."

"I can attest to the fact that residents are a

little overzealous." Jess tucked the empty tray beneath her arm. "When I first moved here, it was as if the entire town adopted me. If you think about how their kids and grandkids have moved away, it makes sense. They're retired and need more to do every day than play checkers."

Mayor Larry opened the door. "Tracy, take him by Snarky Sam's. And the wine tasting will be tomorrow at eleven." He held the door for Jessica and then returned inside.

There was nothing carefree about Chad's expression. He didn't smile or give one of his self-deprecating laughs. His eyes were nearly as black as dark roast coffee beans. "We need a pact."

"You're. Not." She tapped a finger on the tabletop to emphasize each word. "Writing. My. Video."

"Not that kind of pact." He pulled his cinnamon roll in two. "Not a creative pact. A defensive pact. We tell them no one sees the finished product but us."

"Really?" Maybe Tracy could work this to the town's advantage. "You'd let me read—"

"No. That's just what we say."

"You'd lie?" Why was Tracy not surprised? "I won't. Besides, they'll still expect me to be your tour guide."

"And me your video consultant."

The last thing Tracy wanted was for him to witness her talking about personal things and stumbling over words.

"We could make this work," Chad said, shredding his roll again. "If we set boundaries."

He may have said boundaries, but Tracy saw walls. "No."

"Hear me out." He leaned closer, as if worried the hearing aid crowd within the bakery might be eavesdropping.

Which Eunice was. She sat in the window seat staring at them with those unblinking purple eyes of hers.

"I could use a tour guide," Chad said in a low voice that might just as easily have said, *"You look lovely tonight."*

Shocked at her overactive imagination, Tracy popped a piece of cookie in her mouth.

"And I could help you with your delivery."

Delivery? The word brought her to pizza. Tracy glanced across the street to Giordanos Café, which used to be the town pizzeria. "I'm not…following."

"I know a little about speaking in front of an audience."

She bet it was very little. "Don't tell me. To

imagine people naked." Her traitorous gaze slid to his broad shoulders beneath that black leather jacket before she sought refuge in the depths of her espresso cup.

"That naked thing never works." Chad wiped icing from his fingers with a napkin, seemingly unaware of the direction her mind had wandered. "I notice you pause mid-sentence. You should always pause after the first word in a sentence. Don't barrel forward and then lose momentum. You'll only feel self-conscious and look as if you've lost your train of thought."

"That's for stutterers." Tracy tried to hide her disappointment. She'd read as much as she could about speech impediments and treatments. "That won't. Help me." Not that she'd tried it. But why try something that was for those with a different challenge than she had?

He laid a hand on her shoulder. "Look across the street at that shop—Mae's Pretty Things."

In the shop window, one of Eunice's blue baby quilts was draped over a child's rocking chair. Knit scarves and crocheted lace hung from a dried tree branch. Those things were delicate, frivolous. His hand was heavy. His fingers had a purposeful, proprietary hold on her shoulder.

This pact is a bad idea. He was the suave, sophisticated, sinister Happy Bachelor. She was just plain Tracy.

She didn't dare look at him. She swallowed and stared hard at Eunice's baby quilt.

"Take a deep breath, relax and say something," he commanded softly, using that intimate voice that created intimate images in her head. "Pause after the first word."

"I can't." How she hated to admit she had a weakness. It made her body draw in on itself, like a hermit crab retreating in its shell.

He massaged her shoulder, fingers delving deep in her tense muscles. "Think Olympic athlete. Nothing comes easy to them. And yet they triumph. Take a—"

"Will…you stop with the coaching already?"

"That was awesome." Chad draped his arm over her shoulder and gave her an air-stealing squeeze.

No pact. No way.

Tracy shoved his arm off. "Seriously? You're making a move on me?"

"Nope." Chad grinned. *Grinned!* "I was happy for you and I got carried away."

She wanted to slug him. She wanted to shout at him. She wanted to kiss him.

Ouch. That last thought made her want to sink into a hole in the ground, but at the same time she was filled with the unexpected realization that she'd delivered some quick rejoinders. It made her speechless.

His Handsomeness continued to grin.

Time seemed to slow. Leaves blew down the street, tumbling like small, gently bouncing playground balls. The wind tousled his short brown hair. Her toes—which had felt cold earlier—felt as warm as the rest of her.

She drew a deep breath and said, "That was…cool." She frowned, having expected her speech to miraculously be smoother. Should she put his arm on her shoulders again? Like she did with her dad?

Heck, no. His embrace wasn't safe. She was just a chess piece in a game he was playing. She refused to be played. She had the town to think of. A job opportunity to think of. Her heart to think of.

"Practice. It'll take practice," he said. "The energy you're devoting to self-loathing is better spent outwitting your challenges. Now, let's eat and then get a move on." He may have torn his cinnamon roll into bits, but they were bite-size and he ate every one. When he finished his latte and she her cookies, he stood. "Which way is our tour?"

Tour? She'd forgotten all about it. "This way. But…no lying. And no pact." She stood and marched down the street. "Why…did you offer one anyway? You…don't seem like someone who'd cave to others." Not by the reputation of his column. That man was a slick, lone wolf. But his smile said something different. It said, *"I'm a team player. Let's play!"*

"I've had a lot of experience working with stubborn old people." Chad fell into step beside her. "And I like the idea of helping you."

Not helping people. Helping *her. Don't get carried away, girl.*

"My…" she paused to gather herself "…aphasia annoys me."

"You need to think of it the same way you think of that scar of yours. It's never going away, but over time, it'll be better."

This Chad had nothing in common with the Chad who'd written the columns for the *Lampoon*. He was kind and giving and sensitive. But because he was Chad Healy Bostwick, the Happy Bachelor, he was untrustworthy.

He paused on the corner. "Which way?"

"Over there." She pointed to Snarky Sam's, which was across the street and down the block at the entrance to Main Street. Could she believe in him? Could she get over her self-consciousness and speak without a hitch? All the failures she'd made in front of people replayed in her head like a high speed slide-show. Painful, those memories. She stepped off the curb only to have Chad yank her back.

A blue bubble-fendered Cadillac sped around the corner just a yard away from Tracy's feet. She'd been so deep in her own head, she hadn't heard the Caddy coming.

Lilac Miller waved. The ends of the brown paisley scarf she had tied around her short white hair fluttered behind her.

"Slow down, Lilac!" Anger and fear made her legs as weak as melted chocolate. "I thought she stopped driving." And then Tracy shouted, despite Lilac having already disap-peared around the corner toward the bridge. "I thought you stopped driving!"

"She should." Chad took Tracy by the shoulders, peering into her eyes. "You okay?"

"Yes." And no, she didn't want to acknowl-edge how comforting his strong hold on her shoulders was. She, who resented her family's overprotectiveness, didn't want to explorc why she liked it from Chad.

He smiled as he released her. His smile could make a woman forget he was untrustworthy. "Did you notice how well you yelled at Lilac?"

"No. Thank you for saving my toes."

"And your knees and your hips and—"

"I get the idea." She drew a deep breath, tried to relax and remember to pause after every first word. It was easier when she wasn't looking at him. "What…was it you were saying about my scar?"

"Did I say yesterday there was no traffic in town?" He double-checked the street beforc taking her arm and crossing. "I was saying that your scar will always be with you, the same as your aphasia."

"Was that supposed to cheer me up?" She extricated her arm.

"Shift your thinking." He paused to peer into the deserted grocery store window. "It's just like going to the gym to stay healthy and keep the weight off."

"You and your midlife crisis." It was her turn to grin. "Are you drinking light beer, too?"

He smiled back, meeting her reflection's

gaze in the store window. "Why are we going to Snarky's?"

They made an attractive couple in the glass. But it was only an illusion. "Snarky… Sam is last year's gurning champion."

Chad turned and began walking toward Sam's. "Gurning?"

"Making an ugly face." Tracy hurried after him, collecting herself for a long speech. "It's a fall tradition. The…gurning winner at the Harvest Festival is the town's Green Pumpkin for Halloween." *Woo-hoo! That was nice. Could she do it again? Don't think. Pause and go.* "The…Green Pumpkin used to take candy kids didn't want. And give them pencils or books." She spoke! She spoke and spoke and spoke! Tracy barely contained herself from dancing down the street.

"That's cool." Chad didn't acknowledge her success. He just kept on walking ahead of her. "Why don't you do it anymore?"

"There…are only two kids in town since Flynn's nephew moved away. Gregory and Eveline. Both babies." Tracy was happy with her speech. "We…have unusual traditions. No more…unusual than your Bay to Breakers run." *Hello, naked runners and runners in costume.*

"So…gurning." She didn't have to see his face to know he was smiling. It was there in his voice. "Are you competing this year?"

"No. I…don't have enough wrinkles." He'd have to see pictures to understand.

They'd reached Snarky Sam's. The sidewalk in front of the small, bright white building looked more like a junk shop than an antique store with a side business as a pawn shop—or maybe it was a pawn shop with an antique store on the side. Outside there was an old bicycle, a washboard, a wrought-iron gate and a collection of garden gnomes.

Chad reached for the door. Tracy pressed her palm against his chest, pushing him back. "Don't…" *Oh, wow.* He had a firm chest beneath that polo shirt. She drew her hand back. "Don't…make fun of his…" She'd lost her train of thought. She knew the word. She knew the word. He was waiting for her to say it. "…*Stuffed animals.*" She clenched her teeth. That wasn't right.

Chad smiled. "I'm not despicable."

All evidence from his literary past to the contrary. "What about the *Lampoon*?" she asked, because she couldn't let him get away with thinking he was nice. Or let herself think it, for that matter.

"I wrote what the readers wanted. That's it. It doesn't mean it's who I am." There was a slight crease to his brow. "If you read comments on the column, you'd know. No one featured in my write-ups complains." He opened the door and indicated she should enter first.

"That's…probably because they fear you."

"That's probably because their reservations and revenue increased significantly after my articles. I'm a man of influence."

If that was true, she didn't like his source of power.

They stopped just inside. Snarky Sam's smelled like Tracy's dad's closet—in need of an air freshener. The merchandise was dated and dusty. The display by the door held electronics—toasters, food processors, a VCR.

"Stuffed animals." Chad stared at a squirrel dressed like Sherlock Holmes and chuckled. A blackbird beside it was costumed like Dracula. Its wings spread beneath a cape as if it was about to take flight. "You meant taxidermy."

She ground her teeth again.

"No soliciting." Sam sat behind a display case filled with jewelry. He rested an open comic book on the glass. He was a gnarled, wisp of an old man, wearing a faded brown flannel shirt and an impatient attitude.

Used to his attitude, Tracy took a breath and said, "We're...here to see your Gurning Trophy."

Sam tapped the comic book in front of him. "I don't have time for idle conversation. You get me?"

Chad walked over to a shelving unit. "Bowling balls?"

"Are you the travel writer?" Sam peered at Chad. "You can help me. I have quite a selection of wineglasses. You know," he told Tracy as an aside. "Wine and medicine don't mix so well as you get older." He pinched his face in Chad's direction. "I could use a mention in your column about the wineglasses. And the bowling balls, too. I'm overstocked."

"How did you get overstocked on bowling balls?" Chad looked perplexed. "Is there a bowling alley in town?"

"It's Harmony Valley's official sport," Sam said with pride.

"Get outta here." Chad grinned.

Sam and Tracy nodded. Bowling had been an elective in PE at Harmony Valley High School.

"We have three teams in leagues in Cloverdale," Sam said. "It's about a thirty minute drive south."

Tracy pointed to a trophy behind the front counter sitting next to a photo of Sam. In it, he wore green face paint and had contorted and twisted and scrunched his face into something unrecognizable as the pawn shop owner. "That's…uhm…" *Word-word-word.*

"Gurning," Chad supplied, moving closer.

"Won it all last year." Sam's thin chest puffed out. "Ed Schollenburg died a month before. He was a six-time champion of the Gurn." Sam glanced over his shoulder at his photo. "He was a real inspiration to me."

"Don't try this at home," Tracy deadpanned.

"It's a grand English tradition," Sam explained. "A sport only the elderly can dominate. It's why we love it here. You get me?"

"I gotcha." Chad snapped a picture.

They bid Sam farewell and headed back toward the bakery.

"See?" Tracy said as they neared the vacant grocery store. "Gurning. Isn't that unique? And…nothing your bachelor hipsters could relate to."

Chad's grin said he'd found the gurning contest just as unique and special as Tracy did. It was why his next words surprised her. "I hesitate to point out that gurning is also a side-effect of taking drugs like ecstasy or speed."

"What?" Even in college, Tracy had stayed far away from the serious partying crowds and had never heard of the term when it wasn't associated with the Harvest Festival. She stopped in front of the grocery store. Her gaze drifted to their reflections in the glass. "That was the first thing…you thought of? When I told you about…gurning?" They'd stood in this same spot. She'd felt a connection and he'd been laughing inside. Her insides weren't laughing. They were burning with anger.

"Yep." Chad rubbed his hands together like the plotting villain he was. "You're right. Harmony Valley is priceless. My readers are going to love it."

Tracy made a frustrated noise, checked for speeding Cadillacs and left him on the curb.

CHAPTER NINE

TRACY ENTERED THE bakery and stopped just inside the front door, unable to take off her jacket fast enough.

She felt peculiar. Her chest was too tight and her legs too loose. She liked Chad. She hated him. She wanted his life. She wanted to submarine his column. Gurning? Grrr!

What was happening here? She felt as if she'd stepped onto a battlefield without a gun.

She drew a deep breath and tried to forget Chad's skill in turning something innocent into the hugest irony.

And then she noticed all was quiet. "Why… are you all looking at me?"

"Tracy." Felix brushed cat hair from his black polo shirt and stood. "Do you remember the time you helped me collect money for the Fireman's Fund?"

Tracy nodded. "Every…sixth grader had to volunteer."

The retired fire chief waved that observation aside. "But you never complained. It showed your character."

"Thank you?" Tracy crossed the room self-consciously and put her apron back on. There was definitely something weird going on.

Phil shifted his chair to face Tracy. "You used to sit in one of my chairs while I cut your dad's hair. Once, I helped you with your spelling words."

"I remember that," Tracy said kindly. Phil had always given her a sucker and sent her spinning in the barber chair.

The town council had come in while Tracy was gone. They sat at their regular table with the mayor. They shifted anxiously in their seats.

"Tracy." Rose smoothed her white chignon. "I taught you how to jitterbug on my front porch. Dancing teaches you confidence."

Jess entered the dining room, Gregory on her hip. She took one look around and said, "Okay, stop." She dragged Tracy into the kitchen. "They're auditioning for your video."

"It's…supposed to be about me." But they'd all been mentioning something from her past. Tracy poked her head back into the dining room. "No. You…cannot be in my video." She let the swinging door swing closed.

Conversations in the dining room resumed, along with Tracy's stress level about the job opportunity. She was no closer to determining what her three minutes would be about than she'd been yesterday.

Jess deposited Gregory in Eunice's lap. He grabbed a rainbow-colored teething ring Eunice held and began to gnaw on it. There were pans and mixing bowls in the sink. The center island was dusted with flour where Jess usually stood. Everything here looked normal. Everything inside Tracy felt out of sorts.

"I saw that devil put his arm around you." Eunice sighed from her seat in the rocker. Her glasses were askew on top of her head and her eyelids sagged, as if she could use a nap as soon as she put Gregory to sleep. "Devilish men are the best kind."

A few years ago, Tracy might have agreed with Eunice. But this devilish man made her feel inadequate. Except when he was helping her talk without breaks or grinning at her or…

"Men confuse me." At least, one man. Tracy leaned on the island counter near Jess. "Who…ordered these chocolate chip muffins?"

"Christine." Jess picked up a purple sheet

of paper. "Can you drop them off at the winery later?"

"Sure." Maybe on the walk over Tracy would be struck by inspiration for her video. "What are you reading?"

"Eunice has another recipe she wants me to try." There was hesitation in Jessica's statement. She handed the wrinkled purple notebook page to Tracy.

"Jessica never made my Horseradish-Doodles," Eunice said. "This recipe is for—"

"Sweet and Sour Cookies?" Tracy scanned the ingredients: pine needles, wild onions, garlic chili powder, sugar, butter, eggs.

"Don't they sound delicious?" Eunice asked. "Mama was a whiz with a budget. She found a use for everything in our yard in the most creative ways."

"Eunice, I like the bakery to smell of sweet goodness." Jess took the recipe back. "And this…"

"Is not sweet goodness." Tracy couldn't wrap her head around how the cookies might smell or taste. "How…did this recipe come about?"

"I told you." Eunice made it sound as if she'd explained herself a few too many times.

"Mama was a whiz with the budget," Jess

parroted. She cast Tracy a wry glance that said Mama-isms explained it all.

"But...why create a recipe...like *this*?" Tracy began filling the sink with hot water and soap.

"It all started when Daddy trimmed the pine tree in back and refused to burn the needles inside the fireplace. He said they'd smoke up the house—he was right, by the way." Eunice blew a raspberry on the back of Gregory's neck, giving him the giggles. "Anyway, Mama hated anything going to waste. She tried putting the needles in potpourri. She tried sticking them under our mattresses. But there were so many leftover. Finally, she ground them up and put them in things."

Tracy almost hated to ask, "In what?"

"Baked chicken. Pot roast. Shortbread cookies."

Jessica was just as speechless as Tracy. She looked at the recipe and then back at Eunice. "Where did the sour come in?"

"Oh, that." Eunice chuckled. "It's not very nice and I don't tell a lot of people this, but Mama didn't like Aunt Arlene very much." She paused as if Jessica and Tracy should understand this reference. And then she blinked. "You didn't know Aunt Arlene, but Mama said she'd gone sour the moment Granddad wrote her out of the will. But Mama was nice, you see. She didn't argue with anyone. So when Aunt Arlene came to visit, she made these cookies and served them with tea."

"I would've liked to meet your Mama," Jessica said, sounding as if she meant it.

Tracy agreed. Sure, Mama sounded a bit passive aggressive, but in all the stories Eunice had told about her mother, she hadn't been overtly cruel.

Tracy loved listening to the stories the elderly residents told. They were full of human truths and politically incorrect opinions. "Jess…you should put Eunice's story on your blog." Tracy marveled at the nearly effortless sentence. Chad may be a scoundrel, but his advice helped. "With the recipe. Maybe more people would read it." More than the ten to twenty people in Harmony Valley who gave Jess recipes for posting and also knew how to work a computer.

"I don't know." Jess took in the bakery with a harried glance. "I'm so busy and not much of a writer. Christine asked me to work with Claudia to cater and help organize her wedding, plus I've been getting a lot of wedding cake orders lately."

"I could do the blog," Tracy offered, feeling a spark of interest. "What if…all your recipes had stories?"

Just last week, she'd overheard Rose telling Jessica about the origins of her circus casserole. Before Rose made it to Broadway and later the ballet, she'd worked in the circus and had been given the recipe by the Bearded Lady.

The population in Harmony Valley was diverse for a reason. Fifty years or so ago, Flynn's grandfather had spearheaded a letter-writing campaign to attract new residents. He'd written more letters before he died, but the only one to answer was the sheriff.

"You think more people would read the blog if recipes had a history?" Jess trailed her fingers over Eunice's recipe indecisively.

"Yes." Tracy glanced at the cooling rack. Cookies were her weakness, but apparently, weren't enough to distract her into talking smoothly. Leave that to the dastardly Chad.

"I can't pay you." Jess had a soft look in her eyes, the one that said she understood Tracy was getting little more than minimum wage when she'd been used to getting a lot more.

"I don't mind updating the blog for free." Tracy didn't feel Jess was taking advantage.

Besides, there was a cookie that hadn't come out flat. Scrunched cookies couldn't be sold and shouldn't have to wait until after lunch to be eaten. Tracy claimed it. "I love writing." She'd written advertising copy and news segment scripts. She preferred writing to making coffee and selling scones.

"Maybe I'll pay you in cookies," Jess said with a small smile.

Tracy grinned. "That works, too."

"Hey! Travel writer!" A tall man with black hair waved to Chad from the patio of El Rosal. "Come on over. I'll buy you coffee."

An invitation from someone under the age of forty? Chad hurried across the street to the tables outside the Mexican restaurant. Salsa music, black wrought-iron tables and chairs, and tall heaters made the patio inviting and eased the bad feeling Tracy's reaction to his interpretation of gurning had given him. How could she make him want to smile and he make her so annoyed?

"I'm Slade Jennings, part owner in Harmony Valley Vineyards." Slade had a strong grip and the detached air of a seasoned businessman, despite his attire—a black polo and khakis.

Under Chad's scrutiny, Slade rubbed a hand across his jaw, drawing Chad's eye to a thin, curved scar at the base of his neck. There were several reasons for a scar like that, none of them pretty. Chad quickly averted his gaze.

Slade's smile faltered, but then he exchanged a glance with the other man at the table and his smile returned full force. "And I think you met Flynn earlier at the bakery."

"We did." Flynn had a more casual grip and a more casual approach to life. His T-shirt was dirtier than it'd been this morning and sported a beer logo. His black baseball cap proclaimed him a San Francisco Giants fan. "When the mayor sent you on your tour, we cleaned rain gutters at Eunice's house. Luckily, it's a small house." He brushed some dirt off his T-shirt. "Doing some more work around town this afternoon."

Chad sat next to Slade. "I thought you guys were dot-com millionaires."

"Sadly," Slade motioned for the waiter to bring more coffee. "We're also the handful of able-bodied men in a town filled with old people living in homes that have seen better days."

Chad's story antennae pinged with excitement. He immediately downgraded the feeling. His story instincts needed fine-tuning. They'd been on the fritz since he'd gotten here. "What's the nightlife like around here?" As bachelors, they should know.

Slade and Flynn exchanged grins.

"We wouldn't know." Flynn flashed a wedding ring.

Slade held up his hands. "I'm engaged."

"But before…" Chad tried to keep his voice casually indifferent. "I heard you were single."

"Oh, things were exciting here," Slade said with a healthy dose of sarcasm. "We sat on Flynn's back patio, drank beer and watched the river drift past."

"Don't forget," Flynn added wryly. "We also had our handyman chores."

"If you're both volunteer laborers, why aren't you dirty?" Chad asked Slade, curious despite himself. The man looked rather pristine.

"The Prince of Wall Street held the ladder for me." Flynn spoke in the good-natured tone of a friend.

"Be leery of this man." Slade pointed to Flynn. "The next question he'll ask will be about your free time and skill with a hammer."

"So, Chad." Flynn didn't miss his cue.

"Travel writing can't be a full-time occupation. How are your skills with a hammer and what does your day look like?"

"Choose your words carefully," Slade cautioned.

"I'm under deadline. I need to be writing." The gurning bit was priceless and once he sat down at the computer inspiration was sure to strike. Harmony Valley might be a dud, but it'd make for an entertaining column. "And no. I don't own tools other than the basics needed to put together a desk from Ikea." A hammer, a wrench and both types of screwdrivers, all of which were rarely used. He lived in a penthouse suite with a maintenance contract. His dad had been a metrosexual before metrosexual was cool. He'd raised Chad the same way—style before sweat. "I'm game for whatever you're asking." Because being game led to good stories and he couldn't totally ignore his instincts.

"Great. We're patching roof shingles later." Flynn exchanged another one of those private glances with Slade.

A roof? Chad really should collect all the details before accepting man-challenges. "I don't suppose I could hold the ladder."

"Nope. The new guy always has to go up on the roof," Slade said.

"Lucky you." Flynn lifted his water glass in a toast. "It's only a chicken coop."

"I'll help," Chad said. "But only if I can bring my chicken."

CHAPTER TEN

"LADIES, WELCOME TO Harmony Valley Vineyards' chicken high-rise," Slade said.

The winery owner had a dry sense of humor and Chad had been smiling a lot as he helped the two men, despite being on the roof and bending more than his share of nails. He didn't turn to see who the ladies were. Odds being the women were elderly.

"I had Jess bake some chocolate chip muffins for all your chicken coop troubles." There was warmth and laughter in the woman's voice.

"Two stories is impressive," Tracy said. "Hey, is that Henrietta?"

The hammer Chad wielded missed the nail and struck his finger. The nails he'd been holding in his mouth clattered to the shingles and off the edge. Later, Chad wouldn't admit he'd howled, but he wouldn't say he didn't either. His forefinger felt flattened and stung like the dickens.

"Good thing we didn't use the nail gun," Flynn said. "We'd be headed to the hospital about now."

"I knew I should have had Chad sign an accident waiver," Slade said, only half-jokingly. "Come on down. Happy hour is early today."

"Christine, where's your first aid kit?" Tracy was already backpedaling toward the main winery building.

"First aid under the sink. Ice packs in the freezer." The cool blonde juggled a pastry box so she could kiss Slade on the lips. "I should have brought beer to make up for the mishaps."

"You can make it up to me by spending five minutes alone." Slade sounded like a man in love as he took the blonde and the muffins over to a patio with tables and chairs.

Flynn held the ladder while Chad climbed down. "I'd introduce you to Christine, our winemaker, but she needs five minutes alone with her fiancé."

By the time Chad got his feet on solid ground, Tracy was back and breathless. She carried a first aid kit and an ice pack. "I… wasn't sure if there'd be blood."

"No blood." Chad glanced at his finger, which still hurt like heck, was deep red and looked as if it was going to turn a magnificent shade of purple.

"No blood, no foul." Flynn scampered up the ladder like a sure-footed monkey. "No foul, no lawsuit." He surveyed Chad's handiwork.

Meanwhile, Tracy had moved closer to Chad. She slid her palm beneath his and laid the ice pack on top of his finger. At his questioning look, she shrugged. "I'm a farm girl. We take care of our tools, including our appendages."

"Thanks. I need my finger to type." He wasn't—and would never be—a handyman.

She removed her hand and the ice pack. "You can suffer."

She wasn't seriously spiteful. She allowed him to swipe the ice pack from her without a fight.

"I'll…add handyman to your list of weaknesses." Tracy smirked.

"You have a list?"

She nodded. "Sadly. It's a short list."

Chad's smile felt too big given he'd nearly taken a digit off his hand.

And then he spotted Henrietta lying on her side. "Is she breathing? Is she dead?" He rushed over and picked the blue-gray hen up, only to have her flap and squawk and fly out of his arms.

Tracy laughed. "Chickens sunbathe sometimes. She was enjoying the warmth."

Chad reclaimed the ice pack, wiping off the dirt to cover his relief. He'd rushed to the rescue of a fowl. Dad would have laughed for hours.

"Nicely done up here, Chad." Flynn stood on the ladder overlooking Chad's work. "Just a few more nails and Henrietta has a new home. Bandage him up, Tracy. He needs to finish."

"Nope." Tracy gave Chad a critical once over. "He's done swinging a hammer for the day."

Again, Chad was struck by the way Harmony Valley residents absorbed visitors into their routines and made them feel as if they belonged. Tracy and Flynn hadn't asked him his preference about continuing work, although he agreed with Tracy about calling it a day. But there was a silver lining. "I never counted on learning a new skill when I came to town."

"Life is full of turns, Mr. Midlife." Tracy shooed him away from the ladder. "And before you go claiming a skill, you need to be able to participate without hurting yourself."

CHAD KNEW THE moment he stepped into El Rosal for dinner that night he was in trouble. He thought he'd come in early—just after five—and would beat the Saturday crowd. The place was packed. No tables were free. No bar stool was empty. And there was a thirty minute wait for a table. The early-bird specials were apparently quite popular.

He'd only sat outside earlier. He hadn't experienced the full effect of color that was inside the dining room. Red, yellow, blue, green. The primary colors were everywhere—tables, chairs, walls. There was a small convenience store in the lobby selling ice cream, bread, milk and bananas. The place felt cheap.

"Chad! Chad!" The mayor waved him over to a small table near the kitchen door. Wearing a blue-and-yellow tie-dyed T-shirt, he'd almost blended into the color scheme like an aged and wrinkled chameleon.

Chad had to inch his way past wheelchairs, walkers and one high chair. Past exposed liver spots, swollen digits and ankles, and deep coughs. Should these people be out on such a nippy night? Many of them seemed so frail.

He nodded to the young couple with the baby as he passed, and waved to a table with the bakery's checkers players. Tracy was nowhere in sight.

The mayor invited Chad to sit across from him and his empty plate. "You hit the Saturday night rush."

"It's only five-fifteen." Chad squeezed against the wall.

"And by six-fifteen this place will practically be a ghost town." Larry chortled. His face was the wrinkled tan of too much sun and too little sunscreen. In fact, there was a spot near his ear that looked troublesome.

Chad opened his mouth to mention it, but the mayor beat him to the punch.

"I officially roll up the sidewalk at seven-thirty."

"Really? Is there a curfew or something?"

"No." Larry gave him a look that said Chad might be a disappointment. "That was a joke, son."

Hard to tell when things were so very different in Harmony Valley.

A middle-aged woman with a frizzy black bun and a stained apron opened the kitchen door so wide it almost hit Chad. She surveyed the room with the sharp eye of management.

And then she glanced over her shoulder into the kitchen. "Luis, tables need more chips and more water." She caught sight of Chad and said in a neutral voice that could have indicated welcome or intimidation if she'd been smiling or frowning, "Who are you?"

"He's the travel writer, Mayra," the mayor said. "I told Enzo about him earlier."

She smiled a welcome. "Ah, we'll fix you up. On the house." She whisked Larry's plate from the table and disappeared behind the swinging door. But that didn't stop Chad from hearing her yell. "Enzo! Claudia! There is a travel writer at table one. Work your magic."

"Oh, boy." The mayor leaned forward and said conspiratorially, "You're in for a treat. I hope you don't mind sharing a bite or two. I ordered the early-bird special—enchiladas—which are good, but when Chef Enzo and Chef Claudia get to work, oh, boy."

"Chefs?" The table tops were covered in low end, colorful square tiles. Everything about El Rosal said cheap but filling Mexican food. "This place has chefs?"

"Yep. Enzo and Claudia got married last spring. They run the Italian-Mexican café next to Mae's Pretty Things during lunch. And they cook dinner here."

"Impressive." Although Chad didn't have high hopes of being impressed.

"I wish I'd known you were coming. I'd have brought you a T-shirt." Larry tugged at the tie-dyed cotton of his shirt. "I'm in the business. T-shirts, scarves, towels. You name it, I give it a kaleidoscope of color and a lot of good karma."

Chad loaded a chip with salsa and took a bite, saving himself from commenting. Tie-dye was so 1970.

"Have you fallen in love yet?" Larry asked.

Chad nearly choked on his chip. "With who?"

"With the town. Who did you think I meant? Tracy?" The mayor shook his head. "You're a man of the world. And Tracy… Tracy doesn't know it yet, but she's never leaving. Not that that's a bad thing."

Chad sure thought so.

"At one point in our past, we were a refuge for misfits," the mayor went on.

Chad looked around the room. The residents didn't seem like misfits. They just looked old. Arthritic fingers that held forks awkwardly. Sallow complexions that indicated disease. Coughs that could be traced to pneumonia or cancer. Weak legs that needed help standing. Poor eyesight, balding pates, cancerous skin growths. Chad felt their fragility press in on him the same way it had when he'd watched his parents fade into their twilight years.

What was he doing here? Eight more days? There were a handful of people in this room who could kick the bucket by morning.

Chad started to sweat. He tore off his jacket.

A glass of red wine appeared before him and he took a generous gulp, gripping the glass too tight with his injured finger, making it throb in protest.

"Excuse me, Chad." Larry stood. "I see a constituent who needs my help." He hurried across the room to help someone into a wheelchair. And then he wheeled them out the door.

A plate of bruschetta appeared before him. Instead of parmesan cheese it was sprinkled with finely shredded colby-jack. The tomatoes had been coated in a light green sauce.

Chad took a bite. Bread, cheese, tomatoes and pesto with a hint of jalapeño. It was delicious. It went with the red wine. The blending of tastes rivaled five-star restaurants in San Francisco.

But the culinary excellence couldn't distract him completely from his surroundings.

From the gawdy colors and mortality. His heart beat like a snare drum in his chest and he had the distinct urge to flee. Chad stared at the royal blue wall, trying not to see the end facing some of the restaurant patrons.

His mother used to say he'd been a sensitive child. Not exactly the way a man of thirty-five liked to think of himself. But yeah, he could remember battling an opponent for a soccer ball on the elementary playground. His strike at the ball swept the boy's feet out from under him. Instead of taking the ball, Chad had helped the boy up. And then when he was ten, he'd spent Sunday afternoons playing card games with retirement center residents while his mother visited her friends. He'd felt as if he belonged. Until Chad's favorite card player had died. Beau hadn't looked much older than Chad's father. Chad couldn't bring himself to go back.

Once he left Harmony Valley, he didn't think he'd return here either.

Tracy sat down across from him, panting. "Mayor Larry...said you needed help. Right away."

Chad came back to the present and grimaced.

"He called me." Tracy looked at him more closely. "Are you okay?"

"Compliments of the mayor." Mayra set a glass of red wine in front of Tracy.

Chad's mental notebook, the one that never shut down, made note of Harmony Valley's matchmaking tendencies. Quaint, but unappreciated.

"What's wrong?" Tracy lowered her voice. "You look as if someone just died."

"I…uh…" Chad made a weak gesture that encompassed the dining room. "My parents had me at a very advanced age."

"What are we talking?" She hung her jacket on her chair. "Thirties? Forties?"

"Fifty."

"That's not…much younger than my dad is today." Comprehension dawned. "That… would make your dad eighty-five when he died?"

Chad nodded. "My mother passed a few years before Dad of heart disease." His eyes found the one person in the room who had gaunt features and a sallow complexion. How long did that man have? "When I was a kid, maybe the third grade. I noticed kids assumed my parents were my grandparents. And when

I was in middle school, my friends' grand-parents started dying."

Tracy made sympathetic noises.

He concentrated on steadying his breathing, on the sky blue of Tracy's eyes. "I was afraid every time I said goodbye would be the last."

Tracy took a sip of her wine. "So. You look around. And see the Grim Reaper."

"No." He pushed the plate of bruschetta and the wineglasses toward the wall and leaned forward, letting the words and his fears tumble out. "I see kids and grandkids losing sleep over their health—every cough, every stumble, every forgotten word. I see stubborn independent streaks that put their health at risk. I see hospital beds and bedpans and the responsibility of unraveling finances after years of neglect." And then he saw his father's manifesto and felt a surge of anger, still so fresh, it pushed his fears for others aside. "I see the best of intentions from family being taken for granted. Or worse, being feared." Was that why his father had written his postmortem manifesto? Because he'd felt Chad had overstepped his power at *Bostwick Lampoon*?

Tracy pushed his wineglass back to him. "You need another drink."

He took her advice and downed some more. It was good wine and deserving of a slower appreciation.

"You...went through most of your life expecting them to kick the bucket. Before you saw them again." Her gaze was as soft as blue velvet. "That's scary. You're still grieving."

"No." Grief was the last thing he felt. It lagged behind loneliness and anger. The good thing about the anger was Chad was feeling more in control. "I haven't been surrounded like this. Faced with so much inevitability and loss."

"Welcome to Harmony Valley." Her mouth tilted up on one side. "I...never thought mortality would be your weakness."

Chad sat back in his chair and crossed his arms.

"I know. It's not funny. It's a hang-up." Her smile blossomed and her hands rose above the table to accent each word. "Just like me. And the passenger seat. And like my scar. You think too much. About old people dying."

"Yes." But he didn't know how to stop. He raised his glass. "Here's to accepting scars and living life."

She accepted his toast by clinking her glass to his.

"What?" Mayra slid plates in front of them. She jabbed her finger at the uneaten bruschetta. "Our food is so horrible you can't eat?"

"It's delicious. We were having a conversation," Chad said. What felt like an important one.

"Talk later. Eat now."

So they did.

CHAPTER ELEVEN

A BOTTLE OF wine and a shared mini Bundt cake later, and Tracy was talking like the Tracy of old. Wine always helped her speech. It didn't hurt that she felt comfortable with Chad after talking for an hour. "I can't figure you out." Or why she liked him so much.

The dining room had nearly emptied. There were only two other patrons—two elderly men sitting at the bar. The music had been turned up while the staff cleaned the room and set up for breakfast.

"I'm a man of mystery." Chad was leaning in the corner, a content smile on his face. Such a difference from the tense man she'd found earlier. The lost look in his eyes had hooked her and the subsequent warmth in them when he calmed had reeled her in.

"What was your first article about? The very first you ever wrote."

"For the *Lampoon*?"

She nodded, determined to sort through his

layers the way Jess sorted through Eunice's crazy recipes.

"I did a piece on VIP nightclubs in Las Vegas." Pride rang in his words. She supposed he deserved it. He'd risen to the top of his field.

But something about nightclubs nagged at her. "Ah. That's how you knew."

"Knew what." He stared at the bottom of his wineglass and then swallowed the last of the red wine.

"About gurning."

He smiled.

"What was the slant?" She added, "What did you make fun of?" Because he always made fun, in the same way he always seemed to be smiling. Only his humor was often at the expense of others. Often, she found, but not always.

"I contrasted the conversation and the quality of clientele with a dive bar off the strip."

"Clever." She'd have to look that one up. It sounded like a column she'd enjoy reading, unlike many of his more recent ones.

The two old men at the bar put on their jackets and left. Chad and Tracy were the only remaining customers.

Tracy wanted to ask Chad about his in-

consistent slant to his bi-monthly columns—
many were scathing, some weren't—but try
as she might, she couldn't bring herself to ask
him kindly, not when her town was at risk of
becoming his target. "When did you become
the subversive Happy Bachelor?"

He frowned.

"You have to know. Your writing isn't just
clever, it's often merciless." Because of the
wine and the need not to think so hard about
her speech, she refused to filter. "Your...last
column put down people who camp in national parks. I'm sure your article had an impact on the number of visitors to Yosemite or
Yellowstone. When did you write it? What
was going on in your life?"

"Are you serious?"

"Very much so. Your sarcasm level varies.
I want to know why." She leaned forward and
stared into those coffee colored eyes. "It was
like you had a vendetta against campers. You
wrote it seven months ago."

"My..." He shook his head. "My dad's or-
gans were failing." His normal bravado—that
smile, that twinkle in his eye—was missing.

"And the column about the frequent fliers
who would do anything to achieve their status?" They'd even fly red-eyes over the week-

end for no reason other than to log the last few miles to the next level of status. "That one probably didn't encourage more frequent flier sign ups."

"Written when Dad had a setback in his treatment, I think." Chad looked almost as shell-shocked as he had when she'd first arrived. "This is… It means nothing."

"And the one about the cat lady you met in Istanbul?" The tour guide who had ten cats in a five hundred square foot apartment. She'd shown Chad nothing but kindness, and he'd ripped her to shreds on a personal level, not with anything that had to do with the quality and enjoyment of his tour. And wasn't that a lesson Tracy needed to take to heart?

"That one…I wrote after my mom passed away." His face seemed unusually pale. "I remember because I wanted to cancel the trip, but Dad wouldn't let me. It was part of a special edition at the *Lampoon*."

"I don't think the tour guide's bookings went up after you wrote the article, do you?" But it was as if a door had opened and she had a glimpse inside Chad's soul—to the boy who feared he'd lose his parents too soon, to the man who saw death in the feeble. She wanted to take his hand and squeeze it until all the fear and the anger and the biting sarcasm were forced out of him.

But she couldn't go soft on him. He was grieving and therefore still seeking targets. He'd said it himself—he was searching for a story. If he could be made to see his own reflection in the mirror, maybe he'd go away.

"You point out insecurities in others when you feel insecure," she said.

"I reject that." But he frowned.

"If you feel bad inside, go to the gym or take a drive, but don't pick on a target that can't defend itself." *Don't pick on Harmony Valley*.

"You're reading too much into this."

For a moment, she wondered. But she'd read through several years' worth of his columns. "Go back and read your work. Place them against the timeline of your parents' health." And then because she couldn't resist, she asked, "What would you write about El Rosal?"

His dark brown gaze studied the restaurant the same way he'd done upon arriving at Martin's yesterday morning.

"I'll tell you what you should write," Tracy said. "It was excellent. The service, the diversity of the menu—from traditional Mexican to Italian-Mexican. And the dessert was superb." She couldn't help adding, "Especially the drizzled icing."

"You're missing the contradiction." He tapped the royal blue wall with his knuckles. "What are your expectations when you enter this place?"

"About the same as when I approach a food truck with folding tables and chairs. I'm hopeful." It felt so good to talk without constraints, but not good enough to forget why Chad's attitude was dangerous. His influence could help bring new residents and tourists to town or send them away. "You can't judge a book by its cover."

"I can. People like it."

"Write that and Mayra will come after you." The restaurant owner had harbored a long-standing feud with the owner of Giordanos until recently. "Nothing gets past Mayra."

"Did I hear my name?" The owner of El Rosal pushed open the kitchen door and smiled.

"See?" Tracy reassured her they were fine. "Well, it's been fun. But I've got to get up at 4 a.m."

"I'll walk you home." He stood and reached for his wallet.

"Oh, no, you don't." Mayra swatted at him with a dish towel. "I told you it was on the house. And Mayor Larry paid for the wine."

"Then consider this a big tip." He tossed two big bills on the table. "My compliments to the chefs."

How could a man so generous be so unaware of his own feelings? Tracy headed for the door.

Chad caught up to her easily on the brick sidewalk. The old lamps were lit, bathing Main Street in soft light. The wind rustled the remaining leaves on the oak in the town square.

"Go home. I'll be fine." She walked past the bakery.

"Going around the back? That alley looked like it'd be dark at night."

"I'll be fine." There was a light over the back door. And she'd left so fast, she hadn't taken her purse or her keys. No matter, the door would be unlocked.

"Did I say something wrong?"

She turned the corner and quickened her steps. "I don't want Chad Healy Bostwick to write an article on Harmony Valley. End. Of. Story."

"I notice you—"

"Don't say how you've helped me speak better. I had wine. Everything is easier with wine." And easier when she was mad at him, which had nothing to do with him helping her. "But I won't drink my way through life." And Chad wouldn't be around forever.

CHAD SAT AT the desk in his room later that night and stared at his list of ideas for his column: a stiff B&B owner who lived by old school rules, a mayor who did naked yoga in public, a gurning competition.

Those three things made a great start to his column. Even so, he wasn't sure if he should recommend his readers come to Harmony Valley. What hung in the balance? The quality of the wine. That unknown—not Tracy's armchair psychiatry—were what held him back from writing a word. Dud or diamond? Despite the time warp, the old folks, naked yoga and gurning, he still wasn't sure.

He liked people here. He'd never really connected on a personal level to the residents of a place he was writing about before. Was that the problem? He liked and admired Tracy, but it was the elderly people whom he gravitated toward. He didn't need a psychiatry degree to realize who they were replacing. He was man enough to admit he felt more in common with adults over the age of sixty than he did with most people his own age. The elderly were at a point in their lives where their trails had been blazed and they knew what paths they wanted to continue traveling and how they wanted to travel.

Tracy was different. She was trying to find herself. Chad knew what he wanted to do and how he wanted to do it. For him, life wasn't a blank canvas. It was a paint by number, planned work of art. And yet, Tracy was a part of the town's appeal. The promise of what it could be to the younger generation.

The cursor blinked its indecipherable code on the blank page.

Only it wasn't indecipherable. It said, *"Welcome to Harmony Valley,"* because that's what most people said to him. Most of them said it with more sincerity than a hostess at a fine restaurant.

He began typing.

Welcome to Harmony Valley. Love to debate? Come verbally joust with the ice queen. Want to add some adventure to your yoga? Come commune with nature, clothing optional. For you dabblers in recreational drugs, turn that unpleasant side-effect into a trophy-winning skill.

Chad slumped in his chair and pressed the delete key. That had to be the worst thing he'd ever written. He'd crafted a better column for the Seattle underground.

The week after Dad died.

Coincidence. Tracy was wrong. He wouldn't disprove her claim by reading it now.

Irregardless, Chad needed some fresh air.

Tracy sat in one of two kitchen chairs in her small apartment. She'd set the chair back against a pink stuccoed wall. Her video camera was on a tripod several feet away. Running. Recording Tracy in all her silent awkwardness.

Dinner with Chad had left her torn. The man wreaked havoc on a woman—so pretty to look at, so charming to talk to, so annoying in his beliefs and lack of self-awareness. She'd come home and set up the camera in the hopes of being inspired.

Inspired? No such luck. Doubts clung to words and stuck in her throat like peanut butter on crackers. What did she know about producing videos? She had two years experience writing thirty-second commercials and complimentary digital ads. She had six months experience writing thirty-second news pieces. It wasn't as if she'd made a name for herself at either place.

"This sucks." Her words reverberated in the empty space. She'd have to record a voice over in her closet. It had shag carpet and all those clothes minimized sound bouncing off flat, pink surfaces.

Tracy's fingers curled. She longed for a paint brush and the absence of pink.

Pink was optimistic and pristine and feminine. Not jaded or scarred or solitary.

"I haven't worn. A push-up bra. In nearly two years." How was that for putting on record who she was today? She stared the camera down, feeling feisty. "I haven't worn lipstick. Or blush. Or mascara." All the armor women regularly used. She'd let herself become vulnerable. "No heels. No boots. No dresses." No necklines with a hint of cleavage. No dangly, sparkly earrings meant to catch a man's eye and show him how put-together she was. At least, in that she was honest.

Forget Rose's warning about her single status threatening to be permanent. "I'm...an old maid in the making." She was broken. A female Humpty Dumpty. No man wanted a woman who wasn't sure how to put herself together again.

Something struck the front window. In the summer, moths had flown into the glass when she had the lights on at night. But it was too cold for moths and when something hit the window again, she had to assume. It was a rat.

Tracy shut off the camera and opened the sash. Her windows were original to the house. There were no screens. She stuck her head out, but it didn't take long to spot the rodent below.

"Rapunzel." Chad was bathed in the warm glow of a streetlight one story beneath her, looking like a modern day Prince Charming, if he'd been lost, because Prince Charming wouldn't have stopped by Tracy's castle. "Rapunzel, you cut your hair."

"If…you're looking for nightlife, you won't find any here." She groaned. She even sounded like an old maid.

"What's the matter?" He took a step closer. "Indigestion?"

"Keep your voice down. Mayra might hear you." El Rosal was only a few doors away. "I'm not sick. I'm… I hate that I'm broken and different." Different than she was before the accident. She hadn't meant to say that to him. But she still felt some of the effects of the wine.

Chad considered her for a moment. "You've been working on your video, haven't you?"

"Yes." A word laden with self-loathing. And then suspicion struck. "Did you try writing?"

"Yes." He stuffed that short word with the same disgust she had.

"We suck."

He grinned. "Someone once told me it takes dreck to be inspired."

That someone had been her. "Wise words."

"Back to the dreck, then, in the hopes of being inspired." He took one step and then turned back. "You're a good kind of different, Tracy."

His words wrapped around her like a thick stadium blanket. She stood at her window, watching him until he disappeared around the corner.

She was different. Harmony Valley was different. And different was good.

Tracy turned the video camera back on, sat in her seat in front of that pink wall and began speaking.

"I'm not put-together." Just saying it should

have undercut her confidence. It should have had her running to stop the recording. It didn't. Her voice strengthened. "I'm a woman in pieces. Trying to see how what was me—and what is me—fit together. Most people tell me I'll be okay." Few told her she was okay now.

But Chad had.

CHAPTER TWELVE

CHAD HAD TWO days left before he had to send Marty something. All he had was a crappy first draft. Everything hinged on the wine tasting today. He wanted it to be great wine. Except, the column would be so much better if it was as rotten as the pages he'd written.

Breakfast at the B&B was as abysmal as his mood. Leona offered him a high-fiber bowl of cereal with nonfat milk. The coffee had the same bitterness as Leona's attitude. He'd left without touching anything, stopped to chat with Flynn and Slade, who'd been having coffee on the patio at El Rosal with a man called Duffy, the father of the Poop Monster. Little Gregory had also been at their table, bundled up as if he was going on an expedition to the Himalayas. They'd invited Chad to join them, but he declined. Preferring to see what the bakery had to offer.

The usual crowd was at Martin's, minus the trio of town council ladies. The mayor sat at their table, looking a bit adrift without them. There was no line, and Tracy greeted him with a secret smile.

"Ah," Chad said, reading more into that look than he should be able to given he barely knew her. "You moved past the dreck phase." Jealousy pricked at him, stung, and receded, leaving a gentle feeling of something almost like pride.

Her smile blossomed for the world to see and her fingers skimmed the countertop. There was a different kind of energy about her today. A spark of color—

"You're wearing makeup," Chad blurted, as suavely as any middle schooler. He took a second look, leaning over the counter to see she had on knee-high, low-heeled boots, a feminine, flouncy blue blouse that was anchored by her apron, and skillfully applied makeup. She'd transformed from a pretty small-town girl to a sophisticated big-city woman. "Did you do this for me?" To try to get his attention? He never should have tossed pebbles at her window like Romeo clambering for Juliet to come down. He liked her, but he had goals, and he'd be moving on in a week.

Tracy glowered at him. "I was feeling good.

About myself." She stepped back from the counter and crossed her arms over her chest.

"I just…" He was going to say he missed her approachable prettiness, but caught himself just in time. "I'll have a latte and a breakfast quiche." He set a twenty on the counter and retreated to his usual spot next to Eunice. "Keep the change."

"I'm disappointed in you, Chad." Eunice blinked at him, lowered the fuschia quilt pieces she'd been working on and set her glasses on top of her head. "Women don't need a reason—even if there is a handsome man in town—to dress up."

Chad wasn't going to argue. "How pretty you look today, Eunice." She wore a lime green track suit and neon orange sneakers. The colors nearly made her purplish gray hair look normal.

She tsked. "With lines like that, you must not date much."

Never mind that this had been true most of the past three years. "I'm the Happy Bachelor."

"You're misusing your articles."

For a moment, Chad thought she knew who he was.

Eunice leaned closer and lowered her voice.

"You're *a* happy bachelor. And really, your skills are so rusty with the opposite sex, you're probably *one* unhappy bachelor."

Chad should have accepted Flynn's invitation to breakfast. He should be a loyal El Rosal customer every morning. Why was he making himself suffer with old people?

Flynn poked his head in the front door. "Chad, can we count on your help later?"

"You mean now?" Chad stood, more than ready to escape.

"No. After your wine tasting with Tracy and Christine." Flynn disappeared as quickly as he'd come, not waiting for his agreement.

Chad sank back into his seat.

"You're tasting wine with Tracy?" Eunice leaned Chad's way once more. "Let me give you some better lines to use. My heart always melted when a man told me how pretty my eyes are." She batted her lashes nearly as fast as a hummingbird's wings.

Seize the day.

That was Mildred's motto.

Or at least it had been when she'd been racing. But she was ready to hoist the banner once more.

Agnes held the door Sunday morning so

Mildred could enter Martin's Bakery. She wore a sparkly blue blouse over her black polyester pants and white orthopedic sneakers. Rose and Agnes had helped her pick out her ensemble and apply lipstick—Rose's cranberry surprise. Mildred spotted Phil's familiar gray head and strong nose and wheeled her walker his way.

Seize the day.

She was going to ask Phil out. She stopped next to the checkers table. As luck would have it, Felix had gotten up to use the facilities as she came in. "How are you today, Phil?"

"Worried about Leona." Doom and gloom were Phil's co-pilots.

But she could change all that. She sat down across from him. This was perfect. Only a checkerboard separated them.

Seize the day.

Maybe it wasn't so perfect. Phil might have been frowning.

"How about a match?" It felt as if Rose's lipstick was on her front teeth. She rubbed her teeth clean with one finger.

"Mildred," Agnes scolded in hushed tones.

"Sorry." This was why she didn't wear lipstick.

Seize the day.

Be feminine, like Leona. Be decisive, like Leona. Be confident, like Leona.

"Can you see the board?" Phil asked, not unkindly, but it deflated her confidence.

Mildred stiffened, afraid to look at the board. "Of course."

"Then let's play."

It quickly became obvious that Mildred couldn't sec the board.

"That's my checker," Phil said for the third time.

Mildred apologized. Her smile had wilted and her sparkly blouse itched her collar bone. She didn't dare scratch at it. She barcly dared to try moving a checker. Jessica was making something with chocolate. The warm smell should have comforted, but Mildred would need more than familiar smells to feel better.

"Like this, Mildred." Rose stretchcd an arm between their tables and moved Mildred's piece. "See?"

"I've got this," Mildred said through what were almost certainly lipstick stained teeth.

Seize the stinking day.

Phil sighed and jumped one of her checkers. "You're taking all the fun out of the game."

Mildred bent so far over the table, her nose

nearly touched the board. She moved a piece forward. Hers this time, because Phil said nothing. "I used to play checkers all the time when I was younger." Waiting for a race to start.

"You won the holiday tournament one year," Phil said absently, studying the board.

"You remembered." It came out as a sigh.

Phil puffed his chest out. "I can recite all the checkers winners going back forty years."

"Please don't," said Rose.

"Quit eavesdropping." Tracy bussed Chad's dirty dishes. No sneakers today. Tracy wore hard-soled boots that struck the floor confidently and called out where she was in the dining room. "Mildred's...love life is none of your business."

At Tracy's words, Phil stood on unsteady legs. "I...uh...have an appointment." He quickly righted himself and left the bakery.

"Oh, bother." Mildred scratched her collarbone, unable to harbor any ill will toward Tracy since Phil was...well, Phil. "He didn't even finish the game."

"I'm sorry," Tracy said. "That was on me, much as I'd like to blame Chad."

"For the record," Chad said in a loud voice.

"Tracy looks great today. Mildred looks great today. In fact, all the ladies look great today."

"I knew you were coachable," Eunice said to Chad.

"Phil's loss is my gain." Felix sat down across from her. There was a smile in his voice. He set a small plate of what looked like chocolate cookies to the side of the board. In the table's share zone.

Mildred couldn't believe it.

There was still a day to be seized.

AROUND TEN THIRTY, Tracy showed up at Chad's table. "Let's go taste wine. I have a video to make." She marched out the door.

"Is it bad to hope the wine is horrible?" Chad couldn't resist teasing Tracy when he caught up to her. Otherwise, he might spend too much time thinking about how pretty she looked.

"The wine is fabulous." Tracy led him to the bridge where he'd found her singing the alphabet song the day before. "You're just try-ing to annoy me."

He was. He liked it when she argued with him. Besides, his public apology for assum-ing he was the reason she'd upped her appearance hadn't been accepted. "Do you want to tell me about your video?"

"You won't like it." So certain.

Chad smiled, wanting some of her confidence. "Try me."

Like most creative types, she couldn't resist the chance to share. "It's me...trying to figure out me."

Chad's smile faded. "You're admitting your weakness? In an interview assignment?"

"No." Her hands danced passionately through the air. "I'm showing where I am. In life. Creatively. Verbally."

"I'm not sure that's a good idea."

"I. Don't. Care." And she didn't. She was smiling broadly, staring at the pavement beneath her feet.

The emptiness Chad had felt after his father died returned. Oh, not as vast, not as deep, but it was there, nonetheless. Tracy, a woman he'd only met a few days ago, didn't care about Chad's opinion. And yet, he was struck by the desire for her to care.

"I...won't be defined by aphasia. I...will find a creative outlet."

Had he felt Tracy was adrift? He couldn't imagine her so anymore.

The dappled sunlight through the trees.

The gentle gurgle of the river. The confidence of the woman next to him. He wanted to capture the moment.

"Stop," he said in the middle of the bridge.

She turned and glowered at him. "I'm not singing for you."

"I wasn't asking." But he liked how she understood his humor, because he might have. He guided her back against the railing where he'd found her singing, facing upstream. "I need a picture for my column. Something that promises beautiful women can be found here. It's mostly a lie, of course." His reasoning was a lie. She was beautiful.

"Beautiful women fill this town." She crossed her arms, looking as if she wanted to push him off the bridge. "Mildred…Eunice…"

"It's the Happy Bachelor column, not some self-help magazine acknowledging the beauty everyone has within. Think shallow."

She made a derogatory sound.

"Words," he chided. "You're filtering your words." He'd read somewhere that was good for aphasia patients. "Spit out what you're feeling."

"You…are still looking for irony." She turned her back on him. Her blond hair lifted in the brisk breeze. "You don't believe...in the magic in this place."

"That's a nice, sappy sentiment. Give me the reality and bustle and lifestyle of the city any day."

Tracy glanced at him over her shoulder. "Is...there anything you like about this town?"

He snapped her picture. "I like Martin's Bakery and El Rosal, minus the colors. I like some of the old geezers, too." Especially the ones that didn't seem about to expire. "And I like..." *Tracy*. The image of having her arms around him returned. He almost stepped forward and held her. But she'd only see that as a come-on. "Come on." He walked toward the other side of the bridge. "I bet you're a wine connoisseur, what with your brother being part-owner of the vineyard."

On this side of the river there were no sidewalks. Fields of corn bordered neat rows of vineyards. Squirrels scampered with enthusiasm. Tracy lagged behind, booted feet dragging.

"How far away is the winery?"

"About a mile and a half."

"Do your feet hurt? We could have driven." He turned to see her lips pressed firmly together. She wasn't dragging her feet because they hurt. "Ah. So it's not just being a passenger in a car that bothers you. It's driving, too?" He hadn't seen a car parked near the bakery last night, not in the front or the back. He wondered if she even owned a vehicle.

"I liked driving *your* car," she said, nose in the air.

He waited for her to reach him. "Does that job you want require driving? Or is it in the city?"

"It requires driving." Her voice was filled with weary resignation. "I'm a long shot anyway."

"Meaning you won't worry about driving until you think you'll get the job?"

"Correct."

A white truck that hadn't seen better years in decades turned onto the road ahead from a graveled drive. It pulled up next to them and the driver cranked the window down. "How's it going, Sunshine?"

"Good," Tracy said. "Dad... *Ben*... This is the travel writer. Chad."

The travel writer. She'd told her father about him.

Her father had the tan face of one who worked outdoors and the wrinkles earned by middle age. His blond hair was a shadow of Tracy's brilliant gold.

Ben gave Chad a thorough inspection. By the hard look in his eyes, what she'd said about Chad hadn't been flattering. "You're older than I expected."

Ouch.

"Dad," Tracy said in the same tone a teenager used to reply to her father when he told her to behave and be home by curfew.

"He looks like he's bothering you." Ben angled his jaw to the side. "Is he bothering you?"

Tracy's hands came up as if to ward her father away. "Nothing I can't handle."

"My little girl was still in pigtails when you were in college." Ben's words sounded like a warning. "Watch yourself, Chad."

Yep, definitely a threat.

"As if." Tracy laughed as her father drove off, tossing those blond locks in the breeze.

"Why did you laugh?"

"Come on." She set out at a clip that left him behind. "You and me? I'm not into older guys. I…have no patience for midlife crises. Or…falling into a relationship with a man… who's still grieving for his father."

"I'm not midlifing or grieving." According

to her, he'd be writing the brilliant columns his readers had come to expect if he was. "The person who was my dad left his body six months before his body gave out. And I'm not much older than you are." Maybe eight or nine years.

"The car says differently."

"The car says nothing," he snapped, suddenly empty of patience.

"When did you buy it?"

"Months ago." When the doctors told him there wasn't much left of his dad and that his wishes were to be on life support regardless. Chad's steps slowed. Midlife? It couldn't be.

Tracy stopped and turned, waiting for him to say more.

"I'm an only child and taking care of Dad through his battle with cancer was demanding." Standing there on that country road, he felt older than his thirty-five years. "I lived with him after Mom died. Three years. The car was just something I needed to breathe." A breath of youthful vigor in a life focused on old age. "When not even machines could keep him alive anymore, that car was my outlet."

"I'm sorry." Tracy pulled him into a fierce hug. "I don't like you half the time, but losing a parent is awful. My mom died when I

was eleven. It was so unexpected it took years
for me to get through it. A friendly hug always helped."

Chad and his brain were momentarily on
overload. No one had hugged him after Dad
died. He didn't have huggy friends and Dad
hadn't wanted a funeral or memorial service.

Tracy took a half step back, probably intending to release him, but he held on. Not
because he was a letch, or because she felt
soft and warm in his arms, but because she
was speaking so fluently without passion or
anger. "Did all those words come out of you?
Without wine or hesitation?"

She angled herself sideways, so that
her shoulders were under his arm, but she
wouldn't meet his gaze. "It's a proximity
thing."

"You can talk easier when someone hugs
you?"

"Just…um…you and my dad." She bit her
bottom lip, which did nothing to stop the blush
blooming on her cheeks. "Unfortunately…
About the you part."

Chad drew back to get a better look at her,
brushing the hair from her forehead, letting
his fingers linger over her scar. He was dis-
covering more depths to her by the hour. He

wanted to kiss Tracy, her and all her surprises. "I'm honored."

"I'm annoyed." She shrugged, but not hard enough to dislodge his arm. "I can't go through life hugging people to talk without stumbling. Just like I can't drink wine all the time."

"You must feel safe when you hug me." His male ego liked that.

"I feel…" She disengaged herself and took a few steps back. "Like I should tell you. That your car. Is a midlife crisis. And a Band-Aid for your grief." She waved a hand. "Don't argue."

This time, he didn't.

CHAPTER THIRTEEN

TRACY WANTED TO kiss Chad.

And not with a peck on the cheek.

It was bad enough she'd wrapped him in a hug after he'd told her about his dad. But then to stand there and hold on to those sturdy shoulders while they talked? To allow him to drape his arm across her shoulders and think about how nice it was? How nice *he* was? That was stupid. Heart-risking stupid.

Maybe she should take relationship pointers from Mildred. The old woman had made a date with Felix for brunch tomorrow.

I'm not ready to date.

But a kiss would be nice. She missed kissing. But even more, she missed sitting and talking to a man she liked with the quick back and forth banter of adrenaline-fueled attraction. Despite that, she walked without talking the rest of the way to the winery.

"Hey, guys." Christine waited for them on

the winery porch. The chickens were pecking the ground at the bottom of the steps.

Henrietta was the smallest of the flock. She cocked her head at Chad and then strutted over to circle his feet like a cat demanding attention. He tried to be manly while acknowledging the little hen with a pat on her back, but he came across as sweet.

They entered the warmth of the winery. It was elegant in a simple way that fit the farmhouse they'd converted into a small tasting room and upstairs offices. Dark wood, intimate tables for two, dark granite countertops and wine bottles stored in the racks on the wall. Empty wineglasses were set on the bar.

"I don't need to taste wine," Tracy said. Since her brother was one-third owner, she'd had some of Christine's wine already. It was really good. And they were charging a fortune per bottle.

"No one likes to drink alone." Chad nudged her shoulder as if he had every right to, bringing to mind the feel of his arms around her and the wonder about kisses. "Besides, wine smooths the road for good conversation."

"I agree." Christine's smile was wide and welcoming. "We have two blends to taste today. A white and a red." She poured a half glass of white wine and waited for Chad and Tracy to take a sip. "This is a young wine made from grapes harvested last year."

"Crisp," Chad said. "Pear and maybe a hint of brown spice."

"Cinnamon," Christine said happily.

Tracy was feeling out of her league. The wine tasted like wine. Like the kind of wine she could easily drink a glass or two of. "Tastes good." She was afraid she sounded stupidly chipper. Was this how it would be if she landed that job with Three Filmers? Other employees talking up a storm and Tracy waiting for an opening to add a useless word or two?

Chad sat tall on the barstool as if he owned the place. "As long as you enjoy the wine, who needs to list all the nuances?"

He did. Clearly, he did. Tracy gulped what was left of her wine. The embarrassment of a meddling father and her own overly friendly nature—hugging relative strangers?—eased when her glass was empty.

"And the red blend." Christine filled each of the larger wineglasses halfway.

Chad swirled his glass. Tracy was afraid to follow his lead for fear she'd spill. Everything about wine intimidated her, the same as public speaking now intimidated her.

"It's quite round." Chad swirled the glass again and watched the wine drip slowly down the side. "And it has good legs."

Now he was speaking French.

Liquid, people. It's just liquid.

They both looked at her expectantly.

"Tastes good," Tracy said, on cue.

Christine gave Chad a folio with more information on the wine. And then she gave him a red-and-blue tie-dyed T-shirt with the black Harmony Valley Vineyards logo on it—a running horse on a weathervane. Mayor Larry had made the shirts.

"And one for you." Christine pressed the soft cotton into Tracy's hands.

"I have one already." From Will.

"But I didn't give you one." Christine's smile demanded she accept. "And if I'm really nice to you, you'll volunteer for harvest if I'm short-handed." She'd been short-handed two years running.

Christine led them out to the huge barn and began using more foreign terms. "Free run juice... Punch the lees... Ambient yeast."

Tracy drifted over to the big barn doors where she could listen, but not have to engage in conversation. Henrietta came closer and pecked the ground at her feet.

"Let's hop in the truck and head over to the wine cellar." Christine produced a set of keys from her pocket.

She might just as well have waved a gun since Tracy's stomach dropped. She'd have to make an excuse for not going with them. Chad would know she was a coward. It wasn't as if she could ask Christine if she could drive her truck back to town.

"Why don't we walk?" Chad asked without meeting Tracy's gaze. "I had a big breakfast. I could use the extra steps."

That was nice. He was nice.

But he wasn't honest. With others or himself.

Didn't make her want to kiss him any less. *More's the pity.*

"I CAN'T BELIEVE you lost my recipe for Horseradish-Doodles." Eunice reached into her purse for a sheet of purple lined notebook paper. "So I wrote it out for you again."

"Oh," Jess said, shifting Gregory in her arms. As in: *Oh, no.*

Tracy felt sorry for Jessica, who might just have lost Eunice's recipe on purpose.

But she was also feeling sorry for herself, having suffered through Christine and Chad tossing about their wine lingo as if they belonged to a club she'd been banned from. She might have been down in the dumps about it if it hadn't distracted her from wanting to get cozy with Chad.

Demoralized after the wine tasting, she'd stayed downstairs with Eunice and Jess, instead of returning to her apartment and shooting more video. She sat on a stool at the island with her laptop open to Jessica's blog. The master baker had made some story notes on different recipes and given them to Tracy, but something didn't feel right. Tracy was missing an element to make the stories and the recipes come together.

Jessica reluctantly took possession of Eunice's recipe. "Tell me again. Why did your mother create this recipe?"

"Daddy was on a horseradish kick. He wanted it in everything." Eunice held out her hands, palms up to Gregory. He fell into them and she carried him to the alcove and its rocking chair. "So, Mama gave it to him in everything—on chicken, in his clam chowder and in these sugar cookies. She didn't experiment in small batches. She went whole hog and expected Daddy to fall in line."

"I love Mama." Tracy sighed. Mama would have known how to handle Chad and what to put in a video that said, *"Hire me or you'll be sorry."*

"Why was your dad on a horseradish kick?" Jess wasn't as enamored of Mama's story. Or maybe reading the ingredients had depressed her.

"I think the doctor recommended it for his lungs," Eunice said absently.

"Did he eat the cookies?" Tracy wondered.

That brought Eunice back to them. She tapped the counter for emphasis. "He ate a dozen with a big glass of water."

"I'm curious as to how your mother presented the cookies." Jess gazed up at the cake decorating photograph. "I can't see putting them in the case and labeling them as Horseradish-Doodles. They won't sell. What did she tell your father?"

"Nothing. Daddy ate everything Mama ever set in front of him." Eunice was fiercely proud of her parents.

"What about you, Eunice?" Tracy drummed her fingers over the keyboard without pressing any keys. "Did you eat any Horseradish-Doodles?"

"Oh, I don't like horseradish," Eunice said, unperturbed that this poked a hole in the appeal of her recipe. "I like wasabi. I've always heard that if you like one, you don't like the other."

Was she as turned off by Horseradish-Doodles as Jess and Tracy were? And if so, who could blame her?

"I'm not sure anyone who reads the blog will be interested in making them," Jessica said in a gentle voice. "I know I'm not."

"Oh." The disappointment in Eunice's voice tugged at Tracy's heart strings.

"It's got elements of a good story," Tracy said just as gently as Jess.

"Well, I left out the part where we harvested the horseradish." Eunice looked a little sheepish. "We went up to Parish Hill at night when it was a full moon. It's not trespassing if you go at night, Mama used to say." Eunice's sheepish expression turned downright guilty. "Anyway, Mama fell down the bank and landed in a patch of poison oak. She was itching for a week. She'd do anything for Daddy."

Including trespass and steal. Maybe there was something to the story after all.

"I want people to use the recipes I post." Jess wrinkled her brow.

"Can you change it somehow?" Tracy asked. "Maybe take out the horseradish?"

"Oh, don't do that," Eunice said.

Jess was still lost in thought. "Maybe… I could make sweet horseradish biscuits using Mama's recipe as a base?"

"That's…an interesting angle to a recipe post." Tracy felt a thrum of excitement, despite stumbling over words. It was the same adrenaline rush she'd had last night while filming, the same thrill she'd experienced when she'd helped create advertising and found the perfect slant for a client. "It's the flipside, like my Dad's vinyl records from the 1970s."

"You've lost me," Jess said.

"Me, too," Eunice seconded.

"What if…you post the original recipe along with the story behind it. And…then you click to the modern version of the recipe." The story needed to have heart. Not that a little humor wouldn't help, as long as it wasn't the cutting style of Chad's.

"So Horseradish-Doodles to Sweet Horseradish Biscuits?" With a smile, Jess reached for the flour canister.

Eunice perked up. "Do you want me to go up Parish Hill and pick some fresh horse-radish?"

"No!" Jess and Tracy chorused. The last thing they needed was Eunice tumbling down a bank into poison oak.

"I'll use horseradish extract," Jess said firmly. "At least while I experiment."

The bakery settled into the quiet noises of Tracy's fingers tapping the keyboard, Jessica's measuring and hand mixing and Eunice's humming to Gregory.

"Do you think people will like my story?" Eunice sounded uncertain, which was most un-Eunice-like.

"It makes me smile. And it's unique." But fun and unique hadn't swayed Chad when Tracy introduced him to the town's way of exhibiting gurning.

"I like sweet stories." Jessica folded the in-gredients together. "Lillian Harrington had a darling story behind her pancake recipe. She made pancakes for the entire town."

"She made so many, we ran out of syrup." Eunice was rocking in big swoops. Her sneak-ers landed on the hardwood with a slap as she came down. "Maybe we'll run out of horse-radish."

A DOG GROWLED a warning that Flynn and Duffy ignored.

They had that luxury. They weren't under Nina Valpizzi's kitchen sink, on their backs, trying to fit a wrench around a pipe connector in a position where the wrench wouldn't fit. All to find Nina's wedding ring, which she swore had fallen down the drain.

Chad might have chosen his afternoon activities poorly. His time would be better spent trying to polish some life into his column. Now that he knew the wine was excellent, he had a better idea of how to slant the piece. Or he could have been arguing with Tracy. Or maybe not arguing.

Chad smiled.

The growling increased in volume. Two toothbrush-sized paws took up residence on Chad's stomach. Jean's fluffy white Chihuahua continued to disapprove of Chad's presence.

"Hey, guys." Chad kept his voice calm. "The dog." The one that might bite his chin or nose.

"Don't look Farkle in the eye." Duffy gave a wry chuckle, the kind that said he thought Chad was as clueless about dogs as he was about wrenches. "Small dogs consider that a challenge."

"I thought all dogs considered that a challenge." Flynn scuffed the toe of his boot on a bubble in the linoleum.

Chad lost the wrench's grip on the pipe once more, banging his elbows against the cabinetry and making Farkle growl louder. "I'm not even looking at the dog." The sides of the narrow opening cut into his ribs. Chad shushed Farkle and tried again with the wrench.

He'd told Flynn he had no plumbing skills. Flynn's response? Everyone needs plumbing skills and there's no time like the present to learn. Chad suspected Flynn just didn't want to crawl under Nina's sink, which smelled of moth balls and damp.

"Are you sure there isn't a better wrench for this job?" Chad had heard the right tool made all the difference.

"There's definitely a better wrench for tight spaces." Flynn sounded far too pleased with himself.

"Basin wrench," Duffy chimed in helpfully.

"Give it to me." Chad extended his hand,

causing Farkle to jump back to the scuffed, brick-patterned linoleum.

"We don't have a basin wrench."

Chad hoped that was embarrassment in Flynn's voice.

He positioned the wrench and tightened his hold.

The dog crawled on Chad's stomach without missing a growly beat.

Duffy knelt down and picked up Farkle, who immediately quieted. "Have you ever had a dog, Chad?"

"No." They'd been an indoor-cat household.

"Dogs sense fear." Duffy stood, taking the dog with him.

Chad was about ready to toss in the towel when he gave the pipe connector one last yank. Amazingly, it moved. He loosened the second connector until he could swing the bottom elbow outward. Uncapped, the upper pipe spit gunk everywhere, including Chad's face.

Desperate to wipe the slime from his body, Chad did an army crawl on his back until his shoulders were clear of the cabinetry. Or so he thought. He sat up and hit his temple on the upper cabinet frame, hard enough to see stars. He fell back in the cabinet as the world became foggy.

Someone grabbed hold of his ankles and yanked him out.

"Are you okay?" Duffy's voice.

Farkle growled near Chad's ear, which didn't help the ringing.

"Is there blood?" Flynn's voice.

The room came into focus. The dark browns and reds of the 1970s. The velvet wallpaper with a forest scene on the wall by the kitchen table.

"No blood, but there's a bruise." Duffy got a paper towel, filled it with a couple of ice cubes and handed it to Chad. "Hey, Nina. We need a plastic bag."

Chad's forehead stung and throbbed, making Chad reject the idea of any more DIY projects in Harmony Valley. "I'm not cut out to be a handyman."

"Truer words were never spoken." Duffy bent to peer into his face. "How many fingers am I holding up?"

"None."

Flynn made short work of loosening the pipes and removing them from the cabinet. He stuffed a paper towel in the pipe elbow with a screwdriver, forcing the gunk out the other end and onto a newspaper. The smell almost made Chad gag.

"Go easy on him, Duffy," Flynn said. "We've all had our share of fix-it mishaps."

"Yeah, when I was twelve." Duffy was what Chad had always thought of as a man's man. He'd probably come out of the womb with a wrench and a nail gun.

"Do you see the ring?" Chad couldn't.

Flynn flattened the gunk some more with the screwdriver. "It's not here." He looked into the pipe.

"Boys, you won't believe what I just found." Nina entered the kitchen in a loose black top, hot pink leggings and white heels that looked impossible to walk in. She held up her hand and fanned her fingers. "My ring! It was on the bedside table the entire time."

Farkle pranced over to her mistress and danced on her hind legs.

"Put it back together, boys," Duffy said.

"At least we cleared the drain," Flynn said.

If Chad hadn't already hit his head, he might have given himself a serious head-thunk. As it was, he held his tongue until they were outside by Duffy's gray truck. "Please tell me this doesn't happen often."

"Which part?" Flynn hefted the large tool

box into Duffy's truck bed. "The lost ring? The skanky clogged drain? Or the overly affectionate dog?"

"It all happens. That's part of living here." Duffy opened the door to the truck. A shaggy golden dog not much bigger than Farkle wiggled excitedly on the passenger seat, demanding attention. And just like that, Duffy's man's-man image was deflated. "Points to you for not walking out on us. That shows character." His grin was pure joy, the spitting image of Gregory's. It made Chad forget he'd been the butt of most of Duffy's jokes. It made Chad envious. "And now, since I said that, I bet Flynn will go into his speech."

"Great segue, Duffy." Flynn slapped Chad heartily on the back. "You know, you can be a travel writer and live anywhere you choose."

Chad clenched the ice pack with his hammer-flattened finger, because the pain had to make this nightmare go away. "Are you asking me to move to Harmony Valley?" With its plethora of old people.

And Tracy.

"I am if you're interested."

He wasn't, except for the Tracy part. He smelled of Nina's drain. He was banged up and his head throbbed. If he moved here, they'd expect him to tag along on these handyman expeditions. He wasn't cut out for that. He tried to make light of Flynn's offer. "You just want me for my skills with a hammer."

"You have a long way to go for that to be a true statement." Duffy lifted his froufrou dog out of the truck and into his arms. "I heard about the chicken coop."

"Maybe I'm a wrench man." Chad felt the need to defend his handyman skills, despite not having many. "I got that pipe fitting off, didn't I? And without the special wrench."

Duffy stared at Chad and didn't say a word.

Duffy's dog stared at Chad and didn't growl.

Flynn stared at Chad, but he was smiling.

Chad scratched his head. "Yeah…well…"

"Back to the invitation." Flynn settled his black baseball cap more firmly on his head. "I promised my grandfather we'd do something to bring this town back to life. We'd love to have you as a resident." He began ticking things off on his fingers. "We have no crime to speak of. A couple of gourmet restaurants. A friendly bar."

"No commute traffic," Duffy added. "No noisy neighbors."

"Well, the old guard can be nosey," Flynn allowed.

"And the new guard can be pushy." Chad couldn't let that go. He had a flattened finger and a lump on his head because of them.

"Wc appreciate you giving back to the community." Flynn was a good statesman, perhaps better than the mayor. "We're moving on to Mildred's dripping faucet if you want to come along."

"And learn something," Duffy said.

"I've learned enough for today, thanks." He needed some quality time alone with his ice pack.

CHAPTER FOURTEEN

MONDAY MORNING, LEONA set Chad's breakfast in front of him at 8:05. "You aren't taking care of yourself, Mr. Healy. I can see that by the look on your face."

Chad blamed the mattress. He scowled at the small plate and the trio of small powdered donuts—the kind that came from a box. He tilted his head, but the donuts were still as small as silver dollars. Maybe he'd hit his noggin too hard yesterday. That would explain his inability to write last night. He had one more day to send Marty something that would knock his socks off. "What is this?"

"Martin's is closed today." Leona stood with her hands clasped piously. Too bad her expression was that of a serial killer gazing down on her naïve and unsuspecting prey. "I thought you had a sweet tooth."

He wasn't naïve or unsuspecting. He was angry. "Bacon, Leona. I like bacon." He pushed the plate away.

"That's bad for your heart." She whisked his plate away, along with the mug of coffee. "El Rosal serves breakfast with bacon."

He stood so fast his head spun. "This isn't a bed & breakfast." He clung to the table for balance. "This is a bed, no breakfast."

He headed for El Rosal, muttering the entire way about sadistic bed & breakfast owners.

Once more, the restaurant was packed, and not just with overwhelming color.

"Does everyone have a ride who needs a ride?" Mayor Larry was saying as Chad came in. He glanced Chad's way, and then did a horrified double take, pointing to Chad's forehead.

Chad waved his concern off. The large purple lump on his forehead made it look as if he had a third eye, but he wasn't dead.

Felix, the big, burly man who always seemed to have cat hair on his shirt, nodded a greeting to Chad, unable to pull his gaze from Chad's third eye. "You here for the cemetery run?"

It wasn't a polite query. It was a question of disbelief.

"No. I'm here for the bacon." He could smell it and all its greasy goodness.

The Asian man they called Takata sat in his walker seat and rolled his dark eyes. "It's not a race. We're doing a remembrance in the cemetery today." He gave Chad a piercing look that never strayed from his two actual eyes. "Are you afraid of ghosts?"

"No." He was afraid anyone who stayed at the Lambridge B&B would starve.

Tracy walked by on her way out with her dad.

Chad caught her arm. "Nobody told me about this…event."

"You didn't tell him?" The mayor moved closer.

Tracy slipped from Chad's hold, only to take his face in her hands, turning it back and forth. "What happened to you?"

"I introduced myself to Nina Valpizzi's sink." He hadn't gone out to dinner last night because of the way he looked. This morning he didn't appear much better, but he was starving.

Behind Tracy, her father chuckled.

"The cemetery run?" Chad said through gritted teeth. "Is it something my readers would enjoy?"

"No. It's private." Tracy hesitated and then said, "We go to remember our loved ones."

"To the cemetery? The entire town?" Chad took in the standing room only crowd.

"Anyone who's got someone buried there." Tracy's voice was softer than silk, reminding Chad that her mother had died when she was just a kid. At least he'd had his mother most of his adult life.

"We need to go," her father said gruffly. "We're holding up the rest."

With one last glance at Chad's headlight bump, Tracy left.

Ben gave Chad one of those intimidating stares he seemed so fond of. "I should thank you for helping Tracy speak easier." Ben tapped his own forehead and grinned. "But I won't...old man."

Chad was beginning to think he'd been sent to Harmony Valley by a higher power to be taken down a peg or two.

More people funneled past Chad with walkers, canes and boxes of tissue.

Chad couldn't deny he was curious, but he was fairly certain a visit to the cemetery wouldn't be any fun. Besides, with everyone gone, he'd have all that bacon to himself.

"Did Tracy leave you?" the mayor asked. Without waiting for an answer, he shooed Chad out the door. "You can ride with me."

Chad got into the passenger seat of Mayor Larry's Volkswagen bus. It was vintage mint green with a white top and an engine that went put-put.

"I thought you didn't drive. Something about your back…" Chad hid a smile. If the mayor took his yoga seriously, that wiry body was strong and flexible.

"I only drive on special occasions." He sent the bus lurching forward, lacking the seamless shifting skills Tracy had.

The line of cars headed to the cemetery moved as slowly as a funeral procession.

"I'll drop you at the front of the cemetery so you can experience the entire process." Larry made a left turn beneath the arching cemetery gates. "It's hard to bury someone. Harder still to visit them regularly. Once a year, we lend each other support and listen to each others' remembrances."

Chad hadn't been to his father's grave since his death. Hadn't checked to make sure the headstone was engraved and installed properly. Hadn't been able to face the symbol of the man who'd cast him aside.

"My wife is all the way in the back." Larry pulled to the curb. "You can catch up to Tracy and Ben over there."

Ben and Tracy stood near a cluster of head-stones. Ben's arm was across Tracy's shoulders.

Chad couldn't remember his parents keeping him that close as an adult. What little physical affection his parents had given him as a child had disappeared when he reached puberty. Watching the Jacksons now, Chad felt the hollowness he'd managed to lose since the day he'd been fired.

Cars were parking along every curb. Larry pulled away with his put-put engine and the smell of burnt oil. Tracy glanced up and frowned. Ben didn't look up at all. He walked with heavy steps to a nearby bench and sat down.

Chad felt like an intruder. He'd much rather be eating bacon. But he was here and there was a story. Besides, Tracy looked in need of a strong shoulder to lean on.

Tracy had a tissue clutched in one hand. When he reached her, she gestured toward a headstone. "This is my mom. She never took a handout. Never took no for an answer. And she gave the best hugs." She rolled the tissue around her finger. "And…these are my grand-parents—the Jacksons. They were farmers here, like my dad. Grandma was a great card player. Grandpa…knew he always had to lose to her. That way…she'd believe she was the best card player in town."

"Smart man." Chad resisted the urge to put an arm around her in front of Ben. The last thing a cemetery needed was an argument. "I hope Grandma passed along some recipes for your blog."

"Angel food cake with pistachio icing." There was something touching about Tracy retelling her memories.

Chad felt bereft of love and memories. He knew he'd had good times with his mother over the years, and the rarer moments of connection with his father. But he had no time to dwell on them as Ben began speaking.

"These are my grandparents." Ben's voice sounded like a preacher reciting an oft-read eulogy, recycled for the next comer. His words were rote, meant to keep the emotion at bay. "When I was a boy, we farmed with a team of horses and a plow." He stood and held a hand out to Tracy.

"It's tradition to walk to the next visitor and listen to their stories," Tracy said softly.

Chad should have excused himself. He understood why no one in town had told him about this. These losses, these stories—they were intimate. Instead of leaving, he followed the Jacksons to the next group.

Ben put a hand on a headstone, leaning heavily on it as he nodded to Nina Valpizzi. "Your mother made me a green bean casserole for Thanksgiving a few months after my wife died. She helped me keep up the pretense that everything was normal."

"Oh, Ben." Nina's smile for help with her sink hadn't been as thankful as it was today. "Your sweet wife made me a pine wreath to hang on the door when my son was born. She decorated it with plastic blue baby buggies. I still have it in a box in the attic."

Ben smiled softly. Tracy sniffed, and Chad took her hand.

Nina came to Chad, reached for his face, drew it down and kissed a spot to the side of his bruise. "You were kind to a panicked old woman and you were hurt." She patted his cheek. "My mother would have said you were a keeper." She glanced down at Chad's hand clasped around Tracy's and nodded.

Ben's blustery protectiveness had been left outside the cemetery gates. He said nothing. And they all moved to the next group.

And so it went. Small favors were mentioned. Tiny acts of kindness, generosity and honorable acts. The crowd built as they walked to the rear of the cemetery. Chad wondered if his father was buried here if anyone would say anything nice about him. He'd been a tough boss and a tougher parent.

Finally, the session ended with lengthy remembrances of Flynn's grandfather, who had been instrumental in starting the tradition. There were more tears. More hugs. And surprisingly, more laughter as cars were brought around.

"I'm going to walk back, Dad." Tracy gave Ben the truck keys.

"I'll drive the travel writer to town." Ben had probably given kinder looks to crows who snacked on his crop of corn.

"I'll walk." Chad gave him the smile he used for writers who were late with their columns. "With Tracy."

Ben flashed a glance Tracy's way.

"He's harmless," she said. "He hammers his fingers and bangs his head on sinks."

"True." But Ben glared at Chad one more time before he walked away.

Chad wasn't harmless. But he was feeling like a shallow man who didn't honor his parents like these people did. He wanted to crack a joke to lighten the mood—a priest, a rabbi

and a travel writer walk into a cemetery...
He wanted to write a satirical piece on the re-
verse correlation between headstone size and
the number of graveside visitors. But mostly,
he wanted someone to talk about his father as
kindly as others had talked about Harmony
Valley residents. And he wondered...would
someone talk about him with fondness when
he passed away? Maybe only his father's assistant, Doreen.

Cars slowly filled with people and drove
away. Chad and Tracy walked through the
empty graveyard in the chill autumn sunlight
in silence for several minutes.

"I...don't remember much about my
mother's funeral." Her voice was a fragile
thread. Her grip on his hand strong. "I...
know people spoke, but...it's what they tell
me here that I remember."

"My dad didn't want a funeral or memorial
service." At the time, Chad had been grateful.
His mother's service had been difficult, filled
with speakers who were younger work col-
leagues rather than friends or family—most
of her friends had already passed on or were
too frail to travel.

Tracy draped his arm over her shoulders.
At first, he thought it was because she wanted

to be close to him. And then he realized she wanted to talk.

"According to Agnes," Tracy began. "Funerals are for those left behind. But they happen too soon." She spoke in nearly a whisper as if they were in a crowd and she only wanted Chad to hear. "I couldn't have stood up and talked about Mom then. I couldn't have told my dad and brother how much she meant to me." She gripped his hand at her shoulder as if she needed to keep from slipping too deeply into memory. "There was this one time she took me grocery shopping. I must have been five or six. She wanted me to get in the car, but I wouldn't. I'd stolen a sucker and I suddenly knew I couldn't leave without returning it, but I didn't know how." She swallowed, but she couldn't swallow back the raw emotion, the grief and regret. "I started crying. Mom could have spanked me and put me in the car, but she knew there was something wrong. She knew..." Tracy pressed her lips together and blinked rapidly. "She hugged me. I gave her the sucker and confessed. She told me she admired my honesty. She told me I had to be brave and honest with the store clerk. She hugged me and told me good people make mistakes." Tracy looked at him with tear-filled eyes. "All I want is to feel her hug me again."

Chad drew her closer.

"This is a difficult day in so many ways." She put a few inches between them as if suddenly aware they were too close.

He felt as if she was pulling away from who he was on the internet: Chad Healy Bostwick. When she should have been trusting of Chad Healy's embrace, of his ability to give and take in conversation like friends often did. He gathered her close once more and did something he rarely did. He spoke about his father. "My dad was...firm."

"Did he ground you for breaking curfew? Or using the credit card he gave you only for emergencies?" She smiled up at him, clearly pleased that he was sharing as so many people had shared today.

"Not anything that simple." Chad should have gone into town with Ben. It would have been easier than this. But he didn't regret staying. Tracy needed company. "Dad cancelled Christmas once." And that was all he planned to say.

"That's extreme." The smile and teasing note in her voice disappeared. She slipped her arm around his waist, almost as if she was... worried about him.

It had been so long since he'd had anyone worried about him, that he took a moment to let the warmth of it sink into his chest. That warmth loosened the hold he had on the past.

"It was after my mother divorced him the second time." Yes, he'd had an unorthodox upbringing on many levels. "I went to spend the holiday with Dad. Mom had given me my presents beforehand and I happened to gripe about getting up early for church service on Christmas Day. I'd planned on playing my video games all night long." That rebellious statement hadn't sat well. "Dad took everything away—the video game, the flip phone she'd bought me. And the funny thing was, neither one of us went to the service."

"I can see reading that in a column in the *Bostwick Lampoon*."

"His life was full of hypocrisies. It's probably why the *Lampoon* was so successful. Dad recognized irony when he saw it." Chad saw no irony today.

"I haven't read any of his columns. What section did he write for?"

"The news of the day." Front and center. His dad's columns took on issues with meaning. "He wrote about a third-world dictator who touted a simple life but owned a fleet of luxury cars." That had won Dad many awards. "He wrote about a dog breeder who cropped tails and stitched ears, like a canine plastic surgeon in search of physical perfection."

"You loved him." She patted his chest over his heart. "I can hear it in your voice."

"He was my father," he said simply. His dad had made his life difficult—demanding perfection even when perfection wasn't possible. "He taught me about business and writing." And that postmortem… It'd taught him to pick himself up after a setback.

She allowed his words to settle and him to breathe. She was a caring, compassionate woman. He felt caring and compassionate just holding her.

"What would he have written about in Harmony Valley?" she asked.

That was easy. "Dad would have liked what happened today. But he would have returned next year to see if the recollections of people had changed and were still sincere."

"He wasn't very trusting of his fellow man."

"He trusted them to stretch the truth and lie, even to themselves."

"A glass-half-empty approach." They'd reached the cemetery gate. She turned to face him. "And your glass?"

"I'm trying for half full." He was surprised to realize he meant it. He touched his forehead. "It hasn't been working out so well for me."

"It will." She kissed him.

KISSING CHAD WAS NICE. Safe.

Nothing like his smile promised—light-hearted and teasing—and nothing like his articles promised—a complex activity with depths that might make a woman nervous.

It was just… There was no zing.

So disappointing.

Tracy began to pull back, forming an apology in her head. She hadn't been thinking when she'd wrapped her arms around him, at least not thinking any more than that she wanted to embrace half-full-of-optimism Chad. The lips part? Well, that just kind of happened.

But then Chad moved. Suddenly closer.

His arms. Tight around her.

His breath. Mingled with hers.

Tracy's heart pounded out signals as foreign to her as Morse code. Her legs were threatening to melt like butter. And her brain seemed to have forgotten why kissing Chad was wrong.

Just as suddenly as things got interesting, they ended.

There was sun shining on her closed lids. There was a soft wind lifting the ends of her hair over her scar. And there were strong hands on her elbows, holding her steady.

Tracy needed those hands to keep from falling—either to the ground in shock or back into his arms.

She kept her eyes closed, afraid of what she'd see. "Suddenly, I feel like it's me that's having a midlife crisis."

"Let's hope not." He tilted her face up with a finger beneath her chin, and then kissed her nose. "Regrets?"

"Yes." Lots.

He sighed. "Do you think El Rosal is still open for breakfast?"

She opened her eyes. "You're thinking about breakfast?" After they'd kissed?

"There's not much to the Lambridge Bed & Breakfast's breakfast." He rubbed his stomach and turned toward the road. His expensive loafers began the trek back to town as if their bodies hadn't come together, as if their lips hadn't touched, as if they hadn't exchanged the same air.

He was walking away?

He'd been the one to deepen the kiss, turning something that was a whim and vanilla into something that was tempting and to be taken as seriously as the quality of chocolate in Jessica's Death by Chocolate cake.

He was walking away?

That's when it hit Tracy—the painful turn to her stomach, the sickening taste in her throat. This was just like the time she'd belly-flopped in Mayor Larry's swimming pool. The only difference was there'd been no witnesses this time when she'd flopped.

Chad was walking away.

Because she wasn't good enough for him. A man like Chad, who had the world at his feet, would want a woman at his side who people would look at and say, *"Wow. She's perfect for you."*

He moved in circles she could only dream of. She was sure he was embraced by cliques formed by power players, big deals and bigger exposure. Tracy embraced gurning, pumpkin bowling and cemetery runs. She moved through town at walker speed. She needed crutches and concentration to talk without much hesitation.

Tracy wasn't perfect. She was scarred and scared and just a big mess.

Whereas Chad came to the cemetery run and said all the right things to people he barely knew, kissed a woman nearly ten years younger than he was and then wondered about breakfast.

He was walking away, not even looking back.

Oh, she'd belly-flopped, all right. She might just as well sink to the bottom of the pool.

CHAD DIDN'T LOOK BACK, not once on the way into town.

Yup, he'd kissed her.

There were more important things for him to be focusing on than a pretty girl. His future was at stake. His travel magazine was at stake. His pride was at stake.

None of which seemed as important as that kiss with Tracy.

Still, he kept walking. Because being with Tracy made him feel his wineglass was half full and she planned to top it off.

He knew there was no happily-ever-after. Just look at his parents. They'd fallen in love late in life. They'd somehow managed to have a kid when they should have been having grand-kids. They'd loved each other. They'd hated each other. They'd married and divorced and married and divorced and married. All that pain. All that drama. It had all started with a kiss. It all could have been prevented if one of them had just walked away. It had been in her arms that he'd realized he and Tracy were the mirror image of his parents. They smiled at each other. They laughed together. They ar-gued about fundamental principles. He recog-nized the signs: Danger Ahead. And so he left.

Chad's loafers pounded the pavement down Main Street. El Rosal was in his sights.

Agnes and Rose stepped on the sidewalk in front of him.

Agnes regarded him like a kindly aunt spotting a nephew she doted on. "Chad, have you eaten at Giordanos Café yet?"

He shook his head. Bacon was within reach.

Rose and Agnes had other plans. They moved on either side of him, took him by the arm and led him into the café. Agnes' nose was red and her eyes watery. She'd talked about her husband at the cemetery.

Bacon would have to wait.

"Claudia is serving an early lunch because

of the ceremony." Rose squeezed his arm as if this was the best news ever. Or at least of the morning. "Look at the special."

There was a sandwich board sign near the door with a chalkboard. On it someone had written with thick blue chalk: Turkey Chipotle-Flecked Panini with Cheddar Cheese, Guacamole and Bacon.

Maybe Chad wouldn't have to wait for bacon after all. He opened the door to the café for the ladies. They took the last open table in the front corner by the window. In the kitchen, a man and a woman—both with dark hair, both with chef jackets on—were laughing. They exchanged a glance that was filled with the kind of love Chad just walked away from.

I walked away from a kiss. Not love.

The woman, Chef Claudia, it turned out, took their order with a smile. Chad made a mental note to research her background online. It might add some much-needed meat to his article.

"Grief makes me hungry." Rose tore into her second rosemary wheat roll. She'd talked about her husband at the cemetery, too, but she didn't seem as choked up about it as Agnes was.

"It was a nice morning." Agnes sniffed. "I hope we didn't seem too sentimental."

"It was sincere," Chad said, meaning it.

"What are your intentions toward Tracy?" Rose demanded, having eaten three rolls and downed one glass of water. "She grew up with my granddaughter. She's almost like a granddaughter to me."

"She's my tour guide," Chad said sternly, hoping he didn't give anything more away with a smile fueled by a remembered kiss. "Really, ladies. What would Tracy say if she heard you grilling me?"

"She'd tell us to mind our own business," Agnes said.

"But we never do." Rose lifted the bread bowl and shook it at Claudia.

"Is Mildred on her date?" Chad grinned at their shocked looks. "I was there when Felix asked her to brunch." Although when Felix had said "brunch after everything tomorrow morning," Chad had had no idea what he'd meant. Now he knew Felix had been referring to today's cemetery run.

"She's breaking up the band," Rose lamented.

"You guys play instruments?" Now, there was a spin to the story he hadn't considered.

"We sing." Rose answered with the air of one who'd misunderstood the question. "We used to dance on my porch."

"On Sunday nights, Rose puts on one-woman shows," Agnes said with the patience of a saint. "She sings all the parts herself."

"Alto, bass and tenor. I dance and I have costumes, too. I'm quite talented." Rose stated things matter-of-factly, without pretense or grandiosity. Well, maybe a little grandiosity. She had her snowy white hair in a tight bun at the base of her long neck, similar to the way Leona wore her hair. But with Rose, the air was one of accomplishment and comfort with herself, rather than the cold unhappiness of Leona.

"I'd love to see a show," Chad said.

"You must come by next week. I'm doing *Annie*."

Chad's curiosity switch flipped on. "Is this a public viewing? At a theater here in town?"

Rose harrumphed. "Who needs a theater when I have lovely hardwoods at home?"

So much for her productions being column-worthy.

Their lunch was delivered and their table fell silent as they dug in. Chad's panini was excellent, the bacon thick, smokey and satisfying.

"Let's get back to Tracy," Agnes said after she'd pushed more food around her plate than she'd eaten. "And your intentions."

Rose dabbed a napkin to the corners of her mouth. "You're almost too old for her. What are you? Thirty-eight? Forty?"

"Thirty-five," Chad ground out past a bite of bacon stuck in his throat.

"Nine years." Rose met Agnes' gaze. "What do you think? Is he robbing the cradle?

"When he's eighty, she'll be seventy-one." The trip to the cemetery must have hit Agnes hard. She always seemed so upbeat. "One foot in the grave."

"That's a little dark," Chad protested.

"Not necessarily. I was a pip at seventy-one." Rose stared at Chad as if he was a costume she wasn't sure she should wear for one of her productions. "Not so spry at eighty."

"You're still moving around." And she was putting on one-woman shows.

"Yes, but at eighty-nine, chances are you wouldn't be." Agnes stared out the window as if seeing Chad as an old man. "Maybe this isn't such a good idea."

Chad didn't like her reasoning. He was a

spring chicken compared to the age his father was when he got married.

"If you have feelings, Tracy might not know." Rose picked up the remains of her panini. "Back in my day, if a man was interested in a woman, he tossed pebbles at her window late at night. If the woman was interested in the man, she came outside with him."

"And did what?" He knew. He just wanted to see what Rose would say.

"There were all-night dance halls in New York." Rose took a bite of her sandwich.

"Moonlit drives." Agnes sighed. "Parking and talking."

Chad glanced up at the second floor window above Martin's Bakery.

"That's right," Rose said, noticing the direction of his gaze. "We'll expect a progress report tomorrow."

He decided not to tell them he'd already tossed pebbles. Partly because Tracy hadn't come outside with him. And now, she never would.

CHAPTER FIFTEEN

CHAD SAT AT the desk in his room at the Lambridge B&B and stared at the blank screen on his laptop.

There had been words there last night about how forgetful old people were with their possessions and their pasts. He'd erased those this morning. Not because he imagined Tracy's glower, but because it wasn't something that would make readers want to visit the town.

And maybe that was the point, he realized. Maybe Harmony Valley was so saccharine sweet, it wasn't worth visiting.

His chest felt empty at the thought.

There was something to Harmony Valley. There was quirk and irony. There was open-armed welcome and belonging. Why couldn't he put it on the page?

He stared at the blank screen, changed his font style, typed the words: *Welcome to Harmony Valley!* Erased them. And stared at the screen.

Maybe if he looked at some of the other columns he'd written this past month, he'd be inspired. His hand hesitated over the mouse. What if he began reading them and he found out Tracy was right? That he'd written his most cutting work when he felt grief or fear. He'd rather not know.

Tracy would disapprove of his cowardice, especially after he'd helped talk her out of her own.

Although, she'd approved of his kiss.

Which was just a kiss.

And she was just a woman.

But when he combined that kiss with that woman, Chad was exponentially in trouble. He wanted to be with her. But they weren't compatible. She hated the way he wrote. And he was determined to carry the Happy Bachelor forward, even if it meant losing an opportunity to date Tracy.

There was a sound outside. And then another. A shovel cleaving dirt. Leona was digging in the garden. His grave, he suspected.

Chad wasn't going to check. He had a column to write. The blinking cursor laughed at him: ha, ha, ha. A ha for every blink. He knew what that meant. No words would be written until he nailed down the proper angle for his story.

He had about eighteen hours to figure it out.

A shame since gurning and naked yoga had seemed so promising.

Was Tracy right? Was the town too special for his writing style?

Leona shoveled more dirt. She was worthy of an article all her own. And he was desperate enough to give it to her.

Chad grabbed his jacket and hurried downstairs. And there was his muse—in pressed blue jeans and a green crew neck sweatshirt—wielding a shovel like a pogo stick. She positioned the shovel and hopped on it with both feet. She'd harvested all her vegetables. Several baskets were filled with them off to the side. But her shoveling technique...

"Should you be doing that?" There were so many ways her execution could go wrong. A slipped foot. A turned ankle. Lost balance. Broken bones.

"Quit looking at me as if you've never seen someone dig in the garden, Mr. Healy. I'm not burying a body."

He took a step closer, fighting the urge to take the shovel from her and complete the task. Dimly aware that his story radar wasn't pinging about Leona, he couldn't stop himself from asking, "Do you need any help?"

"I'm an independent woman." She jumped and missed the shovel with her right foot. She stumbled back with a soft cry.

Chad took the shovel from her. "You won't be so independent when you break a bone." He slid the shovel blade into the dirt—no small feat since the soil was clay. The clump of dirt he turned over was heavy. Had she just had plants here? If felt more like she hadn't harvested anything from the ground in years.

The shovel creaked. It was old. The blade was rusted. The handle had cracks running down the shaft, as if it'd been left outside for decades. His smashed finger twinged and throbbed in protest.

"Stop shoveling." How like Leona to refuse help.

"I'm not going to charge you for my services." He kept digging, levering up heavy clods of soil so quickly the wood handle expanded as he levered it down and contracted when he eased it up, pinching his palms. He eyed Leona's gloves.

She'd taken them off and was swatting her leg with them as if the gloves were a riding crop.

Regardless, he wasn't stopping. There was only another four square feet of dirt to turn in the garden. He had a rhythm down. He had speed. He had—

Crack!

The shovel handle broke. The wood pinched his palms. He tugged his hands free of the handle with a hiss of pain. Thin red slashes of color crossed his palms in four inch lengths. Another good deed punished.

"Now look what you've done," Leona said in that nefarious voice of hers. She picked up the shovel pieces.

"I'm looking, all right." At blood blisters forming on his palms. He didn't have the ability to help this woman or others, not the way they needed to be helped. Not like Flynn or Slade or Duffy did. "I give up."

But not on his column. He left Leona in the garden and hurried upstairs. He forced words on the page with as much determination as he'd forced the shovel into the clay.

"THE BAKERY…SMELLS like Christmas. Every day." Tracy had the camera set up in the kitchen. The lens captured Tracy on a stool next to Jess, who was kneading dough.

She'd tried scripting things out, but she found words came easier if she had ideas and conversation starters to work with. Besides, when she'd sat down to script things out yesterday, all she could think about was Chad walking away from her. Her spirits had sunk, taking her ability to speak with them.

It was barely five thirty in the morning. A new day. All the lights were on in the kitchen. The smell of yeast and freshly brewed coffee filled the air. Set on preheat, the ovens ticked and hummed. It was warm and intimate, and words oozed from Tracy like frosting from an icing bag—slow and steady.

"The bakery...doesn't care if I lose a word. The bakery...doesn't care if I lose a job." Tracy paused and glanced at Jess. "It's true. The bakery...doesn't judge."

"I felt it the first time I came in here." Jessica's gaze ran lovingly over the kitchen's interior and the many sepia tinted photos of the Martin family on the wall.

"The bakery...doesn't care if you make oatmeal raisin cookies or a multi-layered fondant wedding cake."

Jess nodded, turning the dough again and again. "It just wants to be needed."

"Useful," Tracy added softly, suddenly feeling a strong sense of belonging as if some of the pieces of herself fit here. With Harmony Valley. With Martin's Bakery. With this new Tracy she was becoming. "Wow." She got up and turned off the camera. "The bakery...doesn't care if you aren't perfect."

Jessica placed the dough in a bowl, covered it with a clean white tea towel and moved it to the counter near an oven. "Speaking of useful, do you know who might have keys to the veterans hall? Christine wants to have her wedding reception in town. I think that's the largest venue around."

"It's the only venue around." At least the only one for a large wedding reception. However, given the way unused properties were falling apart in town, Tracy shuddered to think about the condition of the place. "Last I heard...Rutgar is in charge."

"Rutgar." Jessica's gaze turned thoughtful. "I haven't seen him here in a long while."

"I can go ask for the keys," Tracy offered, knowing how much Jess hated to leave the bakery in case a potential order came in. Tracy couldn't sell a bride a cake over the phone. "Tuesdays are always slow." Tracy had planned to fill her day by collecting the stories behind the recipes on Jessica's blog. "Besides. You might not like what you find. Inside the hall."

"I WAS PLAYED." Mildred said when Agnes and Rose picked her up for coffee and asked how her date with Felix went the day before. "He took me home from the cemetery. And then—"

"Did he suggest something frisky?" Rose demanded from the back seat.

"No."

"Did he get frisky in the car?" Rose demanded.

"No. He drove me slower than Agnes does to his house." Mildred hitched around to face Rose, not that she could see the details of her friend's expression. "He drove so slow, I could have driven." Using the curbs as rails.

"His house. Now it gets frisky," Rose said knowingly. "Can I stand the details?"

"Rose!" Agnes and Mildred both cried foul.

Mildred turned to face forward. Agnes parked the car in front of Martin's Bakery. The wind had been intense last night and had blown away the clouds. Mildred squinted more than usual in the bright sunshine.

Rose unsnapped her seat belt and scooched forward, eager for details. "You said you were played."

"He made a lovely brunch." Mildred had expected as much. Felix had been a fireman and the firemen in Harmony Valley had been known to be good cooks.

"Wait." Agnes plucked something from Mildred's blouse. "Is that—"

"Cat hair," Mildred said miserably, brushing at her blouse, not that she could see the hair. "He invited me over to get me to adopt a cat." Not that Dusty wasn't a lovely cat—a champion purrer, a wonderful cuddler and a warm-bed hog. But she'd wanted something more than a cat in her life. She'd wanted someone who could hold a conversation as well as her hand.

"That big…big…hairball," Rose said indignantly. "I see Felix inside. I'm going to give him a piece of my mind."

"Please don't. I'll be mortified."

"We'll stay silent," Agnes promised, glancing back at Rose with what Mildred could only hope was a threat in her eyes. "But we won't forget."

Mildred was no longer going to seize the day. She was going to walk into Martin's and survive the day. Because that was what one did after embarrassment in a small town. You held your head up and carried on.

Mildred repeated the words as she pushed her walker inside a few minutes later: *Survive the Day.* Didn't matter that she'd had her romantic hopes raised by Felix only to have them crushed. Didn't matter that Phil had run away from her a few days ago. Didn't matter if she looked their way now or not. She couldn't see if they were uncomfortable by her presence. She couldn't tell if they pitied her.

"Mildred," Tracy said. "You…look like you could use a pumpkin spice latte today and biscotti for dipping."

"I could," Mildred said, hopes lightening as she reached for her purse.

"Considering…what happened the other day," Tracy said in a hushed voice. "Today's order is on me."

"You don't need to do that. She's old," Rose said right behind her. "She doesn't remember what happened yesterday, much less two days ago."

"So true," Mildred murmured. Her memory wasn't what it used to be. She hoped in time this episode would fade from the annals of her mind.

"I'll bring your order out," Tracy said.

"Has your talking improved?" Mildred asked. It seemed as if it had.

Tracy might have blushed. "My...confidence has improved."

Mildred wished she could say the same. She had to sit in the same seat she always took—directly across from Phil at his checkerboard. She sighed and walked with her head held high.

"Big storm last night." Hiro Takata sat one table over. He used to be the town undertaker. His deep, even voice had been a comfort to many a grieving family. It was a comfort to Mildred now.

"Yes." She and her cat had slept through most of the wind storm.

"A couple of fence boards blew down at my place." Hiro cleared his throat. "How about at yours?"

"Not that I noticed." Not that she could see. She had a relationship with a cat instead of a relationship with a man with two good eyes who could see if her fence blew down or her rain gutters needed cleaning. "I'll check when I get home." She pulled out her chair and leaned on the table as she made the balance transfer from walker to seat.

"I could come by later and look." Hiro cleared his throat again. "I mean, if you don't mind Becca driving me over."

Mildred looked up in the vicinity of Hiro's face. "Why would I mind?"

"Just like love-struck teenagers," Mayor Larry mumbled.

Was Hiro…? *No.*

Hiro couldn't be flirting with her. They'd known each other for decades. He'd been widowed for more than ten years and never said anything to her that even remotely hinted at him wanting something more. He was just being nice. Wasn't he?

She only knew one thing for certain. He didn't rescuc cats.

CHAPTER SIXTEEN

RUTGAR LIVED ON top of Parish Hill. It was about a forty-five minute walk to the top from the bakery. The alternative to walking was driving, but the safe, boxy sedan Will had bought Tracy was at the farm. And if she went to the farm, she'd want to paint something, because Chad's rejection stung.

So Tracy set out on foot. She hadn't even reached the town square when Chad came roaring up in his red convertible, like a handsome prince on his mighty steed, smiling as if he'd just slain a dragon. The image was marred by the bruise on his forehead and the reason behind his smile. It was Tuesday.

"You wrote your column," Tracy surmised.

His grin widened. "Sent it off this morning."

"Pardon me...if I don't share in your joy."

"You should. Harmony Valley will draw lots of tourists. All I need to do now is finish the piece after the festival on Saturday."

Tracy's heart shrank back, struggling for each beat. She'd known he'd write the column. It was just that on some level, she'd hoped it'd be bad and he'd realize it. She should have known the Happy Bachelor would persevere.

"Can I give you a lift?" He leaned across the center console and opened the passenger door.

"Are you kidding me?" Her heart came roaring back to life with a vendetta. "You kissed me, walked away and wrote a cutting article about my hometown." She slammed the door shut. "And now you expect me to hop in the pick-up mobile?"

"Yes." But his smile vacillated from cocky to confused to…was that hurt?

"Oh, don't play the hurt card." She drew a deep breath, prepared to breathe fire. "You kissed me. And left me. Because…I'm not worthy of the mighty Chad Healy Bostwick!"

"You think I'm that shallow?"

"Yes, Mr. Midlife." Tracy crossed her arms over her chest. "I don't trust Chad Healy Bostwick. I thought I trusted Chad Healy, but—"

"I'm just Chad to you." He ran a hand through his hair as if he was frustrated. "When I'm Chad and you're Tracy, everything is fine."

How she wanted to believe that he could separate himself from his public persona. How she wanted to trust the tenderness she'd felt toward him yesterday wasn't a complete misread on her part. Because Chad was like the bakery. He didn't care if she lost a word or a job. He just cared that she tried.

"The trouble is…" Chad began, staring at his palms. "I like you. And I like this town. But the Happy Bachelor makes a living pointing out the ironies in destinations." He turned his head and looked up at her with eyes that shone with vulnerability. "I like it when it's just Chad and Tracy. I'd like to be Chad and Tracy for a few more days. But I'm leaving come Sunday. And when I leave, I'll be Chad Healy Bostwick, the Happy Bachelor."

He was offering to ease a little of her loneliness, and allow her to ease a little of his. Temporarily. The Tracy who'd struggled nearly two years to fit in was tempted. But the Tracy who was fitting the pieces of herself back together knew it was too late. Too late for kisses or the shelter of his arms.

And yet…

Chad had a soft spot for the elderly. And chickens. He helped others when he didn't have to. She'd never heard him complain about getting banged up while volunteering. And he'd been nice to her from the start, despite her speech challenges.

"I'll spend time with Chad." Tracy opened the passenger door. "But no kisses. No hugs. No hand holding. As long as you're Chad… we can hang out."

His expression turned mischievous. He revved the engine and smiled that no-worries smile of his. "Where to?"

Tracy didn't move. She didn't get in the car. She felt the same way when she'd been called about the second interview, as if she stood on a high ledge and was suddenly struck by vertigo. A fall here would be disastrous. He hadn't agreed to her stipulations. "If…you don't like my terms, move on."

"Let's negotiate." His eyes twinkled and tempted. "One kiss a day. It'd be like an apple. Keeping things healthy between us."

"If you don't like my terms—"

"Okay, okay. Where to?" The twinkle was gone, but he was still smiling.

"To talk to Rutgar. About veterans hall." It was a long walk up a steep hill and she was woefully out of shape. And that was the poorest excuse ever given for getting into a man's car. She hesitated.

"Rutgar? The guy from Parish Hill?" Chad gripped the steering wheel and immediately released it, as if burned. "I thought I'd drive up there this morning and see if the boogeyman myth is true."

"It is. He's as territorial as a junkyard dog unless he likes you." She got in the car so Chad wouldn't go up there alone. "Go slow. And…if you make me nervous. You have to stop."

He waited for her to buckle in and then drove slowly down the block in first gear, which meant every time he slowed down the car tried to lurch to a complete stop.

"Please shift. Before you give me… whiplash."

"Work on pausing in the beginning," he reminded her before shifting into second. He drove carefully down the next block, but second gear wasn't for cruising either. "Is this better?"

"You're killing me." Tracy risked looking at him.

"I can go whatever speed you want me to." He spared her a glance, one that said he meant both the speed of the car and their short-term relationship.

Despite their different backgrounds and

beliefs, they shared a bond. It stretched between them like a tangible thing. Empathy for others. A creative bent. He had hang-ups. She had hang-ups. But in the end, there was something real, something she'd threatened to break by overstepping the boundaries of friendship.

Instead of asking him to stop and let her out, she asked him to shift into a higher gear. Soon they were going forty. The wind whipped her hair and tugged at her jacket, but she didn't care. She trusted him to pull over if she needed him to. She trusted him to respect her wishes...when he was Chad.

He slowed to make the turn toward Parish Hill as if he were a driver of eighty-five, not thirty-five. The car could handle speed and corners. It was ten switchbacks to the top. They slowly climbed up the first one.

Tracy didn't feel as if the world was ending. She loosened her grip on the door handle. "Thank you for going slow. Half the fun of driving this road is going fast."

"I'm not here to have fun. I'm here to take you safely to the top." True to his word, they drove conservatively on every switchback. At her direction, he turned down a driveway with a sign that said, *"Trespassers will be shot."*

"That's a joke, right?" Chad asked.

"In theory." Tracy drew a deep breath. "Don't show any fear. When you see his shot-gun."

They drove farther down the drive and the house came into view. It was a log cabin. It had been built on stilts and was painted a dull brown. The porch stretched from one corner to the other.

"Why did I ever think this was a sleepy old town?" He parked the car behind a beat up green truck.

Before they even got out of the car, Rutgar appeared on the porch with his shotgun. He looked like a Viking had dropped into the Wild West—tall, muscular, with long gray-blond hair and a full beard.

"State your business." Rutgar cocked his gun, but didn't point it at them.

Chad reached for the key in the ignition, intending to start the car again.

"Wait." Tracy snatched the keys away before he could do so and got out of the car. "Hey, old man. It's Tracy Jackson. Last time…you threatened to shoot me…I was in high school." She and Emma had left a party and come here trick-or-treating on a dare.

No birds sang. No squirrels chirped and scolded. There was only the rising wind rustling the towering pines and the pounding of Tracy's pulse.

"Tracy," Chad said in a low voice, hurrying around to her side of the car and stepping in front of her. "Get back in the car."

Rutgar walked to the edge of the porch, his booted feet pounding on wood. "State your business."

"The veterans hall." Tracy peeked around Chad's shoulder. "Jessica sent me. We tried calling. But no one answered."

"That's the same baloney the sheriff said yesterday." He narrowed his eyes. "What do you want with the hall?"

"Jessica…wants to see if Christine can hold her wedding reception there. Do you have the keys?" Tracy should have just broken into the hall. Chances were even she could kick the door down after all this time.

Rutgar pointed his gun at the ground. "Why didn't you say that when you first got here?" He stomped into the house.

Tracy made to follow, but Chad held her

back. "I didn't hear him put the safety on the gun."

"Would you...know what that sounds like if he did?"

"No." Chad frowned. "Would you?"

"No. But he's never shot anyone." Even Eunice and her mama, who had trespassed and stolen horseradish, although Rutgar had probably only been a teenager then.

"Yet," Chad emphasized. "He hasn't shot anyone yet."

The big man returned and lumbered down the steps, the gun nowhere in sight. He shook a ring of keys.

"You found them." Tracy hurried to meet him halfway, Chad at her heels.

Rutgar held them to his chest. "I want them back as soon as you measure or whatever it is you need to see. We take pride in that place."

Tracy hoped there was something left to take pride in. She'd seen enough of the neglected insides of buildings in Harmony Valley to know that time wasn't always kind. But she promised and took possession of the keys.

"Do you want us to check your phone?" Chad asked, making Tracy do a double take. "So we can call ahead before we bring the keys back?"

"What happened to your face?" Rutgar stared at the bump on Chad's forehead. "Looks like someone took a hammer to your skull."

"Naw. Nothing that easy." Chad pointed at Tracy with his thumb. "She hit me with the kitchen sink."

Tracy resisted rolling her eyes.

"I like you." A beefy hand landed on Chad's shoulder. "Don't make me regret letting you in my house."

"What are you doing?" Tracy asked quietly, hanging back at the steps when Rutgar went inside.

"His shirt is buttoned wrong. His boot laces are frayed. And his fly is down." There were worry lines on Chad's face where she hadn't seen any before. "He needs help, Tracy. He's isolated out here and probably too proud to ask anyone to help him."

"Okay," Tracy whispered back. "But...you have to tell him his barn door is open." She wasn't going to point out the old man hadn't zipped his pants. And her smile wasn't for Rutgar's fashion faux pas. It was because this was the Chad she adored.

"Wait here." Chad went in first, murmured something she couldn't make out, and moments later called Tracy inside.

"Phone's dead." Rutgar's stormy bluster had reduced to a mild squall.

The house had the feel of a hunting lodge. Exposed wood. The heads of elk, moose, deer and bear hung from the walls. There were cobwebs across antlers and thick layers of dust on the coffee tables and television screen.

Chad was fiddling with the phone.

Tracy sniffed. "What's that smell?"

"Seed medley." Rutgar's eyebrows shot up and he hurried down the hall. "I didn't hear the timer go off."

He was cooking? Curious, Tracy followed him into the kitchen. It was a galley kitchen that opened to a small breakfast nook. "It smells delicious."

He removed two baking sheets covered in sizzling seeds from the oven.

"What are those?"

Rutgar smoothed the beard around the corners of his smile. "Pumpkin and winter squash seeds. I seasoned these with garlic." He loosened them from the sheets with a spatula. "I'll send some home with you if you like."

"I'd like." Jessica would like, too.

"Do you have any six-volt batteries?" Chad

appeared in the doorway holding a small oblong battery. "Looks like your plug isn't getting power and the battery backup is dead. I'm going to use the outlet farther down the wall."

"That bum plug is where a tree fell on the house last winter." Rutgar made a huffing noise and rummaged in a drawer. "Didn't think to test it." He handed Chad a battery.

"Your hall light is out, too." Chad backed into the hallway and pointed up. "I'll change it if you have a light bulb." He returned to the living room.

"I like him." Rutgar rummaged in a cabinet for a bulb and set it on the round oak kitchen table.

"So you've said."

"He seems reliable."

"Only on the outside." He'd walk at the first sign of trouble, just as he'd done when they'd kissed. There were several jars of seeds on the counter. Tracy picked one up. "Are all these the same seasoning?"

"No." He separated the jars. "This one is nutmeg and cinnamon. These are Worcestershire chili lime. And the ones with the darker seasoning are chocolate powder, powdered sugar and sea salt." He tugged at his beard.

"I plan to make some with horseradish tomorrow." He grinned. "You should have been here last week. I made squirrel jerky bites. Froze some for winter and ate the rest."

"Sorry I missed that." Not. "Where...did you learn to make these seeds?" She hoped there was a story behind them.

"My father was an outdoor enthusiast and he wanted foods that didn't spoil."

A hollowed out pumpkin and a winter squash gourd sat on the counter. "Are you... going to do something else with these?"

"I am." He smiled wide enough to flash his teeth past all that beard. "I'm going to put a little milk, spices and honey inside, then triple wrap them in foil and put them in the fire pit out back for a few hours. Comes out tasting just like pie. Do you want to come by for some tomorrow?" He looked as eager as a child waiting for a piece of birthday cake.

"It...would have to wait until I finished work." Tracy would prefer his pie to squirrel jerky. "Did...your dad come up with that recipe, too?"

"Oh, no." He reached for a picture on a shelf in the china cabinet. Based on the grainy quality and yellowed paper, it appeared to have been taken around the same time as some of the old photos hanging at the bakery. "That was my great-grandmother. She was an American Indian. The only thing I remember about her was her cooking on the fire pit in back. We've had a fire pit long before they were ever considered trendy by you young folk."

Tracy peered at the faded and out-of-focus picture. His grandmother was small and stood next to a big fire pit. The landscape was blanketed with snow. "Jessica would love to have these recipes for her blog. Why don't you bring them down tomorrow?"

Rutgar's eyes shifted and his feet shifted. He looked frazzled. "I don't come down much anymore."

"Everyone's noticed. They miss you." She patted his arm. "And coffee's on the house."

Rutgar's gaze steadied. He stopped fidgeting. And he smiled.

CHAPTER SEVENTEEN

AFTER BEING SHOWN the majestic view of the valley from the top of Parish Hill, Chad drove slowly to the bottom, wondering why Tracy was so quiet. "Aren't you going to ask me what my column was about?"

"Nope." Tracy had her left hand on the door handle and her right elbow on the window sill, riding the wind with her right hand. She was looking to the side of the road.

He wanted her to look at him. He wanted her to renegotiate their deal. If they only had a short time together, he really thought one kiss a day was fair. "I thought I was going to add being shot to my list of Harmony Valley mishaps."

"Now...you're just being dramatic." Her lips turned up a bit at the corners. "You haven't had mishaps."

"I disagree." He held up his left forefinger, which was black, and pointed to the third eye on his forehead. Then he showed her one of his palms, which had the blood blister streak across it. All a thinly veiled attempt to win her sympathies. "My elbows are black and blue from climbing beneath Nina Valpizzi's kitchen sink. And now I've almost been shot."

"Unless…you walked on four legs. And had fur or antlers. You were safe with Rutgar." She did a double take. "You're…not going to write about Rutgar, are you?"

"Why not?" He wasn't, but he enjoyed teasing her.

"Your…readers won't come here and experience Rutgar. He's…not a ride at an amusement park." Tracy was working herself up into full glower mode, adding circular hand gestures for emphasis.

She was right. "I wouldn't do that to the old man." Now Leona… She could take it. "Where is the veterans hall?"

"It's near the highway." She instructed him where to turn. "Once…you make the turn from the highway. You…can either head straight to Main Street. Or…take the north fork toward the eastern side of town."

He turned onto the fork before they reached the highway. There were large overgrown trees between the hall and the road. Their branches hung far out over the pavement. The wind was picking up again. The trees closer to the building scraped the roof and walls of the hall. Berry vines had grown through open windows. The parking lot was torn up in spots from roots pushing up the asphalt. The beige building looked dingy and unwelcome.

"I...haven't been by here in a long time." Tracy sounded disappointed.

"For your sake, I hope it's better on the inside."

Chad glanced through the main double doors. Cobwebs draped the open doorway to the main hall. The floor was layered in dust and dirt.

Tracy unlocked the door. Something scuttled inside. And the smell...

"That's not promising." Chad grabbed a broom in the corner and brushed the cobwebs in the doorway clear. He followed Tracy through the next set of doors into the main hall.

It was as large as most hotel banquet rooms he'd seen. The lighting was fluorescent and dim. The walls unfinished cinder block. The stage at the far end had moth eaten black velvet curtains.

"Too bad," Chad said turning toward the exit. "This looks like a bust."

"That's…what they said about me, I bet… when I first was brought into the hospital. I kind of like lost causes." She laughed, but it was one of those what-have-I-gotten-myself-into laughs. "Jessica said the wedding is nearly a year away."

"You'll need more time than that. Might be easier to tear it down and start over."

"Pessimist."

He waited on the main walk while Tracy locked up. The blue, bubble-fendered Caddy that had almost run Tracy over the other day sped by.

"There goes what's-her-name." The scarf tied around her white hair today was red and fluttered behind her like the tail of a kite.

"Lilac." She shaded her eyes and surveyed the dump once more. "With work. It…could be a charming place for weddings. Indoors or out." She scanned the overgrown grounds. Across the highway, neat rows of vineyards marched toward the hills. "It…could be a conference center. Or a retreat. Or something."

Chad shook his head. "You'd need another hotel. More restaurants. A gas station." He could have added to the list. The point was, Harmony Valley didn't have the infrastructure.

"But it would be cool. Wouldn't it?" She

met his gaze squarely for the first time since they'd left Parish Hill. Hers was hopefully naïve. "This place…could become a destination."

Not in her wildest dreams. It was too remote and lacked too many amenities. "You should concentrate on Jessica's blog."

"You read it?"

"I did." Tracy had some skill with the written word. "And the transformation of the old recipe to the new one was brilliant."

She glowed. "It was my idea. See? You should listen. When I make suggestions. About your column."

He was listening. She'd taken up residence in his head without an invitation. He didn't know how to get her out. He'd only been able to shut her out for a short while, long enough to write the column for Marty. He was beginning to think he didn't want her to go.

But that was short-term Chad thinking. The Happy Bachelor had to think of the long-term, earning respect, and the bottom line.

NINA VALPIZZI CAME in to the bakery first thing Wednesday morning. She had on a belted leather jacket and a pair of false eyelashes. If Chad saw her high heels, he'd worry she might tip over and break a bone.

Tracy hadn't seen Chad since they'd inspected veterans hall. They were only friends, after all. That hadn't stopped her from searching the internet for Chad's new site to see if he'd posted the column about Harmony Valley online for his advertisers to see. No dice.

Nina asked to see Jessica. "I was reading the blog this weekend and loved the story about Eunice's mother. So I went back to look at my recipe and remembered a story about my mom." She hugged Jess across the counter, dousing her in musky cologne. "So fitting after the cemetery run. It's like she's still here." She ordered a caramel macchiato.

"You're…my one progressive coffee drinker in town." Tracy tried to inconspicuously rub her cheek where Nina's cologne seemed to linger as she took milk and caramel syrup from the refrigerator. "Almost everyone else takes coffee plain. Or as a latte."

"My daughter got me hooked on them." With her midnight hair color, the caterpillar eyelashes didn't look so bad. They distracted from her pale wrinkles. "Can I get that to go?"

"Certainly."

"I'm driving to Santa Rosa this morning to see my grandbabies perform in a school play." Nina studied her reflection in the bakery case and tugged down her leather jacket. "Do you think if I bring Jessica another recipe that I might make her blog again?"

"As long as the story is interesting…and Jess can make it up-to-date. I don't see why not."

Nina glowed. "Give me a dozen chocolate chip cookies to go along with that. The kids will love them." She glanced around the empty bakery and then leaned on the counter. "What's with you and Chad?"

"Nothing." Tracy snapped a lid on a to-go cup and then handed Nina the coffee.

"I saw you together at the cemetery run. I think you make a cute couple." Nina did a little head and shoulder bobble. "Farkle likes him. You should keep him."

"He's not a stray up for adoption." And wow, didn't that comeback snap out of her!

Nina waggled a finger with purple polish. "Men don't always realize what they need."

In Chad's case, there was no arguing with that.

No sooner had Tracy folded the top of the bag on Nina's cookies than Lillian Harrington came in asking for Jessica. She'd washed her hair with uniform gray dye. It hung in a straight bob that only emphasized how long her long face was. She'd run the post office once upon a time. On lazy summer afternoons, her tall figure delivering mail at the end of the drive had signaled a race to the mailbox between Will and Tracy.

"I can only spare a minute," Jess said when Tracy interrupted her in the kitchen, Lillian on her heels. "I've got pizza bagels in the oven and the timer's ready to go off."

"I love the new blog. It's like I'm a superstar." Lillian handed Jess a stack of recipe cards. "See if any of these recipes inspire you and I'll swing by to tell you my story."

Ever efficient, Jess did a quick perusal of the recipes. "Corned beef and syrup pot pie? Is this a breakfast item?"

Tracy's stomach recoiled. It was a good thing the culinary vision was Jessica's.

"It's better than it sounds." Lillian's blush added a nice touch of color to her cheeks. "Can I tell you how it came to be?"

The timer went off.

"Why don't you tell Tracy? She's collecting the stories." Jess smiled to soften her words.

"She's a better writer than I am. She'll do the story justice."

Tracy took that as her cue and led Lillian to the front, producing a notebook and pen from under the counter. "So...corned beef and syrup pot pie?"

Lillian hesitated.

"Can I...get you something while you tell me?" Tracy was getting good at the upsell.

"A nonfat latte and a vanilla scone." Lillian unzipped her white windbreaker over her white T-shirt and looked down at her white sneakers. "I got that recipe from a pen pal in Ireland... From a man I never met." There was a wistful note in her voice as she talked about her international friend.

Lillian's story didn't have that spark, but she was willing to delve deeper for the "celebrity" of being on Jessica's blog. Or maybe she wanted to reconnect with an old friend. She promised to write a letter to her pen pal to uncover the origins of the recipe. Before Lillian left, she proved her Harmony Valley roots. "I hear you've got a beau, Tracy. I can't wait to meet him."

"Technically," Tracy struggled to keep the sarcasm and hurt from her voice. "He's not mine." And didn't want to be.

"It can always develop into something more." Lillian zipped up her white jacket as Rutgar arrived.

The big man gave Tracy scribbled seasoning recipes for winter seeds and his instructions for squirrel jerky. He was probably one of the few people tall enough in Harmony Valley to lean over Lillian's shoulder at the counter. And then he leaned over the bakery case, closer to Tracy, and pointed to Lillian's drink. His booming voice couldn't quite hit a whisper. "What is that?"

"A latte." Tracy grinned at the idea she was bringing Rutgar into this century. "Coffee in steamed milk."

"I think I'd like to try one." He sniffed and checked out the contents of the bakery cases. "Are you cooking pizza?"

"Pizza bagels. Fresh out of the oven. I can get you one."

"I'll take two." He surveyed the room. "I like it when it's quiet like this. You can almost hear the wind outside. Speaking of… did you hear the wind last night? It was raging up on the hill."

"I tend to sleep like the dead," Tracy said. A hazard of rising at 4 a.m. every day. "Do you mind if I keep your keys another day or so? Jessica and Christine haven't had a chance to see the hall."

"Take your time. It's a great place."

Tracy managed a wan smile.

And then the regulars dribbled in. Phil and Felix arguing over who was the better checkers player. Tracy poured them extra large mugs of black coffee. Mayor Larry entered wearing a red-and-purple tie-dyed hoodie. By the time he got to the counter, Tracy had his coffee with two packs of sweetener ready.

"Good to see the business is growing." The mayor paid and moved to his regular table in the center of the room, waiting for the town council. "So much wind lately. Heard a tree blew down on the highway."

Flynn's wife, Becca, who worked as a caregiver in town, parked and got out to help Old Man Takata inside. Based on their animated faces and moving mouths, there was a debate going on between them. When they entered, Becca said, "Bran muffin, no croissant." And then she left.

Tracy saluted, smiling as the old man worked his walker to the counter. "Black coffee and chocolate croissant?"

"You betcha." He glanced around the room. "No town council?"

"Not yet." Tracy carried his order to a table near the checkers game.

"They say the wind will die down later today," Takata said.

The mayor repeated his information on the downed tree on the highway. Lillian wondered how the mail was going to be delivered. And Rutgar surprised them all by sharing that a tree had fallen at the turn to Parish Hill.

It wasn't cosmopolitan or fast paced, but it was friendly. Harmony Valley was a pretty darn good place to be.

CHAPTER EIGHTEEN

"WHERE ARE YOU GOING, Mr. Healy?" Leona said. "You missed breakfast yesterday and now today. Nine o'clock. Who sleeps until nine o'clock in the morning?"

"I thought we agreed that this was a bed, no breakfast." Chad headed toward the front door. "I stayed up late trying to write a new column." He hadn't been able to capture the snark and sarcasm of the column he'd written for Marty. He hadn't heard a word from Marty either. Had he lost the account? He needed to call.

"If you're hungry—"

Chad paused at the door, curious as to what the ice queen would offer him.

"—the farmers market starts in the town square at nine. There are baked goods, fresh fruits and vegetables and lemonade."

That was almost...nice. Like a recommendation expected from a B&B owner.

Chad stepped onto the front porch and

zipped up his jacket. The wind had abated since last night, but still blew hard enough that he had to lean forward to walk into it. Leaves blanketed Leona's lawn and several other lawns on the street. He hunched into his jacket, pausing to check out the downed fence in Leona's backyard. It looked as if the wind had blown tomatoes and peppers from their vines, too. He supposed he should tell Flynn about it. Of course, if he did, Flynn would want him to help.

He walked toward the town square. Past Nina's house. Past Mrs. Beam's house. Past Duffy and Jessica's house. There were about ten tables set up in the town square. It was a chilly day, despite the sun being out. A few residents roamed from table to table—talking, laughing, making purchases.

There was a craft table with knit items. And shocker! There was a pile of knit scarves very similar to what he'd seen at Mae's Pretty Things. He took a picture of the wool knit lampshade. Unusual, to say the least. And since he was writing another article about Harmony Valley after the festival, it would make an interesting photo.

"Can I interest you in a lampshade?" The woman sitting behind the table looked as if she'd be blown away if she stood up. She made Agnes look like a giant in comparison.

"My lampshade wearing days are over."

She frowned, sending her wrinkles turning in on themselves, not understanding his reference.

"I meant, I'm past my wild days when I would have worn a lampshade as a hat."

"You're never too old to be wild." Her smile had probably charmed many a man in her day, but she was missing a couple of front teeth.

Chad held on to his smile even as he registered the sickly tone of her skin. Was it cancer or kidneys that had taken her health?

He moved on to a table with health aids—canes, walkers, bandages and the like—from a medical supply store in nearby Cloverdale.

"Not much traffic today," Chad said to the man working the booth.

His thin gray hair blew in the breeze. "Wait until they finish their coffee and it warms up a bit." He shrugged deeper into his jacket. "It'll be busy in another fifteen minutes."

There were several tables with produce, but one caught his eye. It had baskets filled with big ripe tomatoes, plump gourds and shiny bell peppers. He'd seen those baskets when he broke Leona's shovel. And here she'd have him believe she didn't care about the town. What a hypocrite.

"All proceeds benefit the Harvest Festival." The elderly woman sitting behind the table smiled at him as if he'd just offered to buy her entire stock.

Chad bought a tomato and tucked it into his pocket. Most likely, it'd have a poisonous pit, but that was the only way he'd get to try something from Leona's garden.

He wandered over to Martin's Bakery. While his creative juices were lacking, Tracy was writing some good stuff for Jessica's blog. Just to torture himself, he'd read more of them this morning. And she was fast. She'd revised twenty yesterday.

When he entered the bakery, people nodded his way and called out greetings. This was more of a welcome than he'd had while working at the *Bostwick Lampoon* and more than anything he'd received from Leona. He got into line behind a couple of old women who had lost most of their hair and what was left was long and scraggly. Made him wonder if Phil had cut it. The man's hands shook as if he was in the midst of an earthquake.

Felix asked Chad if he'd like to play a game of checkers later.

"I wouldn't if I were you, Chad," Rose said with unusual snappishness. "You might end up adopting a cat."

Mildred and Agnes shushed her.

Unfazed, Felix chuckled.

Rutgar waved to him from a table at the back. "Try the pizza bagel."

The last time he'd felt this type of camaraderie, he'd been in school.

"Where's Jessica?" The first woman in line asked. "I loved how she took my recipe for coffee gelatin and made it into something I'd serve for dessert."

Chad had liked that one, too. It was a recipe born from a sugar shortage during World War II. Since there were already gelatin packets in the store, they'd been mixed with coffee, giving it a fruitier taste. Strawberry coffee? Wasn't his cup. Jessica had come up with the idea to replace the amount of water added to gelatin with coffee to make a coffee gelatin mold. Great with whipped cream.

"Jessica's in the back." Tracy's gaze caught on Chad's. Her smile brightened—making Chad feel ten feet tall—and then she toned it way back—leaving Chad feeling bereft. "Can

I get you anything? Jess will…have a moment when your order comes up."

That empty feeling returned to his chest. In the few days since he'd arrived, Tracy was talking smooth, she was writing sharp and she was probably healthier than he was—unbruised and with glowing cheeks.

She doesn't need me.

Chad sagged against the bakery case.

Tracy doesn't need me.

It shouldn't have hit him so hard. But it did, and he moved forward very much aware of his limitations as a man. If it wasn't for the Happy Bachelor, they might pursue a relationship. The entire premise of the column was targeted to smart, single men enjoying the single life.

He glanced at Tracy again. At her sunny hair and soft smile. How had she snuck up on him like this? How had she captured a corner of his heart? Why did he care that she was independent and capable?

Because his parents hadn't been. Not for years.

He looked away, at the elderly clientele. They all needed someone. They relied upon the community here in town.

This is the story.

Chad rejected it, dug deeper, thought about Tracy and his parents. The needing. The not needing. He'd rather be loved than needed or not needed any day. He'd rather be loved by...

His gaze cut back to Tracy, but he wouldn't allow himself to complete the thought.

He was an idiot. He was at a tipping point in his career and she did something to his writing that could undermine every bit of the reputation he'd built.

When it was his turn, he needed to play it cool.

When it was his turn, he needed to keep things impersonal.

When it was his turn, he turned on the charm. "Loved what you did with the blog."

"Thank you." She blushed, which only made her blue eyes seem bluer. "What can I get for you today?"

He didn't like being treated like other customers. She'd kissed him. Shouldn't that mean she'd look at him with longing? Shouldn't that mean she'd smile at him as if he hung the moon? Or make excuses to touch his hand or his shoulder or his face?

He pretended to study the offerings in the case, even though he'd already decided on the pizza bagel to go with his homegrown tomato. "There's a gentle humor in your blog delivery."

"That's the way I approach life." Her smile. It was one he'd seen her give Rose while he was in line.

He didn't want that friend-to-all smile. "Regardless, it's good writing." Not the type he'd contracted for at the *Lampoon*, but she had a knack for telling a cohesive story. Not everyone did.

She frowned as she rang his order. "You don't have to sound so surprised." She moved her hands to emphasize her displeasure, but she managed to take his money without touching him.

"I'm not surprised. I'm envious." He was taken aback that it was true. "Your page visits jumped up when I checked them this morning."

"Really?" There was the smile she'd given him right before she'd kissed him. "I'll have to check."

Their conversation felt mundane. He wanted to remind her he was leaving in a few days and exchange contact information. He wanted her to slip into his arms so she could talk up a storm.

He sat at a table near Eunice and sent Marty an email, asking if he liked the column.

When Flynn came in for a coffee refill, he told him about the fence down at Leona's.

Flynn didn't invite him to help.

Chad had to volunteer.

MILDRED HADN'T OWNED a pet since she was a girl. Being a race car driver, she'd never had the time to care for one. And when she'd moved to Harmony Valley, she'd jumped into life with both feet and created a busy one.

It was nice to have Dusty around the house. He wasn't much of a talker except when he wanted to be fed. The rest of the time he laid claim to Mildred and the house like a king to his castle. Currently, he was wrapped around her neck like an orange, purring muffler.

Agnes and Rose knocked on the front door and then let themselves in. They'd only dropped her off an hour ago.

Mildred stayed in her recliner, lest Dusty be disturbed. The king had conquered her.

Rose came to stand next to her chair. She touched the cat with one finger.

Dusty stopped purring and lifted his regal head to stare at Rose.

"I had to make sure he was real." Satisfied, Rose took a seat on the couch.

"Did I forget something on the schedule?" Mildred tried to keep all their activities straight in her head, because she couldn't see calendar notations. Her vision had gotten so bad, Agnes had begun paying her bills.

Agnes petted Dusty. "That wind storm last night blew the fence down between your backyard and Leona's. Flynn, Slade and Chad are coming by to fix it." She reached in her purse and pulled out something gray, waved it beneath Dusty's nose and then threw it toward the hearth. "Get the mouse, kitty. Didn't you smell the catnip?"

Dusty sighed and laid his head back down on Mildred's shoulder.

Rose went over to pick it up. She sniffed it. "How old is this toy?"

"I just bought it at the vet's this morning." Agnes huffed, which Mildred took as an indication that the mouse was going back to the veterinary office.

Rose gave the mouse to Agnes. "Let's hope that travel writer doesn't hurt himself again."

"He means well, but he doesn't have much experience being handy." Agnes tapped her forehead and tsked. "That bruise."

"They're going to be mending fences," Mildred murmured. "Between Leona and me." She didn't like the metaphor. She and Leona would never see eye-to-eye. Mildred was a stout supporter of Phil's.

"Here they are now." Rose sounded excited. "Look at all that equipment. Power tools and compressors and the like."

"It's warm enough to watch with a jacket on." Agnes disappeared to the rear of the house. "I'll wipe off the patio chairs."

Dusty perked up when he heard the back door open and close.

"I'm supposed to keep Dusty inside for a week so he knows this is his home." There were other reasons Mildred had wanted Dusty to stay inside, but she didn't want to say them out loud for fear of appearing more foolish than she already had for taking the cat home.

"Cat stays indoors. Got it." Rose waved at the men out front. "I'm glad you gave up the idea of dating Phil."

"Why?" Mildred hadn't given up. She'd just been busy with Dusty.

"We're the band!" Rose played air guitar.

"Seats are ready," Agnes called.

Dusty leapt off Mildred's chest.

"Don't let the cat out," Mildred shouted apprehensively.

"Oops." Agnes tskd. "Here kitty. Shoot, he's running across the grass."

Mildred was struck with fear. It had only been a few days. What if Dusty ran away? "Is he coming back?" She lurched to her feet and reached for her walker.

"I've got your coat." Rose trailed behind her.

"He's heading for Leona's big tree." Agnes provided the play-by-play.

Mildred saw the open doorway and the sunlit yard with brown leaves scattered about her grass like confetti in Times Square on New Year's morning. The brisk air washed over her. The tree—the huge pine—was in Leona's yard. That tree was to cats what an eight-cylinder five-speed was to a rookie racer. Back when she could see better, she'd watched cats climb up that tree and sit, waiting for squirrels or waiting for the courage to get down.

"There he goes. Up the trunk." Agnes' announcement was demoralizing.

"Oh, bother." Mildred slowed to lift her walker carefully over the threshold. "Felix said Dusty loves climbing trees and hates getting down."

"He's up pretty high. Maybe thirty feet." Agnes shaded her eyes from the sun.

Mildred's spirits sank. She wheeled her way across the patio, wishing for her binoculars so she might try to spot the cat in the tree. All her eyes registered was a big fuzzy tree. And then she heard a heart-wrenching meow. "Call Felix. Call the volunteer fire department. Call the sheriff."

"What's up, ladies?" Flynn appeared from the side yard, carrying something big, red and bulky.

"Runaway cat up Leona's big tree," Rose summarized.

"Felix said Dusty can't get down from trees," Mildred wailed.

Flynn set down the big whatever-it-was on the patio. "Ladies, let's sit. No reason to panic."

"No reason to…?" Mildred's voice cracked. "My cat is stuck up a tree!" Worse, Leona's tree. "He could fall. He could break something trying to get down. He could have a heart attack from the stress."

Mildred's heart was beating overtime.

Chad appeared before her with a calm

touch on her arm. "How about we sit down?"
His voice was as calm as his touch. Tracy really shouldn't let this one go, even if reporters
didn't make much money. "I've never seen a
dead cat in a tree, have you?"

Tracy shouldn't waste her time with him.
He was a callous lout. "My cat is different."
But Mildred let him help her sit in a chair.
The wind mixed up the leaves on the lawn
and snuck up Mildred's ankles. "Where's my
coat?"

Rose helped her put it on. "Dusty's a brave
one. He went up higher." Rose dragged a
chair next to Mildred, as if Dusty's demise
was going to be good viewing.

Dusty meowed, a cry for help if Mildred
had ever heard one.

"Maybe there's a bird in that tree," Agnes
said.

"Squirrels mostly," Chad said infuriatingly
calm. "I've seen them from my window."

"Maybe he'll kill something and come
down." Agnes wasn't giving pessimism a
chance, bless her.

Birds. Critters. That was another reason
Mildred had wanted to keep Dusty an indoor
cat. Felix claimed he was a mighty hunter.
Her vision was so bad, she didn't think she

could see gutted mice or plucked bird parts if Dusty brought them to the back porch. Or worse—she shuddered—inside. "I never should have taken that cat."

"Nonsense." Agnes sat on the other side of her. "You love that cat and he loves you."

"But he doesn't love me enough to *stay*." Mildred lowered her voice to a whisper. "I need to rethink the Phil thing."

"Let's not start that again." Rose patted her arm. "The band. Think of the band."

"I should have had another child when I retired from racing." Mildred was on the Pity Train, seated in first class. "Then I wouldn't be lonely and I wouldn't need a disloyal cat."

"Didn't you retire when you were forty because of that wreck?" Rose clasped Mildred's hand. "I remember when I first saw you, I thought you looked like death. Chad's injuries look like he's been tickled compared to what you were like after your accident."

"My injuries were bad," Mildred admitted with stiff lips. Alistair McKinney had forced her into a wall to prove women shouldn't race. All he'd done was prove he was pond scum and get banned from the circuit.

"You moved here when you were still recovering." Agnes took her other hand. "You wouldn't have been able to care for a child. You could barely take care of yourself and your baby girl."

"I know. She was five and deserved a brother or sister." Mildred's voice sounded as shaky as Phil's hands. "I could have adopted later. Forty-five isn't too old to raise a baby nowadays."

Chad knelt in front of Mildred. "But you wouldn't have always been there for a child you had late in life. You wouldn't have been there for the majority of their lives."

She knew where he was going with this. "Is it selfish to want to give love unconditionally? Is it selfish to want someone to love you unconditionally in return?"

"No," he said. But the word was so faint, Mildred wasn't sure he'd actually spoken.

"If I thought like you do," Mildred said, gasping because she was on the verge of crying. "I wouldn't have taken Dusty for the simple reason that I couldn't guarantee I wouldn't die tomorrow. But now I've come to love him and he's going to die up there in that tree!"

"Relax," Agnes soothed. "Chad will get Dusty down. Won't you, Chad?"

He stood. "I will."

Mildred sniffed. "If you get him down, I'll put a good word in for you with Tracy."

He hesitated. And for a moment, Mildred thought he was going to reject her offer. Instead, he said, "Thank you."

He walked off and Mildred squeezed both her friends' hands. "It's back to Phil." Because Hiro hadn't said anything to her since their talk about her fence yesterday morning. And at least with Phil, she could be sure he wouldn't climb a tree and try to kill himself.

"WHAT SHOULD WE do about the cat?" Flynn stared up into the branches, which swayed in the wind.

"He'll come down in his own time." Chad wasn't keen on waiting. Mildred's words had touched him. Yes, his parents were selfish to have a child so late, but they hadn't made the choice lightly. He'd been loved the best way they knew how. And yet, he hadn't given his love to anyone other than a pet. He'd held on to his feelings for fear if he gave love to someone, they might disappear too quickly, the same as his parents. Or that he'd experience the same rollercoaster of emotions they had.

He thought of Tracy's determined approach to life and its challenges. He recalled the joy he felt at her smile and the promise he'd sensed in her kiss.

He'd walked away from Tracy?

Yes. And despite what he felt for her, he wasn't sure he wouldn't do it again. His writing defined who he was and it would show the *Lampoon* they'd made a mistake.

"Kitty might go all the way to the top if we turn on the nail gun compressor," Slade said.

"I'm not hammering nails the old-school way." Chad had enough scars and bruises to last him awhile.

"What's going on out here?" Leona demanded, standing in the doorway to her sunroom, looking as if they'd disrupted a most important business meeting.

"Mildred's cat is up your tree," Chad said, noticing that Flynn and Slade had retreated, hopefully to lug the fence boards from Flynn's truck. He didn't fancy adding splinters to his list of woes.

Leona returned inside, leaving Chad to call for the cat beneath the sixty-foot-tall tree.

Chad wasn't worried about the cat. He was worried Mildred might work herself into a tizzy. And the tizzy would lead to something more serious. He was worried he'd continue to let the opportunity for love with Tracy pass him by. And that emptiness would be a permanent state of being.

Leona reappeared. She carried a can of tuna. She banged the can with a fork the same way a wedding guest tapped their wineglass to encourage a kiss. "Kitty-kitty-kitty," she crooned in a voice that sounded almost warm.

"Well, what do you know." Chad chuckled. "The ice queen has a heart."

She scowled at him and kept up her kitty-calling.

That cat was no dummy. There was the urgent sound of claws ripping through bark. The big orange tabby leapt to the ground and circled Leona, rubbing against her legs.

The trio of women on Mildred's patio applauded. Mildred shouted her thanks.

"Pick up the beast," Leona commanded.

Chad hurried over and scooped the cat into his arms.

"Now take him back." Leona shoved the tuna can into his hand and headed back to her big, empty house.

The cat contorted itself to stay in Chad's arms and keep eating from the can. Unfortunately, it dug its claws into Chad's arm and hand, hooking them just beneath his skin.

Add another set of injuries to his mounting Harmony Valley scars.

"You're not so bad," Chad said softly enough that only Leona would hear.

"Don't be so sure," she replied, just as softly, but with a hard note.

When the cat was safely inside and the nail gun compressor had been plugged in, Chad stood back and held up his hands so Flynn and Slade could see his blood blisters and bruised finger. "I'll hand you two the boards." No way was he getting near that nail gun.

Flynn and Slade exchanged glances in that way of theirs that spoke of secret wavelengths no one else could read.

"Nope," Flynn said. "You'll operate the nail gun."

"Given my track record, that's not wise." He clenched his hands to stop them from trembling.

"You've got to learn sometime." Slade had the oddest way of looking at a man. His gaze tallied, totaled and summarized. His gaze said Chad could handle power tools.

Chad had no reason to add power tool wielding to his list of accomplishments. Not unless he stayed in Harmony Valley. Not unless Tracy ever truly forgave him. Not unless he redefined who he was and re-evaluated the risks of loving, and gave Tracy his heart. There were a lot of conditions to him staying. "Okay, I'll work the nail gun, but you guys are driving me to Emergency when I nail myself to a board."

As it turned out, Chad didn't puncture any of his appendages with a nail.

He shot a nail into Slade.

CHAPTER NINETEEN

"THIS IS A MISTAKE." Agnes glanced out her windshield at Phil's barbershop a few hours after Dusty had been rescued from the tree. Mildred's heart thudded painfully in her chest like a big block engine that needed oil.

They'd watched the men fix Mildred's fence while they plotted the seduction of Phil. Their planning had been cut short by the nail gun incident—who knew hands could spew so much blood?—but when they realized Slade would live, the trio had decided to seize the day.

"You shouldn't let Phil cut your hair," Rose said. "His hands shake like the dickens."

Admittedly, the only plan they'd come up with was extreme and Mildred's. But it was a plan and they were putting it into action immediately.

"You can't talk me out of this." Mildred had failed with the checkers match. She would not fail with Phil this time. "It'll just be him and me."

"And his sharp barber scissors," Agnes muttered.

Rose wasn't as subtle. She practically shouted, "He'll cut your ear off."

Fear and longing jolted through Mildred in an unbearable rush. She wasn't sure anymore which was stronger. She had to keep telling herself, "This is Phil." Phil was a professional. He wouldn't hurt her. On purpose.

"You don't have a cell phone." Rose squeezed Mildred's seat back. "How will we know if you need a doctor?"

"You'll hear my screams." It wasn't as if she could see the numbers on a cell phone anyway. "Now, get my walker, please." Mildred got out of the car and stood, holding the door frame for balance.

"Mildred." Rose got out of the back. "When I was a teenager, the circus came to town. I fell in love with a man who was suave, and sexy, and a high flyer on the trapeze."

Agnes set Mildred's walker in front of her. For once, Mildred was grateful she couldn't see very well. If she could have seen the fear on her friends' faces that was in their voices, she might have lost her nerve.

"I, on the other hand," Rose said, her voice unusually somber, "was young and stupid. Enrique put me in tights, put me on the trapeze and caught me mid-air. I thought my heart would burst from my chest."

"What a lovely memory." Mildred felt her fear recede. This was the right thing. She just knew it. She was going to take a leap of faith just as Rose had done. "Thank you, Rose." Mildred gripped the handles of her walker with sweaty palms.

But Rose wasn't finished. "My parents refused to talk to me after I put on those tights. And Enrique dropped me at a show in New York City. I lost everything over a man. Think about this, Mildred. Sharp objects. Shaky hands."

Mildred's palms seemed sweatier. Forward motion halted at the curb.

"Can I help you, ladies?" Phil appeared in the barbershop doorway, looking tall, probably because he didn't hunch over a walker and Mildred stood in the gutter.

For once, Rose and Agnes were silent.

That must have been a sign. Mildred gathered her courage and said, "I need a haircut."

"Excellent." Phil's voice sounded like the mad scientist on the old black-and-white movie she'd watched last night. "Come sit in my chair." He held the door open for her.

Agnes gasped. "Mildred?"

"Did you hear nothing I said?" Rose sniped.

"I'll be right back." Mildred concentrated on the cadence of forward progress. Lift walker. Move it forward. Step, step. Repeat. In no time, she was through the door.

Phil directed her to sit in the red chair in front.

After she was settled with her walker to one side of the cutting station, he put the barber drape over her, snapping it too tightly at her neck. Mildred was too petrified to say anything. Besides, if she spoke, her voice might sound like the shadowy creature on that movie last night. Thick, pained, crazed.

"Just a trim?"

She nodded, making the collar of the drape cut into her Adam's apple.

Phil turned on the clippers.

"I THOUGHT I MIGHT find you here." Chad walked onto the bridge toward Tracy. After the nail gun incident, he needed to talk to her. He felt as if she was important. But he couldn't quite prioritize her importance in his life, not without seeing her.

Tracy was on the bridge with her camera

set on a tripod. She sent him a guarded look. She looked more drained than he'd seen her before. The afternoon sun was drifting to the mountainous horizon to the west, turning a deep pinkish-orange that made Tracy's hair sparkle.

"We need to talk about that kiss," he said, heading her off at the pass by adding, "That kiss was great."

She'd been opening her mouth to say something. She snapped it closed and crossed her arms over her chest.

He took that to mean he should continue. "I just spent the last few hours with Slade at Urgent Care." He pointed out the blood stains on his shirt and pants.

"You almost killed him."

He wasn't surprised she'd already heard about the accident. "In fairness, his thumb wasn't where it was supposed to be." He hadn't figured out what he wanted to say or what he wanted to do where she was concerned. He just knew he had to talk to her. "I shouldn't have walked away the other day."

She pressed her lips together.

He couldn't look at her all closed up like that and open himself up to her. He paced the area of the bridge where she stood. "I was... I am...confused."

She made a huffing noise, which he took as an indicator that he was on the wrong track.

"I haven't had time to just be me in years." The truth of the statement filled him with a confidence that lifted his shoulders and planted his feet before her. "About ten years ago, my father challenged me to get serious at the *Lampoon*. He wanted higher quality articles more in line with the voice of the magazine. I stepped up my game." He'd packed away his laugh, his smile, his appreciation of a joke. He'd become a writer in the image of his father—sarcastic, cutting, ironic. "When we named the column the Happy Bachelor, that's who I was."

He didn't want to be the man in his father's shadow anymore, but he wasn't sure he knew how to be anyone but that man.

Tracy tilted her head and tossed her hands in a way that made him smile and remember how much he liked being with her. He was different when he was with her. He was the smiling, laughing, joking man of his youth.

His youth? He was thinking like an old man. Chad shook his head. "I was increasingly being asked to become more involved in managing the *Lampoon*. And then my dad got sick and…it was all I could do to hold the company and him together. Being compassionate was impossible."

"So that's your excuse…for…shutting down? And…and hurting me?"

"No. It's an apology. It's me saying I'm sorry for leaving."

She turned away, but he caught her hand. It was small and soft, but cold.

He placed his other hand over hers to warm it up. "I'm not grieving, but I'm not sure what I want anymore, except I want to show the *Lampoon* they made a mistake. And I think I want…you."

"You think?" So much derision.

"I hope. And I hope you'll go with me on this." He had a long way to go, and only a vague idea of how to get there. He needed time, no matter how much he wanted to take her into his arms now. Acting now solved nothing between them. "Will you give me a chance to make yesterday up to you? To surprise you with something romantic?"

After a painful moment of silence, she nodded.

"Clippers?" Mildred didn't recognize her own voice.

"I'm gonna clean up the hair on your neck."

Phil was wearing a strong dose of musky cologne.

It made it hard for Mildred to breathe. Or maybe it was the clippers buzzing behind her. "Oh…uh…I like my neck hairy."

He snapped off the clippers, set them on a side table and then picked up a spray bottle.

"No shampoo?"

"I don't do shampoos unless you need a dandruff treatment." He ran his fingers through her hair and then parted it in spots as if looking for lice. "You don't need a shampoo. I haven't washed my hair in weeks."

"Oh, my." Mildred was sorry to hear that, but glad Agnes and Rose hadn't heard.

"Let's take off your glasses and I'll get to work." He removed her glasses and—by the sounds of it—set them on the counter beneath the mirror.

Now she couldn't even see shapes.

She heard him open and close a drawer, snip the air with scissors and position himself behind her.

She didn't have to see to visualize the way his hands shook.

"I changed my mind." Mildred scooted forward, reaching for her walker. Where was it?

Rose would never let her live this one down.

Finally, her hand connected with a handle. In no time, she was up and headed toward the door, mortified, but both ear lobes intact. "I think I'll grow my hair long."

Phil scurried after her like a six-foot-tall mouse with big shuffling feet. He stood in the doorway.

Was he going to trap her here? Rough her up for refusing a haircut? Or take her into his arms and profess his undying love?

Mildred's heart pounded out a desperate tango. She had to stop watching those old black and white films.

"Your glasses," Phil said. He put them on her nose and opened the door. "Sorry it didn't work out."

Mildred trundled through to freedom and safety and continued singlehood. The band was staying together.

"Oh, and Mildred?"

"Yes?" She didn't dare turn around.

"I need my drape." He unsnapped it from her neck, nearly choking her again.

TRACY CAME IN the back bakery door, holding Chad's words closer than her video camera. Chad had apologized. Chad liked her. Chad had once been a real happy bachelor.

She wanted to dance across the kitchen like Rose. She wanted to execute a three-jump checker move and say, *"King me."* She wanted to say something totally outrageous the way Eunice did and get away with it.

Instead, a quiet voice in her head whispered, "Be careful."

Someone came in the front, ringing the bell. Was it Chad?

"Can you get that?" Jess whispered, rocking Gregory in the break area.

Tracy hadn't noticed Jess was there. She ran to see if Chad was at the front door. He wasn't.

Crowing, Rose grapevined across the dining room, just as Tracy had wanted to do.

Smiling, Agnes held the door open for Mildred, whose face was beet-red.

"That was priceless." Rose sank into a chair.

"It was worthless." Mildred sat in her walker, but she had a half grin on her face.

"We need a half dozen snickerdoodles to go." Agnes patted Mildred's shoulder. "You got farther than I would have."

"That's true." Rose caught her breath. "I could never have asked Phil for a haircut."

"What?" Tracy came closer to examine

Mildred for knicks and cuts. "But your hair looks so good."

The three town council women laughed.

"That's because I chickened out when he picked up the scissors." Mildred fluffed her hair. "It was like a horror movie. Snip-snip." She shuddered. "I couldn't get out of there fast enough."

Tracy bagged up their cookies and sent them on their way, returning to find Gregory awake and Jessica pacing. "Where's Eunice?"

"Working the afternoon shift at Mae's Pretty Things. I was hoping to experiment with her recipes without her around." Tracy might have missed the stressful note in Jessica's words if she hadn't seen the pinched lines around her mouth. "I also need to work on transforming the old recipes I've been given into something new. And find time to check out the veterans hall with Christine." Jess smoothed Gregory's dark hair and pressed a kiss to his crown.

The little tyke blinked sleepily.

Tracy looked from the books on the shelf to the baby. "I can read to him." It would be nice to cuddle with the little man.

"Really?" Jess was already moving—out of the chair, across the room, shifting the baby for a hand off into Tracy's arms.

Gregory sensed Tracy's tension. He craned his neck to look her in the eye. His lower lip trembled.

"Oh, no. No crying." Tracy sat in the rocker and picked up *The Cat in the Hat*. "We're going to read books."

Only a few pages in, Gregory tucked his head beneath her chin and pointed at the pictures, with drooly, blubbery commentary. Tracy talked back, as if she understood what he was saying. Neither one cared that her sentences were sometimes stilted.

TRACY SAT AT her kitchen table trying to fit different video clips together in a way that made sense. The trouble with shooting segments without a plan was she had enough digital clips to make four or five videos. The more she worked on it, the less she was interested in boxing herself into three minutes of video. Wasn't that essentially what had happened to Chad? He'd fit himself into the role of the Happy Bachelor and couldn't seem to find his way out of the mold.

Something rattled a front window. Tracy couldn't get to the pane fast enough.

Chad stood on the sidewalk smiling up at

her. "Rapunzel, I couldn't sleep. Come out and play."

There was mischief in his voice and she just bet in his eyes, too.

The mischief and the nip of cold combined to give her a shiver. "It's ten o'clock." She had to get up at 4 a.m. It was already past her bedtime.

"Life doesn't end until at least eleven." Spoken like a true playboy.

Once upon a time, Tracy wouldn't have hesitated. She would have flown down the stairs, danced all night and rolled out of bed in the morning without complaint. "I can't."

"But you want to, don't you?" He sighed. "I want you to, too.

She was a sucker for a suave, good-looking man. "Meet me around back."

When she opened the back door, Chad was there to greet her with a smile. He wrapped his arm around her shoulders and said, "So you can talk easier."

Who wanted to talk? She snuggled closer. He was warm and solid and had promised her romance. She buried the hurt from the cemetery and put her trust in him, hoping he'd figured out the man he wanted to be and the woman he wanted at his side.

They headed toward the town square, crossing the grass and sitting on the bench beneath the sprawling oak tree. The night was clear. Stars shown above in the velvety sky. Bullfrogs sang by the river. It was perfect. He was perfect. She felt perfect in the crook of his arm.

Tracy turned to face him, whispering, "I was promised something romantic."

"Don't confuse that promise with this. I couldn't sleep."

She heard a distant sound, like the bell they used to ring at school signifying the start of earthquake drills. Or maybe the sound was in her head. Tracy pushed the warning aside and focused on Chad. Strong, warm Chad. "Why couldn't you sleep?"

"I turned in a column to one of my advertisers two days ago and haven't heard a word about it since."

"I hope he hates it."

"Somehow, I knew you'd say that." His words rumbled with humor. "But losing an advertiser over content would be disappointing. My success lets the board know it was a mistake to let me go."

She heard the sound again, louder this time.

"Enough talk." His thumb brushed her

chin, her lips. And then he leaned in to kiss her, gathering her into his arms, drawing her into his lap.

There was no awkward tangle of limbs. Her palms found his cheeks. His hands found the small of her back. His lips plundered. Hers surrendered. And her heart pounded happily in her chest.

All too soon a spotlight blinded them. "Excuse me, folks. I got a report of mischief in the area." It was the sheriff.

"Nate." Tracy tried to extricate herself from Chad's arms, but he didn't let her off his lap. "Nothing going on here."

Chad chuckled.

"Got a call from Leona, too," Nate said. "She reported Mr. Healy was unaccounted for."

"Someone is going to be unaccounted for tomorrow," Chad said in a deadly tone. "At the very least, she'll be featured in my column."

His column? The warning bell went off again.

Tracy backtracked through their conversation, overlaying it with their earlier one, realized he hadn't come to her window because he couldn't stop thinking of her or because he couldn't spend another moment without her. He'd come because he needed a distraction from his insecurities.

"Leona wants to lock up." Sheriff Nate clicked off the spotlight. "I'll tell her you'll be back in ten minutes."

"Make it twenty." Chad rearranged Tracy in his lap. "Now, where were we?"

"We were living a fantasy. Or at least, I was." She pushed out of his arms and onto her feet. "You couldn't sleep. You probably couldn't write with the irony you seem to value so much." She paced the length of the bench and back, realizing where they were. "And I... I'm just now remembering this tree." She placed her palm on the cool, rough bark. "This...is where marriage proposals happen. It's...what every little girl in Harmony Valley dreams of." And a couple of the big girls, too. Her brother had proposed to Emma beneath this tree. "I...don't want someone around...who thinks he might want me. I want someone...who knows he wants me. More than any job or stupid column."

Chad got quickly to his feet as if his bachelorhood had suddenly issued a red alert.

Tracy had her answer. She smiled sadly. "I need...to get up early tomorrow." She walked away.

He didn't follow. She couldn't hear any

footsteps in the grass. But he did call after her softly, "Dream of me."

The egotistical, seductive jerk!

"You know." She paused, gathering herself to turn and face him. "The thing about dreams is…at some point they either come true. Or…you realize they never fit in the first place."

CHAPTER TWENTY

LATE THE NEXT MORNING, Jessica assembled the key players in Harmony Valley to assess the veterans hall—Tracy, Christine, Slade, Flynn and Duffy. Somehow, Chad managed to tag along, too.

Tracy wore her sternest attitude where Chad was concerned, and her grubbiest jeans, shirt and work boots. She'd also brought gloves. The gloves she stuck in her back pocket so she could make notes of what needed to be done on a clipboard. Assuming someone decided anything should be done. She hoped they decided to fix the place up. She felt an odd kinship with the once productive spot.

The group stood in the parking lot, taking in the neglect while Duffy's little golden terrier raced around the grounds on olfactory overload.

Since she'd gotten out of Duffy's truck, Jessica had been speechless. She held Gregory close. "I'm trying to be positive inside." She didn't sound as if she was succeeding.

"I don't like the look of this." Slade had a big white bandage on his thumb and a big negative attitude toward the hall. "Not for *my* wedding reception."

"It's a tear-down," Chad said, earning a scowl from Tracy. He deserved more than a scowl, but with so many witnesses, a scowl would have to do.

"We should get Dane and his crew out here for a look." Flynn referred to the construction company that had restored and rebuilt the winery buildings.

So far, that was the only thing Tracy had written down: *call Dane Utley.*

"I'm not financing this," Slade said firmly, in a tone he'd used a lot when he, Flynn and Will had been building the winery. Slade took a hard look at the bottom line. "The partnership is not financing this. It has money pit written all over it."

But his bride wanted a huge wedding locally, so he was going to have to compromise.

"Let's…just do a walk through." Tracy herded them toward the sidewalk. "Trees first. Duffy?"

"Trees need trimming," Duffy said matter-of-factly. Given that he was the vineyard manager, he knew about trees. His little dog, Goldie, snuffled through the blanket of leaves on the ground, giving Gregory the giggles. "A couple of dead branches have fallen and broken windows. A couple more branches are dead up there and could fall at any time on passing cars."

Everyone took several steps back in case the trees decided to fall.

"The parking lot is a loss," Slade said glumly.

It was hard to argue when he was right.

Even Christine was looking doubtful. "It's lacking the wow factor, isn't it?"

Slade looked at his fiancée as if she'd lost her mind. "It never had it."

"Tear-down," Chad repeated, as if no one had heard him the first time.

Tracy clutched her clipboard and fought the urge to defend the hall. During her recovery in the hospital, Tracy hadn't realized Will was her patient advocate. He'd worked behind the scenes to obtain the care and treatment she'd needed to come back to life. The veterans hall had no advocate, no voice, not even Rutgar's booming one.

"Let's take a look inside." Jessica's voice

was resigned. She'd been excited about the hall this morning. A usable rental hall near a bakery that did wedding cakes meant more wedding cakes would be sold. "Tracy, can you unlock the doors?"

She could. But she couldn't do it without stating her case. "Before we go inside…I'd like to remind those who knew me before the accident—" Flynn and Slade "—that I was a tear-down, too. Don't be afraid…of a big challenge. Or of big change."

"Nothing comes easy," Chad murmured, studying her intently.

Tracy felt her cheeks heat. She shouldn't have been surprised that he understood her loyalty to the place. Chad had understood her better than anyone since they'd met. She undid the heavy locks and propped the doors open, because the air inside smelled like a cat litter box left out in the rain and then covered in plastic.

Gregory made a face and buried it against Jessica's neck. Goldie put her nose to the floor and raced inside. It was her idea of heaven. The rest of the group ventured no farther than the first few feet inside the hall.

"What is that smell?" Slade covered his nose.

"Raccoon," said Duffy.

"Squirrel," said Flynn.

"Skunk," said Christine.

Tracy hoped it wasn't all three. "Let's… try to look at this from the positive side—in terms of possibilities."

"That'll be hard to do." Slade tugged on the placate of his polo shirt as if adjusting one of those ties he always used to wear.

Tracy ignored him and launched into her pitch. "The hall is large and open. I've…been to conferences in smaller venues than this. You…could easily fit fifteen hundred people at tables in here. And…still have room for the band. Or DJ. And a dance floor."

Chad was the only person looking at her, not the devastation. His gaze was indecipherable and she had to look away.

"Replace the windows, make sure the roof doesn't leak, refinish the floors." Flynn ventured into the middle of the hall. "It's not *that* bad."

"Don't kid yourself." Slade moved closer to the door. "It's bad."

"Maybe the veterans in town have money in the bank," Chad said, surprising Tracy with a show of support.

"Not enough money." Slade was prevented from backing out the door by Christine's hand on his arm and a look that encouraged him to be patient.

"We could update the lighting. With a wedding budget." Tracy had spent a few days giving it some thought. "Maybe rent light fixtures. Chandeliers." Yes, there was such a thing as chandelier rental. "Maybe…hang wallpaper or drapes on the walls?"

"Oh." Christine perked up.

"Speaking of curtains," Duffy said. "Did the curtains up there just move?"

Goldie was on the stage. She began to bark at the drapes. And then something with red-gold fur leapt from the stage and raced toward the front door. Goldie ran to the edge of the stage, barking, decided the jump was too much for her short little legs, and raced down the stairs.

"Back-back-back!" Duffy yelled, gesturing for them to give the fox room to escape.

Goldie and her short legs were no match for the speeding fox, although she gave it her best effort. Her taking the stairs had given the fox too much of a head start.

Once the fox passed, Duffy stood in front of his dog and yelled, "Goldie, stay."

The little dog skidded to a halt in front of

him, panting and wagging her tail, but sneaking looks past Duffy's legs.

That was most likely the death knell for the veterans hall. Tracy's spirits sank.

"You're lucky you didn't get eaten, mongrel." Duffy picked Goldie up and held her to his chest. She drooped in his arms as if she'd expended all her energy. "If you bring in a pest control company to get rid of the critters, I can help tame the trees. If I have a crew." His gaze took in the men. "If Christine can spare me, we can start tomorrow, midafternoon."

"So what do you say?" Tracy asked. "Do we check into funding? Get a bid to repair the place?" This last was spoken directly to Slade.

Slade looked to Christine.

"I'd love to get married here in town." Christine put a hand at the base of his neck where his scar was. "We can have the wedding on the bluff overlooking the river and the reception here."

"It'll look like a dump." Slade was first class all the way.

"Not necessarily," Chad said, once more Tracy's champion. "I've seen shacks in the desert classed up with wall tapestries and lighting changes. I think Tracy's on to something."

"It'll take a miracle," Slade grumbled, heading toward the door.

"Don't rely on miracles and wishes," Tracy said, half to herself, because she knew how rare wishes came true. "Rely on hard work."

"ARE YOU SURE that's safe?" Chad asked Flynn as they watched Duffy lash himself to a V in a tree trunk thirty feet above the road at the veterans hall the day after they'd toured the facilities with the bride and groom. Chad had offered to help because Tracy was giving him the cold shoulder. She wasn't the only one. He hadn't heard from Marty either. "The other day Duffy talked about dead limbs ready to fall."

"Normally, I'd say no. Not safe." Flynn shaded his eyes as he looked up. "But as a vineyard manager, Duffy is paid to clear out trees and brush. And last winter after we had one heck of a rain storm, he helped clear some gigantic pines that nearly crushed Rutgar's house. I have respect for his chainsaw skills and his knowledge of trees."

"What's not safe is you two standing under the tree," Duffy called down to them, looking like a true professional with goggles and protective earwear. The chainsaw he held roared to life.

They leapt a safe distance back.

Duffy cut limbs with a cool efficiency. When he shifted to another side of the tree, Chad and Flynn came in to drag the branches out of the street. Some were small enough to toss into the back of Flynn's truck. Others needed trimming to fit. Those they stacked on the dried grass that had once been a lawn.

When they had a big pile of oversized branches, Flynn produced his own chainsaw— much smaller than Duffy's—and went to work, leaving Chad to schlep branches into the truck bed. Chad had been banned from power tools.

Duffy dropped several limbs into the street and looked to be shifting his position.

Chad walked onto the road, waded into the knee deep foliage, grabbed a branch big enough not to snap when he dragged it away, and tugged. The labyrinth of foliage didn't budge.

Tires squealed around the corner from the highway. A blue, bubble-fendered Cadillac bore down on Chad and his tangled sea of branches. A brown scarf fluttered in the wind behind the driver's white hair.

"Hey!" Chad yelled and waved at the driver.

There was only about six feet of roadway free between the pile of branches and the opposite sidewalk. Not nearly enough room for a wide Cadillac to clear without driving on the sidewalk. But it didn't look as if she was veering at all. And if she didn't veer and cleared enough branches, she was going to run Chad over.

The Caddy's grill approached like the famished jaws of doom. Chad's shouts didn't rise above Flynn's or Duffy's chainsaws. He tried backing up, but his legs were stuck within the V of one branch and the angled offshoots of the branches beneath it. He stumbled backward and was almost immediately swallowed into the thatch.

Metal protested the scrape of wood across paint. Branches snapped. There was a series of lurching noises. Chad was tossed, poked, scraped, skewered and banged against the pavement like a rag doll in a blender.

And then the engine receded. And the chainsaws stopped.

"Chad! Chad!" Flynn's voice.

Booted feet approached. There was a sound like a two-hundred pound cat climbing down a tree.

"I'm alive," Chad croaked, feeling as if he wasn't.

Branches shifted, cracked, lifted. Hands drew Chad from the mess with more pokes, scrapes and skewers.

"I'm alive," Chad said again, but everything was starting to throb and sting. And he was grateful of Flynn's steadying arm.

"You're okay," Flynn sounded surprised. "I thought Lilac was going to kill you. I thought she wasn't supposed to drive anymore. She almost killed my nephew's dog last year." He blew out a breath. "Really, I thought she was going to kill you. She ran over half the pile of branches and never stopped."

"It's a shame. She ruined that classic Caddy grill," Duffy deadpanned. When they both looked at him as if he was crazy, he shrugged and added, "Don't tell me you weren't thinking it, too."

Chad was getting his sea legs back. He laughed. "I was." In some sick, small corner of his male brain, he'd mourned a vintage car.

"Me, too." Flynn started laughing.

And pretty soon, the three of them were filling the empty street with adrenaline-rush guffaws.

"I need to take you to Leona's," Flynn said when the humor petered out.

"I'm fine," Chad said as evenly as he could, when he felt as if he'd had a bad acupuncture session. "I can walk." That might have been an overstatement. The Lambridge B&B was all the way on the other side of town. The bakery… He might make it there.

"You can't walk." Duffy dragged the remaining branches out of the road, easy as you please. "Take him home, Flynn. He's too stubborn to listen to reason. I'll finish up here."

Slade pulled up in a shiny black truck that had probably never had branches loaded in the bed. "Fred Oliver called me. He lives down the street and saw the whole thing. Am I driving someone to the hospital?"

"Nope." Chad had been shaking out his limbs, just to make sure nothing was broken. Nothing seemed to be. "I just feel like a big pincushion." One that had been pounded several times by a hammer.

"Now you know how I feel." Slade grinned and held up his bandaged hand. "Get in. I'll take you to Leona's."

Chad preferred being taken to Tracy. And what was the point in that? He was standing with one foot in each world—satirical bachelor articles and settled, elderly Harmony Valley. Try as he might, he didn't seem to fit in either place.

He shuffled over to the truck like an old man who'd had his walker confiscated.

Meanwhile, the sheriff pulled up. "Heard Lilac is up to her old ways."

Flynn nodded. "Speeding, reckless driving."

"Jumping the curb," Duffy added.

"Destroying classic automobiles. That's a law, right?" Chad sighed. "Seriously, can you test her for blindness or blind spots?"

"I'm on it." The sheriff sped away.

"Things aren't usually this exciting in Harmony Valley," Slade said, backing up and pointing the truck in the direction of the B&B. "Old people. Who knew?"

Chad did. They could be as unpredictable and protective of their independence as randy teenagers. He stared out the window, on the lookout for a blue Cadillac.

"You don't need to walk me up," Chad said when Slade pulled in front of the large green Victorian.

"I feel it's my duty. I was supposed to be on the crew today and I used my injury as an excuse." He walked next to Chad at a pace that was as slow as Mildred's fastest walker speed. "Are you sure you're okay? No nausea? Double vision?"

"I just hurt."

Leona opened the front door. "I hear Lilac nearly killed someone this time." She eyed Chad as he approached the porch. "He's not bleeding, is he?"

"He's not spurting arterial blood, if that's what you mean," Slade said wryly. "We need to get him comfortable. Acetaminophen, bandages, ice packs." He held Chad's arm up the stairs. "Were you normally this clumsy as a kid?"

"I was worse." He hadn't exactly been the star of the soccer team. Or any sports team for that matter. In high school, he'd been the captain of the debate and chess teams three years running.

Leona blocked the doorway. "Turn around." A royal command.

"Why?" Chad was feeling the need for a pain reliever.

"You can't come in until you're clean." That's when Chad noticed she had a dust broom in her hand.

Slade began to protest, but Chad knew it was no use. "I'll never get in if we argue."

She brushed the remaining leaves and twigs from his back, assured herself his blood wasn't spurting and opened the door for him to come inside. "Mr. Jennings, you may go. Mr. Healy, upstairs with you. I'll be right up with what you require."

Chad doubted that. He watched her disappear down a dark hallway and shuffled into the living room. It seemed as if he'd barely laid down when Leona began shrieking.

"Not on the couch! Not on the couch! Have you no sense of value?"

Chad rolled his head to the side. His body was an aching throbbing mess and he probably looked as if he'd been in a cat fight. "Why is it you don't have any pictures of your family in this house?"

She stopped trying to lift his feet off the couch. "Have you been snooping?"

"No. There are no pictures here or in the foyer or the dining room or on your refrigerator. Why?" He was a columnist. He noticed details. He'd planned on questioning her some other time. But his timing stank.

"My family is none of your concern, Mr. Healy." Leona handed him an ice pack. "I'll

give you five minutes to get off my couch."
She fled the room.

He put the ice pack on the back of one
hand. His parents were old, like her. They
were stuffy, like her. But they'd loved Chad.
They'd had pictures of him on their refrigerator, in their offices, on their phones. He
dragged himself upright, shifting the ice pack
to his forehead, and went to the one place he
knew he'd be cared for.

"WHAT ARE YOU doing up here?" Tracy had
spent the afternoon tracking down women
who'd given Jessica recipes, but not stories.

She'd heard about Chad's near miss with
Lilac's Caddy, but she'd also heard he'd been
delivered safely to Leona's, where speculation
ran high that he'd be tossed to the curb rather
than nursed back to fighting form.

She'd climbed the stairs to her apartment
only to find Chad sprawled across her bed,
plastic baggies of ice positioned across his
body like bulbs sprouting in a spring flower-
bed. Seeing him in her bed, she'd had that
fairy-tale flutter in her heart and recalled his
promise of a romantic gesture. If this was his
idea of romance, where were the rose petals?

Tracy shook Chad's arm. "Are you dead?" If not, he would be soon.

"If I was in heaven, there wouldn't be so much pink." Chad didn't open an eye, but he didn't have to. There was pink everywhere one looked in Tracy's apartment.

"How did you get in?"

"Lucky for me, no one locks doors in Harmony Valley, except Leona."

Now he found something to appreciate about the town? "I'd ask you if you were in pain. But I'd rather know why...you chose to crash on my bed."

"Crash." He forced a laugh. "I'll never abuse that word again."

She leaned over him and brushed a thick lock of sun-kissed hair from his forehead, only to find a scratch from one temple to the other above his green-tinged sink bruise. His hair was damp, as if he'd been sweating.

"It's hot up here," he said, as if reading her mind.

"It's the heat from the kitchen. It felt like an oven in the summer." She catalogued the damage—his shirt torn in several places, the scrapes and gouges although nothing was oozing blood, the angry red bruises already formed on his arms. The danger had been more serious than Flynn had led her to believe. He could have died! The impact of nearly losing him blindsided her. She sat too quickly on the edge of the bed. "I hate to ask if you've checked for damage beneath the denim."

"Just bruises."

"Did Leona toss you out?" If she had, Tracy was going to exchange harsh words with her.

"I'm beginning to feel you've bet money on that event. That's the second time you've asked me." He cracked open one eye. "I rummaged in your medicine cabinet for a pain reliever. I expected to find pink nail polish. All I found was black."

"I've been in a dark phase. Since the accident. The apartment came in pink."

"I also was in your freezer to get ice and your kitchen drawers looking for bags to put it in." He closed one eye. "You don't have enough food in here to feed a rabbit."

"Good thing I don't have any rabbits." Honestly, she lived on baked goods and vegetables. Was that so bad?

"You also don't have any steak. I would've settled for a hamburger." He sighed. "Leona wasn't sympathetic to my wounds and I knew

I couldn't invade her kitchen…at least not without her knowledge."

That was as good as admitting that he'd snooped in Leona's kitchen at some point during his stay. He should have been an investigative reporter.

"My mother used to make me tea when I got injured to calm me down." His voice had that vulnerable note that played on her heartstrings. "My dad used to make me steak to replenish my blood cells."

"They sound like wonderful parents."

"They were. They were just…old."

And firm, he'd said. And angry with each other. They'd had Chad when they were already set in their ways. But that wasn't the issue here. "You…want me to make you tea and steak?"

"Would you?"

"Sure." She struggled to keep the excitement from her voice. "If…I can read your column before you publish it."

"I'll buy you flowers instead."

"There's enough pink in this room without flowers from you."

"I'm not sure I'm going to write the column." His voice fell to failure levels. "My advertising sponsor won't return my calls."

She brushed the back of her hand over an unmarred section of his cheek. "You'll publish it. You're not a quitter." She felt a twinge of betrayal for Harmony Valley, but it was Chad who needed bolstering right now.

"You think I'd buy you pink roses?" He blew out a breath and shifted an ice pack higher on his shoulder. "You like dandelions. You're a daisy girl through and through."

"Plain and simple, like my speech. Is that it?" Plain. His opinion of her stung. Never mind that he was right. Had she always preferred daisies to roses? Or was this a preference that had evolved from her speech de-evolving?

"You're not plain." He'd been so cavalier about his injuries, that the sudden annoyance in his voice made her sit up straight. "In case you haven't noticed, everyone talks in fits and starts. Your stops are just more pronounced than others." He groaned. "Except when you drink or are mad at me."

Or she was in the shelter of his arms. "Then…you should let me read the column early. You know I'll be mad at you. And then I can really test my speech skills."

"Maybe I don't want you to be mad at me."

She didn't say anything, because she'd already built her hopes up too often for this man, only to have them tumble back to earth. He was a fluke. Plain and simple.

"Maybe I need more than steak and tea in exchange."

"I'll…throw in a baked potato and some rabbit lettuce."

A weary head shake. "I was thinking more along the lines of this bed. It's more comfortable than the one I pay for at Leona's."

"If I let you stay here…you'll give me the read?" Tracy glanced around. There was no couch, no daybed, no pullout. This wasn't an apartment for two people who weren't sleeping together. It was more sparsely furnished by Jess than most hotel rooms. Still…how badly did she want to see his column?

"Those are my terms—tea, steak and this bed."

"Deal." She took his hand and shook it. Never mind that they'd made and broken several deals already. She had high hopes for this one.

He opened both eyes. "Really?"

"Yes." She gathered some of her things and stuffed them into a large black leather tote.

He watched her in silence until she moved toward the door. "What are you doing?"

"I'm going to get your steak. I'll cook it for you in the morning." After a good night's sleep in her childhood bed at home.

CHAPTER TWENTY-ONE

THERE WERE SOUNDS in the bed & breakfast.

There were never sounds in the bed & breakfast.

Chad rolled over in bed without a spring squeak or a mattress sag. He would have ignored the sounds if not for a stab of pain on his arm where it was scraped and bruised. He sat up blearily.

Female voices drifted up to him.

Leona never talked to herself. She barely talked to him.

The room was bathed in pink light.

And then the smell of cinnamon drifted to him, grounding him in a pleasant reality. He was at the bakery. It was who-knew-what-time of the morning. It was dark and he was suddenly famished, having not eaten dinner last night.

A few minutes later, he'd showered and borrowed Tracy's toothbrush and showed himself downstairs.

"You…don't look quite so dead this morning," Tracy said, handing him a mug of green tea. She indicated he sit on a stool at the island counter. "You're scabbing over nicely."

Chad took that as a compliment.

"I've got your steak right here." She had the microwave running on the hold-warm setting.

Soon, Chad was eating his steak, drinking his tea and thinking fondly of his parents.

"We're using you as a guinea pig," Jess said, smiling lopsidedly. "Duffy drew the line at tasting these until I had them perfected." She set a plate of two biscuits next to him, along with two pats of butter.

"What are they?" They smelled like rosemary.

Jess turned her attention back to a mixing bowl. "Sweet—"

"Biscuits," Tracy finished for her. She was arranging cookies like dominoes on a display plate.

Chad devoured the biscuit, only belatedly realizing both women had stopped working to stare at him. "Did I belch and not realize it?"

Tracy took a step closer. "How do you like the biscuits?"

"Why?" He stopped eating. "Did you poison them? I was going to order you flowers."

"Forget the flowers." Tracy glowered at him in that endearing way of hers. "We agreed on your column."

"The biscuits are a transformation recipe," Jess explained, ignoring their argument.

"Do...you remember Eunice talking about Horseradish-Doodles?" Tracy's glower downgraded to a frown, and then one corner of her mouth curled upward. "These are Sweet Horseradish Biscuits."

"I don't taste horseradish." Chad swept his tongue around his mouth. "I taste rosemary, but there's a sharpness to it."

"Horseradish," both women said. They high fived.

"Let's try them in the case this morning," Jess said.

In no time, Tracy had the rest of the batch on a plate and disappeared into the dining area with them.

"I feel as if I've been conned," he said, feeling more content in the morning than he had in a long time.

Jessica had a gentle smile that was welcoming. "You shouldn't complain since you liked them."

He had and he was still hungry. He finished the second one off as Tracy returned.

"So today is setup day for the Harvest Festival. What does that mean?"

"Mostly…it means the townspeople get an extra day outside their home to visit with each other." Tracy's sentences were long and strong this morning. "There's…not much setup to do." She plated mini carrot-cake loaves and then took the frosting bag and expertly drizzled icing on top. "There's the stage. And PA system. Chairs to sit on. Tables for activities. Pumpkins to be stacked. The bowling lanes to be marked."

"Tracy is going to win pumpkin bowling and become the Harvest Festival Queen," Jessica teased.

"I'm not competing. But you…" Tracy shook her finger at Jessica. "You have to try it. You've never done it before."

Chad had to ask. "Is there a competition for the king?"

Tracy didn't do a good job of hiding a smile. "It's the nail-driving competition. You have to drive a nail into a piece of wood with one strike."

His finger throbbed just thinking about wielding a hammer again.

"Come back in the summer. We…have a

contest for the cutest male legs," Tracy dead-panned.

"That's more my speed."

Tracy didn't roll her eyes, but Chad knew she wanted to.

"CHAD'S NICE," JESSICA said to Tracy after Chad left to return to Leona's house.

"Don't get ideas. We're barely friends." And didn't that hurt to admit? "He...doesn't know what he wants out of life."

"And you do?" Jessica crimped the edges of a sugar-free apple pie Old Man Takata had ordered.

"Well..." Was it just last week she'd wanted desperately to return to the fast-paced world of advertising? These past few days, her life had felt so full. She hadn't thought about it at all.

Duffy entered, carrying a babbling Gregory. "He's an early riser, just like his mother." He strapped Gregory in a high chair, kissed his son on the top of the head and then kissed Jessica goodbye. "See you ladies at lunch."

Tracy sighed. Two years ago, she'd been at the top of her game in advertising. She'd had a vague idea about family, but couldn't visualize it. But lately, seeing Gregory with

Duffy melted her heart. She could visualize a little boy or two with sun-kissed brown hair. They'd be cheerful, resilient boys. Like their father. And she'd be a good mom, getting them off to school and never missing a dinner for a demanding client's last-minute deadline. Not that she wanted to be the head cook. Take-out would be nice every once in awhile.

Jess put dry cereal on Gregory's tray. "You never answered my question."

"I don't know." The challenge of the video excited her, but the actual job? Not so much. She was no better than Chad, not knowing what she wanted out of life.

"I can confuse the issue further." Jess twisted a dish towel in her hands. "In order to make this place work long-term, I need more business." Her hesitant smile spoke louder than her words about fragile dreams and the fear of failure. "You increased our sales with your blog ideas. You could help me get more wedding cake business, too."

"Be your marketer?" Tracy was flattered. But she was also a realist. "Jess…you can barely afford to pay me now." Her peers in advertising would scoff. And truth be told, Tracy felt a twinge of embarrassment at the idea of introducing herself as a marketing manager for a small-town bakery.

But her peers would already deduct intelligence points for her speech pattern. And she was her own harshest critic. Jess was offering what she'd wished for days ago—a job without a job interview.

"We could work something out—bonuses, commissions—couldn't we?" She wasn't looking at Tracy anymore. She was looking at the pictures on the wall. Generations of Martin's. In a place that didn't judge.

"LATE NIGHT, MR. HEALY?" Leona was waiting for Chad when he returned to the bed & breakfast. A few strands of hair were loose in her normally military neat hairstyle.

Was she worried about him? Or did she think he wouldn't pay her for a night he hadn't slept here? "Spent in the infirmary. I received better care there than you offered." She'd been more concerned with her precious furniture than his health. "I hope you didn't report me missing with the sheriff."

Her nose went in the air. "You're too early for breakfast."

"Already had it, so you can put those store-bought donuts back in their box."

An expression flashed across Leona's face that was half hurt, half anger. "You have two more nights, Mr. Healy. Two more nights."

He went upstairs to change his clothes, but it wasn't until he came back down and was out the door that the finality of it hit him. His time at Harmony Valley was coming to an end. He needed to figure out his relationship with Tracy.

Correction: *He needed to quit screwing up the foundation of what could be a relationship with Tracy.*

The town square was already a beehive of activity. The older generation sat in chairs and in walkers beneath blankets and heavy jackets and tried to direct Flynn and Slade, who looked upon Chad's arrival as one looked upon the cavalry in a foot soldier's losing battle.

"We're putting up the stage first." Flynn gestured to his truck and the big sheets of plywood it held. "How are you with a power drill?"

"Do you ask me these questions just to humiliate me?" Chad had never worked a power drill in his life. "I thought I was banned from power tools."

"A drill really doesn't qualify on my list.

Slade and I are going back to the mayor's
storage unit to load up the bleachers. I don't
want someone—" Flynn gave the high sign
toward the gathering of the elderly on the
lawn. "—to try to assemble the stage and fall
or have a piece of wood fall on him."

"I can't do this on my own."

"I recruited the best." Flynn pointed to
an old white truck pulling into the square.
"Tracy's dad."

"Ben hates me." Chad wasn't proud of the
whine his voice, but he was still working the
kinks out of his bruised body. "Take me to
the storage unit. Leave Slade here."

"Sorry, buddy." Flynn slapped him on the
back, causing Chad to flinch. "And sorry
again. But the mayor doesn't let anyone else
see what goodies he's got stored there. He
certainly won't let a reporter—"

"Columnist."

"—see what's inside there."

"Hey, boys." Ben held a cup of coffee as
if in toast. "I thought you'd have everything
set up by now."

"We've just got to get the stage unloaded
and then you can work your magic." Flynn
hurried over to his truck.

"I'll be assisting you today." Chad was determined not to complain about his wounds in front of Ben, or make a fool of himself, or drill a hole in Ben's appendages.

"We're not performing surgery." Ben finished his coffee and tossed the cup into the trash.

"Just tell me what to do."

And Ben did. They laid out the pieces of the four-foot-tall stage frame and attached the hinges with screws and a drill, until only the last corner was remaining.

"Why don't you put these screws in?" Ben handed Chad the drill and the bag with the screws.

Chad preferred to decline. But at that moment, Tracy showed up.

"Hey, Dad. How's it coming?" She kissed her father's cheek and managed not to greet Chad.

"Good, Sunshine, but I see Rutgar over there fiddling with live wires." His gaze focused across the square. "Can you two finish while I go prevent a catastrophe?"

They both assured him they could.

"Well." Tracy peered at the inside of the stage. "What are we doing?"

Chad pretended he knew what was what. "We need to fit the corners together and screw the hinges on." How had Ben done this? Hinge first on one board? Or one screw on each hinge side? Chad leaned over the three-foot-high particle board and attempted to screw the hinge in upside down. "It went in."

"Don't sound so surprised." Tracy's blond hair tumbled into her eyes. "I guess...that means you've earned the right to put in the next one."

Agnes called Tracy over to a group of elderly in a row of chairs.

Audience gone, Chad felt relieved. He needed to regroup. Should he invite Tracy to the B&B to read his column? Or ask her to dinner?

He leaned over again and tried to screw the hinge on the other corner board. The screw fell to the ground and the boards inched apart. But Chad was determined to get this. He supported the boards with his knees, leaned upside down and tried to put another screw in. The screw slipped. The drill slipped. The tips of his fingers got drilled.

He shouted. He nearly fell over the side of the walls on his head, but lurched back, only to drag his fingers up the plywood and tumble to his butt to the ground. The back of his head bounced off the pavement.

Tracy's face swam in front of his eyes. "Are you okay?"

"Do I have any fingers left?"

"The fact that you're joking means you're okay." She stood and said to the crowd, "Give him space. He's okay." She resumed leaning over him.

"This town hates me. Literally, it's out to kill me." Not any of the people specifically. Just the town in general.

"If that were true…it's doing a horrible job." She took his arm and helped him up. "But…it might be karma from you trying to write one of your belittling columns about it."

"I don't believe in karma." He looked around at the elderly faces. They reminded him of his parents. This was a community he could simultaneously relate to and be concerned for. The contradictions were there. They'd been there the entire time. This was a place where old traditions contrasted with new ways, and where old people coexisted with the young. *This is the story.*

That Pollyana story wouldn't attract any advertisers.

"I'm going to have you sit with Agnes

while I finish up the hinges." Tracy pointed him in the direction of others unable to help setup. Older others.

Chad's head throbbed. He glanced down at Tracy, wishing he could look at her all day. "You know how to operate power tools?"

"Hello?" She patted his arm gently, as if she knew he was battered all over. "I grew up on a farm."

Chad walked away, but not to the peanut gallery. He pulled out his phone and dialed Marty.

"I had you on my list of people to call today," Marty said by way of greeting. His tone was riddled with a bad-news vibe. "That article you sent wasn't the slam dunk I needed."

Chad sat on the curb, rubbing a palm over his forehead, trying not to lose his cool, trying to think fast to avoid disaster.

"What happened to you, man? The slick killer instinct is missing in these pages. It's as if you just wanted to kill the town, nothing slick about it."

Marty had to have misread the column. Chad stood and headed for the B&B at a good clip. "Give me another shot at it." He could edit it into something better.

"I'm sorry, Chad. We're going to have to back out."

"There's a cancellation clause, Marty." Chad's words snapped with anger. If he lost Marty, the rest of his sponsors would almost certainly bail. "It's gonna cost you." Twenty percent.

"You know how this works." Marty's uneven rumble smoothed. "You invoke that penalty and I won't work with you again."

Chad didn't need the advertising money as much as he needed Marty's goodwill. Still, he was mad enough not to bow down. "I'll let you know what I decide on Monday."

News of No Wrinkles backing out would travel fast. Media-buying execs were networked tighter than the small town gossip chain.

Chad returned to the B&B to wait out the avalanche of cancellations he was sure would come. And come, they did.

The *Lampoon* had won this round. If he launched his website on Sunday without sponsors, it'd be like saying, *"I'm nobody."* It'd be like saying, *"Dad won."*

Or it could be an entirely different statement. *"Take that, world, the Happy Bachelor doesn't need anybody."*

THE PEBBLES HIT Tracy's window just as she was thinking of turning off her laptop and starting dinner.

She opened the front window, sticking her head out into the chilly night air. "I should give you my cell phone number before you break a window."

Chad stood below her, more serious than she'd ever seen him. "Have you eaten?"

"No."

"Come with me to El Rosal. The early-bird-special diners have left. My treat."

Tracy hesitated. The man standing below her wasn't just plain Chad. "I'm sorry, but—"

"I still owe you something romantic." Was that desperation in his voice?

Tracy felt her resolve weakening and shored it up. "El Rosal isn't romantic." No matter how much she liked the food.

"Don't let Mayra hear you say that." Chad pulled a small tablet from his inner jacket pocket. "I brought my column."

So much for romance.

A few minutes later, they were seated at a roomy booth and receiving excellent service in the near empty restaurant. If the veterans hall became popular, El Rosal's business would increase. If the winery succeeded, the town's population would increase. If Chad wrote a good column, it could be like a perfect storm of fairy dust and rainbows over Harmony Valley.

Tracy took off her rose-colored glasses. "Let's get this over with." She raised her voice to be heard above the salsa music and reached across the table. "Were you kind? Or did you unleash your inner beast?"

"I wrote it for my audience." There was a defensiveness about him that clung like the smell in the veterans hall had clung to her boots.

His audience? "At the *Lampoon*?"

"I've been hoping to draw those readers over to my site, so yes. *Lampoon* readers." He drummed his fingers over the tablet case nervously. "My advertising sponsor didn't like it. In fact, I lost all my advertisers today." He handed her the tablet.

She hesitated reading it. Sponsors bailing was bad news. Really bad news. Chad looked more beat up than he had after Lilac tried to run him over. But she wasn't here to give him sympathy.

Tracy read the column quickly, with a sinking heart. While he talked with Enzo about which wine to choose, with the press of a few buttons she emailed the file to herself. "This…reminds me of the cat lady piece. You…make us sound like a town lost in time, one that should stay lost."

"I praised the winery, the bakery, El Rosal and Giordanos." He frowned. "Maybe it wasn't my best piece. But it was interesting?"

Tracy hesitated, realizing he was asking her a question rather than defending his work. He'd never *not* defended his work before. "I'm sorry. I don't recognize your voice in this. It's not clever. It's cruel, which makes it hard to read. You liken Leona…to a prudish horror-movie villainess. You posted a picture of Snarky Sam…next to one of a twenty-year-old drug addict mid-gurn. And you wrote naked yoga isn't as pleasurable…with an old naked man as with starlets in Hollywood."

"I admit…it's not my best." He turned his fork over and back, and over and back again. "When you summarize it like that, it sounds bad."

"It is bad." She returned the tablet to him. "That piece…won't help you relaunch the Happy Bachelor. That'll kill the column." If that was what she wanted, why did she long to reach across the table and cover his hand with hers? "Change of topic. I finished my video."

"Really?" He forced cheer into his tone. "What is it that makes Tracy Jackson unique?"

"The usual, boring things—dreck—that make it worth getting up every morning." It was her turn to fiddle with the silverware, to admit something personal. "This town. My family and friends. My scar. My *unique* speech. The knowledge that life can change." She snapped. "In an instant. So why let dreams pass you by?"

"That's awesome. Look how you didn't give up on your dreams and things turned around. Have you sent it in?"

"No," she said flatly. "I'm going to stay here. I'm going to freelance in town. As it grows—"

"You have a college degree and you're going to waste it here?" His disapproval stabbed at her confidence, threatening to puncture it.

She held on to that hard-won confidence. "I've…been looking for a challenge. And I found many. Right here." She tapped the table with her forefinger. "I'm changing my dream. I want to live here. And do work that is fun. And challenging."

"That's quitting." His lip curled. The man she'd known these past few days was gone.

She wasn't sure she recognized the man sitting before her. "Reach higher, Tracy."

"I did reach high." She struggled to keep her voice down. "I succeeded in advertising. I can move on to creating a life that's important to me. I can ask what if. Maybe you should think about moving on, too."

He wouldn't look at her. The happy, smiling man she found so captivating was nowhere to be found. "You're moving backward. I'm moving on."

"You're not." She did raise her voice then, raised it higher than the pulsing salsa music, high enough Mayra could probably hear her in the kitchen. "You're…trying to write the same column you've written for years. You're scared of spreading your wings. Scared of seeing what else is out there. You're hoping this little website of yours will get your job back. But what happens if it does? You're going to be just as unhappy as you were before." She slid out of the booth. "I'm not hungry anymore."

Tracy had known this was what he'd write. She might have hoped it'd be more skillfully written, but she never should have hoped for anything different. And tomorrow at the Harvest Festival, she wasn't going to be silenced.

She was going to let the town know exactly what Chad thought of them.

For his own good.

CHAPTER TWENTY-TWO

CHAD ENTERED THE town square on the morning of the Harvest Festival with a heavy heart.

In his own way, he'd come to love the small town and care for its residents. So his attempt to write a column about them had been a disaster? He'd move on. He'd rebuild. And every so often, he'd think about the handyman gang, Eunice, or Tracy. Especially Tracy. And when he thought of her, his heart would give a painful squeeze and his lungs would feel leaden and he'd wonder what might have been if he'd been smarter or braver or a better writer.

The parking spaces on Main Street were full and there were several generations of people congregating around the town square. The relatives had arrived.

There was Nina Valpizzi with her grandkids. Did they notice her attention tended to wander and she was forgetting things? There was the mayor with a woman who might have been his daughter. They shared the same aquiline nose. Had she noticed the spot on Larry's face that needed checking for cancer? There was Takata with his walker and... Mildred?

Chad couldn't resist walking over. "Hey, you two."

"Don't even say it," Mildred said. "We're just friends."

Takata chuckled. "I'm going to enter the nail-driving competition and she's going to bowl with pumpkins. Wish us luck."

"And good luck to you, Chad." Mildred clasped her hand over his with that unconditional warmth and trust everyone in town had offered him. "We expect great things from you and your column."

Chad didn't tell them there'd be no column He just moved on.

There was plenty of food to be sampled. Martin's Bakery had set up a booth and packaged up cookies, brownies and Bundt cakes for sale. Not to be outdone, El Rosal had a grill going behind their patio. It smelled heavenly.

"Chad." Rutgar slapped him on the back hard enough to dislodge a peanut stuck in his throat. If a peanut had been stuck in his throat. "If you ever want to write an article about living off the land, you know where to find me."

The mayor pumped his hand. "You let me know anything you need to make your column about us shine. We've enjoyed having you here."

After a string of other goodbyes—all expecting great things and delivered with nice words—Chad was saved by Flynn, who handed him a beer and led him over by the grill. "The key to these things," Flynn said. "Is to stay on the sidelines. The older generation really gets into the traditions."

"What does the younger generation usually do?" Try as he might, he couldn't catch sight of Tracy.

"Try not to get involved."

But Flynn's philosophy was hard to live by when Agnes asked Flynn to judge the gurning contest.

Chad laughed.

"You, too," Agnes said sternly to Chad. "Your face is too beautiful for the gurn, but we need judges."

As judges, Flynn, Chad and Duffy had to sit on the stage and try to take the contestants seriously. They failed miserably.

And then Chad caught sight of one of the *Bostwick Lampoon*'s writers in the crowd. Mark Nesbit laughed harder and louder than anyone.

After the competition, which Sam won, Chad worked his way down to his former employee's side. He shook Mark's hand like any civilized man would do, but inside his territorial instincts were snarling. "What are you doing here, Mark?"

"I'm writing the *Lampoon*'s travel column now. We're retitling it The Sophisticated Bachelor." Mark got a good look at Chad's banged up face. "What happened to you, man? Brawl over a woman? Spent the night in the drunk tank?"

"I got run over by a Cadillac."

"There's a story for you." Mark surveyed the crowd with an ear-splitting grin. "I can't believe you were judging that last event. Are you related to someone here? That was one of the tackiest competitions I've ever seen." Considering Mark was in his twenties and hadn't seen a lot of the world, his observation meant little to Chad. But readers of the *Lampoon* might believe him.

Chad felt the first wave of anger wash over him. "Gurning isn't tacky. It's included to give older people something to participate in." His explanation fell on deaf ears.

Mark had the attention span of a gnat. "Did I hear there's going to be pumpkin bowling?"

"Yes."

Mildred was waiting to take her turn. The lane had been marked with chalk powder in the grass. The pins were two-liter soda bottles filled with water and then frozen.

"Smashing pumpkins. Best played drunk, I bet." Mark nodded toward the beer in Chad's hand. There was nothing sophisticated about the little man. He wore a wrinkled beer brand T-shirt, a pair of off-brand blue jeans and sneakers with holes near one toe.

"Actually, it's more a game of skill." The pumpkin stood little chance of surviving against ten frozen pins. The winner was the one who knocked down the most pins without destroying their pumpkin.

"That's a hoot." Mark leaned back and howled at the blue sky, drawing several frowns from the crowd. "This is better than the retirement party they threw for my grandfather at the pork factory." Mark got out his cell phone. "I've got to take video of this. That old biddy is setting aside her walker. I bet she falls."

In that moment, Chad realized several demoralizing things. He didn't like his former employees at the *Lampoon*. And he was afraid Tracy was right. He'd been cruel and callous and without scruples, like Mark. And yes, he was scared to death to spread his wings and try something different, something that didn't rise to the top by putting others at the bottom. He'd been too stubborn to see it, too stupid to get out of his own way.

Of more immediate concern was the possibility that Mildred would fall and Mark would capture it on video.

Chad made a quick decision. He bumped into Mark hard enough to send them both to the ground and dumped his beer on his former star employee. Mark's cell phone clattered to the pavement a few feet away. Chad helped Mark to his feet at the same time he ground his heel on Mark's cell phone. "Sorry, dude. Someone knocked me over."

"Or maybe you've been drinking too much. Now I smell like a brewery." Mark spotted his cell phone. "Oh, man. My screen shattered." He slid his fingers across the screen. It remained blank. "It's broken. How am I supposed to report this now?"

"You're not supposed to, Mark. This story

is not for you. Go back to reporting about politicians who cheat on their taxes. And tell the new editor-in-chief that Harmony Valley is off-limits to the *Lampoon*."

"Seriously? You can't do that." But Mark's laugh was nervous.

"Mark, look at my face—" his beat up face. "—and then tell me I'm not serious. Because otherwise we can head over to that alley and we'll see how you look when we're done."

Mark hurried away.

Chad looked for Tracy. Tracy was fearless. She'd stood up to him from day one. She fought constantly to improve herself and to fly in new directions. She'd be proud of what he just did.

And then he saw her standing in front of the microphone with a look his way that said she was anything but proud of him.

"I HAVE AN announcement to make." The last time Tracy took the microphone on this stage, she'd been the Grand Marshall of the Spring Festival. That was nearly a year and a half ago. She'd been just as scared to speak in front of the crowd as she was now.

Deep down, she knew Chad wasn't a tear down or a throw away. This was her way of helping him. But in doing so, he'd never speak to her again.

Chad came up to the edge of the stage. She could feel his attention on her. She didn't want to watch the impact her words had on him.

"I have an announcement," she said again, much louder this time. "Chad…used to be the editor of the *Bostwick Lampoon*. Do you know what that is?" She glanced around, carefully avoiding making eye contact with Chad. "It's a magazine that makes fun. Sometimes cruelly so. Of pretty much everything." If she'd been expecting Chad to defend himself, she'd been wrong. He was almost docile at her feet. "Chad…didn't come here to write a kind column. He came to make fun. Here's part…of what he plans to publish about us." Tracy looked at her cell phone screen so she wouldn't lose her nerve. "Harmony Valley… is the kind of place you retire to when you want to be forgotten."

Chad seemed to shrink. She had the audience's full attention now.

She scrolled to another line. "You'll find… great amusement in throwback favorites, like Horseradish-Doodles and squirrel jerky. But…I don't recommend trying them unless you're closer to a hospital."

"Oh, Chad." Eunice pouted. "I had such high hopes for you."

Tracy scrolled further. "And…since it's a town for old people. They…need activities old people can participate in. Gurning. Pumpkin bowling. Even naked yoga."

People began to turn and scowl at Chad. Voices were raised. Insults were thrown.

Tracy had to shout above the crowd noise. "The…only nice things he said were about the winery, the bakery, El Rosal and Giordanos." Tracy lowered her phone. "He…never told us he came to write a glowing article. We…were the ones who assumed too much and trusted him with our…" She almost said hearts. Hers had certainly been too trusting where plain Chad was concerned.

The crowd seemed to hold their collective breath.

"Anyway… He…wasn't the only one who held back the truth. Chad…" Tracy finally met Chad's steady gaze, surprised by the acceptance there when she'd expected bitterness. "There is no Lambridge Bed & Breakfast. You came to town. And we needed a place for you to stay."

"Why did you have to tell him that?" Rose tossed up her hands.

Tracy lifted her chin. "Because we shouldn't have lied."

"Especially when he had to stay with Leona," Mildred said, causing the crowd to chuckle.

But the laughter was short-lived. Residents converged upon Chad and everyone wanted to tell him what they thought of him.

Tracy returned the microphone to its stand and slipped away.

CHAD STEPPED INSIDE the Lambridge Bed & Breakfast, which wasn't really a bed & breakfast after all. Stopping in the foyer, he thought about how his column had hurt people's feelings and wounded their pride. Even the house seemed angry with him. It was as cold as his column.

He'd never been somewhere where they'd seen his column before he left town. He'd never regretted writing a column before. He'd let every resident have their say, because he deserved every harsh word. Flynn and Slade had returned from the storage locker in time to hear Tracy's speech. They'd turned their backs on him. That hurt almost as much as Tracy's disappointment in him.

Leona crossed the threshold carrying a

vase of fresh flowers. She set them down on a table nearby. "What's wrong, Mr. Healy?"

"I'm a hated man."

"By..."

"Pretty much everyone in town."

She scoffed. "They've hated me here for decades. I wouldn't concern yourself, especially since you're leaving tomorrow."

"They don't like you because you divorced Phil." Although Chad couldn't understand why they'd been married in the first place.

"Not true. They don't like me because I don't participate in all the tomfoolery that goes on. They've practically adopted every tradition from every country around the world. It keeps them busy and gives them a sense of purpose. And I won't be a part of it. I don't need to be a part of it."

Chad didn't need to either, and yet belonging had made him feel good. But Leona wasn't as heartless or uninvolved as she wanted to appear. "You donated vegetables to raise money for the Harvest Festival."

"I don't know what you mean." Her nose went into the air. She'd never admit to caring.

Which was why her part in the town's deception made no sense. "Why did you agree to this bed & breakfast charade? You hate anyone in your home."

Leona fiddled with the flower stalks and accidentally broke a stem. "I... I..." She was so like his mother, it hurt him. She'd been an enigma, too. "Do you have family, Mr. Healy?"

"Not anymore." Not so much as a distant cousin.

"I don't either, besides my son and grand-daughters."

"And Phil."

She waved a hand as if her ex-husband didn't count. "They say you can't choose the family you're born into, but you can choose the family you make. If that's true, the people in Harmony Valley are my family." She added in a mumble, "Annoying though they may be."

"They might like you better if you told them that."

"I don't care if they like me." She plucked the ruined white carnation from the vase, snapped off the broken stem and handed it to him. "I'm comfortable with my life. But you, Mr. Healy, you aren't."

"Oh, this will be good." And a great way

to forget the pain in Tracy's eyes when she'd read his column.

"You smile and try to charm everyone, but you don't let yourself care. It makes it easier when you move on. You've buried your heart deeper than I have. I almost pity you."

"Almost," he said softly, because her words had hit home.

"Well, you are renowned in a way." Her lips almost moved upward in a smile. "I've read some of your columns. And I'm sure you have fond memories of every place you've been. But since you never let yourself fall in love with a destination, you feel oh-so-superior when you poke fun and leave."

Tracy had said much the same. If Tracy's accusations had pierced the layer of protection around Chad's heart, Leona's shattered it, breaking it into sharp shards that made it hard to breathe.

"So don't go thinking we're alike, Mr. Healy. I stay here and show my true colors every day of the year." She left him in the foyer.

It took Chad a few minutes to trust his legs to carry him upstairs. He had a column to write. He'd planned his website to go live tomorrow and he was going to keep to that schedule. Schedules were the only thing he had left, and by going live he'd be letting the *Lampoon* know he wouldn't be defeated. He logged into the blogging program and stared at the screen, but he couldn't type a word. He couldn't even remember what the lead sheet had said that had sparked the *Lampoon* team's interest in the first place.

He went down to his car and got the box from the office out of the trunk, carrying it back upstairs. He set it on the bed and opened it up. There was the folder with the lead sheet. It said simply: Harmony Valley, too good to be true.

There was a picture of his parents on their thirtieth wedding anniversary five years ago—they counted the years they'd been divorced in their marriage total. He'd taken the picture of them sitting on their balcony overlooking the Golden Gate Bridge. They held each other close.

And there was the crumpled postmortem manifesto. Chad smoothed out the wrinkles.

Chad is not my choice for the job.

That's where Chad had lost it. It had been a day for painful realities. Chad forced himself to read the rest of his father's last wishes.

Chad is a happy person, too happy for the

sardonic vulgarities often required of the Lampoon. I suggest you find a suitable alternative by looking at former students from pompous schools who've lied about their grade point average and other achievements on their résumé. That's the kind of person I was. At least, until I became a father. And then I forgot how much that role means to a child, even an adult one. Chad should never forget.

Chad returned to the desk and stared at the screen. His father had redeemed himself in Chad's eyes. Chad had to redeem himself, too.

He began to type.

THE HARD THING about making amends and doing the right thing was that it often required logistics, which Harmony Valley was sorely short of.

So Chad left town on Sunday morning and drove back to his family's empty penthouse suite in San Francisco, full of memories both pleasant and unpleasant, and began a campaign to win Harmony Valley and Tracy back.

He returned on Tuesday morning and began his campaign with flyers posted on all the businesses on Main Street, including Martin's Bakery. When he was done, he had quite a few copies left. He pushed through the door to Martin's and stopped. The regulars were there, including Tracy. She wore a simple T-shirt, little makeup, and her sunny blond hair looked as if she'd slept until the last minute this morning.

There was a tablet on top of one bakery case beneath a sign that said, "Read Today's Blog!" Someone had written a new note on the chalkboard: *We do wedding cakes! A free pie for every referral.* Tracy had already begun her marketing campaign.

"Well, look what the cat dragged in." Eunice studied him over the top of her black-rimmed readers. "We won't fall for your act again, buster. Better hit the road."

"You people are too smart to fall for the same line twice." Chad distributed flyers to every person in the bakery. Everyone except Tracy. "First off, yes, I wrote the column Tracy read at the Harvest Festival."

Tracy stood behind the counter as if afraid to move. Where was the fierce and fearless woman who'd won his heart?

"Tracy had an advanced copy that I gave her," Chad said.

"Thank goodness she did." Rose shook her

finger at him. "Wait. Why were you stupid enough to give it to her?"

"Because I trusted her." He willed Tracy to look him in the eyes. "I still do."

Her startled glance flew to his.

He nodded. "But I didn't publish the column she read." He held up the remaining flyers. "This is the travel column that was posted this morning. Feel free to read it."

"Read it to me, Hiro," Mildred said.

The patrons at Martin's began to read. Hiro's low, steady voice didn't carry beyond one table over.

"I don't understand," Tracy said, holding out her hand for a copy of the column. "You were convinced that was the right column for your career."

"That was before I realized what an empty career it was." Chad hugged the flyers to his chest. "That was before I decided what I wanted to do with my life next. You were right about the story from the beginning, but I was just too stubborn to listen. I wrote this column before I left town Sunday morning. By Monday night, I had a new set of advertising sponsors and a new name for my website: The Happy Bachelor Settles Down."

Tracy's expression was stuck stiffly between wonder and disbelief.

"I want to retire to Harmony Valley." He'd begun the process of selling his shares in the *Lampoon*. He'd put the penthouse up for sale. And made other changes, too.

Tracy scoffed. "You're too young to retire."

If anyone else heard their conversation, they didn't react.

He brought out his most reliable smile, the one the Bunko ladies had loved. "I've already had a midlife crisis, I don't know why I can't retire."

"Hey," the mayor said. "This column is nice. This column should get picked up by a big city newspaper for sure."

"It's funny. I like to hear about Roxie and her chickens." Despite her black framed readers, Eunice held the column close to her nose. "And look! There's a mention of Mama and her Horseradish-Doodles."

"I like how you reference squirrel jerky and living off the land," Rutgar rumbled from the back.

"From the first time I saw you, Tracy, you made me smile. And somewhere along the way, I learned a thing or two from you." Chad couldn't stop smiling at Tracy. He moved closer to the counter, close enough to take one of her hands in his. "How to be fearless and how to be kind. How to be just plain Chad."

"You aren't really going to retire, are you?" Blue eyes wide, Tracy searched his face for some clue.

"For a while. Maybe I'll get restless and write some travel columns about the nice, joyous discoveries that can be found in the most surprising of places." He leaned over the counter and touched the hair over her scar. "Of course, I'd need a travel companion, someone who's willing to keep me honest and point out the unique, sweet character of a place."

She leaned forward until her lips were within kissing distance. "Who did you have in mind?"

"Eunice." He grinned.

The room erupted with laughter. They'd all been shamelessly eavesdropping.

Chad didn't mind at all. "And maybe… sometimes… I'd find room in my minivan for my wife and kids to come along."

"Minivan?" Tracy glanced outside the window. "You went from a sports car to a minivan?"

"Well, sweetheart, if you expected me to

buy a truck and fill it with tools, you are sadly
mistaken. If I accompany Flynn and the guys
on their rounds, it'll be as an assistant lug-
ging the tool box." He gave her a gentle tug,
so that they were back in the shared space in
the middle of the counter. He was a long way
from winning her over forever, but he felt his
empty places being filled already. With Tracy
by his side, he'd have days filled with smiles
and laughter and jokes. "Wouldn't you rather
load a minivan with our kids?"

She answered him with a kiss that was far
too short, because everyone in Martin's, and
everyone they called to Martin's, wanted to
celebrate the newest couple in Harmony Valley.

After Mildred and Hiro, that is.

* * * * *

LARGER-PRINT BOOKS!

GET 2 FREE
LARGER-PRINT NOVELS
PLUS 2 FREE
MYSTERY GIFTS

Love Inspired®

Larger-print novels are now available...

YES! Please send me 2 FREE LARGER-PRINT Love Inspired® novels and my 2 FREE mystery gifts (gifts are worth about $10). After receiving them, if I don't wish to receive any more books, I can return the shipping statement marked "cancel." If I don't cancel, I will receive 6 brand-new novels every month and be billed just $5.49 per book in the U.S. or $5.99 per book in Canada. That's a savings of at least 19% off the cover price. It's quite a bargain! Shipping and handling is just 50¢ per book in the U.S. and 75¢ per book in Canada.* I understand that accepting the 2 free books and gifts places me under no obligation to buy anything. I can always return a shipment and cancel at any time. Even if I never buy another book, the two free books and gifts are mine to keep forever.

122/322 IDN GH6D

Name _____ (PLEASE PRINT) _____

Address _____ Apt. # _____

City _____ State/Prov. _____ Zip/Postal Code _____

Signature (if under 18, a parent or guardian must sign)

Mail to the **Reader Service:**
IN U.S.A.: P.O. Box 1867, Buffalo, NY 14240-1867
IN CANADA: P.O. Box 609, Fort Erie, Ontario L2A 5X3

**Are you a current subscriber to Love Inspired® books
and want to receive the larger-print edition?
Call 1-800-873-8635 or visit www.ReaderService.com.**

* Terms and prices subject to change without notice. Prices do not include applicable taxes. Sales tax applicable in N.Y. Canadian residents will be charged applicable taxes. Offer not valid in Quebec. This offer is limited to one order per household. Not valid to current subscribers to Love Inspired Larger-Print books. All orders subject to credit approval. Credit or debit balances in a customer's account(s) may be offset by any other outstanding balance owed by or to the customer. Please allow 4 to 6 weeks for delivery. Offer available while quantities last.

Your Privacy—The Reader Service is committed to protecting your privacy. Our Privacy Policy is available online at www.ReaderService.com or upon request from the Reader Service.

We make a portion of our mailing list available to reputable third parties that offer products we believe may interest you. If you prefer that we not exchange your name with third parties, or if you wish to clarify or modify your communication preferences, please visit us at www.ReaderService.com/consumerschoice or write to us at Reader Service Preference Service, P.O. Box 9062, Buffalo, NY 14240-9062. Include your complete name and address.

LILP15

LARGER-PRINT BOOKS!
GET 2 FREE LARGER-PRINT NOVELS PLUS
2 FREE GIFTS!

⟨H⟩ HARLEQUIN®

super romance®

More Story...More Romance

READERSERVICE.COM

Manage your account online!

- Review your order history
- Manage your payments
- Update your address

> ### We've designed the Reader Service website just for you.

Enjoy all the features!

- Discover new series available to you, and read excerpts from any series.
- Respond to mailings and special monthly offers.
- Connect with favorite authors at the blog.
- Browse the Bonus Bucks catalog and online-only exculsives.
- Share your feedback.

Visit us at:

ReaderService.com

RSI5